HUNTED PAST REASON

The Beardless Warriors
Bid Time Return
Earthbound
Fury on Sunday
Hell House
I Am Legend
Journal of the Gun Years
Now You See It . . .
The Path
Ride the Nightmare
7 Steps to Midnight
The Incredible Shrinking Man
Someone Is Bleeding
Somewhere in Time
A Stir of Echoes
What Dreams May Come

HUNTED PAST REASON

Richard Matheson

A TOM DOHERTY ASSOCIATES BOOK / NEW YORK

This is a work of fiction. All the characters and events portrayed in this novel are either fictitious or are used fictitiously.

HUNTED PAST REASON

This book is printed on acid-free paper.

Design by Heidi Eriksen

A Tor Book
Published by Tom Doherty Associates, LLC
175 Fifth Avenue
New York, NY 10010

www.tor.com

Tor® is a registered trademark of Tom Doherty Associates, LLC.

Library of Congress Cataloging-in-Publication Data

Matheson, Richard.
    Hunted past reason / Richard Matheson.—
1st ed.
        p.   cm.
    "A Tom Doherty Associates book."
    ISBN 0-765-30271-3 (alk. paper)
    1. Wilderness survival—Fiction.   2. Male
friendship—Fiction. 3. Mentally ill—Fiction.
4. California—Fiction.   5. Camping—Fiction.
I. Title.

PS3563.A8355 H86   2002
813'.54—dc21
                                          2001050768

First Edition: July 2002

Printed in the United States of America

0   9   8   7   6   5   4   3   2   1

With deep gratitude to Don Congdon,
My literary bulwark for forty-five years

Acknowledgments

My deepest gratitude to Lee Holloway for her invaluable contribution to the creation of my story's antagonist.

Most of the information about plant and tree life in northern California comes from the excellent book *California's Sierra Nevada* by George Wuerthner, published by American and World Geographic Publishing.

To die is nothing.
To live is everything.
—LLOYD PLAYDON

Sunday

2:07 PM

"This is as good a place as any," Doug said, leaning forward on the backseat.

"Okay." Marian started to slow down the Bronco as it turned a curve to the right.

"By that fallen big-leaf maple'll be fine," Doug told her.

"Right." She eased the Bronco toward the right side of the road and braked slowly. The carpeting of yellow leaves crackled under the tires before Marian stopped the Bronco by the fallen tree.

"Perfect," Doug said.

Bob drew in a sudden, involuntary breath. "And so the adventure begins," he said, trying to sound pleased.

Marian looked at him as she switched off the engine. "You all right?" she whispered.

He nodded, smiling. "Fine," he said.

Doug opened the back door of the Bronco and got out. He stretched his arms upward, groaning as he arched his back. "Oh . . . *boy*," he muttered.

Marian looked worriedly at Bob. "Are you *sure* you're all right?" she asked.

"Yeah, why do you say that?" He managed a grin.

"Well—" She gestured vaguely. "You didn't sound too certain there."

"About what?"

"And so the adventure begins," she quoted.

"Oh." He laughed softly. "I'm a little nervous of course. I'm no kid. But I'm sure it's going to be fine."

In back, Doug had unlocked the hatchback door and was starting to lift it.

"You're comfortable then," Marian said.

"Oh, sure." He leaned over and put his arms around her. She responded and they held on to each other tightly.

"Okay, lovebirds," Doug said from behind the car. "Time to unload our gear."

Bob and Marian drew apart, smiling at each other. They opened their doors and slid out, standing on the leaf-covered ground. "My God, the leaves are so *big*," Marian said, picking up one that was more than a foot across. After a few moments, she dropped it, the golden leaves crunching under their shoes as they moved to the rear of the Bronco where Doug was pulling out his backpack.

"Here, I'll get yours," Marian said, pulling at Bob's backpack. "Holy! *Moses*." She had lost her grip on the pack, which thudded down on the ground. "It weighs a bloody *ton*," she said. "How in God's name are you going to carry that for four days?"

Bob forced a smile. "It's really only three, honey. There's not that much left of today."

"Two *hours* would be too much for carrying that," she said, gesturing toward the fallen pack. "You're forty-five, not twenty-five."

"*Honey*..." He gazed at her reproachfully.

"Oh..." She sighed, looking guilty. "I'm sorry. I'm not saying you can't do it. It's just..." She made a face. "It's so damn heavy."

"He'll get used to it," Doug told her. "And it'll get lighter every day as the food goes."

"I suppose." She watched Bob pick up the pack and move it away from the Bronco, then turned toward the back of the car.

"You're not taking this, are you?" she asked, picking up a red flare.

"Sure." Doug's smile was teasing. "To light our campfires."

Marian put down the flare, smiling. "What's this?" she asked, picking up a length of chain. "You don't need *this* on your hike, do you?"

"No." Doug took it away from her and put it back in the car.

"What's it for?" Marian asked him.

"Protection," he answered.

She opened her mouth as though to speak, then closed it again. "Oh," she murmured, watching him take a long leather carrier from the Bronco. "What's that?" she asked, trying to cover her feeling of embarrassment about mentioning the chain.

"A bow," he said.

Bob made a sound of strained amusement. "You're taking a bow?"

"I always do."

"And arrows, I presume."

Doug gave him a look.

Bob asked, "Why? Do you hunt while you're out?"

"Not necessarily," Doug said.

Bob and Marian exchanged a look. "Which means...?" Bob asked.

"Bob." Doug turned to him with a mildly accusing look. "We're going into wilderness. There are black bears out there. Mountain lions. Coyotes."

"Oh, now, wait a minute," Marian said abruptly. "Nothing was said about black bears or mountain lions or coyotes." She looked at Bob in concern. "Now I'm not so sure this is a good idea."

Doug laughed. "Marian, I'm not saying we're going to run into one of them. The bow is just a precaution."

She stared at him, her expression one of worried doubt.

"A precaution," he repeated.

"How many times have you used it while—" She broke off. "Scratch that. How many times have you *had* to use it while backpacking?"

"Once," he said, smiling.

"Black bear or mountain lion or coyote?" she asked uneasily.

"Rabbit," he said, repressing a grin.

"Rabbit?" She looked startled. "You shot a rabbit?" As Doug nodded, she asked, "How come?"

"I lost my pack in some rapids and I had to eat," he told her.

She looked at him in silence for a few moments.

"There aren't any grizzly bears up here, are there?" she asked apprehensively.

"Used to be," Doug answered. "Wolves too. Until they were killed off by stockmen—traps, guns, poison."

Marian winced at his words.

"Honey, I'm sure it's going to be—" Bob started.

"All right, let's put it this way," Marian broke in. "How often do you *see* black bears or mountain lions or coyotes?"

Doug chuckled. "Marian, you're too much," he said.

"Well," she insisted, "how often?"

He groaned softly. "Once in a while, dear girl," he said with labored patience. "But they don't want to have anything to do with us any more than we want to have anything to do with them. You leave them alone, they leave you alone."

"Marian, come on," Bob chided.

"All right, all right." She nodded several times. "I'm just . . ." She gestured vaguely with her hands.

"I should never have mentioned it," Doug said. "Believe me, it's nothing to be concerned about. Okay?"

"Okay." She smiled awkwardly. "I'm just . . . an apprehensive frau, that's all."

Doug's responding smile was a sad one. "Too bad I don't have a frau to be apprehensive about me," he said.

"Oh . . ." Marian moved to him and kissed his cheek. "I'm sorry, Doug. You're really doing something nice taking Bob on this . . . what, hike?"

"Adventure," he said with a teasing smile.

She smiled back at him. "Right, adventure," she agreed.

"All right. Now." Doug looked serious. "You're okay with the Bronco?"

Marian nodded, smiling. "Okay."

"And you understand my map."

She nodded again.

"Well, I'm not the world's greatest mapmaker," he said.

"It's fine," she told him.

"Well, just . . . follow the yellow Hi-liter route."

"To Oz," she said.

His lips puffed out in a sound of partial amusement. "Yeah, right," he said. "It's about . . . I'd say forty miles or so.

Two things to keep in mind. Turn off the main road after you pass the Brandy Lake sign. And most important, keep an eye out for the two Pine Grove signs, one for Pine Grove Street, the other for Pine Grove Lane. You turn right on Pine Grove *Lane*; it's the second sign you'll come to. Got it? The second sign."

"Got it," she said.

He raised his hands, palms forward. "I'm only being a pest about this because we've had to go out searching for a lot of guests who turned right on Pine Grove Street."

"I'll remember," she said.

"Okay. Good. You have the keys to the cabin?"

"In my purse."

"Right. And you understand about the propane tank for the stove. And turning on the water."

"I do." She nodded. "I'll be fine, Doug."

"Well . . . I just want to be sure. We won't be there until Wednesday afternoon."

She nodded. "I'll be fine," she reassured him.

"Sure you will," he said. "You'll enjoy the cabin. There's a nice big deck in back that overlooks the forest. Sit there with a drink, you'll love it."

"I'm sure." Marian nodded, smiling.

"You'd better be on your way then so you have plenty of light in case you make a wrong turn. Driving up there in the dark can be a bitch."

"I'll be fine," she said once more.

"Good." He kissed her on the cheek. "We'll see you on Wednesday then."

"On Wednesday." She was silent for a moment. Then she said, "I'm going to say good-bye to my husband now."

"You mean auf Wiedersehen, don't you?" Doug said with a grin.

She pointed the index finger of her right hand at him. "That's up to you," she told him.

His grin widened. "Don't worry, I'll take good care of him."

"I know you will."

She took Bob's hand and led him several yards away, to the other side of the fallen maple tree. She put her arms around him and held him close. "You take good care of yourself now," she said.

He embraced her. "I will."

"Be careful."

"I'll avoid the black bears and the mountain—"

"Stop that," she interrupted softly. "I'm going to be uneasy enough without worrying about wild animals chewing on you."

Bob laughed softly. "Don't be uneasy," he told her. "Doug has backpacked dozens of times."

"Well, *you* haven't," she said. "Take it easy. Don't let him push you."

"Why would he do that?"

"Well . . ." She blew out a heavy breath. "He's so . . . physical; you know that. He's an actor, he's done westerns . . . action pictures. He's . . . tuned up."

"What, and I'm out of tune?"

She sighed. "I don't see you going to the gym very often. Or swimming."

"I walk, don't I?"

"Your one saving grace." She squeaked as he pinched her back. "Well, anyway, I mean it: *please-take-it-easy*. Don't let Doug push you. He won't do it on purpose," she added quickly, cutting him off. "He might just do it without thinking."

"I'll collapse at regular intervals," he said.

"Oh . . ." she sighed again. "You aren't very reassuring."

"I will be careful," he promised. "I will take it easy. I will avoid wild animals."

The grip of her arms tightened. "Please do," she said quietly.

After several moments, she drew back and looked at him intently. "Honey, are you sure you want to do this?" she asked.

"I have to, sweetheart. How am I supposed to write a convincing novel about backpacking if I've never backpacked once?"

She nodded, sighing again, then made a face of mock pleading. "Please, sir," she said in a little girl's voice, "couldn't you write a novel about drinking chi-chis and lazing around in Hawaii with your wife of twenty years?"

He chuckled. "Maybe the next one I—" he started.

"Bobby, we have to go," Doug called.

"I wish he wouldn't call you that," Marian said, "as though you were ten years old or something."

"He doesn't mean any harm," Bob said. He drew her close and pressed his lips to hers, lingering on the kiss.

"Dear God, that was like farewell," she said, tears appearing in her eyes.

"Don't be silly, sweetheart. We'll be at the cabin on Wednesday afternoon. Have a vodka and tonic waiting for me."

"If I don't drink up all the vodka, worrying about you."

He laughed softly and took her by the hand, leading her back around the tree.

"Farewells all completed?" Doug said.

Marian managed a faint smile. Doug's smile became one of sympathy. "Really, Marian, there's nothing to be worried about. Your husband will be sore as hell in every muscle, that I guarantee, but otherwise he'll be intact."

"Okay, okay, I'm going," she said. She kissed Bob briefly on the lips, then moved to the Bronco and got in behind the steering wheel. She turned on the engine and pulled out onto the road, raising her right hand in farewell. Bob had the feeling that she didn't look back because she was crying. Oh, sweetheart, he thought, smiling sadly.

As the Bronco disappeared around a curve, he picked up his pack with a grunt at its weight. "Okay, let's go," he said.

"Whoa, whoa, not so fast," Doug told him.

"What?" Bob looked at him, curious.

"We have to check out our gear before we leave."

Bob frowned. "Now?" he asked.

"Sure, now."

"Why didn't we do all that before we left Los Angeles?"

"It's a good idea to do it now," Doug said. "Double-check before we leave."

"What if I don't have everything I need?" Bob asked. "What can I do about it now?"

"Well, I gave you a list of things you need. I assume you got all of it," Doug said. "I *was* going to go to the supply store with you—as you recall. But you were in New York attending a big meeting."

"Mm-hmm." Bob nodded, wondering why Doug felt the need to call it a "big" meeting. It wasn't that and Doug knew it.

"Oh, well," he said. "Let's do it then."

Doug looked at him questioningly. "Are you sure you're up to this, Bob?" he asked.

"Sure," Bob said. "I'm looking forward to it."

"Are you really?"

It didn't sound like a question to Bob. Doug's smile bordered on disbelief. He chuckled. "Okay. You got me," he admitted. "Naturally, I'm a little apprehensive."

"A lot apprehensive," Doug answered.

"Well, maybe," Bob said. "I'm not exactly John Muir."

"Not exactly." Doug's smile was amused now.

"I'm counting on you to lead me through the wilderness without incident," Bob said.

Doug shook his head, laughing softly. "I'll do my damnedest, Bob," he said. "Okay. Let's see what you've got."

Bob leaned his pack against a tree to open it.

"I see you got a side packer," Doug said.

"Is that bad?" Bob asked. "The salesman said it was easier to get into."

"Did he tell you it would leak more in the rain?"

"Well . . . no," Bob answered. "Are we expecting rain?"

"Y'never know," Doug said. "Did you try it on for comfort?"

Bob nodded. "Yes, I did. The salesman even put a sandbag in it to show me what it would feel like when it was loaded."

"And—?"

Bob chuckled. "It felt heavy," he said.

"Damn right." Doug nodded. "Well, let's see what you've got inside."

Bob unzipped the bag and took out the first item.

"What the hell is that?" Again, Bob felt that it wasn't a question but a judgment.

"A stove," he said.

"That wasn't on the list I gave you," Doug told him.

"The salesman talked me into it," Bob said. "He showed me how easy it was to use. What would you rather have at the end of the day, he asked, cold cereal or hot chicken à la king over rice?"

"You have chicken à la king with you as well?" Doug said, laughing as he spoke.

Bob sighed. He was getting a little weary of Doug's belittling tone. "You never took a stove with you?" he challenged.

"Yeah, sure I did," Doug answered. "Nothing wrong with having a stove. I was just trying to cut down on the weight you have to carry."

"Okay." Bob nodded.

"Canister stove's heavier too," Doug told him. "And you'll have to carry out the canister."

"Oh, no." Bob looked dismayed.

"Oh, yes," Doug said, nodding and smiling again. "Those are the rules of the game, Bobby. You don't leave anything behind. Except for piss and crap, of course."

Bob made a face, nodding. "I understand."

"Do you?" Doug looked at him almost sternly. "There *are* rules, Bobby. It isn't just a stroll in the park we're going on, you know."

All right, all right, Bob thought, He felt like saying it but didn't want the hike to start out on a strained note.

"Before we look at what else you have in your pack—" Doug started.

Oh, God, what now? Bob wondered.

"You're not wearing cotton underwear are you?"

The unexpected question struck Bob as funny, making him laugh. Doug frowned. "I'm sorry for laughing," Bob said. "I just didn't expect that question."

"Well, it's not an unimportant one," Doug told him. "Cotton underwear gets wet from perspiration, feels lousy."

Bob nodded. "I understand. I have on poly prop-whatever-underwear."

"Polypropylene." Doug nodded. "Good. And thin polypropylene socks under your wool socks?"

"Right."

He must have sounded a bit apathetic, he realized, because Doug frowned again. "Bob, these things are important," he said.

"All right. I understand." Bob nodded.

"Okay." Doug looked serious again. "You have three complete sets of socks."

"Mm-hmm."

Doug started to speak but Bob interrupted him. "What do *you* use for a stove?" he asked.

"Two logs close together over the fire," Doug said. "I put my grate across them." He grinned. "Of course, now I have a stove to use."

The hell you do, Bob thought, after making fun of it? He sighed. Well, let that go, he decided.

"Very often, I've just eaten what Muir did—uncooked food, hot tea or coffee," Doug told him.

Well, he *is* trying to be helpful, Bob chided himself. And, after all, Doug didn't *have* to offer to take him on this hike, helping him get background material for his novel.

"All right, getting back to your clothes," Doug continued. "Let's take a look at your boots." He knelt in front of Bob. "Did you know that every mile you walk, each foot hits the ground almost two thousand times?"

"No. Jesus." Bob was impressed.

"And each foot has twenty-six functional bones," Doug continued.

"No kidding," Bob said. "How do you know all this stuff?"

"I can read too," Doug said.

What the hell does that mean? Bob wondered.

"All right, they're leather, that's good. You never buy plastic."

Plastic? Bob reacted. Who in the hell would buy plastic shoes for hiking?

Doug was running his hands over Bob's boots. "Lightweight, that's good," he said. "You won't need heavyweight boots for a hike this short. Ankle-high, good. Padded ankle collar." He grimaced a little. "Well . . . nylon uppers don't need any break-in, but—"

"What?" Bob asked.

"I prefer leather uppers, they last longer, have more resistance." He stood up, grunting. "No matter. Yours'll be fine. You told the salesman to give you an extra half inch of toe room, didn't you?"

"No." Bob frowned. "You never told me that."

"I must have forgotten," Doug said. "It's nothing fatal. Although it *does* help to have that extra half inch when you're doing steep downhill hiking. You *did* wear a pair of thick socks when you were trying them on, didn't you?"

"Yep." Bob nodded, trying not to sound bored, which he was getting.

"Water seal the boots?" Doug asked.

"Yes."

"Cut your toenails?"

"What?" Bob laughed at the question.

"Not a joke," Doug said. "You're going to be doing a lot of walking. Overlong toenails can cause problems."

"Oh, Jesus." Bob made a face. "Well, I don't think they're too long."

"We'll check 'em later," Doug said. "I have a clipper in case you need it."

Bob repressed a sigh but not enough. Doug looked at him with mild accusation. "Bob," he said, "I'm not talking just to hear the sound of my voice. I've been backpacking for years. Everything I'm telling you is pertinent."

"All right, all right, I'm sorry again, I apologize. I realize you're just trying to help me."

"Good." Doug patted him on the shoulder. "Just a few more things and we'll be on our way."

"Shoot," Bob said. "Not with your bow, of course."

Doug gave him a token chuckle, then went on. "Got gaiters?" he asked.

"What?"

"Gaiters. Like leggings. Helps keep your lower pants dry, safe from thorns. Keeps sand and dirt out of your shoes. Rain."

"Rain again," Bob said. "You know something I don't?"

"No, no," Doug answered. "Just a precaution. I *did* mention gaiters, though."

Bob nodded. No, you didn't, he remembered.

"You have polyprop long johns?" Doug asked.

"Uh-huh." Bob nodded. Let's *get* on our way then, he thought.

His mind blanked out a little as Doug ran through what seemed to be a lecture about using the "layering" system to dress; each item of clothing working in combination with the others to deal with any change in the weather, hot or cold.

Lower layer, the long johns, socks; middle layer, shirt or vest, pile pants; outer layer, windbreaker, jacket, boots. Bob's jacket was quilted, not down; that was good. If down got wet, it took forever to dry. Was Bob's jacket seam-sealed? Bob didn't know; he did not attempt to repress a sigh. Doug went on as though he didn't notice. No snaps on Bob's poncho, not good. In a wind, it would blow out like a boat sail. Snaps would prevent that. What kind of weather we planning on? Bob asked. Never know, was all Doug answered.

"Are we ready to go now?" Bob asked.

"No, no, no, no," Doug said scoldingly. "There are several more important things."

"Jesus, Doug. Are we going to have any time to walk before dark?"

Doug looked at him in silence.

"I know. I know," Bob said apologetically. "Important things."

"You doubt it?" Doug said irritably.

"No," Bob sighed. "I'm just . . . anxious to get going, that's all."

"So am I, Bobby, be*lieve* me," Doug said gravely. "But if we go off half cocked, you'll regret it. I know how to do all this. You don't. So, for Christ's sake, show a little patience. You'll be glad later about what we're doing now."

Bob nodded, looking guilty. "I know, I'm sorry. I'll say no more."

"Don't worry, we'll be on our way in no time," Doug reassured him. "Let's just get through it."

"All right. Lay on, Macduff."

Doug chuckled. "Let's check your food supply," he said.

"Right." Bob took out what he'd brought. "Monologue time," he said. "All food in plastic bags, a few small boxes of orange juice, no cans. Cereal. Beans. Powdered milk. Sugar. Powdered eggs. A packet of cheese. Instant coffee. Nuts. Chocolate."

"Good," Doug said. "Chocolate has all kinds of valuable ingredients. B vitamins. Magnesium. Good for you."

"Marian would be happy to hear that," Bob told him.

Doug chuckled a little. "The powdered milk is good too," he said. "Lots of protein and calcium. Phosphorous. Vitamin D. Perfect in a survival situation."

"A survival situation?" Bob asked. "I thought we were just going for a hike."

Doug looked at him askance. "Just a phrase," he said.

"Glad to hear it," Bob answered.

"So what else you got?"

"Raisins. Powdered potatoes. A little bread. Two oranges, two apples. Energy bars. And, of course, my chicken à la king with rice, turkey tetrazzini, beef almondine."

"Actually, you may have more food than you need," Doug told him.

Bob made a face. "Don't tell me that," he said.

"No tragedy," Doug told him. He picked up a pamphlet from Bob's pack. "What's this?"

Bob took the pamphlet and looked at it, laughed.

"What?" Doug asked.

"*Survival in the Wilderness.*" Bob read the pamphlet's title. "Marian must have slipped it in there when I wasn't looking."

"Doubt if you'll need it," Doug said with a snicker.

"I doubt it too." Bob slipped the pamphlet into his shirt pocket.

"Well, you seem to be in pretty good shape, food-wise," Doug told him. "Plenty of carbohydrates—the staple of a hiker's diet. You have enough water to see us through the afternoon?"

Bob showed him his filled water bottle.

"It'll do, I guess," Doug said dubiously. "I think I told you to get a wide-mouth halgene bottle though. Easier to clean. Easier to fill from a stream or spring. Easier to get a spoon into."

"They didn't have any," Bob said quietly.

"All right, all right, no tragedy," Doug replied. "I see you have some water packets too. They're good in a pinch. What else have you got?"

"Pair of folding eyeglasses. Not that I think I'll be doing any reading."

Doug snickered. "Doubt it," he said.

"And a small pair of folding binoculars," Bob told him.

Doug made an indeterminate sound. "Won't hurt," he said. "You might get some use out of them. How about toiletries?"

Dear God, this is going to go on forever, Bob thought. We'll end up camping right here for the week. He took the plastic bag out of his pack. "Toothbrush. Toothpaste. Skin lotion. Sun block. Multivitamins."

"Let's see." Doug held out his hand and Bob handed him the small container. He read the ingredients. "Not bad," he said. "Two, three hundred milligrams of Vitamin C, Vitamin A, good. Vitamin B-1. Vitamin D. Potassium. Sodium. Calcium. Iron." He tossed the container back. "It'll do," he said in a tone that indicated it really wasn't good enough.

My cup runneth over, Bob thought.

"And—?" Doug asked.

"Uh . . . oh," Bob said. "Water purification tablets."

"Safer to boil the water," Doug told him. "Boiling time varies with height above sea level. Best to boil it for ten minutes wherever you are. And remember, drink *before* you get thirsty. Thirst is an alarm signal. Don't wait for it. Remember, when you sweat it's ninety-nine percent water."

"Do I—?"

"Use your urine color as an indicator. If it's darker than usual, you're not drinking enough."

"Okay." No point in asking questions, Bob thought.

"Pint every half hour," Doug told him.

Bob nodded.

"What else you got?" Doug asked.

"Oh . . . toilet paper," Bob told him. "Deodorant."

"Deodorant?" Doug chuckled. "You afraid your b.o. will offend the squirrels?"

"Just a habit," Bob said.

"All right, no tragedy."

Tragedy? Bob thought. How could using a deodorant be a tragedy?

"What's that?" Doug said, pointing.

Bob took out a plastic bag with six mini-bottles of vodka in it. "Thought it might be nice to have a little drink at the end of the—"

"Not a good idea, Bob," Doug broke in. "Alcohol impairs

the judgment. Dehydrates the body. Decreases the appetite. Not good."

"Jesus, Doug, one mini-bottle before dinner? That's hardly boozing one's way through the forest primeval."

"Well." Doug shrugged. "Okay. Your call. You'll have to carry out the bottles though, you know."

"Oh, Christ, I forgot about that."

Doug chuckled. "Law of the wilderness, Bobby," he said. "You'll remember all this next time." He chuckled again. "If there *is* a next time."

"You don't think there will be?" Bob asked.

"Let's just say I hope you rented all this equipment." When Bob didn't reply, Doug made a face of mock pain. "Ooh," he said, "that's a lot of money for one hike." He gestured vaguely. "Though I suppose you'll get a hell of a lot *more* money when you sell your novel."

Bob didn't know how to respond to that. It crossed his mind how ironic it was that Doug had decried the mini-bottles of vodka. He'd seen Doug put away two six-packs of beer on more than one occasion.

"What about cookware?" Doug asked.

Without a word, Bob showed him the two small aluminum pots nestled together with a lid that could be used for a frying pan.

"Should be marked for measurements," Doug said. "However. Cup?"

Bob showed him his metal Sierra cup. Doug made a face. "Should have gotten a plastic one like I told you. This one could burn your lips as well as cool down hot liquids too fast."

Backpacking One, Professor Crowley, Bob thought. Was there going to be a written exam after all this?

"Okay, you got a spoon and knife," Doug said. "You have a hunting knife too?"

Bob opened his jacket to show the knife in its sheath.

"That's not a knife," Doug said, imitating Crocodile Dundee. "This is a knife."

He reached into his pack and pulled out what looked like a small machete. "Golak," he told Bob.

"Jesus," Bob said. "Are we going for a hike or a war?"

"Never know," Doug answered.

For Christ's sake, what does *that* mean? Bob wondered. He decided not to ask.

"A few more things," Doug said, "but I have them with me so you don't have to worry about them. Flashlight with extra bulbs and batteries. I see that you have one too—that's good. Waterproof matches. First-aid kit, whistle; I have two, I'll give you one of them."

"Whistle?" Bob asked.

"In case you get lost, Bobby," Doug said. Marian was right. Doug sounded exactly as though he were talking to a ten-year-old.

"Trowel." Doug held it up.

"What's *that* for?" Bob asked.

"You plan to bury your shit with your hands?" Doug said. It was hardly a question. He grinned at Bob. "You'll borrow mine," he said. "It'll bond us."

Bob had to laugh at that.

"You have your sunglasses," Doug went on. "One more thing before we get our packs on. Your sleeping bag."

Bob showed it to him. Doug shook it open. Oh, Christ, Bob thought, it took me long enough to get it folded right.

"Down-filled mummy bag, yeah, that's good," Doug said. "I'm glad you listened to me on that anyway."

That's right, I ignored everything else on the list you gave me, Bob thought. Christ.

"Not too much loft," Doug said, patting the mummy bag.

"Loft?" Bob asked.

"Insulation," Doug told him. "The more air there is between you and the ground, the warmer you'll be. It's pretty heavy though, should keep you warm. Heavier than it needs to be actually."

Make up your mind, Dougie, Bob thought.

Doug checked the sleeping bag more closely. "Should have a zipper at the top *and* the bottom," he said. "Helps cool you off on a warm night."

Jesus! Bob thought. Which one will it be, staying warm or staying cool?

"Well, pack up and we'll be on our way," Doug told him.

Thank *God*, Bob thought. He started to roll up his sleeping bag. Please don't tell me I'm doing it wrong, he thought. I'm sure I am.

Doug sat down on a boulder, yawning and stretching.

"What you have is an internal-frame backpack," he said. "Pretty compact, fits better. Makes it easier to maintain your balance no matter what kind of ground you're walking on. Most backpackers prefer the internal frame."

Which means, of course, that you don't prefer it, Bob guessed.

"I prefer the external-frame type," Doug said. Bob was glad his back was turned away so Doug wouldn't see his cheeks puff out in a stifled laugh. "Better air circulation on the back.

Easier to pack. Can carry more weight. Though God knows that isn't what you'd want right now."

No, not at all, Bob thought in amusement as he started to repack his bag.

"No, you wouldn't want more weight, you'd want less," Doug went on.

Yes, sir, Professor Crowley, Bob thought.

"They say a pack for any kind of extended trip should be about a third of the hiker's weight. What do you weigh, Bobby?"

"Two hundred."

"That would be—" Doug was quiet for a few moments before saying, "about sixty-five pounds." He chuckled. "You'd last about twenty minutes," he said.

"Doug, I'm not *that* weak," Bob told him, trying to not sound irritated.

"Not saying you are, kiddo," Doug said. "You just don't know what sixty-five pounds on your back would feel like."

"I suppose." Bob was trying to repack his food supply compactly.

"Fortunately, I'll be carrying the tent and the ground pads," Doug said.

"Yes, don't forget to tell me what I owe you on them," Bob told him.

"For the tent, nothing, I already own it," Doug said. "I'll get you on the ground pad later." He chuckled. "And the whistle."

"And the whistle," Bob said good-naturedly.

"Here, put it in your pocket," Doug told him.

"Okay, thanks," Bob said. Doug knows a hell of a lot about all this, he told himself. Be grateful for his knowledge. So he is a little abrasive about it, so what? He's doing me a hell of a favor taking me on this hike. Appreciate it; don't keep niggling at his little lectures. They don't matter, not at all.

Anyway, what do I have to complain about? he thought. I need to know all this stuff for my novel. I should stop the internal kvetching and take notes, for chrissake.

"Yeah, if you manage twenty-five, thirty pounds you'll be doing good," Doug said. "Make sure you put stuff you'll only be using when we camp *inside* the pack. Anything you might want to use on the trail, put in one of the outer pockets. Put things in the same places all the time too so you don't have to search for them every time you need them. And make sure you pack the stove and fuel in an outer pocket in case there's a leak, you got that?"

Bob tried not to sigh. "Got it," he said.

"All for your safety, buddy," Doug reminded him.

"I know. I appreciate it," Bob said. Say no more, he told himself.

"Okay, let's try it on for size," Doug said, standing.

"Right." Bob picked up his pack and tried to swing it around his right shoulder. "Whoa!" he cried as the weight of the pack pulled him over, almost making him fall.

"And that, class, is the wrong way to don your backpack," Doug said. His smile was smug but Bob laughed anyway. "Guess I could use a little instruction here," he said.

"Guess you could." Doug took the pack from him. "Now watch what I do," he said.

"I'm watching."

"First you loosen your shoulder, load lifter, and hip stabilizer straps a little bit. They're all padded, that's good."

Bob nodded as Doug loosened the straps slightly.

"Got that?" Doug asked.

"Yeah."

"You have to establish a routine for fitting the pack each time you put it on," Doug told him. "Next you bend your knees like *so* . . . swing the pack onto your thigh and—slide under the shoulder straps in one quick movement. Got it?"

"Got it." Bob nodded.

"All right, the pack is on your back. What comes next?"

"With me, probably collapse."

"Come on, Bobby, I'm trying to tell you something here."

"Yeah, okay, okay. I presume you tighten the straps back up."

"Not yet," Doug said. "First you lean forward and cinch the waist belt . . . like so. It should sit right above and on your hips. Next, you straighten up, settle the pack on your hips, *then* pull your shoulder straps tight."

"Whoa," Bob muttered.

"What?"

"Complicated."

"No, it isn't." Doug shook his head. "Do it a few times and you'll do it without thinking. All right. Next you buckle the sternum strap . . . so. Then you tighten—you did try this pack on, didn't you?"

"Sure." Bob nodded. "The salesman never told me all this stuff though."

"They never do," Doug said. "All right, next you retighten the load lifter straps and hip stabilizer straps—that'll keep the pack from swaying while you're walking."

"Hope I remember all this," Bob said, looking confused.

"You will," Doug told him. "Otherwise, you'll end up with raw spots on your neck and hips and God knows where else."

With movements so fast Bob couldn't follow them, Doug was out of the pack and holding it out. "Okay, let's see you do it now," he said.

3:58 PM

My God, it's gorgeous, Bob thought as he walked along the trail behind Doug. The forest was deeply green with splashes of glowing gold from the maple leaves. One of them fell now and then, fluttering to the ground in slow, vivid loops. The only sound was that of pine needles crackling beneath their boots as they walked; two miles an hour on flat ground, one mile an hour on harder terrain, Doug had said.

Bob drew in a deep lungful of air. Like a fine white wine, he thought, crisp and pure. He smiled at the image. He was glad he had come. Now that all the lecturing was done, Doug had been quiet for more than a half hour except for asking Bob to let him know when he felt the need to stop and rest. So far, he'd said nothing even though his legs were starting to feel a little tired. The pack on his back seemed to grow heavier with every minute. Carefully packed, riding high, no more than twenty-five pounds he estimated, it still felt as though he were carrying an anvil on his back.

To hell with it, he told himself. He'd keep on as long as he could. What am I, a wimp? he challenged himself. Undoubtedly, he thought, but I'm going to fight it.

He concentrated on the forest again. Patches of sunlight dappled the trail ahead. As the trail curved to the right, he saw, again, the mountain that was their first landmark, Doug had said. There was a little snow on its peak, glistening in the sunlight. If it stays like this, he thought, I won't need to see my poncho blowing out like a boat sail. He chuckled softly to himself, imagining that sight.

So far, except for the pack, the walk had been nothing but pleasant. They'd passed a fast-moving stream, its crystal-clear water splashing off rocks, sometimes forming momentary rainbows with the sunlight. He'd seen a mule deer grazing on a small meadow, looking over at them, apparently unconcerned because it returned to grazing a few moments later.

These are the things I want to remember for my novel, he kept thinking. All of them.

"Sure you don't need to stop and rest?" Doug asked, looking back.

Bob didn't answer at first. Why doesn't Doug ask me if I want to stop and rest, not if I need to. These were the little digs that annoyed him. He was going to say no, he was fine. Then common sense prevailed. Don't be a macho idiot, he told himself.

"Yeah, I guess I would," he said, "I have to pee anyway. All that water you made me drink."

"Need plenty of water," Doug said, moving off the trail to another spot with a fallen oak lying across it. "At least a gallon a day."

Bob joined him on the open ground and, moving around the fallen tree, opened his pants and emptied his bladder. "Oh, *that* feels good," he said.

"Pause that refreshes," Doug responded.

Bob walked back around the tree and slumped to the ground, groaning.

"You dying?" Doug asked, half smiling.

Bob snickered. "Not yet," he answered.

"Put your pack on that little boulder," Doug told him. "Take all the weight off your back."

Bob shifted over to the boulder and laid his backpack on it. "Oh, you're right," he said, sounding pleased.

"Usually am," Doug said, "about backpacking anyway."

He took the compass out of his jacket pocket and looked at it.

"We still going in the right direction?" Bob asked.

"Yup." Doug put the compass back into his pocket. "If this was unfamiliar country, we'd use a topographic map but here we don't need to."

"How many miles to your cabin?" Bob asked.

"Hard to say," Doug answered. "Never figured it out. A good three days though. Four if you get real bushed and we have to slow down."

Jesus, Doug, do you have to keep harping on this? Bob thought.

"You're gasping for breath a little bit," Doug told him. "That's to be expected. Be sure you exhale all the way, get the carbon dioxide out of your system, make lots of room for oxygen. Concentrate on your exhaling."

"All right." Bob nodded. *Good advice,* he thought.

"I'll probably lose some weight by Wednesday, don't you think?" he asked.

"Don't plan on it," Doug said warningly. "You're going to need all the energy you can muster. Don't worry about gaining weight on a high calorie diet. You won't."

"I understand," Bob nodded.

"What do you do for exercise, Bob?" Doug asked.

Bob felt inclined to exaggerate, then decided against it. "Walk," he said.

"That's all?"

"And swim in the summer," Bob added.

"Oh, that's right, you have a swimming pool."

Bob felt himself bristle a little. Doug knew very well that he had a pool; he and Nicole had gone swimming in it.

"No weight lifting?" Doug asked.

"I used to," Bob answered. "I stopped."

"Why?"

Bob exhaled wearily. "I got bored with it," he said.

"Bicycle ride?"

"I used to," Bob said, wishing the line of questions would end.

"Tennis? Handball?"

"No, Doug, no," he answered.

"Well—" Doug gestured with his hands. "I'm only asking because it applies to hiking. Ever take the twelve-minute test?"

"What's that?"

"You see how far you can walk or run in twelve minutes," Doug said. "If you can cover a mile and a quarter to a mile and a half in twelve minutes you're in fair condition."

"And good?" Bob asked, wondering why he was asking; he knew that the answer would only aggravate him.

"Good is what I do," Doug said. "A mile and a half to a mile and three-quarters in twelve minutes. You do that, you're ready for anything."

Well, bully for you, Bob thought.

"Have to keep that cardiovascular system humming," Doug said. "Strengthen the muscles."

"Mmm." Bob nodded. "Well, I'm . . . obviously not ready for the Olympics. But I'm not ready for the undertaker either. I don't smoke. I drink sparingly. Watch my diet, take vitamins."

"Uh-huh." Doug's nod was dismissive.

"What are we gonna see on this hike?" Bob asked to change the subject.

"Oh . . ." Doug gestured vaguely. "Forest. Meadows. Cliffs. Streams. Rivers. Finally, the old Wiley place."

"What's that?" Bob asked.

"Deserted lodge. Built back in the twenties. When we reach it, we're almost to the cabin."

Bob nodded. Doug fell silent again and he racked his mind for another question. Otherwise, Doug might start lecturing again.

"What kind of trees are those?" he asked, pointing.

"Douglas fir," Doug answered.

"Got a tree named after you, very impressive," Bob said.

Doug showed no sign of amusement but became silent again, closing his eyes.

"Wow," Bob said, "look at that big bird up there."

Doug opened his eyes and looked up. "Red-tailed hawk," he muttered.

"It's beautiful," Bob said.

Doug grunted. "I suppose." He yawned. "You'll see all kinds of birds out here. Hawks. Owls. Jays. Chickadees—"

He broke off and Bob caught his breath at a strange, clattering noise overhead. Looking up, he saw two animals running through the trees. One of them soared between two branches.

"They're not squirrels," he said.

"Pine martens," Doug told him. "They like to chase each other."

Bob chuckled as the two thick-legged martens disappeared in the overhead branches, making bark dust and twigs rain down.

He started to speak when Doug said, "I'm going to take a ten-minute nap." Laying his head back, he closed his eyes again. *Ten minutes?* Bob thought. Could he do that?

He stared at Doug for almost a minute. Doug was handsome enough: well-proportioned features, full head of black hair, athletic build. But he sure could be a pain in the ass.

He lay his head back and closed his eyes.

Was this a mistake after all? he wondered. His past relationship with Doug had never been a close one. He and Marian had gone once to the cabin when Doug and Nicole were still married. Doug had been doing reasonably well then: a small, running part in a detective series; it was on that set that he'd become acquainted with Doug.

The weekend had been a tense one. Doug and Nicole were obviously getting close to a divorce, their behavior during the weekend not easy to experience, filled with arguments—about their son Artie, about Doug's limited career, hints (from Nicole) about Doug's womanizing.

Doug tried to cover it all with laughter and charm; he could be charming when he wanted to. At least he was on that weekend.

Bob had made the mistake—he felt now that it *was* a mistake—of mentioning the backpacking novel he was planning to write. When he spoke about the research he'd done, Doug had insisted that the only proper research he could do would be to actually take a backpacking trip—and he was the one to take Bob on it. Bob had expressed interest and gratitude at the offer. Now he wasn't sure it was a good idea after all. Since things had been going poorly for Doug's career (he was back working with a building contractor again) his disposition had darkened somewhat.

And I have three whole days ahead to be with him, he thought, maybe four.

Yippee.

He twitched as something landed on his lap. Jerking open his eyes, he looked down and saw an energy bar lying on his right leg.

"Time for a snack," Doug told him. "Eating while you hike should be one long, endless snack—a piece of candy or fruit, a sip of juice, an energy bar. Something to raise the blood sugar level."

"Thanks," Bob said. "Can't say I'm crazy about these things. Marian loves them but I don't."

"Eat it anyway," Doug told him. "You should take in three ounces of carbohydrate every two hours. Don't want to let your glycogen level get too low."

And so the lectures begin again, Bob thought; Professor Crowley on the podium.

"If we were home, I'd kill you if you spent a lot of time eating candy and flour products, sugar, big-time carbohydrates. Out here though, go for it. You need the energy."

"Okay." Bob tore off the wrapping, looked at it for a few moments, then put it in his pocket.

"That's a good boy," Doug said. "Never litter."

Bob started to chew on the energy bar. Yuk, he thought. Dates.

"Fat is good too," Doug told him. "Nuts. Cheese. Meat." Bob looked at his watch. Ten minutes, sure enough. He was impressed.

"Here, swallow this," Doug told him, tossing over a white tablet. "Salt tablet," he said as Bob picked it up off the ground. "Better than fake sweat."

"Fake sweat?"

"Gatorade, that kind of thing. Supposed to supply you with sodium chloride." He made a scornful noise. "Salt tablets are better."

"It's really beautiful up here, don't you think?" Bob asked after he'd washed down the salt tablet with a sip of water.

"Sure," Doug answered. "Why do you think I come here?"

"The blue sky, the clouds," Bob said. "The air. The stream. The incredible colors of the leaves. Those yellow trees aren't maples, what are they?"

"Dogwood," Doug told him.

"They certainly are beautiful," Bob said.

"Chlorophyll draining," Doug said. "They're dying."

Bob chuckled. "Well, that's one way of looking at it," he said. "Not too aesthetic, but—"

"—true," Doug broke in. "I'm not a sentimentalist, Bob. To me, nature is a challenge. Something to conquer."

"You really feel that way," Bob said.

"You bet." Doug nodded. He looked at his wristwatch. "We'd better get on our way. We want to set up our campsite before dark."

"Right." Bob took off his green corduroy cap and scratched his head. "Move on, Macduff."

He groaned as he stood, the pack still feeling like an anvil fastened to his back.

Doug made a sound of amusement. "Good thing we're on government land," he said. "Don't have to be prepared to make a dash from the hunters."

"Hunters?" Bob looked surprised.

"It *is* hunting season," Doug told him. "If this wasn't government land, we'd be wearing bright red jackets and track shoes."

"Well, I hope the hunters know it's government land," Bob said uneasily.

"Sometimes they don't give a damn whose land it is," Doug replied.

4:21 PM

As they started on, Doug picked up a twig and after rubbing it off, started to move one end of it inside his mouth.

"What are you doing?" Bob asked.

"Brushing my teeth, nature style," Doug answered.

Bob grunted, smiling slightly. "I'll use my toothbrush," he said.

"Well, so will I, dummy," Doug told him. "This is temporary."

"Ah." Bob tried not to take offense but barely managed it.

"Just remember it in case you *lose* your toothbrush," Doug said.

"Yes, sir. I'll remember." He was sure that Doug could hear the edginess in his voice.

They were approaching a meadow now. As they started to cross it, Bob said, "Odd-looking grass."

"Not grass, Bobby, sedge." Doug's tone was friendly now. Is he sorry he called me "dummy"? Bob wondered. It would be the way Doug would indicate an apology: not in so many words but in attitude. "All kinds of sedge," he went on. "Short-hair sedge, black sedge, brewer's sedge, alpine sedge, beaked sedge."

"Whoa," Bob said, accepting Doug's tone of voice as apology. "A lot of sedge."

"They look like grass," Doug explained, "but they have triangular stems and leaves in groups of three."

"Uh-huh."

"If this was spring, you'd be seeing lots of flowers too. Purple owl's clover. Larkspur. Paintbrush poppy. Lupine. Meadowfoam. Popcorn flower. Baby blue eyes."

"Jesus, how do you *know* all these things?" Bob asked, too impressed by Doug's knowledge to hold a grudge against him.

"You forget, I've been coming up here for years," Doug said. "And I *can* read, you know."

Oh, God, here we go again, Bob thought.

The thought vanished as something big buzzed past his head. "My God," he said, "that bumblebee's enormous."

"Not a bumblebee, a rufus hummingbird."

"Ah-ha." No point in fretting about Doug's manner, he thought. He was here to learn and Doug was teaching him. What more could he ask?

He started to say something, then broke off at a noise in the distance—what sounded like someone blowing across the top of an enormous pop bottle. "What the hell is *that*?" he asked, fully expecting that Doug would know.

Which he did. "Blue grouse," Doug said, "I've never seen one but I've heard them many times."

As they started back into the forest, Bob asked about the
trees up ahead. They hadn't run across their like before.

"Live oak, blue oak," Doug told him. "Deciduous, of
course."

Bob repressed a smile. Of course, he thought. "What about
those trees?" he asked, pointing. "They look black."

"They're called black oak," Doug said. "They grow really
fast after a fire."

Bob nodded. "What kind of trees are mostly found up
here?"

"Oh, pine, of course," Doug said. He *does* enjoy letting me
know what *he* knows, Bob thought. "Ponderosa, sugar, Jeffrey,
white, Douglas, and white fir. Ponderosa knows how to protect
itself from fires too, its bark is real thick."

Bob was about to speak when Doug stopped and raised
his right hand. Bob stopped abruptly, looking at him. Trouble?
he thought.

"What is—?" He broke off as Doug whispered *"Shh"* and
pointed upward with his right index finger.

Bob looked up and caught his breath.

Lying on an outcrop of rock on the hill to their right was
a mountain lion. It was lying on its left side, stretched out in
the sunlight.

For a few moments, Bob felt a tremor of uneasiness. He'd
seen mountain lions before but in cages or confined environments. To see one so relatively close—at least it seemed close
to him—and in the open . . . it was something that made him
feel uncomfortable, even menaced.

But as moments passed and the large, tawny-furred cat lay motionless, obviously sound asleep, the discomfort faded.

"What a gorgeous animal," he whispered.

"Lots of good steaks in there," Doug whispered back.

Bob gave him a look. "Come on," he whispered. "You don't mean that."

Doug punched him lightly on the arm. "Just teasing the animal activist," he said.

Their conversation continued in whispers as they gazed up at the sprawling mountain lion. Its flanks rose and fell slowly as it slept, a faint breeze stirring the light-colored fur on its right flank.

"I'm not an animal activist," Bob said, "I just think it would be criminal to harm a beautiful creature like that."

"It *is* beautiful," Doug agreed. "Sleek. Quick. Powerful. Deadly." He made a clicking sound of admiration. "The perfect predator."

Oh, Jesus, Doug, you're hopeless, Bob thought. He decided to keep it to himself.

"Well, let's keep going," Doug whispered, turning onto the path again.

Bob looked across his shoulder at the sleeping mountain lion as they moved away from it. Briefly, he imagined the cat waking up, spotting him, and with a frightening roar, leaping to its feet and off the rocky ledge, bounding toward him, muscles rippling, eyes intent on his.

Oh, shut up, he told himself. It wants to be left alone, no more. He looked ahead again. Doug had increased the length between them.

"Doug?" he called as softly as he could; no point in waking up the mountain lion unnecessarily.

Doug stopped and looked around.

"I've got to pee again."

"All right," Doug said. He stopped and waited while Bob stepped behind a tree.

"Drink more," Doug told him. "You've been pissing out a lot of liquid."

"All right," Bob answered. "My bottle's getting kind o' low though."

"There'll be plenty of water in the lake," Doug told him. "Drink."

"Yessir." Bob emptied his bladder on the trunk of the tree. "Hate to pee my way across the entire countryside," he said.

"Don't worry, it's biodegradable," Doug's voice reached him.

He finished and walked back to the path, drinking water. "Warm," he said, frowning.

"I forgot to tell you," Doug said. "Carry the bottle inside your pack wrapped in a piece of clothing. It'll keep your water cooler."

"Oh." Bob nodded.

"I've noticed, you're not walking erectly enough," Doug told him. "Don't slump. And don't lean forward. All of that's bad for your back. And keep a steady stride. Not too fast, but steady."

Yes, Professor, Bob thought. He almost said it aloud, then changed his mind. Doug was telling him these things to benefit him, not harass him. Just listen, nod, and *fermez la bouche*, he instructed himself.

"Try not to lift your feet any higher than you have to," Doug went on. "Swing your arms; good for circulation. And keep a steady, rhythmic pace. You'll get less tired that way. Slow and steady wins the race."

What race? Bob thought. Are we in a race? He put the thought from his mind. Just listen, ordered his brain.

"I hope you've done a lot of walking to toughen up your legs," Doug told him.

"Quite a bit," Bob lied.

"Well, let's be on our way," Doug said. "Got to keep moving or your muscles will cramp."

Muscles? Bob thought.

The stream was wide and fast-moving, a fallen tree across it covered with deep crosshatches. "Makes it easier to cross," Doug said. "Incidentally, since you're so curious about trees, those cinnamon-colored bark ones are incense cedars."

Bob nodded. Thank you, Professor, he thought.

Doug bent over and broke a twig off the tree. "Watch," he told Bob, tossing the twig into the stream. It was almost immediately swept out of sight. "That can tell you how fast the water's moving," Doug said. "So if the stream looks deep to you, don't try to cross it, the current might knock you down. Keep going farther downstream and look for a spot where you can cross diagonally."

He shook his head with a grim smile, remembering. "That's how I lost my backpack that time I mentioned before," he said, "I loosened my straps and unhooked my hip belt, of course, you're supposed to do that. But I miscalculated the velocity of the stream; it was probably a small river actually. And *boom*! I was in headlong and my pack was gone, washed over a damn waterfall. I was lucky I held on to my bow case." He grinned. "That's when I shot the rabbit for food. Okay, let's cross."

Bob tried to be as careful as he could but the weight of

his pack pulled him off balance and he started to fall. Doug, close behind, grabbed him and pushed him across the tree trunk. He was startled by the ease with which Doug moved him. "Easy does it, Roberto," Doug said, laughing a little.

As they continued along the trail, not only did Bob's back ache and his legs feel heavy, he started getting breathless as well.

"You should be getting your second wind by tomorrow," Doug told him.

And now you'll tell me what that is, Bob thought.

"It's a surge of energy that follows the period of time it takes you to get used to hard exercise," Doug said. "You'll feel more comfortable, be able to move faster."

"I'm looking forward to it," Bob said wearily.

Doug laughed. "You *are* in piss-poor condition, aren't you?" he said.

Bob didn't feel like arguing. "Yes, I am," he agreed. "Can we move a little slower?" he asked, "I'm losing my first breath."

"We're getting up a little higher, that's why," Doug explained casually.

Bob kept laboring for breath. That's it? he thought. We're *up* a little higher? I'm still having trouble breathing.

"Doug, I gotta stop again," he said.

"What, already? The water's running through you like a sieve."

"No, it's not that, I just need to rest a little while."

"Oh." Doug's tone was remote. He's already sorry he invited me on this hike, Bob thought.

Doug looked at his watch as they sat down. "Getting late," he said.

"I know, I'm sorry," Bob answered guiltily. He leaned his back against a tree trunk, groaning uncontrollably.

"You really think you're going to make this, Bob?" Doug sounded honestly curious, marginally concerned.

"I will, I will, I just—" Bob swallowed and closed his eyes. "How fast do you usually go?" he asked, feeling that he ought to, at least, maintain some level of conversation, especially if it gave Doug a chance to brag a little.

"At least a dozen miles a day," Doug told him. Bob wondered if he knew why he'd asked the question. "Beginners usually . . . a mile a day, no more," he added, sounding bored.

"Always measured in miles?" Bob asked. He really didn't care to know but still felt compelled to let Doug be impressive.

"Not always," Doug said; he sounded a little more interested now. "It can be hours a day too. Most packers give out after four or five hours. I've hiked ten to twelve with no problem."

"Ten to twelve?" Bob opened his eyes and stared at Doug with genuine awe.

"Once I went sixteen, once nineteen," Doug told him.

"That's amazing, Doug." He wasn't trying to cater to Doug now, he was truly impressed.

Doug seemed to lighten up at that. "I know it's hard for you," he said, "but I'm really trying to take it easy on you, give your muscles a chance to loosen up, get your pulse rate up to snuff."

"I appreciate that, Doug," Bob told him.

"You might try relacing your boots," Doug suggested. "See if they're on too tight; you don't want to pinch your feet."

"Okay, I will. Thanks."

He started at the strange noise overhead, deep, throbbing, uneven. "What in the hell is *that?*" he asked.

"Blue grouse again," Doug told him, "up on the mountain."

Bob felt himself going to sleep.

There were at least seven coyotes circling them, maybe eight. There were no trees to climb. The ground was open and bare.

"What do we do now?" he asked fearfully, turning to Doug.

Doug wasn't there.

"Oh, Jesus, only *he'd* know what to do," he muttered.

He stared at the growling, slavering coyotes as they moved in slowly.

He jolted and opened his eyes. Doug had just shaken him by the shoulder. Bob stared at him groggily.

"You fell asleep," Doug told him.

"Oh, jeez, I'm sorry, Doug," Bob said, a pained expression on his face.

"Look," Doug said, "what I'm going to do is go on by myself, set up camp for us."

Bob stared at him blankly. "I don't understand," he murmured.

"It's getting late," Doug said. "It takes a while to set up camp. I can go on ahead and get it ready."

"Well . . ." Bob looked alarmed. "Leave me alone?"

"Bob, all you have to do is follow the trail," Doug said with a chuckle. "You can't get lost. And when you get to the camp, the fire will be burning, the tent set up, the sleeping bags ready. I'll take yours with me—and your stove, give you less weight to carry. I'll even take some of your damn chicken à la king with me so it'll be ready to eat by the time you arrive. Take you maybe two hours to get there. Maybe less."

"But . . ."

"Have to do it this way, buddy," Doug said. "We're behind schedule."

"What if I get lost?" He was aware of sounding like "Bobby" now, a panicking ten-year-old.

"Bobby, you *can't* get lost," Doug said. "Just follow the trail. Okay?" It was more a demand than a question.

"Okay." His voice sounded timid to him. He swallowed dryly. "There's no chance I could wander off the trail?"

"None," Doug said, "and if it gets a little dark, use your flashlight. You reversed your batteries, didn't you?"

"What?" Bob felt helpless and stupid. "What do you—?"

"Keeps them from running down if the flashlight accidentally gets turned on," Doug told him.

"Oh." Was he going to just *agree* to this, let Doug leave him behind in the woods—hell, the forest!—the very first afternoon they were out?

He tried to struggle up but the pack was too heavy on him and pulled him back; he thudded against the tree trunk.

"You'll have less weight now," Doug told him, strapping Bob's stove and sleeping bag on his pack. "You'll be fine—able to move a little faster."

Bob felt as though his mouth was hanging open, his expression appalled as Doug turned away and started walking briskly along the trail. Don't! a voice cried in his brain. What about the mountain lion?!

That seemed to break the spell of dread. The mountain lion, for Christ's sake? he thought. What did he think, the mountain lion was going to trail him and have him for supper? *Grow up*, Hansen, he ordered himself. Grow up, get up, and move your ass. This isn't goddamn *Deliverance*, you know.

Maybe if I start after him right away and move as fast as I can, I'll be able to catch up to him, he thought abruptly. Good idea. Doug couldn't be walking *that* fast.

He tried to stand quickly and fell back, landing clumsily. Yeah, that's great, Hansen, he mocked himself. Real deft.

He tried again and fell back awkwardly once more. Jesus Christ, he said he took some weight *off* my pack! he thought. It feels as though he added rocks to it instead.

No. No. He calmed himself. On your knees first, then stand slowly. Got it? He drew in a quick breath, nodding. Got it, he answered.

Carefully, he turned himself and rose to his knees, then slowly, arms outstretched to keep himself in balance, rose to his feet. There, he thought. That wasn't so difficult now, was it? He tried not to pay attention to the painful drag of the pack on his back, the aching in his legs. Go, he told himself. Move.

He started to walk along the trail as rapidly as he could. Stand erect, he reminded himself. Don't slump. Don't lift your feet too high. Walk with a steady stride.

His brain reacted with unexpected irritation. Goddamn it, how am I supposed to remember all that crap? What am I, John Muir? No. He tried to settle his mind. It's already been established that you definitely aren't John Muir. Just walk erect, don't slump, steady stride. It's not that fucking hard, you idiot. Thanks for the kind words, he thought and had to grin.

He concentrated on keeping a steady stride. Doug was right, that did work better. But then Doug was right about everything. Backpacking-wise anyway. Life? A little different.

Odd how the forest, which had seemed exquisite and inspiring before, was now beginning to take on the aspects of an ominous entity around him. The tall, thin pines looked like spears, their foliage thick and gray-green, large, scaly cones on the ground beneath them. The huge leaves of the maple trees now looked like random splashes of yellow amid the dark green canopy. Was the green really that dark or was the light starting to fade? That would be all he needed: to be alone in the forest in the dark. Wonderful, he thought. He tried to visualize the possibility with amusement but his involuntary shiver belied it. Great, he thought. Alone in the forest in the dark. And I don't even have my sleeping bag now! he suddenly realized. I'd goddamn freeze to death! They'd find my skeleton twenty years from now, lying under—

Oh, shut up! he commanded himself. And straighten up for Christ's sake, you're slumping! "Oh," he muttered gloomily. He fought away anxiety. Just—follow—the—goddamn—path; that was all he had to do. He wasn't in the great North Woods. This was a national park in California and he was on a trail. A *trail*, Hansen, he reminded himself.

No, wait. Goddamn it, I am slumping again! There must be some way to control—

Yes! His face lit up as he moved to a fallen tree and found a branch on it with the right thickness. Taking out his hunting knife, he started to saw away at it so that it would be about five feet long. Oh, great, he thought, the knife was just about sharp enough to slice its way through butter.

He hacked and pulled at the branch until it broke off, then cut off the twigs (sure, those the damn knife can cut off, he thought) and did the best he could to level the end of the branch.

He began to walk again, using the branch as a staff. Not bad, he thought. It did help keep him more erect. Now just move at a steady pace and you'll—

"Jesus Christ!" He stopped and jerked around as something rustled noisily in the brush to his left. Just before it vanished, he saw that it was a fleeing rabbit.

"Oh . . . God." He swallowed dryly, then opened his bottle and took a drink of water. His heartbeat was still pounding. Is it going to be like this the whole time? he wondered. I thought it was something big, something dangerous. A rabbit, for chrissake. He groaned at his vulnerability. Just keep going, will you, Hansen? he suggested. Yes, by all means, he replied politely to himself.

He started walking again. It did seem easier to stay erect and keep a steady pace using the staff. For a few moments, he visualized himself as a proficient woodsman striding through his familiar wilderness. After all, he had only to follow the very obvious trail. Soon enough, he'd reach the campsite. Doug would be waiting there, a cozy fire burning. Dehydration or no dehydration, he *would* partake of one of his little bottles of vodka.

He seemed to be going uphill more now. At least the strain of walking seemed to be increasing and it was becoming more and more laborious to breathe. Well, he could manage that. If only it wasn't getting so shadowy. The more shadowy it became, the more menacing the silence seemed.

Ordinarily, he loved silence. Where Marian and he lived in Agoura Hills, it was deathly silent, far from the freeway noises; and he enjoyed it immensely, they both did. Sitting on their deck at sunset, having drinks, they often commented on how quiet it was. There, quiet seemed peaceful and comforting. Here . . .

Well, it's the unknown, he tried to reason with himself. Just . . . keep moving and stop worrying about it. It ain't gonna kill you.

"I hope," he muttered. He frowned at himself. "Shut up," he said.

He had to stop and empty his bladder again, then take another drink of water. The bottle was getting pretty empty, he saw. What if he got lost and ran out of water?

"Oh, for God's sake, shut the hell up," he ordered himself. Drawing in a deep, he hoped, restoring breath, he continued walking.

As he got into a rhythmic stride, he began to think about Doug.

Was it really necessary for him to go on ahead and leave me behind? he wondered. After all, how much more difficult would it have been to set up camp if they'd gotten to the place together, wherever it was?

This was their first day out too. Doug knew he was uneasy. He knew that Marian was uneasy. Was it really thoughtful of him to hurry on ahead to make camp? Or had there been something mean about it, something actually a little cruel under the circumstances?

He thought about the few years they had known Doug

and Nicole, then, limitedly, Doug by himself. They were never really close. They'd had a few laughs together but their personalities didn't really blend that well. Nicole was pleasant enough, very beautiful (she'd been a model), but a little cut off and remote. And, from the very start, she'd obviously been unhappy about her marriage to Doug. The death of Artie had really torn what threads were left intact in their relationship.

What Doug and he had shared most in common was their knowledge and attitudes toward the motion picture and television business. They were both highly dissatisfied and frustrated by it, Doug more than him because, as relative as the pain was, actors did have it worse than writers. He could, at least, submerge his disappointments by writing a short story or a novel. Doug could only do a little theater that while creatively fulfilling involved no monetary satisfaction at all.

In other words, Bob thought—in other words, had there always been an edge of envy, even resentment in Doug? And had he just demonstrated a small bit of that by leaving him behind in the woods?

"The forest," he said. "The *forest.*"

It wasn't any charming, sweet, endearing woods.

It was BIG. Powerful. Unyielding. A massive, silent being that could and had swallowed men alive.

That's a charming image, he thought.

But he couldn't dispel it.

Well, here's another goddamn thing he didn't tell me about, he thought.

He stared glumly at the fast-moving stream in front of him. On its opposite shore, the path obviously continued.

Now what? he thought. It was definitely getting darker and there was no way he could see to cross the stream: no fallen tree trunk, no stepping-stone boulders.

"Well, what am I supposed to do *now*, Dougie boy?" he asked loudly.

Breaking a tiny piece of twig off his staff, he tossed it into the stream and watched it be swept away by the bubbling, splashing current. Great, he thought, his face a mask of annoyance. Now I know it's moving fast. Thank you, Douglas, for that enlightening bit of woodlore. It changes everything.

He drew in a quick, convulsive breath. This isn't funny, Bob, he told himself. What was he supposed to do, *walk* across the stream, get his boots and socks and trousers soaking wet? Screw that.

"Well . . ." Grimacing, he started walking along the edge of the stream, hoping to find a narrower part of it.

Up above, a wind was starting to blow in the high pines. Great, he thought, a storm.

He shook that away with a scowl. Stop being a baby, he told himself. Doug got across the damn stream, so can I.

For a while, he imagined Doug coming up with a rope from his pack, hurling one end of it across the stream, encircling a branch with it, and swinging across like Tarzan.

"Not likely," he muttered, moving guardedly along the stream edge so he wouldn't stumble on a stone.

About twenty yards down, he came across a tree trunk fallen across the stream. "Ah," he said. "Ah." You might have mentioned it to me, he said to Doug in his mind. You know this goddamn forest, I don't.

As he crossed the trunk, it shifted with him. "*Oh, God,*" he muttered. Flailing at the air for balance, he lost hold of the staff and dropped it in the stream. By the time he'd fallen to one knee on the tree trunk, grabbed hold of it, and regained his balance, the staff was long gone, washed downstream by the leaping current. Great, he thought as he made it finally to the other side of the stream. Easy come, easy go.

He walked back along the stream until he reached the trail and started along it again. This is a goddamn national forest, he thought as he walked. Why didn't they put some kind of bridge on the stream so the trail could be followed more easily? It might have been considerate to novices like me.

He concentrated on walking erect, not slumping, lifting his feet, keeping a steady stride. Well, he should be at the campsite soon. He swallowed uneasily. He'd better be. The light was fading fast. At least, it seemed to be. Maybe it was because of the thick tree growth.

Just keep going, he told himself. Erect. Feet lifted. Steady stride. He walked through the deep, silent forest, trying to remain convinced that he would reach Doug soon, have that vodka, dine on chicken à la king, and, most of all, rest his weary bones.

5:13 PM

"Good God," he muttered.

Just ahead of him, the trail split.

He stared at it in utter dismay. For the first time since he'd started after Doug he felt a genuine sense of fear. What was he supposed to do now? Doug did it on purpose, he found himself thinking.

He'd gone on ahead, not to set up a camp but to leave him behind, hopelessly lost.

A spasm of coldness shook his body. No, you're being paranoid, he thought. Would Doug have taken him all the way up here for some kind of terrible revenge? Revenge for what? Envy, okay, maybe so. A little jealousy. But this?

"No," he said. "No. No." He shook his head. He was being ridiculous. There was some other reason. Doug hadn't been up here for a long time. He'd forgotten that the trail split, that was all.

"In that case . . ." he murmured.

He looked at the bushes and trees around the dividing trail. A piece of paper, a note, a scrap of rag. Something to mark the trail he was supposed to follow.

There was nothing. It was shadowy beneath the trees but surely he'd see a rag or piece of paper if Doug had placed one to mark his way.

He drew in a deep, trembling breath. Dear God, he thought. He really didn't know which way to go. And Doug had not left any sign to help him.

He swallowed dryly. His throat felt parched. Removing the top of his water bottle, he took a sip. Not too much, he cautioned himself. You don't want to run out of water.

"Sure," he said cynically. That's what really matters. I can be totally lost in the forest, but so long as I have water, I'll be fine. "Damn," he muttered. "Stupid idiot."

All right. All right. He straightened up, a look of determination on his face. Maybe this was a test, a goddamn test. That sort of thing Doug *would* do. He was setting up a situation where logic could tell him which half of the trail to follow.

All right, think, he thought; think, you moron.

The right-hand trail looked as though it was beginning to

angle downward. That would indicate that it was heading toward the lake Doug had mentioned. Was the answer as simple as that?

No, the left-hand trail could also be leading to the lake. Couldn't it? The lake could be to the left, not the right.

Which leaves me right back where I started, he thought. He tried to find some measure of amusement in the thought but couldn't really do it; the situation was too potentially serious to be amusing in any way.

Well, for Christ's sake, make up your mind! he ordered himself. He couldn't just stand here like a bump on a log and—

He had to snicker at the memory. A bump on a log? He hadn't thought of that phrase since he was a boy. His mother had used it often.

"All right," he said firmly, "which way, Hansen, right or left?"

The right-hand path seemed the most likely. It *was* angling down and that would indicate it heading toward the lake. And Doug *had* said it might take him less than an hour to reach the campsite. So the right path was the most logical one to take. There you go, Bobby, he imagined Doug telling him when he reached the campsite. You just passed your first test in Woodlore I.

"Yeah, yeah," he muttered, starting forward onto the right-hand trail.

The trail kept getting steeper as he moved along. He found himself tending to lean back, trying to center the weight of the pack so it wouldn't pull him forward.

The path was also getting darker as he walked. Looking up, he could see, through rifts in the tree foliage, that it was still light. You'd never know it down here, he thought.

He kept looking to the right, trying to catch a glimpse of the lake. But all he saw was endless forest. Was this the right way after all? Had he made a mistake? Maybe—

He gasped out in shock as something rolled beneath his right boot and he found himself lurching helplessly to his left. "No!" he cried, starting to fall, thrashing, into some brush.

His right palm, flung down automatically to brace himself against the fall, hit the ground and was scraped across it, making him hiss in pain. A jagged streak of pain stabbed at the right side of his back as he thudded to a halt, a bush twig raking across his right cheek, making him hiss again.

He lay motionless in the brush, gasping for breath. Oh, Jesus, what if I've broken something? he thought, terrified. What if I'm on the wrong path and I've broken a bone?

The sound he made, intended to be a despairing laugh, came out, instead, as a sob. "Jesus, Jesus, Jesus," he murmured, eyes tearing. What am I doing here? he thought. His throat felt dry again. He lay immobile, aware of his body twisted into a heap. I'm finished, he thought. I'm gone.

He forced air into his lungs. Shut up, he told himself. Just shut up. He'd taken a clumsy tumble, nothing more. It's not as if that mountain lion is about to pounce on me and bite off my face.

He grimaced at the thought. Great imaging, he told himself.

"All right, get up, for chrissake," he said irritably. "Get off your ass—or whatever you're lying on. Night is going to fall too if you don't get moving."

Laboriously, with slow, groaning movements, he struggled to his feet. His back felt sore and tender, his right palm hurt. But, at least, he didn't appear to have any broken bones.

He got back on the trail and stood still, wondering what to do.

"Doug?!" he shouted. He had to clear his throat, took a sip of water, then shouted again. "Doug! Doug!"

Was that an answer? he thought, suddenly excited. He shouted Doug's name again and again, finally realizing that what he was hearing was the echo of his own voice.

"Oh . . . shit," he muttered.

The whistle! he thought suddenly.

Fumbling through his jacket pockets until he found it, he blew on it as hard as he could. He had to drink more water; his mouth felt dry. He blew on the whistle again, struggling to make the sound as loud as possible.

There was no response.

"You bastard," he muttered. "You lousy bastard."

He continued down the path, moving with cautious steps. What the hell had rolled beneath his boot anyway? A twig? A rock? A pinecone? Whatever it was, it had sure made him take a real flop into the brush. For a few moments, he visualized John Muir accosting him and saying, "Bob, if I were you, I'd go back to Los Angeles, you really don't belong out here," and him replying, "Mr. Muir, how right you are."

Twelve minutes later, he reached the lake and the end of the trail. The open area of water made the light brighter; it wasn't that close to darkness after all.

Neither was it any spot for a campsite. There was thick growth all the way to the shore, no possible flat, open areas anywhere in sight. So the trail had been the wrong one after all. Great. Sorry, Bobby, you just failed test number one in your Woodlore course, Doug told him in his imagination. Try again.

"You son of a bitch," he said. "You miserable son of a bitch, not letting me know which trail to take."

He winced as he realized how his right palm hurt. Looking at it, he saw dried blood streaks across it, imbedded dirt, scrapes, and scratches.

Kneeling—the movement sent a streak of pain across the right side of his back that made him cry out softly—he put his palm in the cold water of the lake, and removing his handkerchief, he rubbed it on the palm as gently as he could to clean it off. "Oh . . . Jesus," he said, his face contorted from the stinging pain.

How am I supposed to write a convincing novel about backpacking if I've never backpacked once, he heard himself telling Marian. He sighed heavily. Would that I *had* written that novel about Hawaii she suggested I write, he thought.

He straightened up with a grunt of pain and effort.

"Doug!" he shouted. "Damn it, where *are* you?!"

This time, the echo was more distinct. What, the open water? he wondered.

"What's the difference?" he said as he started back up the trail. Now how long was it going to take to reach the campsite? he thought. Would it be dark by then? He blew out hissing breath. Good ol' Doug, he thought. My pal.

He stopped to take another sip of water, then continued up the trail, leaning forward to keep the weight of the backpack centered. His water was really getting low now. What if he still wasn't able to find Doug? What if Doug *did* do all this to lose him? He shivered, grimacing. Come on, he told himself. Don't be goddamn paranoid. You do this all the time. What was that song Mel Brooks composed for *The Twelve Chairs?* "Hope for the best; expect the worst," he sang softly. Something like that. And that was him. "You're a goddamn pessimist, Bob," he informed himself. As if I didn't know, he thought.

When he reached the split in the path and started along the left one, he tried to see what time it was but it was too dark in the heavy shade for him to read the watch face. He stopped and retrieved his flashlight. Don't forget to reverse the batteries, he thought. Oh, fuck you, he answered himself, switching on the flashlight and pointing the beam at the face of his wristwatch.

"Oh, my," he said. It was seven minutes after seven. This time of year, it was going to be dark soon now. Thank God they hadn't left after daylight savings time had ended or it'd be dark already. Damn you, Doug, he thought. Why did you do this to me on the very first day? It was unconscionable, really unconscionable.

He became aware that he was limping slightly as he walked. All I need, he thought. Days of hiking ahead and a limp. "Swell," he muttered. He was really getting angry with Doug now. What the hell right did he think he had to leave him alone on the first day of their hike?

His anger kept mounting as he limped along the trail. By the time he saw the glow of the campfire ahead, there was nothing left in him to react with relief at the sight. He was all anger.

"Hey, there he is," Doug said as Bob walked up to the campsite.

"Don't-ever-do-that-to-me-again," Bob told him in a low-pitched, shaking voice.

"What?" Doug looked perplexed.

"Do you have any idea what I've been through?" Bob demanded. "You don't tell me there's no way to cross that stream at the trail. You don't tell me there's a goddamn *split* in the trail."

"Bob—" Doug said.

"So I go down the right-hand trail and fall because it's so damn steep! I hurt my back, I scrape my palm! I find the lake and there's nothing there but water!"

"Bob!" Doug cried. "Take it easy. Let me—"

"Take it easy?!" Bob almost yelled. "I was fucking terrified out there! Terrified! I screamed your name as loud as I could! I blew your goddamn whistle until I was out of breath!" He knew his voice was breaking and he sounded on the verge of crying but he didn't care. "What the hell was wrong with you, leaving me alone like that?! You know I've never done this sort of thing before! You know it goddamn well!"

Doug tried to grab Bob's arm. "Bob, will you kindly let me—"

"Why didn't you tell me there was a split in the trail?!" Bob shouted.

"I didn't remember that there was!" Doug answered sharply.

"Oh, well, great, great!" Bob said. "What was I supposed to do, guess which trail to follow?"

"No, Bobby, no," Doug said, sounding angry now. "I did mark the left-hand trail! I *did* mark it!"

Bob felt struck dumb by Doug's words. Then suspicion struck again. "How?" he demanded. "There was no note, no piece of paper, no piece of rag."

"Did you look at the ground?" Doug demanded back.

"The ground?! It was so dark there I could barely *see* the ground!"

"Well, if you had—if you'd thought for a moment to shine your flashlight at the ground, you'd have seen that I made an arrow out of stones there! Pointing toward the left-hand trail!" Doug was glaring at him now.

Bob stared at him, speechless.

"And even if you *hadn't* seen it—which you obviously didn't—I'd have gone back to find you after a while. Do you think I'd have just *left* you out there, for Christ's sake?!"

How strange, was all Bob could think. How instantaneously rage could turn to guilt.

He tried to speak but couldn't; his throat felt so dry and raw. He took a sip of water, noting that his hand shook holding the bottle.

Then he drew in trembling breaths.

"I'm sorry," he said. "I didn't know, I didn't understand." He couldn't lose all his anger though. "You really shouldn't have left me alone though. I was scared to death, Doug. Alone in the dark forest? Jesus Christ. I didn't know *what* to do."

Doug's expression had softened now. "Okay," he said, "I probably shouldn't have left you alone. You just weren't up to it."

That's right, make sure you get a little dig in, have the final word. Bob pushed aside the thought, he was so relieved now that the nightmare (albeit minor) had ended.

"I know what it's like in the forest after dark," Doug said. "Although it wasn't really dark yet. It's just getting dark now."

"Under those trees it was dark," Bob said.

"Granted." Doug nodded. "It can be hair-raising. All the noises."

Bob managed a weak chuckle. "I even imagined that mountain lion getting me," he said.

Doug's smile was perfunctory. "I told you they don't want anything to do with us."

Bob sighed. "I know you did," he said. Can't help getting in one more little lecture, can you? he thought.

"Here, let's get that pack off you," Doug said.

Bob groaned with intense pleasure as Doug removed the pack and put it on the ground. "Now I know what Quasimodo must have gone through," he said.

He saw that Doug didn't get the point and let it go.

"Here, let me get that scrape on your cheek," Doug told him.

"Scrape on my cheek?" Bob looked confused. "Didn't know I had one." He'd forgotten all about it.

He sank down with another groan of pleasure as Doug got a small plastic bottle of alcohol, a cotton ball, and a tube of ointment from his pack. "That for me to drink?" Bob asked.

Doug made a sound of vague amusement and got down on one knee before Bob. "Take your cap off," he said.

Bob removed his cap and lay it on the ground as Doug opened the small bottle of alcohol and, up-ending it, wet the cotton ball.

"This'll sting," he said.

Bob stiffened with a faint cry as Doug wiped the cotton ball over his cheek. "Not too bad a scratch," Doug told him.

Bob nodded as Doug took hold of his right hand and lifted it up, palm raised. "This is going to sting too," he said.

"Oh!" Bob jerked, eyes closed, teeth clenching as Doug wiped the cotton ball over his palm. Are you enjoying this? he thought, then frowned at himself for the uncharitable thought.

He sat quietly, gazing at Doug's intent expression as he spread salve on the cheek and palm. I've wronged him, he thought. He never meant for me to come to harm. It was my own fault. It would have been better if Doug had stayed with him. Still, there *was* a camp now. Doug's tent was up. He saw their sleeping bags inside, the pads underneath them. And, of course, the fire. The crackling yellow-orange flames and radiating warmth were really comforting. Especially after what he'd been through.

Doug finished applying the salve and looked up with a slight grin. "That should do it," he said. "Try not to fall down again."

Bob thought for a moment that Doug was razzing him. Then he let it go, smiling at Doug. "Thank you, Doctor," he said.

"No problem," Doug answered, "I'm sure the Writers Guild insurance will pay for it."

"Yeah." Bob chuckled, taking it for granted that Doug was joking.

"Well, I guess you could use one of your little bottles of vodka right now," Doug said.

You got that right, Bob thought.

8:23 PM

Bob leaned back against his pack with a sound part groan, part sigh of pleasure. "I feel alive again," he said. He took a sip of the instant mocha coffee he'd brought along. They had cooked and shared the chicken à la king, two slices of bread, and, for dessert, two cookies and an apple each. He hadn't even minded that Doug had made fun of him for putting some of the condiments that Marian had packed for him on the chicken à la king.

"A little bit of civilization in the north woods, eh?" Doug had said with a teasing smile.

He hadn't even responded.

"Too bad you didn't bring a pair of slippers," Doug said; he had brought a pair and was wearing them.

"Yeah." Bob nodded. Of course you never told me to, he thought, but then I suppose I should have thought of it myself.

"How's the blister?" Doug asked.

When Bob'd taken off his boots, he'd become aware of the blister on his right big toe. Doug had put a bandage on it, one with a hole in its middle so as not to irritate the blister itself. While he was putting it on, Bob asked him, only half jokingly, if there was anything about backpacking he didn't know.

"Not much," Doug replied and proceeded to inform him of ways of knowing direction while hiking.

Moss grew more thickly on the shadiest side of the tree, which would be the north side of trees that were fairly out in the open where sunlight could reach them all day.

Vegetation grew larger and more openly on northern slopes, smaller and more densely on southern slopes.

You could prevent yourself from traveling in circles by always keeping two trees lined up in front of you.

Then, at night, there was the north star . . .

"Enough," Bob said, chuckling. "I'll never remember any of it."

"Well, you might need it someday," Doug told him, "you never know."

"I know," Bob said. "This is my one and only backpacking hike."

"Oh." Doug nodded, an expression of remote acknowledgment on his face.

Bob tried to soften what he'd said by remarking that he could see how wonderful backpacking must be; he was just not inclined toward it, but Doug's nod was no more than cursory.

Doug had been quiet for a while, staring into the fire, and Bob decided that he really must have offended him by so casually negating any possibility of him ever backpacking again. Doug didn't have to do this; it had been and was a generous offer. He had to try to say something to lighten Doug's mood.

"What made you pick this spot for a campsite?" he asked.

"Oh." Doug shrugged. "A number of things."

"Like what?"

"You're not really interested," Doug told him.

"Yes, I am," Bob insisted. "I know I'm a dud as a hiker but I *would* like to know as much as I can for my novel."

"Your novel," Doug said. He looked at Bob without expression. "Is there a movie in it?" he asked.

Ah, Bob thought. The entrée to peace. "Probably," he said, "there are four good male roles in it, two females."

"Why not just do it as a screenplay then?" Doug asked.

"Oh, no," Bob said. "I don't want to put you through all this just for a screenplay. If it gets fucked up—assuming it gets made at all—there's nothing left to show for it. But if there's a novel . . ."

"Yeah." Doug nodded, conceding. "I understand. That way, if it's good, you make money from both the novel *and* the screenplay."

"Right." It wasn't what he'd meant but he let it go. "And, when the time comes—as I hope it will—for the story to be filmed, I'll certainly suggest you for one of the parts," he said, playing his trump card.

"Well, I'd love to read the screenplay when you've written it," Doug said, sounding considerably more cheerful now.

"Sure," Bob said, nodding. "There *is* a good part for a villain, but he's a man in his sixties."

"That's nothing," Doug said quickly, "I played a father in *Our Town* and he had to be a man in his late fifties."

"Oh." Bob nodded. "I'll remember that."

Doug nodded back, smiling, then made a clucking sound. "So you need to know about what constitutes a good campsite."

"Yes, I'd like to."

"Okay." Doug seemed to think about it for a few seconds, then began.

"Well, to start with," he said, "it was no problem in the nineteenth century, even the early part of this century. You could cut brush for a campfire, cut logs, drink and wash in the water, have all the room in the world because there were so few campers. Now——" He made a hissing sound of disgust. "Thousands of people every year, screwing up everything."

"I know." Bob nodded glumly. "Ruining the environment."

"I'm not talking about the environment," Doug said, "I'm talking about camping and backpacking."

"Oh." Bob nodded. Should have known, he thought.

"Well, anyway, first of all, proximity to water," Doug said, "that's a must, absolutely basic, which is why we're by a lake. Also the site should be on a gradual slope—well drained. That way, if it rains——"

"You think it's going to rain?"

"No, no." Doug waved his hand impatiently. "Just let me finish."

"Sorry," Bob apologized.

"If it does rain for any reason, you're safe from runoff. A meadow would be a bad place to camp, for example. Also, there's a nice breeze here. Keeps away the bugs."

"My God, you think of everything," Bob said.

"Better than being miserable," Doug replied. "But shut up, I'm a long way from being done."

"Sorry again," Bob said, smiling.

"Surrounding trees to break up any wind that rises," Doug continued.

"I apologize for interrupting," Bob said, "but why are we so far away from the lake?"

"So there isn't any chance of contaminating it," Doug told him. "A lot of idiots camp right by the water and piss and crap all over, polluting what's supposed to be fresh water."

Bob nodded. "Got ya." *I should be taking notes,* he thought. *Was he going to be able to remember all this?*

"Open ground," Doug went on, "no vegetation, rotted trees."

Bob wanted to ask about the rotted trees but decided to remain silent as Doug continued.

"Up a little high to avoid cold air, which flows downward. Slope facing east, protected from a west wind and getting the sun in the morning, which you'll find makes it a lot easier to get up."

"Douglas, I am damned impressed by your knowledge," Bob broke in, thinking that Doug wouldn't object to being interrupted in that way.

"Tricks of the trade, Bobby." Doug grinned at him. *I was right,* Bob thought.

"Tent needs to be well staked, of course," Doug said, "so

the wind won't blow it away. Use one with a dome top; gives with the wind. Double wall. Full-cover rain fly."

I won't even *try* to find out what *that* is, Bob thought.

"Outer shell waterproofed," Doug continued. "Repels rain and prevents condensation from forming on the inner walls. Curved walls to prevent wind flap, a vestibule to keep rain from blowing in."

"A vestibule?" Bob asked, visualizing the vestibule of an apartment house in Brooklyn he'd lived in when he was a boy.

"Need a little entryway," Doug told him. "Wind and rain can blow in through a simple opening. As for the ground cloth, it should be exactly the size of the tent floor. If it sticks outside and it rains, the ground cloth can direct water under the tent. Did you put your iodine tablets in your water?"

"Yeah?" Bob more asked than said.

"Don't forget to do that all the time," Doug told him, "*Giardia lamblia* can kill."

"Jesus, what's that?"

"Parasite," Doug answered. "Deadly little bastards. Use your iodine tablets always."

"Ooh," Bob said.

"What's wrong?" Doug asked.

"The chicken à la king has done its job," Bob answered, making a face.

"Just as well," Doug told him. "Good time to teach you bathroom regulations anyway."

"Regulations?" Bob laughed softly.

"Oh, yeah," Doug said, "very important." He got up. "I'll show you where to go. Come on."

"Okay." Bob winced a little at the pressure in his bowels. "Not too far, I hope."

"Far enough," Doug said.

Bob pulled on his boots and got to his feet with a groan. "Stiff," he said.

"You'll loosen up," Doug told him. "Get your flashlight and toilet paper."

He led Bob away from the camp, walking up the slight rise. He walked and walked. "How far are we going?" Bob asked.

"Far enough," Doug said again.

Bob couldn't believe how far they were walking away from the campsite. "Jesus, I'll need a compass to find my way back," he said, grimacing; he really had to go now.

"Okay, this should do," Doug said. Turning, he looked back at the faint glow of the campfire. "About two hundred or so yards," he estimated. He held out his trowel; Bob hadn't noticed that he'd brought it with him.

"Okay," he said, "behind that boulder would be good. Dig a cat hole six to ten inches deep. Squat over the hole and shit. Then, when you're done, fill the hole back up and tamp the soil down good."

"What about the toilet paper?" Bob asked.

"That you can't bury," Doug told him. "Either you burn it at the campsite or you pack it out."

"Pack it out?" Bob stared at him incredulously.

"So burn it," Doug said. "Just make sure the smoke isn't blowing in my direction."

Bob nodded. "What if the ground's too hard for digging?"

"Cover your crap with dirt or leaves or dead bark or whatever you can find. Just don't leave it uncovered. Some animals might eat it."

"Oh, Jesus," Bob said, moving behind the boulder. He

started to undo his trousers, watching Doug's form moving back toward the camp.

"What if I have to take a leak during the night?" he called after him. "Do I have to schlepp all the way back here?"

"No," Doug said across his shoulder. "Just move a decent distance from the campsite." After a few moments, he added, "And try to pee downwind."

Fifteen minutes later, Bob gave up trying to move his bowels. Maybe tomorrow, he told himself.

When he got back to the camp, except for his slippers, Doug was completely naked.

"Whoa! What's going on?" were the first words that occurred to Bob.

Doug chuckled. "Bath time," he said. "What did you think, I was going to seduce you?"

"Uh . . . try to seduce me," Bob replied.

Doug laughed. "Right," he said.

"Bath time?" Bob asked.

"I like to do it every night," Doug told him. Bob noticed that he'd filled a cooking pot with water and was heating it on the grate.

"I thought we slept in our clothes," Bob said.

"You can." Doug's tone was dubious. "But dirt and body oil can collect on the inside of your sleeping bag that way. Eventually find its way into the fabric, eventually into the fill and break down the bag's insulation ability."

"Ah." Bob nodded, averting his eyes.

"This embarrass you?" Doug asked him.

"No. I just—" He broke off. Don't be so polite, he thought.

"Well . . . yes, sort of. Outside of my son, I haven't seen a naked man since college gymnasium."

"Don't know what you been missing," Doug said. Bob glanced up at him. What the hell did *that* mean?

Doug laughed again. "Jesus Christ, Bob, I'm just kidding."

"Oh, okay." Bob nodded, trying to smile.

"If I'd known this was going to bother you, I'd have done it behind a tree. It's a little warmer by the fire though."

"Yes. Of course." Bob was aware of trying to sound casual and failing.

"Not that I need the fire," Doug told him. "I'm exothermic; it's easy for me to release heat. My hands and feet are always warm."

"Not Marian," Bob said, still averting his gaze, "her hands and feet are always cold."

"She's endothermic then," Doug told him.

"Ah-ha."

Doug said no more but took the pot off the grate, using his washrag for a pot holder. Setting it on the ground, he soaked the washcloth in the water. "Whoa. Hot," he said. Taking the washrag out of the pot, he wrung it out gingerly, then started rubbing soap on it.

"You gonna do this?" he asked.

Bob sighed. "I dunno. If we were going out for a couple of weeks, I suppose so. But three or four days . . ."

"More likely four or five the way we're going," Doug told him.

Again, the little jab, Bob thought. "Isn't this where you were planning to camp the first night?" he asked.

"Yeah," Doug said, soaping under his arms and over his chest. "But only because I figured we'd never get any farther."

He chuckled. "You almost didn't make it here."

"Mmm." Bob had sat down by the fire now.

When Doug didn't respond he glanced up. Doug was soaping his stomach and groin, leaning forward slightly. Bob had seen him in a Speedo bathing suit when Doug and Nicole came over to the house to swim. Seeing him entirely naked though made him aware of how muscular Doug was, his stomach flat, his abdomen muscles clearly defined.

For a moment, he thought of telling Doug how well built he was, then decided against it. He wasn't sure how Doug would react to such a comment. He was aware of how uncomfortable he felt.

Doug seemed to read his mind. "Sorry if this makes you uncomfortable," he said.

"No, no. It just . . . caught me by surprise, that's all."

"How *do* you plan to wash up?" Doug inquired. "It's not a good idea to keep wearing the same underwear. You *do* have some extra long johns packed, don't you?"

"Sure." Bob nodded. "And some packages of moist towelettes to wash myself off with."

"Well, that'll have to do if it's all you want," Doug said. He was bending over now, soaping up his legs and ankles, then his feet.

The silence bothered Bob again.

"I, uh, see that that boulder over there is kind of black. Why didn't you use that same spot for the fire?" he asked.

"Stupid thing to do," Doug said. He was rinsing the soap off his body now. "That black will be there for centuries. That's why I make a fire ring with stones. Which I'll dismantle in the morning. You'll be helping with the fires so remember never to use wet stones, they can explode in a fire."

"Oh, my God." Bob winced a little.

Silence again. He glanced up involuntarily and saw Doug drying himself with a towel, arms raised. He swallowed, wondering if Doug had done this deliberately to embarrass him.

Oh, don't be stupid, he told himself.

"I notice that you didn't dig a fire pit," he said to break the silence and divert his mind from more uncharitable thoughts.

Doug chuckled. "You've been reading," he said.

"Yeah, well . . . yeah, it did say that in the backpacking book I read."

"It's a good idea in windy weather," Doug said. He was getting into a clean pair of long underwear now. "It's also less visible and won't bother other campers. But since it isn't windy and there *are* no other campers, there's no need for a fire pit."

"Got ya," Bob said.

Doug put on his slippers again and crouched by the fire, palms extended to the heat.

"You use only squaw wood to burn," he said.

"Squaw wood?"

"I guess they call it that because Indian squaws made the fires," Doug answered. "It's wood that's lying on the ground. You never use living growth for burning. Start the fire with fallen leaves or twigs or pine needles. And if there's not enough dead wood on the ground, break off dead limbs or branches on fallen trees. Or living ones; just make sure the limbs or branches are dead. Got that?"

"Got it," Bob said. I hope, he thought.

"You notice that I built a small wall of stones on that side of the fire," Doug said, pointing. "That's to keep the smoke rising in that direction. Don't ask me why that works, I have no idea. It does though."

Bob smiled. "I didn't notice that before," he said.

"Tricks of the trade, Bobby," Doug said. "By the way, don't ever try to put out a fire by pouring water over it. That can make rocks explode too. Knew a guy who got blinded that way."

"Jesus." Bob grimaced.

"Fires are tricky," Doug said. "Getting them lit is one thing, keeping them lit is another. They'll do anything you want—burn slow, fast, anything—but you have to know what you're doing. Flick the coals one way and it's a goner. Flick them the right way and you've got a fire that'll burn for hours."

"Well, you're the expert, I leave campfires up to you."

"No, no, it'll be one of your chores," Doug said. "I'll show you how to start a fire tomorrow."

"My chores," Bob said.

"Sure, you didn't think this was going to be a free ride, did you?" Doug said, his tone hardening slightly. "You'll do the fires, do cleanup work. I'll take care of the sleeping arrangements, keep us supplied with purified water." His smile seemed vaguely unpleasant, Bob thought. "In addition to being your guide and protector."

Bob only nodded. "Okay," he said then.

"I think from now on we'll use my grate to cook on," Doug said. "Easier than your stove."

"You mean I brought it for nothing?" Bob asked, looking pained.

"Well, Bobby, I didn't tell you to buy it, did I?"

"No." Bob's tone was glum. "That damn salesman..."

"You can use the stove on your own if you want," Doug said. "There's just not much point to it."

"Yeah." Bob nodded. Sighed. "And I suppose I can't just leave it here," he said.

"No, no. What you pack in—"

"—you pack out," Bob finished.

"Exactly," Doug said.

9:38 PM

The fire was low now, little more than glowing embers with a few small tongues of flame licking upward.

"Have you checked for ticks?" Doug asked.

"Ticks?" Bob answered, wincing.

"Yeah, ticks," Doug said. "If you find any attached to your body, cover them with something that'll cut off their air supply—Vaseline, oil, *tree* sap if you have nothing better. That'll make the tick release its grip and you can remove it. Make sure you get the whole tick though. Grasp it where the mouth parts are attached to the skin. *Don't squeeze its body.* And wash your hands after touching it. It has fluids that cause lyme disease."

"Oh, Jesus Christ," Bob said grimly.

Doug chuckled. "Don't despair. It probably won't happen. You have on long pants and a long sleeve jacket, a hat. Tuck the hems of your pants into your socks for protection."

Now he tells me, Bob thought. "I can see it all. I'll get lyme disease, catch rabies from some demented squirrel, get bitten by a rattlesnake, torn to pieces by a mountain lion."

Doug laughed loudly. "Well, you have a lot to look forward to, don't you?"

"A lot."

"See, there's one," Doug said. Reaching out he brushed a tick off Bob's hat. "All there is to it. Now get out all your food."

"What?" Bob looked at him, not understanding.

"Your food, your food," Doug said, "we have to hang it up so the bears can't get at it."

"Oh, Jesus, bears too?" Bob reacted. "How many of them are out here?"

"Not that many," Doug told him, "but they can smell food if it's anywhere around."

Bob swallowed, nodding. He felt as though he were sinking into a pit. What next? Attack by Indians? An earthquake? A volcanic eruption?

He opened his pack and started taking out the food he had in plastic bags. "Plastic bottles too?" he asked.

"May as well," Doug said, "I've seen bears open bottles with their teeth. I don't know how they can smell what's *in* the bottles but . . ."

His voice faded as he started removing plastic sacks from his pack.

"Why the different colors?" Bob asked.

"Breakfast, lunch, snack, and dinner," Doug told him. "And coffee, of course. All double-sacked; I notice you didn't do that."

You never told me to, Mr. Crowley, sir, he heard himself kvetching in his mind.

"You can also put different kinds of food in different sacks—soup powder, beans, whatever."

By now, he had taken two heavy cloth bags and a quarter-inch nylon rope from his pack. He tossed one of the bags to Bob. "Put your food in there," he said. "They're called stuff packs. For an obvious reason, I guess."

He was finished filling and tying up his pack before Bob. Taking hold of the rope, he coiled it and began tossing the end of it at an oak limb about twenty feet above them. On the third try, he got the rope end over the branch so that it hung down in two lengths in front of them.

"You notice I'm putting the rope about ten feet from the trunk," he said. "Not that that'll stop a really acrobatic bear but it's better than hanging the bags close to the trunk."

He chuckled. "I've never seen it myself but some guy I met once told me that he saw a mother bear stand on her hind feet and her cub stand on her shoulders, trying to knock down a food bag."

"No," Bob said incredulously.

"That's what the guy told me."

Bob laughed. "What a sight that must have been."

Doug nodded, chuckling again. "That's for sure," he said. "Like some greaser kid trying to knock down a piñata."

Greaser kid, Bob thought, frowning. Just how prejudiced *was* Doug? They'd never had a conversation revealing it in any way. Was that because Marian was almost always there?

Tying his bag to one end of the rope now, Doug pulled it up close to the limb. Then, taking Bob's sack, he tied it to the other length of the rope, reaching up as high as he could and looping up the excess rope. Bob noticed that there was a monofilament line on that end of the rope. "What's that for?" he asked.

"In case there isn't a stick or a branch to pull them down,"

Doug said. He tossed the bag with Bob's food in it up toward the limb. The other bag dropped down so that both bags now hung about twelve feet from the ground.

"That should do it," Doug said, "unless a twelve-foot bear comes by."

"If it does, I'll have died of a heart attack long before it can get our food," Bob said.

Doug snickered. "You and Marian," he said. "Oh, before I forget. Cover your pack with your pack cover in case it rains. And make sure you leave the pockets open so mice and raccoons can check them out without chewing their way in."

"Anything else we can expect?" Bob asked. "A pack of coyotes maybe?"

Doug only shook his head. "A backpacker you will never be," he said solemnly.

That's for *damn* sure, Bob thought.

"Take anything into the tent you might need during the night," Doug told him. "Flashlight, water bottle, toilet paper, et cetera."

As they started for the tent, Doug reached up and broke off a small branch hanging above its entrance.

"Aren't you despoiling Mother Nature now?" Bob joshed him.

Doug didn't seem to get it. "Would you rather have your eye poked out if you get up to piss during the night?" he asked, tossing aside the branch.

Bob watched as Doug clambered into the tent, carrying his bow and arrow holder.

"In case of Indian attack?" he said.

Again, Doug didn't seem to get it—or chose not to get it— as a joke. "Bear," was all he said.

"Doug, you keep on mentioning bears," Bob said as he crawled into the tent. "How likely *are* we to see one?"

"They like to prowl around at night," Doug told him. "But as long as there's no smell of food around the tent, they'll usually move on."

"Usually?" Bob asked.

"Don't worry about it," Doug said, "I've never had a problem with one yet. Except for the time one of my buddies got eaten by one."

"*What?*" Bob looked at him, aghast.

Bob laughed. "Jesus," he said, "you and Marian are two of a kind. Real worriers."

Bob drew in a shaky breath. "I presume that was a joke then."

"You presume right, sir," Doug answered with a dead-on imitation of Ed McMahon.

That was his idea of a joke, Bob thought as he put aside the articles he'd brought with him, slid his way into the sleeping bag, and zipped it up. He was glad that Doug had told him not to sleep in his clothes. He did feel more comfortable in a clean pair of long underwear after washing himself off with some of the towelettes Marian had bought him. A clean pair of socks felt good too.

He released a long sigh, then yawned.

"You won't have trouble sleeping tonight," Doug said.

"That's for sure," Bob replied. Abruptly, he wished he'd thought to bring along some Valium to relax his muscles. Oh, well, he thought. Let nature take its course. Whatever that means, he thought. He stretched out his legs, then let them relax.

He watched as Doug began to shake out his sleeping bag vigorously.

Richard Matheson

"What are you doing now, checking for rattlesnakes?" he asked, repressing a grin.

Doug didn't even smile. "Fluffing it up," he said as though Bob had asked a serious question. "Getting the maximum loft. Traps air in the fibers. Helps to keep you warm."

Jesus, but he knows a lot, Bob thought. I suppose I should do the same thing, he told himself. He was too damn tired though. The hell with it.

"Did you bring a woolen cap to keep your head warm while you're sleeping?" Doug asked.

You *know* you never told me that, Bob thought. "I'll use my corduroy cap," he said.

"Not as good. But... if that's all you have..."

Anything else I'm going to need you haven't told me about? Bob thought.

"Important to keep the top of your head warm," Doug told him. "I'm going for a walk now."

"A *walk*?" Bob looked astonished.

"Better than having a warm drink. You want to go with me?"

"No, thanks, I am very comfortable in here," Bob told him.

"Okay, suit yourself. I'll be back in a few minutes."

Before Bob could respond, Doug was out of the tent and gone. Jesus Christ, what if something happens to him? he thought; he falls, gets mauled by a bear, anything? He'd be alone then, with no way of finding the cabin. Did Doug know he'd react this way? He wouldn't be at all surprised.

He lay silently—and tensely—listening for the sound of Doug returning. What was with him, anyway, going for a walk in the forest at night? Even with a flashlight that he must have taken with him.

88

Bob exhaled heavily. Was Doug doing all this to torment him? Why *should* he? They were friends, weren't they? Or were they?

Minutes passed. He grew more and more tense. Jesus, what if something really *had* happened to Doug? What would he—?

A sudden thrashing noise outside, a crazed growl. He stiffened, face a mask of terror.

Doug lunged into the tent, shining his flashlight beam into Bob's face. Seeing Bob's rigid expression of dread, he burst into laughter. "Oh, shit," he said, "you're too easy."

Bob looked at him in fury. "If I'd had a gun, you'd be dead now, you fucking idiot!"

Doug snickered, shaking his head. "Calm down," he said, "it was just a joke."

"A joke that would have killed me if I had a bad heart," Bob told him. "It's still pounding."

"Okay, okay, I'm sorry," Doug said, "I didn't think you'd react *this* hard." He slipped into his sleeping bag and started thrashing his legs.

"What are you doing *now?*" Bob asked him, irritably.

"Isometrics," Doug answered. "Gets the blood flow going."

My blood flow is turned off for the night, Bob thought. Anyway, he felt warm enough. He put on his corduroy cap. He hadn't planned to wear it while he was sleeping but if it helped . . .

The two of them lay silently for a while. Then Doug said, "I haven't seen you in a while. What have you been up to?"

At first, he wasn't going to reply, he was still so angry with Doug. Then he thought: Well, what the hell, maybe he *did* think it was a joke. There were still days ahead of them being together, Doug in total control of the hike. He couldn't afford being resentful the entire time. He closed his eyes and instructed himself to calm down, forget the incident.

He sighed. "Well, mostly I've been schlepping through the forest primeval with a joker I know, doing research for a novel."

"No screenplays lately?" Doug asked, ignoring the remark. "Teleplays? Series work?"

"I haven't worked on series episodes in five years," Bob told him.

"Oh, that's right, you don't have to do that sort of thing anymore," Doug said.

Why was it, Bob wondered, that almost every other comment by Doug seemed to verge on insult?

He decided not to make an issue of it. "I was never very good at it anyway," he said. "I can adapt novels okay or make up stories, but I was never able to get a fix on already established characters in already established environments."

Doug grunted. "No screenplays? Teleplays?"

Bob knew very well what Doug wanted. He was still bucking for available parts. "I did a screenplay about . . . oh, it must be nearly a year ago. They haven't made it yet though, don't know if they even intend to. That's the only project I've been working on this year. I sold a novelette to *Playboy* but I don't think there's a film in it. That's why I decided to take a crack at this backpacking novel."

"You don't want to do it as a screenplay though," Doug said, sounding vaguely accusing.

"No," Bob said. "Novel first. Screenplay later—if it happens. What about you?" He hoped he wasn't treading on Doug's toes. If things weren't going well for him . . .

"Oh, I did a commercial. Ford SUV."

"That pays well, doesn't it?" Bob asked, trying to sound impressed.

"Not bad," Doug said. "It isn't acting though."

"No, of course not," Bob said sympathetically. "Any little theater?"

"I'm supposed to do a Simon play in Glendale," Doug said. "Not sure I want to though."

"Why not?"

"Oh . . . it's a long way to drive. A rinky-dink operation. And the director seems to be an idiot."

"That's no fun," Bob said.

Doug grunted scornfully. "Especially if you're trying to do Neil Simon," he said.

Bob racked his mind for something else to mention. "What about that . . . hospital show you were trying out for?" he asked.

"Not *that* hospital show," Doug said. "*The* hospital show—*ER*."

"Oh. And—?"

"I'm still waiting to hear," Doug told him. "The director and I didn't exactly hit it off. He wasn't interested in any of my ideas about the character."

"Ah." Bob nodded. Another strikeout, he thought. It was too bad too. He'd seen Doug act on television and the stage and he had a definite presence, a charismatic masculinity. He didn't understand why Doug wasn't further along. Oh, the hell I don't, he thought. Acting is on a par with bond-servanting. Too often, talent had little to do with it. It was who you knew; it was good representation; it was sheer good luck. At least for someone like Doug; he wasn't exactly Robert De Niro or Dustin Hoffman. And even they had their problems. It was a merciless business.

"You're a lucky son of a gun, you know that, Bob," Doug said.

"How so?" Bob asked, genuinely curious as to what Doug was getting at.

"You're a good-looking man," Doug started.

"Well, Jesus, so are you," Bob broke in. "Me times ten."

"Yeah, much good it does me," Doug said. "You also have a good marriage. Marian is a hell of a lady."

"I buy that," Bob said, trying to prevent this conversational approach from dipping too low.

"You have two healthy, successful kids," Doug continued, making Bob wince. He really didn't want to get into that area; it was too raw. He closed his eyes, wondering if Doug would be offended if he fell asleep on him. Probably. He opened his eyes again.

"Life has gone well for you, no doubt about it," Doug said.

Bob didn't want to start a hassle but he felt compelled to answer Doug's remark.

"Well, you know, I had to work awfully hard to get where I am," he said. "Marian and I had some damn lean years when we were first married. I had that night job in the supermarket, I was a bank messenger for a while, I worked in a hardware store for more than a year. It wasn't exactly going that well back then."

"No, but it worked out well," Doug said. "You have your career, your marriage, your kids. I have shit."

"Doug, it's not *that* bad," Bob said. Well, we're into it now anyway, he thought. No help for it. Continue. "You're a handsome, talented actor—"

"—out of work," Doug interrupted.

"You know the way the business goes," Bob said, "a month from now you could be in London costarring with Emma Thompson."

"Not bloody likely," Doug said. "And even if I was, I don't have the rest. No Nicole. No Jenny." His breath faltered. "Artie gone."

Bob swallowed. Well, this was going nowhere fast, he thought. He should have gone to sleep as soon as he'd gotten into the tent. It wasn't that he didn't sympathize with Doug. He did—all the way. But what more could he do that he hadn't done already? He felt a heavy sigh coming on and held it down.

"How old are you, Bob?" Doug asked.

Bob hesitated, then answered, "Forty-four."

"I'm forty-two," Doug said. "How old is Marian?"

"Oh, now, you know I'm not allowed to answer that," Bob said, conscious of still trying to lighten the moment.

"Why not? Nicole is forty," Doug said. "How old *is* Marian? About the same?"

"About the same," Bob conceded.

"Sex still good with her?" Doug asked.

Bob felt himself twitch. What the hell made Doug think that up out of nowhere?

"Well, is it?" Doug asked as though he couldn't understand why Bob wasn't willing to answer the question.

"Well . . ." Bob didn't know what to say.

"I imagine it is," Doug said. "She's a hell of a fine-looking woman."

Bob didn't care for the direction Doug had taken the conversation but he said, "Yes. She is."

Richard Matheson

"Nicole and I had a great sex life," Doug said. "We screwed like maniacs. She used to really get turned on by being handcuffed to our bed and raped."

"How nice." Bob knew it was an inappropriate response but couldn't think of anything else to say. Like maniacs, eh? Handcuffs and rape? By Jove, good show.

Doug didn't seem to notice the inappropriateness of his reply. Or chose to pay no attention to it. "I can't say I blame her for feeling the way she does," he said. "Most actors' marriages are wrecked by the conflict between career needs and marriage needs. Actors have less time to devote to their marriages than almost any other group of men. The woman who marries an actor has to pretty much dedicate her life to her husband's profession. Not easy."

"I'm sure it isn't," Bob said. He wouldn't say anything about how difficult it also was for a woman to be married to a writer.

"Add to that," Doug continued, "actors are exposed to more opportunities to fool around than other men. Actresses— I *refuse* to call them *actors*—almost *expect* actors to make a move on them. It's part of the fucking game—and I do mean fucking."

Bob had to admit to himself that Doug had more insight than he gave him credit for. For a few moments, he felt a sense of strange ambivalence. Here they were, lying in the dark wilderness, discussing things no primitive man ever discussed— or thought of for that matter. It was as though they were contemporary men lying in an ancient, timeless environment.

"Ever cheat on Marian?" Doug asked, instantly demolishing the odd ambivalence.

For Christ's sake, are we having a goddamn sex seminar here? Bob thought.

"No," he said.

"Oh, come on," Doug said, totally dubious. "Never?"

"I had the opportunities. I didn't take them," Bob answered.

"Jesus," Doug said. "Assuming that you're telling the truth, you must have gone spiritual at a damned early age."

"It has nothing to do with being spiritual," Bob said. "It's a matter of loyalty. Respect."

"Yeah. I suppose," Doug responded. He made an amused sound. "I guess you know it was my catting around that made Nicole divorce me."

"Well, I—"

"Also because my career was going down the toilet, of course," Doug said bitterly. "I wasn't making enough money for the bitch."

Bob winced. So much for Doug's insight, he thought. I want to go to sleep, not listen to this.

"Ever think about going to bed with a man?" Doug asked.

Bob stiffened. Oh, my Christ, he thought.

Doug seemed to know what he was feeling because he snickered and patted Bob on the shoulder. "Relax," he said, "I didn't bring you all the way up here just to make a move on you."

Bob's breath shook before he could answer. "Glad to hear it," he muttered.

"Well, I saw how uptight you were before when I was bathing and I thought maybe it was a problem for you."

"No." Bob wished his voice didn't sound so faint. What the hell brought all this on? he wondered.

"I did it a few times when I was about twenty," Doug said casually. "Then I decided that I liked pussy a hell of a lot more."

Bully for you, Bob thought.

"Well..." Doug clucked. "We'd better get some sleep. Here."

Bob twitched as something landed on his chest. Opening his eyes, he saw that it was an energy bar.

"I already brushed my teeth," he said.

"Eat it anyway," Doug told him. "Help to keep you warm."

Bob grunted, then, obediently, ate the energy bar, visualizing the nuts and peanut butter in between his teeth all night. He'd get out of the sleeping bag and out of the tent and brush his teeth again if he wasn't so tired.

"Here," Doug said.

He took what Doug was holding out: a twig. "More protein?" he said.

"*No,*" Doug said as though Bob really thought that. "Clean your teeth with it."

"Oh, yeah."

"Well, good night," Doug said, closing his eyes and sighing. "Long day tomorrow," he added.

Bob made a face, crossing his eyes. Looking forward to it, an insincere voice remarked in his head.

10:31 PM

Good God, he thought. He would have sworn that, by now, he'd be sleeping like a dead man. Conversation before with Doug had seemed in doubt because of his exhaustion. Now Doug was asleep, it was quiet, and here he was still awake.

Quiet? he thought. It sounded as though half the wildlife in the forest was prowling around—in search of food no doubt.

He saw now the value of Doug suspending their food from that limb. At one point, he heard something clawing at, he assumed, the trunk of the tree the food was hanging from. What had it been? A raccoon, he hoped, not a grizzly bear. No, Doug had said there were no grizzly bears in this area. Black bears though. Their claws and teeth were just as rending as those of a grizzly. He'd lain in rigid silence, trusting that the creature, whatever it was, would get discouraged presently and move on, which it did.

Little noises persisted though. Crackling, snapping, gnawing sounds. Mice? He hoped so. He visualized them crawling in and out of his backpack pockets, scavenging for food. Well, it's their territory, he told himself. We're the interlopers. It didn't help to alleviate his uneasiness.

But it was more than prowling critters that kept him awake; he was well aware of that. His side ached. He'd taken a Tylenol for that—and for his scraped palm that seemed to alternate between itching and hurting. He didn't dare scratch it though; that would only make it worse. And he *was* extremely tired. His entire body seemed to ache, mostly his legs. I need to rest! he thought in angry desperation. Why *couldn't* he?

Two reasons, his mind told him, one physical, one mental—or was it emotional? It could very well be.

First of all, he wasn't sure that, physically, he was going to manage this hike. It was only the end of the first day and already he felt as though he'd gone through a round with Mike Tyson. What if he, literally, conked out before the hike was completed? Hell, before it was half completed? What could he do, ask Doug to carry him to the cabin? Sure, absolutely.

And yet they couldn't go back. What good would that do?

So they made the spot where they'd started out. Then what? Wait for a car to pick them up? It was October. Traffic was not likely to be too heavy. They'd seen one car after they'd reached the park.

Anyway, he couldn't bear the thought of how Doug would look at him if he quit now.

Doug.

That was the second thing, of course, and more than arguably the worst one.

To be honest with himself—and he was trying to be—he wasn't sure about Doug. He was pretty rough on me today, he thought. Endless little digs and criticisms, all unnecessary. Bob had made it clear from the start that he was uneasy about the hike. He wanted to do it very much, he'd made that clear too. It would make his novel more authentic if he'd taken a backpack trip personally. But uneasy? Yes, he was. Not a problem, Doug had assured him. They'd take it easy, be in no rush. It wouldn't be that difficult.

No rush? he thought. Then why had Doug left him alone to hurry on and get the campsite ready? He must have known—he must have—that it would be unnerving for him. But he'd done it anyway. And, by God, it *had* been unnerving. An arrow made of stones? How the hell did Doug expect him to see that in the shadowy gloom of the forest?

But it was more than that, again of course. It was Doug's personality. They'd never spent more than a day or two together—and that always in the company of Nicole and Marian.

Three days—possibly four alone with Doug? He realized that he didn't know Doug well at all. And there had been hints—more than hints—clear signs—of aspects in Doug's behavior that, frankly, made him nervous. What, actually, was going on in Doug's head? That he was embittered had become more than clear. He'd always known that Doug had felt frustrated about the lack of real success in his acting career.

Now he realized—he'd only suspected it before—that Doug was also bitter about his divorce from Nicole. Even though Nicole had had every reason to divorce him because of Doug's—openly admitted—numerous infidelities. He knew that Doug had a pretty shaky relationship with his daughter. And as for Artie . . . Well, he hoped the subject never came up again.

Did Doug resent him? Clearly, his words had made it obvious that Doug envied him. But was the envy verging on the border of dislike, perhaps intense dislike? Why had Doug brought up the idea of him being lucky because of his career, his marriage, his parenthood? Why call it luck? He'd earned it with hard work and dedication. Goddamn it, he thought, was Doug going to make the next three days a penance for him? Doug had all the trump cards in his hand. He could make the entire hike a nightmare if he chose to—and all in the name of being Bob's "guide and protector."

He was aware of how knotted his stomach muscles felt. God*damn* it, he wished he could take a Valium.

Then reaction set in. Don't be so damn melodramatic, he told himself. So Doug might be a pain in the ass for a few days. Period. By the end of the week, he and Marian would be home with all this angst forgotten. End of story.

It seemed to help. He closed his eyes and started to use fractional hypnosis on himself, starting with his stomach muscles. Your stomach muscles are relaxed, relaxed. All tension gone. Relaxed. Relaxed.

Just before he drifted into sleep, he heard the distant howling of a coyote. The wilderness speaking, he thought with a faint smile. *Canis latrans*, he remembered reading somewhere. "Barking dog."

Darkness soon enveloped him.

Monday

7:01 AM

It was an odd sensation.

He knew he was asleep but he could hear the bedroom door opening and knew, somehow, that it was Marian. Even more odd was his awareness that she was carrying a breakfast tray for him—freshly squeezed orange juice, crisp bacon and eggs, a well-toasted English muffin, and freshly brewed coffee. He could actually smell the amalgam of delicious aromas.

Then she was beside the bed and putting the tray down quietly on the bedside table. He tried not to smile so she wouldn't know that he was awake enough to know she was there—even though (how really odd) he still was actually asleep.

"Sweetheart." He heard her gentle voice.

He pretended that he barely heard by making a soft noise. He stretched his legs and sighed. He felt so wonderfully comfortable. After that damn hike with Doug, this was sheer heaven—the warm, inviting bed, the soft pillow. Never again, he thought with regard to the hike.

"Honey?" she said, a little more loudly now.

"Mmm." He knew he was smiling now. So let her see.

"Wake up. Breakfast in bed," she told him.

He made a sound of pleased amusement.

"Come on now," she said. She put her hand on his shoulder and nudged it a little.

No, he thought. Did he say it aloud? He couldn't tell and that was odd too.

Abruptly, she grabbed his shoulder, digging in her fingers, and shook him hard. "Come *on*," she said.

He jerked open his eyes and saw Doug's face hovering above him, his expression one of tried patience.

"What?" he asked.

"Rise and shine, boy," Doug told him, "time to get going."

Bob stared up groggily at him. "What time is it?" he mumbled.

"After seven," Doug answered. "I knew you were tired so I let you sleep late."

This is late? Bob thought, almost saying it aloud before deciding against it. "Okay," he muttered.

Doug started to back out of the tent.

"How long you been up?" Bob asked.

"About an hour," Doug told him.

Oh, Jesus, Bob thought. I'm gonna love this hike. He sighed and tried to sit up, wincing and making a hissing noise at the pain in his right side. He reached up and out of the sleeping bag to unzip it, wincing again at the tenderness of his right palm. He looked at it, grimacing. Blood was crusted on it and it looked discolored in spots. He blew out breath. *Oh, what a beautiful morning,* his brain sang, off-key.

"Come on, Bob, up 'n at 'em," Doug said.

"Yessir." Bob unzipped the bag and got out of it, wincing once more at the pain that lifting his legs caused. And he took offense at Marian's comment that he wasn't "in tune." I am completely *out* of tune, he thought.

He started dressing slowly, almost infirmly it seemed.

"You getting dressed?" Doug asked.

"Getting dressed," he answered.

"Early bird gets the worm, Bobby," Doug said.

Don't want a worm, he thought. "How about some coffee?" he asked.

"Later," Doug told him. "We have to get going."

Bob rubbed some water on his face and dried it with a paper napkin.

When he crawled out of the tent, he saw that Doug had dissembled the fire pit, taken down the food bags, and reloaded both their backpacks. "Thanks for putting my food away," he said.

"Just today," Doug told him. "Tomorrow morning, you'll do it yourself."

"You didn't have any coffee?" Bob asked.

"Sure I did, an hour ago," Doug said.

"Well . . ." Bob didn't know what to say. Finally, he asked, "You have breakfast too?"

"Yep," Doug nodded.

"Well . . ." Bob looked disturbed.

"We can't start cooking again," Doug told him. "We have to get going. Eat an energy bar while we're walking. When we stop to let you rest, you can make some coffee for yourself."

Bob frowned but didn't speak.

"Tomorrow I'll wake you up when *I* get up," Doug told him. "Then you can have a nice warm breakfast before we take off."

"Yeah," Bob said quietly. What's the goddamn hurry? he thought. Doug was acting as though this were a military operation.

"We need to make some mileage before we stop for coffee," Doug said.

Stop where? Bob thought. Is there a Starbucks run by bears out there?

"I'm kind of hungry, Doug," he said. "Isn't there something I can have before we leave?"

Doug's sigh was one of strained acceptance, his expression put upon.

"So . . . put some instant cereal in a plastic bag, add powdered milk and water and shake it up, eat it while we're walking."

Sounds really wonderful, Bob thought. He felt compelled to say something. Was it really necessary for Doug to be so rigid about all this?

"Doug, why do we have to rush off?" he asked, watching Doug take down the tent. "Why can't I have that nice warm breakfast before we go?"

"We will—tomorrow," Doug said, his movements brusque as he folded up the tent. "This is a backpacking hike, Bob, not a gourmet tour."

A gourmet tour? Bob thought. Just something warm for breakfast?

"You can have a nice lunch," Doug told him. "Make yourself some hot soup or something."

Bob sighed. "Okay." He scratched his right cheek, wincing as he touched the scrape; he'd forgotten about it.

"I put the refuse in your pack," Doug said.

"Refuse?"

"The apple cores, the aluminum foil from your chicken à la king dinner," Doug said. "The cardboard we burned, the foil has to be packed out."

"How come?" Bob asked.

"You want some animal to eat it and die?" Doug said; it wasn't a question. "We take out anything that can't be burned.

Tomorrow you'll collect and pack the refuse. Don't just stand there, get your sleeping bag ready."

"Oh. Yeah." Bob made a face as he moved to where Doug had left the sleeping bag. I hope to God that blister doesn't make walking a pain, he thought.

"I'll let you pack out all the refuse," Doug told him. "Since I'm handling the extra weight."

"Right." No point in arguing, Bob thought. It was only fair. Yet, for some reason, he wondered if Doug was really the dedicated environmentalist he seemed to be presenting. He certainly wasn't going to make an issue of it, but he felt that Doug probably hadn't packed out every single scrap of refuse when he had backpacked in the past. It just didn't seem like Doug, and he wondered if Doug was doing it now to impress him with his concern for Mother Nature.

Oh, well, he thought. Let it go.

"Don't roll up your sleeping bag," Doug told him.

"What do you mean?"

"I *mean*, don't roll it up," Doug said. "You stuff it, not roll it. Rolling compresses the fibers in the same place over and over and eventually breaks them apart."

In three days? Bob felt like saying. He remained quiet and did what Doug told him to do.

As he stood up, groaning, Doug said, "I'll carry your sleeping bag too."

"You don't have to do that," Bob told him.

"I think I do," Doug said, "you're as stiff as a board. I'd better have you do a few stretching exercises before we take off."

I'd rather have a pancake and a cup of coffee, Bob thought.

He tried to copy Doug's stretching exercises for the arms, the shoulders, the back, and the legs. He kept hissing at the effort. "You are in some rotten shape, buddy," Doug told him.

"I know, I know," Bob muttered. What next? he thought. A lecture on my general failures as a human being?

"That help any?" Doug asked when they were through.

"Yeah," Bob lied. It helped make the areas of pain more specific, he thought. He swallowed a multivitamin with a sip of water.

They got their packs on, Bob trying not to grunt in discomfort at the weight; it would only give Doug more ammunition for his criticisms.

"From here on in, we leave the trail," Doug told him.

"How come?" Bob asked.

"You want experience at backpacking for your novel, don't you?" Doug said. "If we follow trails all the way, it's not a hike, it's a stroll."

Yeah, right, Bob thought. He wondered worriedly if he was really going to make it through the hike. Not that he had any choice in the matter. The ship was launched. Either it sailed to its port or it sank.

Very reassuring, Hansen, he told himself. He pressed his lips together. I am going to make it, he vowed. Let Doug lace at him, he wasn't going to let it break his spirit. He made an amused sound. That novel is going to be pretty grim, he thought.

8:21 AM

Is it my imagination, Bob thought, or is Doug taking me on the hardest route he can possibly find? Or already knows about? They had been moving on sloping ground almost since they'd started out, through meadows thick with dry grass and woods so dense that Doug had to use his golak to hack an opening through the underbrush. Already, he felt tired and aching but didn't want to mention it to Doug, knowing the look he'd get and likely the sarcastic comment.

What *was* Doug up to anyway? He hadn't said a word since they'd started out—except to tell him once that, in a pinch, he could eat the dandelions they were tramping through. I'd rather have a cup of coffee, he'd felt like saying. The cereal in the plastic bag had been a waste of time. He couldn't walk easily holding the bag in one hand and a spoon in the other. After a few mouthfuls—and more spills—he'd finally given up and emptied the cereal onto the ground. Sorry, Professor Crowley, if I'm profaning Mother Earth, he thought. I'm putting the plastic bag in my pack, isn't that good enough?

The knowledge that he was all alone in the wilderness with Doug was, to say the least, discomfiting, to say the most, unnerving. Doug, it became more and more obvious, was a loner. He obviously needed to be given his separate "space" now and then. He didn't ask for it, just subsided into silence and walked ahead. Most likely, he already regretted having made his offer to guide Bob through the hike. Obviously, he preferred being on his own, responsible to no one but himself, enjoying solitude, not required to interact with anyone, least of all the total novice Bob was.

Had he done it only to keep the channels open between them in case a role came up that Bob could recommend him for? He was beginning to think that was the case. They had never really had much in common, very little grounds for conversation.

Still . . . he had to remember that Doug *was* doing him a favor. Not enjoying it, God knows, he thought—but doing it nonetheless.

So just sweat it out, Hansen, he ordered himself. Keep up your spirits. Be of good cheer.

Endure.

He didn't want to but he finally had to speak.

"Doug?" he said.

Doug kept moving through the underbrush as though he hadn't heard. Was it possible that he *hadn't* heard? He certainly preferred that possibility to thinking that Doug had heard and was ignoring him.

"Doug!" He felt awkward shouting, but at the same time he wanted Doug to know the urgency of his call.

Doug stopped but didn't turn. Was there a look of irritated disbelief on his face? Was he thinking: Oh, for Christ's sake, now what?

Then he turned, his expression unreadable. He said nothing.

"I'd really like to stop and rest and have that cup of coffee now," Bob told him.

The deliberate way in which Doug lifted his left arm and pushed back his jacket sleeve to look at his wristwatch made his reaction obvious.

"I know it hasn't even been two hours yet," Bob said.

"It hasn't even been an hour and a half," Doug answered.

Bob sighed. Not another painful exchange, please, he thought. He knew he couldn't just be polite. Doug had to know how he felt.

"I'm in rotten shape, you said so yourself," he said firmly. "I need to rest. I need that cup of coffee. I'm sorry if I'm being a burden but give me a break."

Doug's expression eased and he gestured mollifyingly. "All right, all right," he said. "I'm not paying attention. I'm used to moving fast. We'll stop."

"Thank you." Bob nodded. Bless you, sir, and all your kin, he thought. No, stay away from that, he reminded himself.

To his surprise, Doug turned back and started forward again. What the hell? Bob thought. Has he changed his mind already?

Several minutes later, Doug reached a small clearing in the forest and stopped. He was sitting with his pack propped on a small fallen tree by the time Bob reached him.

"Don't step on that scat," he said.

"Scat."

"Coyote shit." Doug pointed at the ground.

"Oh. Thanks for telling me." Coyotes, Bob thought. No point in expressing uneasiness about them; Doug would only tell him he was being paranoid.

With a grateful groan, he sank down heavily and propped his backpack on the same fallen tree so that he and Doug were sitting side by side. "Feels good," he muttered, thinking: That's the understatement of the week.

"Look up on that hill," Doug said, pointing.

Bob looked in that direction, tensing slightly at the sight

of a black bear sitting on its haunches, eating something.

"What's it eating, another backpacker?" he said.

Doug snickered. "Who knows?" he replied. "Could be anything—nuts, berries, insects, maybe a squirrel. Could even be tree bark, they'll eat that too."

"That their usual diet?" Bob asked.

"Hell, no," Doug said disgustedly. "Their usual diet is discarded hamburger buns, fruit, cookies, candy, anything stupid backpackers leave out in the open."

Bob nodded grimly, looking up at the bear.

"Does he know we're here?" he asked.

"I don't think so," Doug answered, "unless you make coffee and he smells it. They can smell anything from a mile away."

So much for coffee, Bob thought, then immediately changed his mind. Slipping out of his pack, he got his cup and spoon and plastic envelope of instant coffee out. Pouring some water into the cup, he spooned in some instant coffee powder and sugar and began to stir it. "So I'll have iced coffee," he said.

"Better not clink the spoon too hard," Doug told him. "They have good hearing too."

Bob stirred the coffee mixture as quietly as he could. "Can he hear us talking?" he asked.

"I doubt it," Doug answered. "He's pretty far away. As long as we don't talk too loud."

"Don't worry, I won't," Bob said. He finished dissolving the coffee powder and, removing the spoon, took a sip. "Uh!" His face contorted with distaste. "That's hideous."

Doug only smiled. What do you care? Bob thought. You've already had your hot coffee. What else did you have, a fucking Belgian waffle?

He forced himself to keep sipping the coffee despite its bitter taste. Doug sat silently staring straight ahead. Waiting for me to finish? Bob wondered.

"There aren't any grizzly bears here, right?" he asked.

"Only black," Doug answered.

"How do you tell one from another?" Bob asked, conscious of speaking softly, almost murmuring, so the bear couldn't possibly hear the sound of his voice.

"Grizzlies have big shoulder humps," Doug told him. "And their faces are concave. They're bigger too. Have longer claws."

"Remind me never to meet one," Bob said.

Doug's chuckle was more derisive than amused. "Oh, you'd know if you met one."

"I'd run like hell," Bob said.

"It wouldn't do you any good," Doug told him. "They're too fast."

"So what do you do, just say a prayer and let him slaughter you?"

"Only thing you *can* do is lie on your stomach, put your hands behind your neck, and pretend you're dead." Doug grunted. "Which you probably would be in less than half a minute anyway."

Bob grimaced at the thought. "Ever see a grizzly?" he asked.

"Several times," Doug answered, "in Colorado. Guy I knew was actually caught by one."

Bob bared his teeth in a reacting wince. "Got killed?"

"Got lucky," Doug said. "Curled himself up into a fetal position and the bear only cuffed him around a few times before leaving."

"Jesus." Bob drew in a shaking breath.

"Of course those few cuffs broke his collarbone and laid his shoulder open to the muscle."

"He died?" Bob asked queasily.

"No, his friends got him to a hospital in time. Left him with a hell of a scar though. And limited use of his right arm."

"I presume he didn't go backpacking anymore," Bob said.

"Sure he did." Doug's tone was casual. "He wasn't going to let a little thing like that keep him from doing what he enjoyed."

"He's a better man than I am," Bob said. "If that happened to me, I'd join a monastery."

"Well, you're a different kind of cat," Doug said. Bob wasn't sure if it was an observation or another dig.

"You'd do the same thing, keep on backpacking?" he asked.

"Why not?" Doug said. "We all have to go sometime."

"Yeah, but I'd rather go in my bed than lying on a forest floor with a grizzly bear cuffing me around."

"To each his own," Doug said.

Bob kept sipping at the coffee, finally eating a cookie with it to improve the taste.

When Doug relapsed into what seemed to him to be glum silence again, he asked, "Are black bears as dangerous?"

Doug drew in a deep breath that seemed to, once more, point out his regret at having made the offer of this hike. Bob was going to say something about it, then decided not to.

"Black bears are different," Doug told him. "More skittish. If one of them comes at you, you yell and throw rocks at it, grab a branch and take swings at it. That'll usually scare them off. I've done that two or three times. Grizzlies they're not."

Bob nodded. "I'll remember that. Assuming I don't faint if I see one coming at me."

Again the ambiguous chuckle but no comment from Doug.

"This . . . route we're taking," Bob said. "Is it the most direct?"

"Not really," Doug answered casually.

"How come we're . . . taking it then?"

"You want to know what it's like to backpack, don't you?" was all Doug said.

Bob started to respond, then didn't know what to say. Scrap that, let's take the easiest route? Doug was probably right. This *was* the best way to give him a true backpacking experience. The novel may end up as a horror story but at least it will be an authentic one, he thought.

"You still a Democrat?" Doug asked.

Where did *that* come from? Bob wondered. "Yeah," he said. "Limitedly."

"What does that mean?" Doug asked.

"I'm not too keen on either party," Bob answered. "It doesn't seem to matter much which party wins, the corporations stay in power."

"So what do you want the government to do, go communist?" Doug asked.

"I presume that's not a serious question," Bob said with a smile.

"Hell, it's not," Doug told him. "If you're not a Democrat and you're not a Republican, what are you?"

"A liberal conservative," Bob answered.

"No such thing."

"Sure there is," Bob said. "I believe in conserving the social values that are worth conserving. If they're not, I believe in liberal pragmatism. Drop what doesn't work, put something else in instead."

"Like what?" Doug challenged.

"Like anything that benefits society rather than damaging it."

"That sounds like communism," Doug persisted.

"Doug, come on. Don't you believe in helping mankind lead a better life?"

"Not if *I* have to pay for it," Doug said stiffly. "Not if they just sit around on their asses, living off my taxes."

Bob drew in a quick breath. "Well, I'm not advocating a total welfare state either," he said.

"You work for your money, you keep your money," Doug said grimly.

"And not pay taxes?" Bob asked.

"Of course, pay taxes," Doug said irritably. "But not such high taxes that I'm paying for the lazy bastards who'd rather take it easy on welfare than put in an honest day's work."

"Well ..." Bob nodded. "I don't disagree with you. But that's the trouble with our country. We can't have a real democracy until voters govern themselves, not expect politicians to take care of everything. As long as people avoid real involvement in the political process, that's how long politicians will run it badly. The voters don't really *want* honest politicians. They say they do but, by and large, they keep electing politicians who lie to them, tell them how much they're going to help the people. Has a politician ever spoken the truth and nothing but the truth? Some have. And they invariably lose by a landslide. What did Jack Nicholson say in that movie? 'You can't *handle* the truth.' That's pretty much the case with the electorate."

Doug was silent for a few seconds before he said, "When you planning to run for office, Bob?"

They both laughed so loudly that Bob felt a twinge of uneasiness, looking toward the spot where the black bear had been. The bear was gone though.

"Didn't mean to make a speech," Bob said. "The entire thing is simple though. The majority of people aren't self-responsible—certainly not in the political arena. So they keep electing politicians who disappoint them."

"That's for sure," Doug said, "fucking bleeding heart liberals. Trying to take away our constitutional right to own guns. Shoving affirmative action down our throats, giving jobs they aren't qualified for to spics and niggers."

Oh, boy, Bob thought. *Oh, boy.* What am I doing here with this man? Three more wonderful days in his company. Jesus.

"I know you don't agree with any of this," Doug said. "Let's just agree that most politicians aren't worth shit."

Bob nodded. Especially the politicians who believe what you believe, Doug, he thought.

Doug looked at him intently. It seemed as though he meant to continue the conversation. Then, instead, he stood. "We'd better move along," he said.

Both of them looked around suddenly at the sound of shots in the distance—two in a row, a pause, then two more. "Son of a *bitch*," Doug muttered angrily.

"A *hunter?*" Bob asked, appalled.

"*Sure*, a hunter," Doug replied angrily. "In a goddamn national forest too. If we run across him, I'll wrap his fucking rifle around his neck."

"I'll hold your jacket while you do," Bob told him.

There was no amusement in Doug's smile and Bob had

the definite feeling that Doug *would* assault the hunter if they met him.

"Did you know that more than sixteen million hunting licenses are issued every year?" Doug told him. "Most of them to *idiots*. Two guys in a canoe were mistaken for a swimming moose by one of these idiots and both were shot, one of them fatally. Another idiot brought a dead mule into town, telling everyone he'd shot a moose. The mule still had its iron *shoes* on, for Christ's sake."

"That's incredible," Bob said, grateful that there was something they could agree on.

"Some farmer got so bugged by idiot hunters that he painted the word 'COW' on his only cow. Guess what? The fucking cow got shot."

10:52 AM

For a while, as they'd moved through the forest, weaving their way through a heavy growth of slender trees, Bob wondered if there was any possibility of them being shot by the hunter. Stupid bastard, he thought, coming into a national forest to shoot animals. He should be put in jail, the mindless idiot.

He'd felt uncomfortable, his skin almost crawling, as he walked, half expecting to hear a shot and feel a bullet tearing into his chest. Great way to end the "adventure," he'd thought grimly. Mrs. Hansen? Sorry to inform you that your husband was shot by a hunter while he was walking through the forest. His head is now on display above the hunter's mantelpiece. Visiting hours are one to five on Sunday afternoons.

He'd had to drop the dark fancy, then, in order to try to empty his bowels.

It hadn't worked at all, his system refusing utterly to co-operate. Stress? he'd wondered. Not enough water? No vege-tables? No way of knowing.

When he'd gotten back to Doug, he was about to speak when Doug, pointing at him, said, "There's a scorpion on your pants leg."

Bob stiffened, looking down. The scorpion was almost four inches long, clinging to his trouser leg.

"Don't hit it," Doug said quickly.

"What?" Bob looked at him worriedly.

"Flick it off, flick it off," Doug told him. "If you swat it, it'll sting you."

Bob swallowed dryly, reaching up slowly to remove his corduroy cap. Gritting his teeth, he slapped down at the scor-pion. It took two slaps to dislodge it; it scurried away into the brush. "Good God," Bob said.

"No big deal," Doug told him. "They're all around."

Super, Bob thought, imagining a giant scorpion crawling into his sleeping bag at night.

"Any luck?" Doug asked.

At first, Bob didn't know what Doug was talking about. Then he did. "Well, I'm lucky the damn scorpion didn't sting me on the ass," he said. "I wasn't lucky about the rest. I'm probably constipated."

"You bring an enema with you?" Doug asked.

"No," Bob said, frowning. "You never mentioned that."

"Well—" Doug shrugged. "You'll probably have trouble crapping. It usually happens; especially the first time out. Inhibition if nothing else. Not used to shitting in the woods. Try drinking something warm when you wake up."

I'd love to if you'd *let* me, Bob thought.

"Anyway, a few days of constipation won't kill you," Doug told him.

"I guess not," Bob said.

"You burned your toilet paper, didn't you?" Doug asked.

Bob nodded. "To a crisp," he said.

"I forgot to tell you," Doug continued, "if it's uncomfortable squatting, dig your cat hole on the opposite side of a log and use the log as a john seat, or dig the hole where there's a small tree with low branches you can hold on to while you're taking your crap."

"Trying to take my crap, you mean," Bob said.

"Yeah." Doug grinned. That seemed to genuinely amuse him. My compassionate wilderness guide, Bob thought.

Now he had managed to work himself into a steady pace, maintaining the same distance behind Doug, across meadows and through the forest. Doug must have taken his comment to heart, because it wasn't all uphill now. He was able to walk almost without feeling the blister on his foot, the aching in his side. His eyes went partially out of focus as he moved. He lost track of time, his mind going blank.

Then, up ahead, Doug stopped abruptly. "Jesus Christ," he said; it was close to a snarl.

Bob walked up beside him to see what Doug was looking at.

Lying sprawled among the small trees was a doe. There

was a dark hole in its side, blood oozing out of it and trickling down its tawny flank to stain the dead leaves it was lying on.

Bob started forward to look at the deer more closely, gasping in surprise as Doug reached out and grabbed his pack, yanking him back. "What—?" he said.

"It could still be alive," Doug told him. "If it kicks you, you'll be sorry."

"Still *alive*?" Bob looked at him, appalled, then turned to look more closely at the doe. He caught his breath, seeing a slight movement of breathing on its side. "Jesus Christ, it *is* still alive," he said in a sickened voice.

"Yeah," Doug said. "Stupid fucking hunter. Four shots and all he can do is wound it."

Bob looked at him in disbelief. That's hardly the point, is it? he thought.

Then he looked back at the wounded doe, groaning as he saw the dazed fright in its eyes. It was trying to get up but couldn't, barely stirring on the ground.

"What do we *do*?" he asked, his tone pained.

"What do you mean, what do we do?" Doug said irritably. "Put it out of its misery, what else? What would you suggest, taking it to a vet?"

Bob drew in a deeply shaking breath. He knew Doug was right but it angered him the way he was expressing it. "Yeah," was all he could say.

Doug looked around, grimacing. "Shit," he muttered.

"What?"

"I need a rock to hit it on the head," Doug said, sounding more aggravated than concerned.

Bob swallowed dryly. Need a drink, he thought. A *drink*?

he assailed himself. Is that all you can think about right now?

"Let's find one then," he said. He started to move around, searching for a rock.

He hadn't gone more than a few yards when he heard a loud, thudding noise and the blood-chilling sound of the doe crying out in shocked pain. Twisting around, he saw Doug standing over it, holding his golak. He'd struck the doe across its neck, cutting in so deep that blood was pumping from the gash.

"Oh, Christ," Bob said.

"Oh, Christ, what?" Doug demanded. "It had to be done, didn't it?"

Bob drew in another trembling breath through his nostrils, a shudder running through him. "Yes," he conceded. "It had to be done. I just don't know how the hell you were able to do it."

"What would you do if you were alone here?" Doug asked.

I will never be alone here, Bob's mind reacted.

"Just leave it?" Doug challenged.

"I don't know," Bob answered. "I just don't know. I've never been exposed to such a thing."

"Well, think about it sometime," Doug told him. "You never know what you might come up against out here."

I will never *be* out here again, his mind answered.

"Well, I admire your ability to do what you did," he said. "It's . . . very brave in a way. The poor thing *did* need to be put out of its misery and you did it."

"You could never kill anything, could you?" Doug said; once again—Bob was getting used to it by now—it was more a statement than a question.

"Doug, I just don't know," Bob said. "It's never come up."

"Well, I killed *men* in Vietnam," Doug told him. "Lots of them."

Bob sighed heavily. "I guess you had to," he said.

"Damn right," Doug said. "Those little gook bastards were everywhere."

Bob nodded, feeling a sense of uncomfortable ambivalence about what Doug was saying. He didn't believe in killing anything; Doug was right about that. But then he'd never *had* to kill anything and hadn't the remotest concept of whether he could or not. He just hoped to God the necessity never came up.

"You want some venison for supper?" Doug asked casually.

"What?" He looked at Doug incredulously. "You're planning to *butcher* it now?"

"Oh, come on, Bobby, grow up," Doug said. "The deer is dead. It's going to get eaten by something—a bear, a mountain lion, who knows? For that matter, we'd better move on before something picks up the smell of its blood and comes charging in, looking for lunch. You want some venison or would you rather just stick with your little chicken à la kings?"

Doug, if you don't stop insulting me, I'm really going to get pissed, Bob thought, tensing.

"Let's just move on," he said curtly. "I don't want any venison."

"Suit yourself," Doug said. He wiped off the blade of his golak on the deer's flank and put it back in its sheath. "So let's be on our way."

As they continued on into the forest, Doug said, "You didn't go to Vietnam, did you?"

"No, I didn't."

"Oh, that's right, you had psoriasis, didn't you?" Doug said. His tone was close to mocking.

"I didn't *ask* to have it, Doug," Bob answered coolly. "It's genetic. And I didn't make the rules about what constitutes physical rejection by the army."

"Yeah, whatever," Doug said disinterestedly.

12:02 PM

We have to stop for lunch soon, I am *starving*, Bob thought. He had eaten an energy bar, a cookie, and a small apple but it had only delayed his hunger. He was getting ravenous now.

He was about to speak when Doug stopped ahead and pointed upward. Bob looked up through the foliage and saw a large number of big birds circling in the sky.

"Vultures waiting for us?" he suggested.

Doug didn't react to the attempted joke. "Hawks," he said. "A storm is coming."

"Oh, great, that's all we need," Bob reacted.

He saw Doug sniffing exaggeratedly. "What do you smell?" he asked.

"The ground," Doug said. "It always smells odd before a storm."

Bob inhaled as deeply as he could through his nose but couldn't tell if the smell of the ground was any different. For that matter, he had never smelled the ground at all. Was Doug pulling his leg? He wouldn't be surprised.

"Take off your cap," Doug said, removing his.

"Why?"

"Just do it," Doug told him.

Oh, shit, Bob thought. He took off his corduroy cap. "Yeah?" he said.

"Does your hair feel thicker?" Doug asked.

Bob had to chuckle at that. "That would be nice," he said.

Doug laughed. "Your hair *is* thinning a bit, isn't it?" he asked, he said.

" 'Fraid so," Bob answered, looking at Doug's thick shock of black hair. Although he was sure that Doug dyed it for professional reasons. And maybe ego reasons too; no way of knowing.

Looking up again, he noticed now a huge towering cloud in the distance. "Oh, that looks ominous," he said.

"Cumulus nimbus," Doug informed him. "Thunderhead cloud. We could be in for a real storm. We'd better find us a place to stay dry."

Super, Bob thought. Just what I was hoping for, a thunderstorm. "Lightning too?" he asked.

"Oh, sure," Doug answered, looking around. For a hotel, I hope, Bob thought.

"Let's head for that cliff," Doug told him. "Could be a cave there. We'll have to move a little faster though. No way of telling how soon the storm's going to hit."

"Can we eat soon?" Bob asked. "I'm pretty hungry."

"Cave first, lunch second," Doug said. "Let's go. Keep up with me now. And if you think a lightning strike is imminent get down as low as you can, sit or crouch on your pack to avoid ground currents."

Oh, God, this is a fucking nightmare, Bob thought.

Doug had turned to the left and started toward what looked to Bob like a good-sized mountain. His stride was rapid. As the undergrowth thinned and the stands of trees began to diminish, he moved faster and faster. Bob did his best to keep the same distance between himself and Doug but kept falling farther and farther behind. Should he call after Doug and ask him to slow down? He did agree that they'd need some kind of shelter if it was going to rain hard, especially if there was going to be lightning. Still, he found himself getting more breathless by the minute, partially because of the speed Doug was going, partially because the pack felt so heavy. In addition, he was becoming increasingly aware of the ache in his side and the pain of the blister on his foot. Can't we just set up the tent? he thought.

Fortunately, the ground, as they approached the foothills, grew more and more open and he was able to keep Doug in view even though the distance between them was getting constantly larger. Doug never looked back.

Does he even care if he loses me? Bob wondered. Why, oh why, did I ever decide to write this goddamn novel? Marian was right, a hundred percent. They could be lolling on a Hawaiian beach right now, sipping—what had she suggested?— yes, chi-chis. Instead, here he was lurching and limping as fast as he could through a national forest, trying to overtake Doug while an impending thunderstorm gathered overhead.

It *was* impending too, he saw, wincing. Now that he was almost out in the open, starting to move up an incline (which only made him more breathless, more tired, more achy), he could see that the sky was darkening rapidly, the huge cloud drifting over them. Oh, Christ, don't let it start before we find a cave or something, he thought.

Up ahead, Doug turned to look back. "Use a rest step!" he called.

"A what?!"

"Rest step, rest step!" Doug said impatiently. "Lift your left leg, move it forward, and put it down with no weight on it! Pause a few seconds, keeping all your weight on the right foot! Then shift your weight to the left leg and move the right leg forward, with no weight on it! Then start with your left leg again! You got it?!"

"Yeah! Yeah." Bob had only a limited idea of what Doug was talking about but didn't want to ask for a repeat explanation. He wanted to find that cave—assuming it existed—before the deluge hit.

He continued up the slope, trying to approximate what Doug had told him and having little success. He grimaced, listening to the roll and mutter of thunder that seemed to get closer every minute.

His right hand was leaning on a boulder, trying to brace himself as he climbed, when there was a tremendous roar overhead and, suddenly, a blinding flash of light that made him gasp, then cry out in stunned terror as he felt an electric shock run up his arm on the boulder. I've been struck by lightning! he thought in shock. He shuddered, horrified, seeing that the hand that had been on the boulder looked ashen with a bluish-gray tinge. I'm going to die! he thought. He felt himself slip to one side and crumple to the ground. I'm paralyzed, he thought with a sob. Dear God, I'm paralyzed!

It seemed as though, almost instantly, Doug was kneeling by him, a look of concern on his face. "Jesus, Bobby, you got hit by lightning."

"No kidding," he said weakly.

"Can you move your arms and legs?" Doug asked.

Bob tried, and with some help from Doug, who rubbed and moved his arms and legs, he found that he wasn't paralyzed after all. "Jesus Christ," Doug said, strangely amused it seemed—it must be relief, Bob thought. "When I heard that boom and saw that flash and heard you scream—"

"I screamed?" Bob murmured.

"Like a stuck pig," Doug said. Bob could see now that his smiles of amusement *were* relief. "Then, when I saw you flop on the ground, I thought, Oh, Jesus Christ, what am I going to tell Marian, I took your husband on a hike and got him killed by lightning? Jesus!" He shook himself as though ridding himself of dismay. "Whoa," he said, "I don't know why you weren't fried. I'm glad you weren't though."

"So am I," Bob muttered. Jesus Christ, he thought. Struck by *lightning*. How could such a thing happen?

He jumped as another roar of thunder sounded overhead. Doug pulled him up. "Crouch on the balls of your feet," he said quickly.

He had barely done so when another bolt of lightning flashed, this time farther away.

"We'd better get to that cave," Doug said.

"What cave?" Bob asked.

"There's one not far up," Doug said. "Come on."

It suddenly began to rain. "Oh, boy," Doug said.

He helped Bob put on his poncho, then threw on his own. "Let's go," he said. He chuckled unexpectedly, reaching out to touch one of Bob's eyebrows. "They got singed," he said.

Bob grunted and they started up the slope. The pack seemed to get heavier with every stride. He still felt dazed and unreal after the lightning strike. He screwed his face into a grimacing mask as they climbed, starting at each crash of thunder, each crackling flare of lightning. Will this ever end? he thought. Have I died and gone to hell? He swallowed dryly again and again. Believing in life after death wasn't much of a comfort when you didn't know if that death was coming at any second—sharply, violently, unexpectedly.

"Hold on," Doug told him as they reached the cave.

"Why?" he asked but his voice was drowned out by a roar of thunder. As quickly as he could, he pulled off his pack to sit on it. Before he could get it off, a bolt of lightning struck about a hundred yards away. Thank God for that, he thought.

Why can't we go in the cave? he wondered. He was getting soaked.

A few seconds later, he knew why as Doug emerged from the cave, a headless, flopping rattlesnake in his left hand, the golak in his right. Oh, Jesus, he thought, seeing how big the snake was as Doug flung it away. He grimaced at himself. Marian, don't ever listen to me again, he thought.

They were in the cave now. It was reasonably big and Doug had placed their packs away from them so the metal frames couldn't conduct electricity if lightning hit near the cave. He had placed their sleeping pads and sleeping bags under them to insulate them against ground shock and told Bob to keep his hands off the ground. Bob's appetite seemed to be considerably lessened by the lightning strike. He wondered if there had been damage to any of his organs. His hand still looked a little ashen although the bluish-gray tinge had faded. I survived a lightning bolt, he kept thinking. Maybe he should write an article for the *Enquirer*: "Author Struck by Lightning and Survives!"

He tried to listen to what Doug was telling him, probably to get him back to feeling normal after what had happened. But he kept drifting off mentally, unable to get over what had happened. Doug had said something about how ordinarily a cave was the worst place to be in a lightning storm but this one was okay because of its height and depth, six to seven feet in each dimension. Any smaller and lightning was actually attracted to caves; something like that.

The only thing Doug said that stayed with him was his account of a forest ranger named Roy Sullivan who more than earned the nickname "Dooms," because he'd been struck by lightning seven times over a period of thirty-five years, one strike even setting his hair on fire and heating his body so much that he had to pour a pail of water over his head.

"But none of them killed him," Doug finished his story. "He died of something else entirely."

"That's comforting," Bob said.

It didn't help much when Doug informed him again that a cave wasn't really all that safe a spot in a lightning storm. Or when he told Bob that he should listen for high-pitched zinging sounds because they indicated that a strike was near.

"Did you know that the odds of being struck by lightning are one in six hundred thousand?" he asked.

"No, I didn't know," Bob answered wanly. "Nice to know I'm special."

He made the mistake of asking if they could set up the stove so he could make himself some soup.

"Put a metal stove right next to us in a lightning storm?" Doug said.

"No, of course not," Bob replied, nodding feebly.

Doug patted him on the back. "You're a lucky man, Bobby," he said. "You were only splashed by the lightning. If you'd been hit directly, two or three hundred million volts would have gone through you."

Bob shivered. I'd rather not hear any more about lightning if you don't mind, he thought.

"If *that* had happened, you'd probably have amnesia, be temporarily blind or deaf, your blood vessels spasmed, your skin mottled. You were lucky."

"Yeah," Bob said, "I feel lucky."

The thunder and lightning had passed but it was still raining hard.

Doug set up the stove and heated soup for the two of them. That it was his soup didn't bother Bob. He sighed in pleasure as he ate it with crackers. Bob used his pot to boil some water for coffee. Bob felt a lot better with some hot soup in his stomach and sipping on a cup of hot, sweetened coffee, eating some oatmeal-raisin cookies with it. He still felt disoriented by the shock he'd gotten but—remarkably he was certain—he hadn't been really injured in any way.

To his surprise, Doug took a small flask from his pack and unscrewed its cap. "Some brandy in your coffee?" he asked.

"I thought alcohol impaired the judgment," Bob needled him without thinking.

Doug looked at him askance. "You want some or not?" he asked.

"I want some definitely," Bob answered. "It can't impair my judgment any more than being struck by lightning."

Doug chuckled. "That's for sure," he said, pouring a small amount of brandy into Bob's cup. "Anyway, I only thought you weren't used to backpacking and the vodka might make it more difficult for you."

"Got ya," Bob said. He raised his cup in a toast. "To you, Douglas."

Doug smiled a little. The hot, brandy-laced coffee tasted wonderful to Bob, making him sigh.

"Well, the weather's giving you a chance to rest, isn't it?" Doug said.

"For which I am intensely grateful to the weather," Bob responded.

"Well, I just hope Marian doesn't get upset if we don't get to the cabin when she expects us," Doug said.

Oh, that's right, Bob thought; it *would* worry her. He sighed. "Well, I guess it can't be helped," he said.

The gas flame of the stove, now turned off, had warmed the cave a little. It seemed cozy now, especially with the brandied coffee warming his stomach. He leaned back against his pack, sighing with pleasure.

After a few minutes, he looked over at Doug, feeling, for some singular reason, a sense of affection for him. Sure, there was still that pain-in-the-ass quality to his behavior, and their politics were worlds apart. Still, Doug *was* taking him on this hike after all and he *had* seemed genuinely concerned about the lightning strike—correction, splash, he told himself.

Now he felt a genuine curiosity as to what had made Doug the contradictory man he was. He'd never asked before. The only times he'd been with Doug was when the two couples were together. Now he was alone with him, he felt warm and comfortable (if still a little woozy) and wanted to know more about his hiking companion than he knew. For that matter he knew nothing at all about Doug beyond his animated social behavior and his rather overbearing conduct during this hike.

"Tell me about yourself," he said.

"Tell you about myself?" Doug turned it into a question.

"Yes," Bob said.

"Tell you what?" Doug asked.

"Your childhood, for instance," Bob replied.

"Oh, you don't want to hear about that," Doug told him.

"Why not?"

"Because it was a fucking nightmare," Doug said.

"That bad." Bob wondered if he'd made a mistake bringing up the subject. He'd only wanted to learn a little more about Doug. But, instead, if he'd opened up old wounds . . .

"I'm sorry, I didn't mean to pry into—"

"My childhood," Doug said as though he were reading the title of a book. "By Douglas Crowley, formerly Douglas Crowlenkovitch."

"That was your name," Bob said, surprised. "I presume you changed it when you became an actor."

"Obviously," Doug said. He took a sip of his coffee and sighed. "Well, it wasn't anything like your childhood, that I'd bet on."

"Where did you grow up?"

"On the outskirts of Pittsburgh," Doug answered. "My old man was a steel worker."

"Were you an only child?" Bob asked.

Doug made a sound of scornful amusement. "I should be so lucky."

"How many of you were there?"

"Four sisters and me," Doug said. "They got the princess treatment, I got treated like some dog they'd found in a lot."

"Really?" Bob said, wincing.

"Yes, *really*," Doug said; sounding almost contemptuous. "They had the two extra bedrooms, I had the cellar."

"The *cellar*?" Bob looked at him in pained amazement.

"That's right. While you had a nice room all to yourself, I'm sure, my old man threw up some plywood and made me a—what would you call it?—a cell, an enclosure, a fucking *closet?* You can imagine how cold it got down there in the winter. The only time it was comfortable was in the summer."

"Jesus." Bob looked distressed at the image Doug had created in his mind.

"Jesus was nowhere around," Doug said. "Just my old man and my mother—who was drunk most of the time."

"Oh, for God's sake," Bob said, wincing again.

"He wasn't around either." Doug's smile was thin and bitter. "My old man used to beat the shit out of me," he said.

"Why?" Bob asked.

"Why?" Doug repeated. "For any damn thing he wanted to. Bad grades in school. Not doing my chores fast enough to suit him. Once, one of my sisters came on to me. She was lying naked on my cot, telling me to fuck her when my old man found us. Who got blamed? Her? My ass. It was all *my* fault. She was thirteen, I was nine, but it was *my* fault and he got that old belt out toot sweet and walloped my bare ass until I couldn't sit down for three days. Bastard. And what about Lenora? She cried tears like the professional crocodile she was and got away with the whole thing—even my mother bawled me out. I wasn't too crazy about Lenora after that. For that matter, none of my sisters cared much for me. My oldest sister Angela wasn't too bad; she, at least, stood up for me once in a while. But not very much."

"Did your father drink too?" Bob asked.

"Not during the week, he had to work," Doug said. "But on weekends . . . watch out. That's when I got most of my beatings. He beat my mother up once in a while too. But never the girls. I don't know what the hell kept him clear of them. Hell, maybe he *was* screwing them, it wouldn't surprise me a bit to find out that he was."

Bob didn't know what to say. He really was sorry now that he'd brought up the subject. Then, again, maybe it was doing Doug good to let out some of his painful memories.

"When did you leave home?" he asked.

"House, you mean," Doug said. "It was never a home." He paused to take a drink of his coffee, then went on. "I was about fifteen. I'd become a real 'tough guy' by then. Hung out with 'the wrong crowd,' don't y'know. Got caught trying to rob a liquor store with a couple of my buddies. We all got sent to a reformatory. I was there two years. Got raped a dozen times or so until I beat up the 'big guy' there. Then they left me alone. Would you believe that's where I got into acting?"

"How so?" Bob asked, surprised.

"Some jerky social worker started a dramatics program there. Most of the guys thought it was only for fags but I tried it and I liked it. That got some of the other guys into it too—they knew *I* wasn't a fag. So we put on shows and I found out I was pretty damn good at it. So after I got out, I went to Philadelphia, got a job in a lumberyard, and went to acting school."

"That's very interesting," Bob said.

Doug looked at him suspiciously. "You jerking my chain?" he asked.

"Well, I don't know what that means," Bob answered. "But if it means am I pulling your leg, no, I'm not. I think what you've told me *is* very interesting. You've survived a lot of hard times."

"That's for damn sure," Doug said.

"So when did you come to California?" Bob asked then.

"Went to New York first. Another acting school—I couldn't get into The Actors Studio; guy who ran it didn't like me. But I got a few parts in off-Broadway shows. Enjoyed the hell out of it because I had my choice of all the actresses; most guys in acting companies are queer. Which is amusing because most of the so-called famous lovers of the stage are queer— which, of course, the audience doesn't know."

"What brought you to the coast?" Bob asked.

"Some Hollywood agent saw me and told me I should come to Los Angeles; he thought he could get me some television work." He exhaled hard. "End of story," he said. He looked outside. "If it doesn't stop raining soon, we'd better try to move on anyway."

"Oh, all right." Bob didn't want to leave the comfort of where they were but knew that Marian would start to fret if he was days late.

Doug poured some more hot water into his cup, added coffee powder to it, stirred it up, and added a little more brandy to the cup. "You want some more?" he asked.

Bob was going to say no, then thought: Oh, what the hell, it's making Doug more genial, making me feel good, and, most importantly, delaying their possible departure into the cold rain.

"Sure," he said. He made himself more coffee and Doug added a little brandy to his cup.

"So that's the story of my fucking life," Doug said. "Excluding a few minor details like my marriage to Nicole, my two kids, Nicole moving out on me, my total alienation from Janie, my acting career in the fucking doldrums, and my son—"

He broke off abruptly and Bob hoped the subject of Artie would be dropped. He knew the pain Doug still felt about it and knew that there was very little he could say to lessen that pain.

"You believe in life after death, don't you?" Doug surprised him by asking.

He hesitated for a few moments, then nodded. "Yes, I do."

"So tell me"—Doug was looking at him almost challengingly—"you think Artie's there, okay then?"

Bob swallowed. "Yes, of course he's there," he said. He'd never tell Doug what he believed about suicides.

"Even though he was a druggie?" Doug asked.

"It doesn't matter what he was," Bob told him. "He's still there." Where that "there" was he hated to consider. But he could, in honesty, say that he believed in Artie's survival.

"You've been reading about this stuff for a long time, haven't you?" Doug said.

"A long time," Bob agreed. "Hundreds of books."

"And you're convinced of this . . . survival thing," Doug probed.

"Totally," Bob answered. "I believe that we're more than body and brain, that we possess a higher self that survives death."

"Survives for what?" Doug asked.

"To come back and try again," Bob answered.

"Oh, shit," Doug said. "We have to go through everything *again?*"

"It'll be different," Bob said. "We'll be different people. But we'll still be the same basic soul working out our problems. Trying to anyway."

Doug grunted and took a sip of his coffee. He bared his teeth, remembering. "That means I'll have to pay the price for what I did to Artie," he said. "Or what I *didn't* do."

"We all have problems that we need to solve," Bob said.

"Not *you*," Doug said, his hostile tone startling Bob. "Your life is a fucking utopia compared to mine. A wife who loves you. Two kids doing well. A successful career. You're even handsome, for Christ's sake. Who the hell *were* you in your last lifetime, the fucking son of God?"

Bob tried to react as though Doug wasn't being totally serious even though he knew that he was. Did Doug resent him *that* much? Was that why he'd been so rough on him? Was it going to get worse? The thought appalled him. Out here, he was completely at the mercy of Doug's backpacking skills.

"Well," he said, forcing a smile. "My life isn't quite that perfect."

"Has *your* wife walked out on you?" Doug demanded. "Has your daughter written you off completely? Has your career gone into the toilet? *Has your son put a pistol in his mouth and blown his fucking brains out?*"

"Doug, take it easy, will you?" Bob tried to calm him down. "I *know* you're having problems in your life, I know—"

"*Problems?*" Doug almost snarled. "Is that what they are? Fucking *problems*? Something I can solve with a fucking slide rule?!"

Bob didn't answer. He returned Doug's glare with what he hoped was a sympathetic look, at least unprovoked. Finally, he said, "I'm sorry if my life infuriates you. I didn't design it that way."

"It doesn't infuriate me," Doug said, obviously lying. "I just don't think you know what misery feels like. Not with the way your life has gone."

"I'm sorry, Doug," Bob told him quietly. "I really am. If I've said anything stupid or anything that hurt you, I'm sorry, I apologize."

He'd hoped that his words would mollify Doug. It only made him fall into a morose silence, sitting and sipping his coffee, staring out through the cave entrance, his expression one of bleak depression. Bob didn't dare say any more. He sat in silence himself, hoping—almost praying—that the rest of the hike wasn't going to be jeopardized because of this conversation.

Doug, I hope this isn't going to spoil the rest of our hike, he imagined himself saying to Doug. And Doug replying: Don't bet on it, Bobby.

2:24 PM

Something hit him smartly on the chest and his eyes popped open. Doug was looking at him with a stiff expression. "Gotta go," he said.

Bob looked at him confusedly. "What did I do, fall asleep?"

"*Naturally.*" Doug's tone was critical.

"I'm sorry, I—"

"Come on, we have to move," Doug cut him off.

Bob looked groggily toward the entrance of the cave. "Has the rain stopped?" he asked.

"Enough," Doug said. "Come *on*. Let's *go*."

"Okay. Okay." Bob frowned. Are we starting in again? he thought.

He looked around. Doug had already packed the sleeping bags and pads. How did he get them out from under me? he wondered. Was I sleeping that heavily?

139

Richard Matheson

"Let's get your pack on," Doug told him. His movements were hurried as he pushed Bob's arms through the strap loops. *"Oh."* Bob winced as Doug twisted his right arm.

"Sorry," Doug said. He didn't sound it.

The pack felt heavier than ever. Because it was wet? Bob looked worried. "Isn't the ground outside muddy?" he asked.

"Bob, we cannot stay here all day," Doug told him. "We have to reach a campsite before it gets dark."

Why? Bob thought. Why not stay right here until the rain stops? Even if it means staying here all night. It's warm, it's comfortable.

"All right, let's move," Doug said.

Bob tried to lift himself, then fell back, feeling slightly dizzy. *"Whoa,"* he said. "That lightning must have done more to me than I thought."

Doug looked at him without expression. What? Bob thought. Am I supposed to feel guilty about getting splashed by lightning now?

The way Doug was looking at him—almost with contempt it seemed—made Bob's temper snap abruptly.

"All right, for Christ's sake, go on without me then. I'd rather be lost than badgered to death."

"Who the hell is badgering you?" Doug looked surprised.

"You are," Bob said. "You're taking advantage of the fact that you know exactly what to do out here and I don't know the first damn thing about it." As he spoke he felt a sudden coldness in his stomach. What in God's name would he do if Doug took him at his word?

"Calm down, for Christ's sake," Doug told him. "You're just feeling rattled because of the lightning splash."

"Maybe so," Bob answered. "I'm sorry. I *do* feel rattled."

"Listen. Bob," Doug said, "I have an idea."

"What?" Bob asked, uneasily.

"Why don't you go back to where we started from? I'll move on fast to the cabin, get the Bronco, and come back and pick you up."

At first, it sounded like a good idea. Then Bob remembered all the ground they'd covered. He'd undoubtedly get lost. Immediately, he said so.

"No, you wouldn't," Doug said as though addressing a child. "I'll give you the compass. You follow it and you'll be back there by dark."

"How could I *possibly* be?" Bob demanded, his voice rising in panic. "It took us more than a day to get *here*."

"So you'll sleep one night in the woods, it won't kill you."

A collage of bears and mountain lions and coyotes painted itself across his mind. "Doug, that is ridiculous," he said. "I'd never make it."

"Bob, you just asked me to leave you here."

"I didn't mean it, for Christ's sake. I just lost my temper."

Doug nodded, looking unconvinced.

"Bob, this isn't working out," he said. "It could take us three, four days more the way we're going. Your wife is going to lose her mind, worrying about you."

"She'll lose her mind a lot more if I get eaten by a goddamn mountain lion," Bob retorted.

"Oh, jeez, the mountain lion thing again. You aren't going to run into a mountain lion. All you have to do is—"

"No," Bob interrupted adamantly. "You saw what happened to me yesterday. I'm not going to let you dump me again."

"Dump you?" Doug looked incredulous. "I'm trying to

help you. This hike was a mistake, you know that. You aren't up to it."

"I *will* be up to it," Bob said, sounding almost frightened now. "Just don't leave me on my own again. It scared the hell out of me."

Doug didn't reply. He looked at Bob as though regarding the child who wouldn't listen to reason. *Is that the look you gave Artie all the time?* the thought occurred to Bob.

Doug's cheeks puffed as he blew out a surrendering breath. "Okay. Okay," he said. "So it takes us a week to reach the cabin. So we'll run out of food and have to eat squirrels. So your wife will become convinced that you *were* eaten by a mountain lion. If that's what you want, okay, so be it."

He pointed at Bob. "Which doesn't mean I'm going to slow down to a crawl," he warned. "We still have to move at a reasonable clip if we're going to make that campsite by dark."

"Okay." Bob nodded, feeling such relief that he didn't even think of how difficult it was going to be to keep up with Doug. As long as he wasn't alone, that was what mattered. He never wanted to be alone in the forest again.

He braced himself against the slight dizziness and continuing weariness as he made his way out of the cave. It wasn't raining hard, something slightly more than a drizzle. They put on their ponchos and Bob drew in a deep breath. He was not going to give Doug any more reason to be aggravated with him. He'd make this damn hike and make it successfully, then go home and burn the backpack, sleeping bag, ground pad, and every other damn piece of equipment he'd bought. I'll dance around the bonfire, naked, he visualized himself, repressing a smile. I'll bellow a farewell chant to all of it and stay in luxury lodges in the future if I ever want to be exposed to Mother Nature again.

"All right, let's go," he said crisply. At least, he tried to make it sound crisp. He had no idea how convincing it was to Doug.

Probably not at all.

They were crossing a tree-dripping glade, Bob twenty feet behind, when Doug suddenly stopped and, reaching back across his shoulder, snatched an arrow from its quiver. Oh, my God, he's going to kill me! Bob thought in shock. Freezing in his tracks, he stared aghast as Doug grabbed his bow and quickly fitted the arrow's neck into the bowstring.

Instead of whirling though, Doug kept looking ahead, drew back the string quickly, and shot the arrow at something Bob couldn't see.

He moved up to where Doug remained standing. "Why'd you do that?" he asked.

Doug pointed toward the ground ahead and Bob looked in that direction.

Lying on the ground, twitching feebly as it died, was a large raccoon. Its fur is so beautiful, was the first thing Bob thought. "How come you killed it?" he asked, trying not to sound in the least bit critical.

"Rabies," Doug told him.

"How do you know it had rabies?" Bob asked.

"Raccoons aren't in the habit of coming straight at you in broad daylight," Doug said. "And doing it fast. They avoid people; they don't attack them."

"He was attacking?" Bob asked, incredulous.

"My call, Bobby," Doug said curtly. "I didn't care to take the chance that it was just being friendly."

Bob nodded immediately. "I understand," he said.

"Do you?" Doug responded. "Do you know that wildlife-related cases of rabies have more than doubled in the last ten years? Do you know what a rabies attack can be like? Hallucinations? Swallowing so painful you can't eat or drink? Muscle spasms in the face and neck? A raging fever? Probable death? You wonder why I killed the damn raccoon?"

"No, no—I understand," Bob said hastily. God forbid he got Doug ranting again. "You did the right thing."

"Damn right." Doug slung the bow across his shoulder and, without another word, started quickly across the glade.

Bob stopped for a few moments to look down at the dead raccoon. It looked as though it had been in perfect health. He couldn't get over how beautiful its fur was—all silvery and black.

As he started after Doug he was unable to prevent himself from wondering if the raccoon really did have rabies or whether Doug was trying to impress him—hell, intimidate him—with his skill at using the bow and arrow. Oh, don't be paranoid, for chrissake, he told himself—but he couldn't help mulling over the suspicion. Was he missing something here? Was Doug actually a menace to him? He didn't want to believe that for a moment. Still, the tension between them seemed to be increasing all the time. Just how *did* Doug feel about him? It had better be benign because if it was something more, he was a pretty helpless prey.

Oh, come on, he ordered himself angrily. Just because you're having arguments doesn't translate into murderous intent on Doug's part. For Christ's sake, Doug may well have saved your life if the raccoon really was rabid.

It *was* rabid, he tried to convince himself. Shape up, Hansen. By the weekend you'll be home with Marian and all this will be nothing more than an unpleasant memory.

Doug had stopped at the base of a steep slope, waiting for Bob to catch up.

What now? Bob thought, looking up the slope. It was much steeper than the one they'd climbed to reach the cave. "What are we—?" he started.

"We have two choices," Doug interrupted. "Either we go around this and add miles to the hike before we stop. Or we climb it and save ourselves a lot of time."

Bob drew in a shaking breath. "Well, I'm not too confident in my ability to do mountain climbing," he said.

"Mountain climbing?" Doug sounded as though he couldn't believe what Bob had said. "Jesus Christ, this is a slope, not a mountain."

Bob didn't want to try it. But, even less, did he want to generate another conflict between them. So he nodded unconvincingly and said, even more unconvincingly, "Okay, let's *do* it."

He was sure Doug knew that he didn't mean a word of it but acted as though he wasn't aware of it. "Good," Doug said. "Use that rest step I told you about and it won't be too hard." Without another word, he started up the slope.

Bob followed, boots slipping on the brush, roots, and mud surface of the slope. Jesus, are my clothes going to be filthy, he thought. He kept trying the rest step but the ground was just too slippery for it to work; he kept falling to his knees, getting mud on his hands, hurting his right palm.

As he labored up the slope—the backpack starting to feel like an anvil on his back again—he recalled the pleasure with which he'd accepted Doug's offer to take him on a backpacking trip. That was a great decision, Hansen, he derided himself. One of the best you ever made.

Looking up, he saw that Doug had stopped and was looking back at him. "Going to make it?" Doug asked dubiously.

"I'll be fine," he answered breathlessly.

He stiffened, seeing a boulder, loosened by the rain, rolling directly at Doug.

"Look out!" he cried.

Doug jerked around and saw the boulder rolling down at him. He made a sudden move to avoid it and slipped, banging his elbow against a rock, hissing at the pain.

Bob had no idea where the strength came from. But, surging upward abruptly, he grabbed Doug's pack and jerked him out of the way of the boulder. Not all the way though. As the boulder rumbled past, it grazed Doug's right shoulder, hitting his backpack and jolting him around in a quarter spin. *"Jesus!"* Doug cried.

They crouched together on the muddy soil, looking at each other. Doug kept wincing at the pain in his shoulder and elbow. "Damn," he muttered. "Damn it."

"You all right?" Bob asked. He panted a little as he spoke.

"I dunno," Doug said. He rubbed his elbow, grimacing. "Shit," he said.

Bob struggled to his feet, thinking: Well, don't thank me, Doug, I only saved your life.

To his amazement, Doug *didn't* thank him. "That was really something," was the closest he came.

"Yeah. It was," Bob said. He was astounded that Doug expressed not one scintilla of gratitude. Instead, Doug got up and said, "We'd better move or it'll be dark before we reach the campsite."

Yeah, right, Bob thought. Your appreciation really warms the cockles of my heart, Douglas.

As though to prove that the injuries had no serious effect on him, Doug moved on up the slope at an even faster pace than he'd been going before. Jesus God, what kind of childhood did he really have? Bob wondered. Proving his mettle seemed to outweigh everything else, even gratitude for someone who may have saved him from critical injury.

He couldn't restrain himself. "Doug, I might have just saved your life, you know."

"No, no, I would have gotten out of the way by myself," Doug answered casually.

Why, you ungrateful son of a bitch, Bob thought. I should have let the fucking boulder crush you into jam.

Shaking his head, he continued climbing the slope. Incredible, he kept thinking. Simply incredible.

"There, you *see*?" Doug was at the top of the slope now, pointing at the ground.

Bob reached the top and found Doug standing beside another dead raccoon. This one was swarming with maggots. Bob made a sickened noise and averted his face.

"Rabies," Doug told him.

Bob nodded, starting past him. After a few paces, he stopped abruptly at a loud, clashing sound in the distance. "What's *that*?" he asked, turning back to Doug.

"Probably a couple of horny stags fighting for a female. They butt their heads together, it makes their antlers clatter."

That's right, lecture me again, Bob thought disgruntledly. Can't get enough of that, can you?

He waited until Doug had passed by him, then followed, looking at the back of Doug's head with a resentful glare.

4:32 PM

It was more than a stream this time. Closer to being a river, Bob thought. Fast-moving, frothing, and bubbling, its current so rapid that in striking boulders it flung up explosive sprays of water drops. It looked very cold and threatening to him. "No log bridge here," he said.

"No more log bridges, buddy," Doug told him, "we're backpacking now, not taking a stroll through the park."

Bob sighed. You already said that, Doug, he thought. "So what do we do?" he asked.

"We cross, what else?" Doug said.

"How?"

Doug looked at him as though he couldn't believe that Bob had asked the question. "Wade, Bobby, wade," he said.

"Wade," Bob murmured. He couldn't see how they could possibly wade across such a rushing stream.

Doug started to remove his backpack.

"Think it might be less wide a little farther downstream?" Bob asked hopefully.

"I presume you mean *upstream*." Doug's smile was thin.

"Upstream, downstream, what's the difference?" Bob snapped.

"Upstream gets narrower; downstream gets wider," Doug told him.

"Okay, okay, it'll be less wide in *one* of those directions."

"Not necessarily," Doug said. "Take off your pack."

"How do you *know*?" Bob asked.

"Bobby, this isn't the first time I've *been* out here, you know. Take my word for it, it doesn't get any narrower farther down or farther up. Besides, the campsite we'll use is that way." He pointed across the stream.

Bob nodded reluctantly. Just stop calling me Bobby, will you? he thought. Marian was right. It did definitely sound as though Doug was talking to a ten-year-old. Maybe that's how he sees me, he thought. With another sigh, heavier this time, he started to unbuckle his backpack straps.

Doug had his pack off now. Moving to the bank of the stream, holding on to its straps, he turned himself halfway around, paused, then took a deep breath and flung the backpack across the stream. It landed several yards from the opposite bank.

He turned to Bob. "I told you how I lost a pack once in a stream like this. I don't intend to take a chance on it happening again."

"Uh-huh." Bob nodded. His pack was off now. He looked at Doug questioningly.

"Well, go ahead, throw it," Doug told him.

Bob winced. "What if I don't make it?" he asked. "I'd lose everything."

"It's not that wide, Bobby," Doug said edgily.

"I know, but—"

"Just sling the damn thing," Doug told him.

Bob hesitated. If his throw was short, he'd be obligated to Doug for everything. The prospect was more than a little daunting.

"Oh, for Christ's sake," Doug snapped. Pulling the pack

out of Bob's grip, he moved to the bank of the stream, cocked his arm, and threw the pack. It landed about a foot from the opposite bank. Great, Bob thought. You didn't try as hard with my pack, did you?

"Doug," he said.

"Yessir." Doug's tone was irritated.

"Why are you expecting me to act like a professional back-packer?"

Doug scowled. "Didn't think that tossing a backpack across a stream is something only a professional backpacker could do."

"Okay, okay." Bob nodded. "Now what, do we jump across the stream in one leap? Oh, no, you said we wade."

Doug was already sitting on the ground, unlacing his boots. He glanced up at Bob. "Do *likewise*, Bobby," he said. He bared his teeth, pulling at the laces of his boots. "Unless you'd prefer getting your boots soaking wet. They take a hell of a long time to dry, let me tell you."

"All right," Bob said. He felt like sighing again but repressed it. I could be home, sitting in my chair, enjoying a vodka and tonic with a slice of lemon, he thought. He sat down and started to unlace his boots. Instead, I'm here, doing research for a goddamn novel. Why didn't I go all the way and write a novel about a Welsh coal miner and work in a mine for a couple of weeks?

"Tie the laces together," Doug told him, "and put your socks inside the boots, roll up your pants. I warn you, the water's going to be cold."

Thanks for telling me, Bob thought. The colder the better. I love wading in fast-moving ice water. The next book I write will be about an Olympic swimmer who trains in Antarctica. He couldn't restrain another sigh.

"All right, let's go," Doug said, standing. "Stay behind me and feel your way ahead as you cross. There could be rocks on the bottom that move under you."

"Right," Bob said. Anything you say, Dougie boy, his mind added.

Doug walked over to a fallen tree and broke off two thick branches. "To brace yourself against the current," he said, handing one of the branches to Bob. "Cross facing upstream so you have a triangle of support."

"Okay," Bob said, not sure he understood what Doug had just said.

Doug moved to the edge of the stream, swung his boots around a few times by their laces, then threw them across the stream. They landed beyond his pack.

"You want me to throw yours?" he asked.

No, goddamn it, I can throw my own boots, thank you, Bob thought resentfully. "I'll do it," he said.

Immediately, he visualized both boots landing in the fast-moving water and being carried off by the swift current. Or, just as bad, the laces coming untied and the boots landing separately, maybe one in the water, one on the other side of the stream. Then he'd have to hop his way through the forest, he thought, visualizing himself doing that for the next two or three days.

He held out the boots by their tied laces. "I changed my mind," he said.

He knew Doug's smile was one of disparagement but let it go. Better a little disparagement than one or both of his boots flying down the stream like lost canoes.

Doug took the boots from him and, twirling them twice by their tied laces, flung them across the stream. They bounced off the ground several feet beyond Doug's boots. The winner and still champion! Bob thought.

His first step into the stream made him cry out involuntarily. "Jesus!"

"I told you it was cold," Doug said. If the temperature of the water bothered him, he wasn't showing it. Or would rather die than show it, Bob decided. *Macho Man!* his mind sang out.

"Lean a little against the current," Doug told him. "And use your branch."

Bob tilted himself a little to the left, feeling the strong push of the current against his legs, bracing his branch on the bottom to help remain balanced. He hadn't folded his pants up far enough, he realized, the rolled-up bottoms were getting soaked even though he'd raised them above his knees.

Doug waded slowly but steadily across the stream using his branch to fight the current. Bob followed, feeling as though, at any moment, the force of the water might knock him over. Then what? he wondered. Would he be carried off like a piece of wood? Or just be sprawled on the stream bottom, getting soaked from head to toe?

"Watch out, there's a rock on the bottom that's loose," Doug said across his shoulder; his voice was drowned out by the loud noise of the torrent.

"What?" Bob asked loudly.

"I said—!" Doug started.

Too late. Bob stepped on the rock, it rolled beneath his foot and suddenly, his balance gone, the branch was out of his grip and he was falling to the right.

He gasped in shock as his body hit the rushing stream. It

began to move him as he floundered in the current. He tried to cry out and a burst of icy water filled his mouth. Gagging and spitting, he rolled over once, trying desperately to push up with his hands, but every time he tried to rise, the force of the stream knocked him over again. Oh, God, am I going to *drown?* the panicked thought struck him. He struggled to get up again and managed to raise onto one knee on the stony bottom. Then he started to fall again. This is *it!* he thought, terrified.

Doug's hand suddenly grabbed the collar of his jacket and began hauling him to his feet. "Try to stand!" Doug shouted.

Bob's legs thrashed clumsily, both feet trying to reach the bottom of the stream. He slipped again and fell into the current. Doug's grip on his jacket collar was abruptly gone, and he tumbled over in the cold, rushing water. I *am* going to drown! he thought with incredulous terror.

But Doug now had him by the jacket collar again, then grabbed his right wrist with a grip so hard it made Bob cry out in pain. He felt Doug dragging him across the bottom of the stream, then onto the bank on the other side of the stream, continuing to drag him onto dry ground. "My wrist!" he cried, grimacing with pain.

But Doug held on to it until he was completely out of the water and onto dry ground. Then he let go of Bob's wrist and sat down hard on the ground beside Bob. "Jesus Christ," he muttered. Bob could see that Doug was almost as soaking wet as he was.

"Well, now we're even, pal," Doug said, breathing hard.

He *does* remember, Bob thought. He knew I saved him before and this was his appreciation.

"Thank you, Doug," he said. "I don't know whether I

could have gotten out of the stream by myself."

"You couldn't have," Doug answered. "You were tumbling along like a piece of wood."

"I know I was," Bob said.

They sat side by side, panting, regaining their breath.

Then Bob said, "Well, at least our shoes stayed dry."

The way Doug looked at him, he half expected a punch in the nose.

Instead, Doug chuckled, looking downward himself. "Yeah, at least they stayed dry," he said.

After a short while, Doug got to his feet, wincing. "Well, you're in luck," he said. "We'll have to set our camp up right away. We're too damn wet to go on."

"My fault," Bob apologized. "I'm sorry."

"Sorry, hell, you're delighted," Doug answered.

Bob looked at him in silence for a few moments, then laughed weakly. "You're right, I *am* delighted," he said. "Let's go cook my turkey tetrazzini."

Doug made a scoffing sound. "Yeah, let's do that," he said.

5:19 PM

There was an open piece of ground about sixty feet from the stream where Doug had said they'd camp for the night. It had made Bob wonder if Doug had intended to camp there all along and only told him that they were setting up a campsite now because they were too wet to go on. He decided to let the suspicion go. After all, Doug may well have saved his life.

Doug told him that he'd planned to have him start the fire, but under the circumstances—both of them wet and the air growing cold—he'd start it himself.

Quickly, Doug had formed a fire ring of stones while he sent Bob to find dry evergreen needles, lichen, and twigs to start the fire with, bigger fallen wood to increase it. He'd erected a cone of twigs over the pine needles and lichen and a larger cone of logs above it. Lighting the kindling with a lifeboat match, he'd begun the core of the fire. As it burned away, the outside logs slumped inward, feeding the heart of the fire.

Soon the fire was burning steadily and they took off their wet clothes, wrung them out as much as they could, and hung them from a line of thin rope that Doug suspended between two small trees. They put on dry long johns, sweaters, and their socks and boots and sat before the fire, warming themselves.

"I think a sip of brandy wouldn't hurt right now," Doug said and got the small flask from his backpack. The brandy made Bob cough but felt comfortingly warm going down his throat and chest and into his stomach.

"Okay, come on with me," Doug said unexpectedly.

Bob looked at him, curious. "Where?" he asked.

"To find something better than your goddamn turkey tetrazzini," Doug answered. He was on his feet now. "Come on."

Bob hated to stand again but didn't want another unpleasant exchange with Doug. He pushed to his feet with a groan and started after Doug who was heading back toward the stream. Bob opened his mouth to ask Doug a question, then couldn't think of one and followed in silence.

Doug led him to a quiet section of the stream and pointed. "Fish like to gather at the shallows in the evening, in a pool, in the shade of bushes, around submerged logs and rocks."

Bob nodded, thinking: My God, the man knows *everything*. He wasn't going to say it though; he was still irritated by Doug's behavior.

"All right, now watch. You may have to do it yourself someday."

Not bloody likely, Bob thought. Still, he watched in interest as Doug rolled up his long john sleeves and stretched himself out, looking down into the still water of the pool.

"And there's our supper," he said. "What I'm going to do now is reach down and very gently work my hand under its belly until I reach its gills."

Bob watched, unable to believe that anyone could catch a fish that way. Doug seemed to be absolutely motionless. But then he said, "Now I'm going to grasp it firmly just behind the gills and . . . Voilà!" Suddenly he yanked his arm out of the water and Bob looked in amazement at the plump trout thrashing wildly on the ground.

"I'll be damned," he said.

"And now, the coup de grâce," Doug said, picking up a sharpended twig and impaling the trout on it.

Bob watched as Doug took a frying pan from his pack and set his grate across two logs on the fire. Doug got a small plastic bottle from his pack, unscrewed the top, and poured a little bit of liquid into the frying pan.

"What's that?" Bob asked.

"Olive oil," Doug answered, returning the plastic bottle to his backpack. He removed a small plastic bag of what looked like flour and after laying the trout in the frying pan, sprinkled some of it on top of the trout.

"You don't need to skin it?" Bob asked.

"Waste of time. Just pick the flesh out of the skin."

Bob nodded.

"Anyway, the valuable fats and oils are right under the skin," Doug said.

"You've done this before," Bob said.

"Many times." Doug got a fork from his pack and turned the trout over, sprinkling flour on the other side of it.

"Did you know you were going to catch a trout here?" Bob asked.

"Well, I have before so I figured there was a good chance I'd catch one again."

Bob inhaled deeply. "Mmm," he said. "It's already starting to smell good."

"I'll let you provide the vegetables," Doug told him.

"Will do." Bob moved to his pack and checked his food supply. "Carrot and celery sticks okay?" he asked.

"That'll be fine," Doug said.

Bob placed his backpack behind himself to lean against as he sat down again.

"That sure does smell good," he said. "Nothing like it."

"Except for fresh shrimp cooked on a beach," Doug said.

"Never had that," Bob replied.

"Never been to Mexico?" Doug asked.

"No, never," Bob answered. "Marian and I have always been leery of catching Montezuma's revenge."

"That's dumb," Doug told him. "I've been to Mexico a dozen times and never caught it once."

"Really." Bob nodded.

"Guess you and Marian go on fancier trips," Doug said.

Oh, boy, here we go again, Bob thought. Goading time. "Not always," he said, trying to keep his tone even; he didn't want to start another hassle. "We like to stay in lodges in northern California and Oregon a lot."

"Uh-huh." It was clear that Doug didn't believe him. "Fancy lodges, I suppose," he said.

"Not always." It was becoming more difficult to sound easygoing.

"Where *have* you gone?" Doug asked.

Do I tell him? Bob wondered. Is he really interested? Or does he just want more ammunition for his convictions about the disparity between our lifestyles?

"Oh . . . a few places in Europe," he said, hoping to get over this conversation as quickly as possible.

"We went to Paris once," Doug said. "I was doing a feature."

"Oh, that's a fascinating city," Bob said, conscious of attempting to sound enthusiastic. "You must have had a wonderful time there."

"Not really," Doug said. "I was shooting most of the time and Nicole was bitching most of the time because we weren't 'doing the town,' " he finished scornfully.

"Oh, that's too bad," Bob said. Change the goddamn conversation quick, he told himself.

"Smells like it's almost ready," he said.

"Not quite." Doug's voice sounded glum.

"Can I interest you in some vodka?" Bob asked.

"No, I'll stick to my brandy," Doug said. He took a sip from his flask. Oh, Christ, don't drink too much, Bob thought worriedly. He had the definite feeling that Doug would not be an amiable drunk.

Bob opened one of his mini-bottles of vodka and sipped on it, watching the trout sizzle in the frying pan. He wondered if the slight dizziness he felt was a leftover from the lightning—what had Doug called it?—"splash." He hoped not. It's sure been a super hike so far, he thought. I get lost, fall down, get a nice big blister on my toe, get hit by lightning, and almost drown. And it's only the second day. What was still in the offing? A mountain lion or bear attack? An avalanche? A blizzard?

He had to smile to himself. I'm some great backpacker, I am, he thought.

"What's funny?" Doug asked.

He started in surprise. He hadn't realized that his smile was that apparent.

"Oh, I was just thinking about all the things that have happened to me since we started out yesterday."

"It's the way things go, Bobby," Doug said. "You wanted to backpack."

I didn't plan on being struck by lightning, Bob thought. He didn't say any more. There was no point to it. It was obvious that Doug always wanted the last word.

He rubbed his wrist, flexing his fingers, the effort making him wince.

"Wrist hurt?" Doug asked.

"A little bit," Bob answered. "You . . . kinda twisted it before."

"Would you rather I'd let you go downstream?" Doug asked, his smile disdainful.

"No, no, of course not. It just—" He broke off. No point in mentioning it any longer, he realized. Doug's reaction wasn't going to change.

"I think that trout is going to be delicious," he said.

The trout *was* delicious. Along with the vegetable sticks, washed down with cold fresh water it made what Bob's mother had always called a "scrumptious feast."

He was leaning back against his pack now, feeling relaxed. He'd eaten a small chocolate bar and was now chewing on some dried apricots and sipping on a cup of coffee. "Hope my innards do their duty soon," he said.

"They may not," Doug said. "Sometimes it takes days for the bowels to cooperate."

Thanks for the encouragement, Bob thought.

It was getting colder now and since their jackets were still drying, they had unzipped their sleeping bags and wrapped them around themselves. The tent was up and Doug had hung their food supplies from a high branch. Bob was a little drowsy but didn't feel like trying to sleep yet. Sitting with the sleeping bag around him, looking into the glowing coals of the fire, he was content to just lean back against his pack and enjoy his relaxation.

"This part I really like," he said.

Doug grunted. "Artie didn't like anything at all about backpacking," he said. "God knows I tried to make him like it often enough."

I bet you did, Bob thought. Best not to reply aloud, he thought. Maybe Doug would let it go with his first remark.

He didn't. "Took him backpacking, camping, fishing, hunting, you name it. He hated all of them."

"Well, some kids like different things," Bob said automatically, instantly regretting that he'd made the comment because Doug replied, bitterly, "*No.* It was *Nicole.* She babied him. Turned him into a weakling. I wouldn't be surprised if he was a fag."

Oh, God, please don't, Bob thought. This is such a nice moment. Don't ruin it.

His shoulders slumped as Doug said, "You really believe in life after death, huh?" There was an obvious edge to his voice.

What do I say? Bob thought. How can I end this and not get into another corrosive discussion?

"Well?" Doug asked demandingly. "*Do* you?"

"Yes. Yes." Bob nodded. "I do."

"Well, I *don't* believe in it," Doug said. "I think it's a load of shit."

"That's your privilege, Doug," Bob told him. "Everyone's entitled to their own opinion."

"Damn right," Doug said. "And my opinion is that it's a load of shit."

"Well . . . okay," Bob responded. "I'm better off than you then," he added.

"How do you figure that?" Doug asked suspiciously.

"Well . . . look at it this way—if there is no life after death—"

"There isn't," Doug interrupted.

"Okay. Say there isn't. When I die, I'll never know I was wrong because it'll all be oblivion."

"And—?" Doug demanded.

"If there *is* life after death, you'll have to adjust to it."

"Yeah, sure." Doug made a scornful sound. "Life after death. Reincarnation. It's all a load of shit."

"Well—" Don't lose your temper now, for Christ's sake, Bob told himself. "If you don't believe in life after death, you naturally wouldn't believe in reincarnation because they go together."

"How's *that*?" Doug asked, his face a mask of disdain.

"There isn't much point in life after death if it's only a one-shot deal," Bob said. "The world would truly be a nightmare if that was the case."

"The world *is* a nightmare," Doug responded.

"That's undoubtedly true," Bob said, "but it would be *worse* without reincarnation."

"Come on, Bob, what the hell are you talking about?" Doug sounded angry now.

"I'm *saying*, Doug, that the world is a nightmare of injustice if there isn't reincarnation."

"What do you—?"

This time Bob interrupted. "A man lives his entire life doing harm to others. He cheats, he lies, he corrupts, he may even kill or *have* people killed. Then he dies in his mansion bed surrounded by his loving family. Is that justice?"

"Who said it was?" Doug answered.

"Then life is meaningless?" Bob replied, *his* voice on edge now. "A baby gets hit by a truck and killed. Is that justice? Government leaders oversee massacres. Is that justice? They start wars, they abuse their population, they create havoc because they're greedy and cruel and never have to pay for it. Is that justice? So many criminals never have to pay the price for their crimes. So many people pay a price for crimes they didn't commit. Is that justice? Does equity exist at *all*? Well, not a hell of a lot if all these crimes go unpaid for, unpunished. That's why I believe in reincarnation. So justice *can* exist. If not in this life then in the life to come. Or the lives to come."

Doug stared at him in silence. Finally, he said, "Jesus, pass the basket, preacher."

Bob chuckled. "Sorry," he said, "I get carried away some-times."

"I never heard you do it before," Doug said. "So this is—what?—your philosophy of life?"

"I have a double-edged philosophy," Bob told him. "I'm almost completely cynical about what goes on at this level."

"This level," Doug repeated.

"Life," Bob said. "I don't see very much that's positive in it. Schools closing. Teachers undervalued, underpaid. Child care limited or nonexistent. Homeless people mounting in number every year. The wealthy growing wealthier. The poor growing poorer. Drug sales rising. Violence in the streets. Corruption in politics, in business, in law-keeping. Military spending higher all the time. The infrastructure left to collapse—roads, highways, bridges, airports, sewers, water systems. Air pollution. Mass destruction of the environment. International chaos. Endless wars. That's how I see the world and my philosophy regarding it is a bleak one, a very nearly hopeless one."

"And—?" Doug sounded almost intrigued now.

"And, the other side of my philosophy is that I believe in ultimate justice. No matter how cruel or brutal or greedy or stupid things are on this level, there's a higher level on which justice is inevitable, restitution inescapable."

"For all of us," Doug said.

"Well, sure for all of us," Bob answered. "What kind of system would it be if it didn't apply to all of us."

"*How* does it apply?" Doug demanded.

"I don't know exactly how. But—" he added quickly to cut off Doug's interrupting response, "I think that, when we die—"

"*Pass on*, you mean," Doug broke in, smirking.

"Right. Pass on. When we do, we carry with us a packet of negatives and positives, how much of each depending on the life we've led. This packet provides the blueprint for our next life. Our long-range task is to eliminate all the negatives and clear up the packet altogether."

"And that's it, huh?" Doug said.

"Pretty much," Bob answered. "Nothing is lost. We pay the price—or enjoy the reward—for everything we do in life. Not in afterlife, I don't believe that. In our next life, though."

"How? How would you know you were paying the price or getting the reward?" Doug was barely containing his scorn.

"I have no idea," Bob said. "It would all take place behind the scenes."

"*Behind the scenes?* That's bullshit!" Doug snapped. "A big cop-out. You don't have to prove anything. It's all 'behind the scenes.' Well, bullshit, Bobby, bullshit! Your philosophy is pure bullshit!"

Bob sighed. "I don't think so," he said.

"All right, tell me this," Doug said, "if God is so damn great, how come He allows so much misery in the world? *Hanh?*"

"Why does almost everyone assume that God created the world to be permanently wonderful?" Bob asked. "What if He created it as a place to grow in, to become responsible in? I don't believe God has anything at all to do with the misery in the world. *Man* caused it, not God. Saint Augustine said that the root of all evil lies neither in Satan nor in God; it lies in *man*."

Doug stared at him in silence for a while. Then he said, "And everything happens for a reason."

"I believe that."

"So there are no such things as accidents," Doug said.

"I believe that too."

"And everything works out in the end."

"I think so, yes," Bob answered. "In the long run, cause and effect become clear, justice prevails."

"So Artie really died because of something wrong he did in his last life, is that it?" Doug said.

Oh, Christ, Bob thought. Is that all this signified to Doug? Some way to take the blame off himself for his son's suicide.

"I don't know, Doug," he said quietly. "I don't know how the details of reincarnation work, I told you that. I just know I believe in it."

"Then you have no idea whether Artie fucked up in his last life—maybe killed somebody so that's why he had to kill himself in this life."

"No." Bob looked at him, astounded. "How could I possibly know that?"

"But it could be, right?" Doug challenged. "And my life is a fucking mess because of something *I* did wrong in my last life?"

"Doug, you're asking me impossible questions," Bob told him.

"So all these fucking beliefs you have add up to nothing, don't they?" Doug said. "You don't even know if what goes wrong in this life happens because of something we did wrong in our last life."

"Doug, we do things wrong in this life too," Bob said, knowing, in the instant he said it, that it was a mistake.

"So I fucked up my life this time around too." Doug almost snarled the words.

"Doug, we all make mistakes. We're human," Bob said.

"Oh, *no*." Doug shook his head, a look of pseudosympathy on his face. "Not you. You're fucking perfect. Everything works out for you. Your marriage. Your career. Your kids. All perfect. Perfect!"

"Doug, let's drop this. Please," Bob said.

"No, no, let's examine all the facts in your perfect life."

"Doug—"

"First off, you're a successful short-story writer. Then you're a successful novelist—"

"Doug, please."

"Then a successful movie writer, a successful television writer. Then a successful husband, a successful father, a successful citizen in every way."

Bob sighed heavily. Was this ever going to end?

"Now you're a successful philosopher," Doug went on, his voice tight, embittered. "You have this wonderful successful philosophy of life. You have all the answers, all the fucking answers in the world."

"I don't," Bob told him wearily. "I'm just trying to get a handle on—"

"A *handle*?" Doug said angrily. "Is that what your philosophy of life is, something you can get a *handle* on?"

"Come on, Doug," Bob responded. "Stop jumping on every damn word I use. Try to understand what I'm saying. Try—"

"Now I can't understand what you're saying," Doug broke in.

"Doug, I'm not saying that," Bob told him. "I just—"

"Too bad I'm not as religious as you are so I *could* understand," Doug interrupted again.

"Goddamn it, I am not religious!" Bob said loudly, "I don't subscribe to any particular church! I have a belief system, that's it! A belief system!"

"Which you talk about all the time."

Bob looked flabbergasted. "Like hell I do! You're the one who started this conversation! What I believe is the foundation of my life, okay. But I don't talk about it or even think about it any more than I talk and think about the foundation of my house."

Doug was glaring at him steadily. We have got to end this conversation, Bob thought. I can't afford to enrage this man; he's holding all the cards.

"So what you're saying in a nutshell is that *I'm* responsible for every lousy, fucking thing that's happened in my life," Doug said.

"Doug, we are all responsible for what happens in our lives," Bob replied.

"Which means that what you've done is right and what I've done is wrong!"

"Oh, for Christ's sake, Doug." Bob looked at him almost pleadingly. "Nothing is that simple. You know that."

"You're saying that my life is all fucked up because of me, not because of anyone else!" Doug suddenly raged.

"Well, what the hell do you want me to say, that everybody in your life is at fault, that nothing you've done has anything to do with anything? Be honest with yourself, for God's sake."

"So says Mr. Perfect," Doug snapped.

"Oh, goddamn it, Doug! Nobody's further from perfection than me! I try, that's all! The same as you! The same as everyone! We try, we *try*!"

Doug didn't reply. His face hard and implacable, he poked randomly at the fire coals with a twig. What the hell is he thinking? Bob wondered. And what the hell am I doing out here all alone with him?

8:29 PM

It had been at least an hour since they'd spoken. Bob had kept trying to think of something to talk about that would lighten the mood of the evening. He couldn't think of anything. Finally, he'd muttered, "G'night" and got up to enter the tent. Doug didn't respond.

Bob zipped up his sleeping bag and got inside. Oh, shit, I forgot to brush my teeth, he thought. He opened his water bottle, rinsed out his mouth, and spit the water onto the ground. Very sanitary, his mind commented. Oh, shut up, he answered it.

After a while—he couldn't tell how long it was—Doug crawled into the tent beside him and zipped himself into his sleeping bag, exhaled heavily, then fell silent. Bob closed his eyes. What's it going to be like tomorrow? he wondered. And the day after. How far were they from Doug's cabin anyway? The prospect of two to three more days like today made him more than disturbed, it made him apprehensive. Doug obviously had undercurrents in his personality he'd never known about. How could he have? Their relationship had been, he realized, very shallow, very superficial. He was starting to see the inner workings of Doug's mind now and what he was seeing did not reassure him about the remainder of the hike.

He was almost asleep when Doug spoke, his voice making Bob's legs twitch in surprise.

"You think there are evil people?" Doug asked.

Bob opened his eyes, blinking. He had no idea what to reply. "What d'ya mean?" he mumbled.

"What I said," Doug responded, his voice tightening. "Are there evil people?"

"Well—" Bob tried to gather thoughts together. "You mean . . . pure evil?"

"Can evil be *pure*?" Doug said. Was he challenging? Goading? Bob couldn't tell.

"I mean . . . evil without any cause," he said.

"Now I don't know what you mean," Doug said.

"I mean . . . someone—we call evil—when there seems to be no explanation for that evil. No cause, no background."

"*Are* there people like that?" Doug asked.

Why is he asking these questions? Bob wondered. Why had he—out of nowhere, it seemed—brought up the subject of evil?

"Well . . . no, I don't think so," he said. "I . . . suppose it's possible. But if you look into the background of what people call evil, you usually find a good cause."

"A good cause?" Doug *was* challenging now.

"I mean an understandable cause." He hoped that if they got into a nonconflicting discussion, it might end the tension between them.

"I saw a documentary on cable a while back," he continued. "It was called *Evil*. The narrator said that there were at least twelve different definitions of evil so there was no way to know which one of them was the real one. It's a value judgment, nothing more."

"What's *that* supposed to mean?" Doug asked, sounding irritated.

Don't give it back in kind, Bob told himself. Stay cool.

"It means . . . it's a matter of opinion. It's more a label than a definitive identification. By and large, all the absolutist judgments about who's evil and who isn't come from laws and courts, politicians, religious figures. They declare that someone—or something—is evil and the majority of the people buy it. They've been brainwashed."

"So what do *you* think evil is?" Doug asked. "What have you been brainwashed to think?"

"Well, I hope it isn't having been brainwashed. I hope it's a rational decision on my part."

"Which is—?" Doug demanded.

"Which is that pain and suffering, deliberately inflicted for no acceptable reason, is evil."

"That's it?" Was that disdainful smile on Doug's face again? "Pain and suffering inflicted for no reason, that's evil?"

"That's my opinion, anyway," Bob said.

"Well, my opinion is that someday—I'm convinced of it— evil people will all be explained away in terms of heredity and environment, period. The word 'evil' will be scrapped. 'Evil' people will all be called dysfunctional people, nothing more."

"Possible," Bob said. "An interesting notion, anyway."

"Tell me this—" Doug started. Bob was relieved to hear that Doug sounded interested now, not just scornful. "Why are evil people more interesting than good people?"

"Good question," Bob answered. "I don't really know. Except that they arouse more dark reactions in people than good people do. They . . . how shall I put it . . . stir up . . . activate whatever deep-seated, negative emotions people have. And those emotions are more . . . colorful, you might say. More intriguing."

"Damn right," Doug said. "I've played good guys and bad guys in films and on television. Guess who audiences always— *always*—find more interesting?"

"Well, of course," Bob said. "Who do audiences find more interesting? Hamlet or Richard the Third? Romeo or Macbeth? Othello or Iago?"

"No contest," Doug agreed. He was really into the discussion now, Bob saw—and thank God for that. "I played Iago in a little theater once and I'll tell you, *he* was the one the audience responded to, not that—goddamn moonstruck Moor."

Bob heard Doug moving and glanced around, seeing Doug's dark shadow raised on one elbow. He *was* really into it—and definitely thank God for it. Maybe they could spend the remaining days in stimulating discussions and avoid the other stuff, the friction-laden stuff.

"Audiences like to call these people 'evil,' " Doug went on, "but they enjoy the hell out of watching them. They relish all their monstrous deeds but convince themselves that those 'evil' people are different from them—even though they're not. They're all hypocrites, pretending to be above the villains they love to watch. And they're not."

Bob was impressed by Doug's insight; it had come unexpectedly. Maybe the next few days would really be interesting after all.

"You know what I don't like about your so-called philosophy of life?" Doug said.

So-called, Bob thought. They weren't out of the personal woods yet. "What?" he asked.

"I don't believe in an outside system of justice and law," Doug said. "I believe that will—individual will—is what counts in this world. *Triumph of the Will* that film was called by that German actress. Not that I'm defending Hitler, for Christ's sake. You want evil, there you got it, big time. But it's evolution, not divine law. Survival of the fittest. The strong win. The weak lose. Simple as that. As far as our so-called system of morality goes, it isn't written in stone. It's an agreement. A contract. And those who are strong enough to break that contract get away with it until somebody stronger puts them down."

"But no—outside rule?" Bob said. "No higher imposition of justice?"

"Right," Doug said. "You know what the Holocaust was? Political reality. Nothing more. Imposition of will. The Germans won, the Jews lost. Evil had nothing to do with it."

Bob felt his skin goose-fleshing. "You really *believe* that?" he asked. "You don't think it was evil? You think it was just a matter of political reality, political will?"

"You got it," Doug said.

Oh, Jesus, Bob thought. The prospect of interesting discussions in the next few days had just collapsed like a house of cards in a high wind.

"Too bad Hitler was a maniac," Doug went on. "With his power of will, he could have accomplished anything."

"He did enough," Bob said quietly.

"Sure as hell did," Doug answered. "Conquered most of Europe. If he hadn't made the same dumb-ass mistake as Napoleon and invaded Russia, he might well have won the war and our fucking national anthem would be—" Abruptly, Doug sang, *"Deutschland, Deutschland, Uber Alles,"* then laughed sardonically. Oh, God, Bob thought. Who am I out here with?

"Not so crazy about the Jews myself," Doug said. "After all the shit I've gone through with them in the business."

Oh, God, dear God, Bob thought.

"All right, look at me," Doug said. What was he going into now? Bob wondered. "If I did evil things, wouldn't people say, 'Well, it was all because his old man was a boozer and beat the shit out of his son and hated everything in the world and that's why Douglas Crowley is an evil son of a bitch.' "

"I don't believe you're evil," Bob told him, aware of a certain lack of conviction in his voice.

"Well, that's where you're wrong," Doug said. "Didn't you know I brought you up here to kill you?"

Bob had never felt so cold so quickly in his life. He could not repress a convulsive shiver. "That's not very funny," he said.

"Oh, I wouldn't just *do* it," Doug said. "I'd give you a good head start, and if you reached the cabin before I caught up with you, I'd let you live. Otherwise—"

"For Christ's sake, Doug," Bob broke in. "Haven't we had enough friction without you—"

"Oh, you think I'm kidding," Doug interrupted. "Bobby boy, I'm not."

Bob felt his stomach muscles spasming. He couldn't speak. Dear God. It was all he could think.

He started at the sudden glare of Doug's flashlight.

Doug laughed, sounding delighted. "Just wanted to see the look on your face," he said. "I can see you really believed me."

Bob exhaled shakily, averting his face. "For Christ's sake," he said. "Why did you do that?"

"Did I scare you, Bobby boy?"

"Of course you scared me. What do you think?" Bob shuddered. Jesus Christ, he thought.

"It was just a joke," Doug told him.

"Some joke."

Bob gasped as Doug grabbed him by the arm. "But I really meant it!" Doug cried.

Bob gaped at him. Doug was silent for a moment, then threw back his head, laughing raucously. "Oh, shit, you're too easy to fool," he said. Letting go of Bob's arm, he switched off the flashlight and lay back down. "Good night, old boy," he said.

Bob lay motionless, feeling the heavy, rapid beat of his heart. For God's sake, he thought. What kind of man *was* Doug that he could do such a thing?

Despite the exhaustion, it took him more than an hour to fall asleep.

1:19 AM

Bob twisted around in his sleeping bag. His right arm had come out of the bag and it flopped over to where he believed Doug was sleeping.

His arm hit the ground. His eyes popped open and he looked around uneasily, suddenly wide awake.

Sitting up, he leaned over and drew back the tent flap. Doug was hunched over by the low-burning fire, staring into the coals.

As he watched, he saw Doug raise the flask to his lips and take a sip of brandy. How much had he been drinking? Bob wondered. And why wasn't he sleeping? Why was he sitting up this late, just staring into the fire like that?

He raised his wrist and read the luminous dial. Close to one-thirty in the morning. My God, he thought. Was Doug going to wake him up at the crack of dawn even though he wasn't getting any sleep?

He twitched as a log fell into the fire, shooting sparks into the air. As the fire flared momentarily, he saw Doug's expression. It was not a reassuring one.

After several minutes, he laid back down again and began to shiver in spasmodic waves. Was it the cold?

He knew it wasn't.

Tuesday

9:37 AM

Bob opened his eyes and stared sleepily at the tent wall. After a few moments, he thought: Well, good, I woke up by myself today. No need for Doug to rouse me with a jostle. He smiled faintly. Is it possible I'm catching on to this thing?

He took his left arm out of the sleeping bag and held it up to see what time it was.

At first, he thought his watch had gone wrong. Almost twenty minutes to ten.

He blinked and shook his head to make sure. The second hand was still turning. It *was* almost twenty to ten.

"What the hell?" he mumbled. What happened to getting up at the crack of dawn, getting an early start? Yesterday, by seven o'clock, Doug was waking him up impatiently, everything ready to go, the campsite disassembled except for the tent. Doug wouldn't even let him have a cup of hot coffee before leaving. Now this?

He twisted around and sat up, startled to see that Doug was still asleep, breathing heavily.

Bob looked at him, half curious, half worried. What time had Doug finally gone to sleep? And how much brandy had he drunk?

More to the point, he thought, what now? Should he just let Doug sleep? Sleep it off, you mean, his mind added. Or should he wake him up?

He thought about Marian waiting for him. Obviously, their

schedule was way behind what Doug had intended. How long was it actually going to take to reach the cabin? He felt extremely uneasy about Marian alone there, undoubtedly to worry when he didn't show up in time.

He scratched his head. Clearly, Doug had stayed awake a long time. This was totally in opposition to his backpacking, let's-get-on-with-it persona. That worried him too. How disturbed was Doug by their conversations? Certainly enough to let their disciplined schedule lapse completely.

Jesus Christ, what now? he thought.

Well, there was no help for it, he decided. He couldn't just let Doug sleep on uninterruptedly. They had to get going.

Reaching out his right hand, he laid it on Doug's uncovered right shoulder—Doug was lying on his left side—and shook it gently. "Doug?" he said.

Doug didn't stir, his sleep was so heavy. Great, Bob thought. He drew in a deep breath and moved his hand a little harder on Doug's shoulder. "Doug," he said.

Doug made a grumbling sound but didn't move. Shit, he must have polished off that brandy, Bob thought. Here we go on yet another first-class backpacking day.

"Doug," he said more loudly. He shook Doug's shoulder even harder.

Doug twisted around with an angry sound. Bob stared at his face. Even in sleep, it looked morose now. Was he dreaming badly?

Well, to hell with it, he thought. We have got to get on our way.

"Doug, wake up." He gripped Doug's left shoulder and shook it.

Doug's eyes fluttered open and he stared at Bob as though he hadn't the remotest idea who he was.

"We have to get going," Bob told him. "It's almost ten o'clock."

He expected Doug to jolt up in surprise. Jesus Christ, we gotta get out o' here then, he heard Doug's voice in his mind.

Doug only looked at him with the same expression, that of a man regarding a complete stranger.

"Doug. Did you hear what I said? It's almost ten o'clock."

Doug cleared his throat. "So?" he muttered.

"Well—" Bob's voice broke off. Doug's reply had flabbergasted him. "I thought—" Again, he broke off.

"Thought what?" Doug said. His voice was guttural, raspy.

Bob tried to smile. "That we had to get on because it's— taking too long. Because I've been holding things up," he added, trying to put the blame on himself.

Doug sat up and rubbed his face with both hands. He hissed, feeling at his right shoulder.

"Shoulder hurt?" Bob asked sympathetically.

"What d'*you* think?" Doug asked through clenched teeth.

"I'm sorry," Bob said. He tried to smile again. "I've got quite a few sore spots myself."

"Yeah," Doug muttered as though he couldn't have cared less.

Was Doug going back to sleep again? he wondered. They did have to leave. Otherwise, they'd never reach the cabin when Marian was expecting them.

"I . . . saw you sitting by the fire last night," he said to prevent Doug from dozing off again. "Couldn't sleep?"

"Don't need that much sleep, I told you," Doug muttered. "Three twenty-minute naps better than an hour's sleep. You saw me take a ten-minute nap yesterday, do it all the time. Don't need that much sleep. I've gone for days on two hours sleep a night."

"That's . . . very impressive," Bob said. He braced himself. "But shouldn't we get going? Marian will—"

He broke off as Doug made a growling sound, got out of his sleeping bag, and crawled from the tent. Bob started to follow him, almost bumping into him. Doug was standing just outside the tent, urinating on the ground. What happened to sanitation? Bob thought.

When Doug was through, Bob got out of the tent and moved to the hanging clothes, feeling them. "Not bad," he said. "A little damp." He started pulling on his trousers, expecting Doug to do the same.

His expression glum, Doug was stirring the coals to build up the fire. Why's he doing that? Bob wondered.

He watched as Doug moved over to the rope that held up the food bag and untied it. The food bag thumped on the ground as he let it fall the last few feet.

"What are you doing?" he asked.

"What does it look like I'm doing?" Doug said, giving Bob a stony look.

"Well . . ." Bob finished with the fasteners on his jacket. "I don't know, Doug."

"You don't know?" Doug said caustically. "You're the one who wants a piping hot breakfast before taking off."

"Well . . . yes. I do," Bob said. "But yesterday, you wouldn't even let me have a cup of hot coffee before we left, and that was seven o'clock in the morning."

"Yesterday was yesterday," Doug muttered. He was taking what looked like flour and dried milk from his food supply. He got his jacket and put it on—the morning air was chilly— then poured some of the powders into a small metal bowl, added water to it, and began to mix it all together with a wooden spoon. Bob watched him in concern. How long was this going to take?

"Well, what are you looking at?" Doug said.

"I'm . . . just wondering what you're—"

"—making?" Doug interrupted. "Isn't that obvious? We're having pancakes. Now make us some coffee."

Oh, Jesus, Bob thought. This is going to be one hell of a day, I can see it coming.

"Sorry, I don't have any Canadian bacon to go with your pancakes," Doug said scornfully.

Bob sighed. Just don't speak, he told himself. No matter what you say, he'll take it the wrong way, that's for certain.

He finished dressing and put on his jacket. He sat down to pull on his socks and boots.

"Well, how about the *coffee*, Bobby boy?" Doug snapped.

"As soon as I get my boots on," Bob told him.

"I don't have *my* boots on," Doug said.

Well, what the hell am I supposed to do about that? Bob thought. Utter a lament?

He finished lacing his boots. Doug had placed the frying pan on the grate and added some oil to it. It still had fragments of trout in it. Shouldn't we clean it first? he heard himself asking Doug. That would be a mistake. So he'd eat his pancakes with trout fragments in them. Better that than agitating Doug any more than he was already agitated.

"You want a little orange juice?" he asked.

"No thanks," Doug responded flatly. "I *would* like a cup of fucking coffee though."

Jesus, he *is* pissed, Bob thought. At what though? Everything? Was this day going to be a total nightmare?

He poured some water in his pan and put it on the grate next to the frying pan. He almost winced, seeing the bubbling pancake batter because the frying pan looked so begrimed. But would he dare tell Doug he'd rather not have any pancakes? That would only set Doug off again.

He opened one of his small boxes of orange juice and drank some. It tasted very good to him, tart and refreshing. He washed down a multivitamin with a second swallow.

"Sure you don't want some of this orange juice?" he asked, trying to be amiable.

"Did I say *no*?" Doug demanded.

Bob was going to repress his reaction. Then abruptly, he decided that the two of them simply could not go on like this for days on end.

"Doug, what's the matter?" he asked.

Doug didn't answer, flipping over the greasy-looking pancakes with his small spatula.

"If it's something I've said, I apologize," Bob told him, wondering if he really felt a genuine concern or was just trying to mollify Doug because he was becoming more and more unnerved by him.

Doug said nothing, his lips pressed together. Bob drew in a quick breath. Let it go? he thought. Or confront it?

He chose the latter, even though it troubled him to consider the possibility that it would only rile Doug further.

"Doug, we can't just go on like this for the rest of the hike," he said.

"The hike?" Doug snickered. "What hike?"

"Doug, I know I'm a total flop as a backpacker, but—"

"That you are," Doug cut him off. "Total."

Bob felt himself getting angry now. Menace or not, he couldn't see himself enduring these endless gibes from Doug.

"All right," he said. "A total flop. But we still have to get along for the next two or three—"

"Why?" Doug demanded.

Bob stared at him in disbelief. "Why?" he repeated Doug's challenge. "Are you prepared to let it go like this the rest of the time? Nothing but tension?"

Doug didn't answer. He poured some instant coffee in his cup and added hot water, wincing as the lifting of the pot of water made his shoulder hurt.

Bob made himself a cup of coffee and took a sip. Now what? he thought. Should he pursue this? Or was it better just to leave it alone? Get through the next few days in alien silence? Somehow manage to survive it as it was?

Doug put two of the small pancakes on a paper plate and tossed it on the ground in front of Bob. "There you go," he said. *"Specialité de la maison."* One of the pancakes flopped onto the ground.

"Thanks," Bob muttered.

He tried to eat one of the pancakes but it was still doughy, almost tasteless except for the fragments of trout.

Doug obviously noticed his distaste for the pancake. "What's the matter?" he asked. "Not up to your usual gastronomic expectations?" For some reason, Bob felt that Doug was quoting a line from some movie or teleplay he'd been in, maybe a stage play. He wasn't used to hearing such fancy language from Doug.

"Doug," he said.

"Mr. Hansen," Doug responded.

"What the hell is wrong?" Bob said. "Why are you acting like this?"

"Like *what*?" Doug countered.

"Doug, you're acting like you hate my guts. That the way it is? If so—"

"Oh, shit," Doug muttered, looking past Bob.

Bob turned to see what Doug was looking at.

A black bear was standing near the edge of the clearing staring at them.

"Oh, my," Bob whispered. He felt as though his breath had stopped.

Doug shoved to his feet, screaming, causing Bob to twitch in startlement. "Get out o' here, you son of a bitch!" Doug shouted, waving his arms. "Get the hell out o' here!"

The bear drew back a little but didn't leave, answering Doug's shouts with low, moaning growls and a popping of its teeth, a noise that sounded like dead sticks breaking. Doug picked up a stone and hurled it at the bear. It flew past the bear's head, making it snarl.

"Well, help me for Christ's sake!" Doug snapped, picking up another stone and pitching it at the bear. Bob tried to stand but his legs went limp beneath him and he fell back on the ground. He'd never seen a wild animal so close before. This wasn't zoo time, this was real.

Doug kept yelling at the bear and throwing stones in vain.

The bear began to pace, back and forth, swinging its head from side to side, grunting like a pig.

"Get out o' here, you black bastard!" Doug yelled at it. "Go on! Go on! Get out o' here!" He glared at Bob. "Well?!" he demanded.

Bob managed to get to his feet and started to wave his arms at the bear. Doug glared at him, teeth clenched. "Yeah, that's going to help a lot," he said. He threw another stone that hit the bear on the shoulder and made it jerk back, baring its teeth and growling.

"Well, why the fuck won't you go, you bastard?!" Doug shouted at it.

"Go on, go away," Bob said, his voice sounding thin.

"Yeah, that's gonna scare the shit out of him," Doug said furiously. He hurled another stone. "Goddamn you, beat it!" he yelled at the bear. "Get out o' here!"

The bear moved forward slightly, growling.

"Son of a bitch, they don't usually act this way," Doug muttered. He screamed at the top of his voice, waved his arms wildly, threw two more stones. In vain. The bear wouldn't leave. It started edging forward again.

"Fuck it, I'm gonna *kill* the bastard," Doug said breathlessly, moving quickly toward the tent.

"*Kill* it?" Bob look at him in disbelief. "No," he muttered. "No."

He never knew what made him behave as he did. It wasn't that a sudden burst of daring had filled him. It was more, he conjectured later, that the idea of the bear being killed for doing what came naturally to it was too painful for him to accept.

Richard Matheson

Whatever the reason, he found himself walking forward toward the bear, arms at his sides. "You have to go," he told it. "You'll be killed if you stay. Go on. Please leave. Please." He wondered later at the gentle, soothing quality of his voice as well. Basically, he knew that he was terrified. Maybe it was the kind of mad reaction terror sometimes brought on. But he simply couldn't bear the idea of the bear lying dead and bloody with arrows sticking out of it. He kept on walking slowly but steadily toward the bear. I'm going to die, it's going to kill me, he thought. But he couldn't stop himself, kept approaching the bear with small steps, speaking to it constantly. "Go on. Please go. I don't want to see you killed. Just go. Turn around and walk away. *Please.*"

The bear growled, pawing at the ground. Then it started walking to and fro, emitting odd coughs and high-pitched growls, gnashing its teeth and raising and lowering its upper lip in what looked like ominous grins.

"Please go away," Bob told it, "just go away."

The bear made huffing, puffing noises now, body lurching back and forth with small jerking motions, clawing at the ground brush like a bull. He's getting ready to attack, Bob thought numbly. Why was he still approaching the bear? It seemed totally insane but something kept him advancing, slowly but steadily. "Don't hurt me. Please," he said. "Just go. If you stay, you'll die. I don't want you to die. This is your home. You live here. Go—please go."

The bear stopped growling now and stared at him in what seemed to Bob to be confusion.

"Go on now. Go," Bob told it quietly.

Then Doug yelled from behind him. "Get the fuck out of the way, you idiot!" he said. "You want the arrow in *you*?!"

Deliberately, Bob eased to the right so that he'd be blocking Doug's line of fire. "Go, please go," he said to the bear. "I don't want to see you killed."

"Goddamn it, Bobby, I am going to shoot!" Doug threatened.

Bob gazed intently into the bear's eyes. "Go," he pleaded. "Go. Please *go.*"

To his astonishment—he realized later that he had never really expected it—the bear turned abruptly and moved off into the forest.

Bob felt his legs suddenly lose strength beneath him and he flopped down into an awkward half-sitting, half-lying position. Jesus, he thought. Jesus Christ. What did I do?

He flinched as Doug ran by him holding the bow with an arrow set in it.

"Don't!" Bob found the strength to cry. "He's gone!"

Doug ran a few yards into the forest, stopped, stood motionless for twenty seconds, then turned back, a look of incredulous disgust on his face.

"Are you fucking crazy?" he said. It certainly wasn't a question. Obviously, Doug thought that he *was* crazy. He wasn't so sure it wasn't true.

"Who the fuck do you think you are, Doctor Fucking Doolittle or something?" Doug demanded angrily. "I could have killed you, you dumb bastard."

"I didn't want you to kill the bear," Bob told him, his voice shaking.

"And almost got yourself killed instead," Doug said with angry scorn.

The look on Doug's face, the tone of his voice, the emotional reaction to what he'd just done suddenly caused an eruption of fury in Bob. It felt like something hot and thick rushing up from his insides.

"What's the matter, are you upset that you couldn't kill it?!" he raged. "Did I spoil your goddamn sport?!"

Doug didn't respond in kind. The look he gave Bob caused a chill to snake up his back.

"You really think you're hot shit, don't you?" Doug said in a soft, cold voice.

The rage had vanished as suddenly as it had appeared. "No, I don't think I'm 'hot shit' as you put it so colorfully," Bob said. "I was just trying to save the bear's life, that's all. It lives here. It was only doing what comes naturally to it."

"Oh, now you're a fucking wildlife expert," Doug responded acidly. "I'm impressed. Where did you pick up all this wildlife lore? At the Bel Air Hotel having a power breakfast with some big-time producer?"

"Oh, for Christ's sake, Doug, let's not go into that kind of talk again," Bob said. He tried to push to his feet.

To his startlement, Doug pushed him back so that he landed hard on his tailbone. "Ow!" he said. "What are you doing?"

"I wanna talk about it," Doug said angrily. "About your big-time career in the biz. About how you could give a shit if I succeed or not."

"Wait a second, wait a second, what are you talking about?" Bob demanded. Again, he tried to stand up and, again, Doug pushed him back. "Goddamn it, stop that," he said. "What the hell's the matter with you?"

"Nothing *you* can help," Doug told him. "Nothing you'd care to help."

"What are you saying?" Bob asked, trying to understand.

"That I'm somehow responsible for you having trouble in the business?"

"You haven't been any help, that's for sure," Doug snarled.

"Doug, I have tried to help you—"

"Bullshit!" Doug cut him off. "You've said you tried to help me, but I don't remember any jobs I got because of your help. You think I'm not aware of all the parts I might have played in your scripts that I never got called on to audition for? All you ever recommended me for were a few Mickey Mouse bit parts, a few lines here, a few lines there."

"Doug, I recommended you for any role I thought you were right for, no matter what the length."

"Bullshit," Doug said, scowling. "You never recommended me for any part worth a damn."

The anger, hot and unavoidable, was surging up in Bob again.

"Maybe if you didn't always come on like the greatest fucking actor in the world, you might have gotten some of those roles."

"Oh, so now it's my fault," Doug snarled through gritted teeth.

"No, Doug. No. Of course not. Nothing at all in your life is your fault. It's all been just rotten luck. Your marriage, your career, your kids, everything. Someone else is to blame, not you. Just rotten luck, that's all. Just crappy karma slapping you down at every turn." Bob knew he was jeopardizing their relationship but couldn't stop himself. He was fed up with Doug's everyone's-responsible-but-me attitude.

He had no idea how much he'd jeopardized their relationship. Not until Doug said quietly, in a malignant voice, "You're right, Bobby. I *do* hate your guts."

Bob was conscious that his mouth had fallen open in reaction to what Doug had said. He couldn't speak at first. Then he swallowed dryly, trying to draw himself together.

"Well, that's great," he said. "Just great." He drew in labored breath. "How many days left to reach the cabin? Two? Three?"

Doug didn't answer. He kept staring at Bob, his expression hard, disquieting.

Bob inhaled again. He seemed to be having difficulty getting enough air in his lungs.

"I suggest we pack up and get on our way," he said. "Go as far as we can before dark. I'll try to hold myself together so you won't be inconvenienced anymore. I suggest we travel and don't talk. We seem—"

"Oh, is that what you suggest?" Doug broke in. "You're running the show now? How odd. I thought I was running it."

Bob fought for patience. "Doug, you *are* running it. I'm just trying to suggest how—"

"Well, don't suggest," Doug said with a sneer, and Bob became even more distressed.

"Doug, anything you say," Bob told him. "Just let's get going. When we reach the cabin, we'll go back to Los Angeles. Or if you want to stay at your cabin, I'll phone for a car."

"A limo, of course," Doug said contemptuously.

"Jesus, Doug," Bob pleaded. "Can't we—?"

"Well, there *is* no phone," Doug interrupted. "It's not a fucking lodge, you know. I'm not successful enough to afford a phone."

Bob tried to reply patiently but firmly, "Then you can drive us to the nearest town and leave us there," he said.

"Oh, is that what I can do?" Doug asked. Amazing how his questions were rarely questions, Bob thought.

"I'll get ready," he said, starting to push up.

Doug flat-handed him on the shoulder, knocking him back on the ground.

"Is that necessary?" Bob asked quietly.

Doug didn't respond.

"Let's just get out of here," Bob said. He pushed to his feet and started toward the tent. Again, Doug flat-handed him, this time on the back, this time with greater force. Bob lost his balance, stumbling forward. It took several yards before he could regain his footing. He turned angrily. "Is that really *necessary?*" he demanded.

"Maybe it is." My God, was that a smile on Doug's lips? "Maybe it is, Bobby boy."

"Oh, God," Bob muttered.

"He can't help you here, big man," Doug said. "Your income doesn't matter here. Neither does your big success."

"Oh, Jesus, Doug," Bob said, turning back toward the campsite.

"Oh, Jesus, what, big man?"

Bob heard Doug moving toward him and twisted around.

This time Doug flat-handed him so hard on the chest, it made him reel back and topple over, landing on his hands; he hissed at the pain on his infected palm.

"What the—?" he began, then broke off, tightening as Doug lurched toward him. Grabbing Bob by the jacket collar, he hauled him to his feet.

"Is this the way it's going to be?" Bob asked, but before

he'd finished the sentence, Doug had slapped him hard across the left cheek, wincing at the pain it caused him on his shoulder.

"Bastard," Doug snapped. Bob wasn't sure if Doug meant him or the pain.

He stared at Doug incredulously. "What the hell is happening?" he asked, his voice shaken. "Are you—?"

He gasped in surprise and pain as Doug slapped him again.

"What's the matter, haven't you got the balls to defend yourself?" Doug challenged scornfully.

"What the hell are we, two kids in a schoolyard?" Bob demanded. "Are we supposed to—?"

He broke off with a cry of stunned pain as Doug slapped him again, his face contorting from the pain it caused him in his shoulder.

"Goddamn it, cut it out," Bob cried, shoving out his palm at Doug's face.

Was it just bad luck, he wondered later, that the flat of his palm hit Doug squarely on the nose? Doug cried out, startled, blood starting to spurt from both nostrils.

"Son of a bitch," Doug snarled, jerking up his left index finger to press beneath his bleeding nostrils.

The blow caught Bob completely by surprise. Fisting his right hand, Doug hit Bob violently in the stomach, doubling him over. Bob couldn't make a sound at the pain, his breath knocked out. Gasping for air, he hitched up slowly, an expression of astonishment on his face. "What the hell are you—?" he started, his voice wheezing.

He cried out in dumbfounded shock as Doug hit him again in the stomach. Gagging, he flopped over quickly, pressing both hands at his stomach, unable to breathe, shooting pain in his stomach. Everything went blurry as his eyes teared. He tried to hold himself rigid in case Doug meant to hit him again.

After almost a minute had passed, he straightened up, sucking feebly at the air. His eyes, filled with tears, saw Doug as a watery figure standing in front of him.

"Well, are you going to defend yourself, pussy?" Doug asked, his voice sounding completely vicious now. "Or are you just going to stand there, crying like a baby?"

Bob realized that tears were running down his cheeks and reached up to brush them away, his fingers trembling. "Are you crazy?" he said, barely able to speak.

"Right, I'm crazy, little man."

Bob tried to back off as Doug moved toward him suddenly. He could only stumble back a foot or so before Doug was on him, knocking him over. Bob grunted as he fell, then cried out in pain as he crashed to the ground, Doug on top of him.

"You aren't going to fight, you gutless shit?" Doug said, his features twisted. "Why don't I just kill you then, put you out of your fucking misery?"

"Why?" Bob asked in agony, staring up at Doug's distorted face. Dark blood was running over Doug's chin.

"Why?" Doug jolted once on Bob, making him sob in agony again. "Why, you pitiful son of a bitch? I'll tell you why. You already know why. I hate your fucking guts. I hate everything about you. You think you shit gold, don't you?" Bob's face jerked to the side as Doug slapped him again. "You're everything I despise in a man. Man, my ass. You're a pussy, a coward." He sniffed hard, running fingers under his nose. "Afterlife, you superstitious motherfucker? Reincarnation? I'll give you a fast trip there and you and Artie can sit around on a fucking cloud, discussing what a bastard I am."

Bob tried to pull Doug's hands away but couldn't, they were too strong, clamping hard around his neck. "You thought I was joking, did you, Bobby boy, Bobby fucking boy? I'll show you how much I was joking, motherfucker."

Bob clutched at Doug's tightening hands, thrashing helplessly beneath him. He couldn't breathe, darkness crowding at the corners of his vision. "Doug," he pleaded in a barely audible whisper. I'm going to die, the thought ran through his mind. It seemed completely unbelievable to him even as it was taking place.

Doug jerked his hands away. "Oh, no," he said, "oh, no. Too easy. Much too fast. I'll kill you but I want it to last—and last. Having trouble breathing, Bobby boy?"

Bob made faint choking sounds in his throat. He looked up at Doug, not knowing him at all. Doug's face was totally unfamiliar, now the face of some demented stranger. How could this be happening? he thought. How in the name of God could this be happening? He kept trying to swallow, to clear what felt like dry obstruction in his throat. Doug looked down at him, smiling. "Time for fun," he said with relish. "Time for big fun, Bobby boy."

Jumping to his feet, Doug jerked a handkerchief from his jacket pocket and dabbed at his nostrils. "Son of a bitch," he said. "You'll pay for this."

Bending over, he grabbed Bob's jacket and hauled him to his feet, beginning to drag him across the ground. Bob tried to struggle with him but he still felt dizzy, weak, unable to breathe. "Doug, don't," he mumbled.

"Doug, don't. Doug, don't," Doug repeated in a mocking,

falsetto voice. "Don't worry, I'll take care of you, my pretty. And your little penis too." Bob felt swallowed in some nightmare dream. Had Doug just imitated Margaret Hamilton, paraphrasing her speech from *The Wizard of Oz?* Had he gone completely insane?

He tried to pull away from Doug but couldn't. Half stumbling, half dragged, he was pulled over to a tree and shoved against it. "Don't move now," Doug told him. He was actually amused by all of this, Bob realized. He *had* gone insane. Dear God.

Feeling Doug let go of him, he tried to back off from the tree.

"I said—!" Doug snarled.

Bob almost screamed as Doug punched him hard below the ribs, driving lines of sharp pain through his back and chest.

"Now do what Daddy says and don't move, little boy," Doug ordered. "If you move again, I'll really have to hurt you and I certainly wouldn't want to do that because you're my friend, aren't you, Bobby boy? You're my good friend."

Bob gasped as Doug grabbed his hair and jerked his head back. "Aren't you, Bobby boy?"

Bob could only sob, grimacing with agony, tears dribbling down his cheeks.

"That's a good boy. I'll be right back," Doug told him. "Stay right there now."

Bob held on to the tree, his body a cluster of shifting pains. He still couldn't breathe normally. What am I going to do? he wondered. He couldn't just let Doug torture him like this. The realization made him shudder violently. That was what Doug was doing, torturing him.

He started to look around to see what Doug was up to.

Richard Matheson

"Anh-anh-anh," Doug warned him. "Don't you move now, Bobby boy, or Doug will get pissed at you."

A few moments later, Bob heard Doug's returning foot-steps. "Doug, whatever you have in mind—" he started weakly.

"Just shut up, pussy," Doug interrupted. "Whatever I have in mind is what I'll do, you get it? *Pussy?*"

"Doug, don't do this!" Bob said, pleading.

Doug didn't reply and Bob reacted with a gasp of alarm as Doug began to run the thin rope around his back, then around the tree.

"For Christ's sake, Doug, what are you doing?"

"Shut *up*, Bobby," Doug answered in a singsong voice.

"Doug, please. We're grown-up men, we're not—"

He broke off with a gasping cry as Doug flat-handed the back of his head, making him jerk forward, his forehead hitting the rough bark of the tree. "Jesus!" he cried, grimacing in pain.

He said no more, trying to restore his breathing as Doug kept wrapping the thin rope around his back and around the tree. How could this be happening? he kept on thinking. How could Doug have hidden all these years the hatred he was showing now? He wanted to try to reason with Doug, try to bring him back to his senses but he hurt too much in too many places, he didn't dare speak again.

Doug finished tying him to the tree, tightening the rope so much that his breath was cut off again. "I can't breathe," he said in a wheezing voice.

"Oh, sorry," Doug said as though he really was.

Bob cried out weakly as Doug pulled the rope even tighter.

"All right, kill me then!" Bob cried hoarsely.

"I will, big boy," Doug told him. "But not right away."

Bob sucked in a choking breath as Doug loosened the ropes, then used the ends to tie Bob's hands together by the wrists. "There we go," he said. He sounded pleased.

Bob leaned his forehead against the tree and closed his eyes. What now? he thought. Oh, God, what now? For a few moments, he had a vision of Marian standing in the clearing, staring at Doug, aghast at what he'd done.

"All right, Bobby boy," Doug said. "It's time to clear out the bullshit."

Bob stiffened as Doug pulled down his pants a few inches and lifted up the bottom of his jacket. "Now," he said.

Bob's breath cut off with a gasp as he felt something sharp pressing at his back. "I guess you know what that is," Doug said. "My trusty ol' golak. One hard shove and you're a dead pussy. So tell me, Bobby boy, you think you'll just be fast-forwarded to paradise? Or only be a corpse hanging off this tree?"

Bob drew in shaking breath. "What do you want me to say?" he asked.

"The truth, baby, the truth. You're as scared of dying as the rest of us. Your goddamn stupid philosophy doesn't mean doodley-squat to you right now with the point of my golak right at your back." Bob hissed as he felt the sharp point of the blade breaking his skin. "*Does* it, Bobby boy?"

Bob closed his eyes, teeth clenched. "You're wrong," he said. "You—"

He cried out faintly as Doug jabbed the blade end into his flesh. The flare of pain made him press his teeth together tightly.

"You're wrong," he said in a sudden blind rage. "You want me to renege—"

"Want you to what?" Doug demanded. He hitched the blade to the right. Bob sobbed at the pain and felt a trickle of blood down his back.

I won't, he thought. He wasn't going to give Doug satisfaction.

"Killing me won't change what I believe," he said in a tense, guttural voice. "I'll go to afterlife, I still believe that. You're the one who'll really suffer in the long run." He could barely finish as Doug turned the blade tip again, making him groan at the pain. "Go on!" he cried, mindless with fury. "Do it! Murder me! I'll still believe what I believe! I won't be dead, but you'll be damned!"

He waited for the final thrust, the burst of pain, the darkness of death.

It didn't come.

"Well, well, well," Doug said. "I must say I'm impressed. You really do believe in afterlife. I admire your conviction, Bobby boy."

Bob felt the tip of the golak blade removed. The pain decreased but he could still feel warm blood dribbling down his back.

"So you're not afraid of dying," Doug went on. "Well, I can understand that. Even if you didn't believe in afterlife, dying would end the pain."

Bob felt himself tightening. What was Doug talking about now?

He knew immediately as Doug said, "Maybe living is something you'd rather not do. Maybe I was offering you an easy way out by threatening to impale you on my golak. Maybe staying alive is worse than dying. Right, Bobby boy? Maybe living . . . but with *pain*."

Bob braced himself for the beating he was sure Doug was about to inflict on him. He closed his eyes and pressed his lips together tightly. Maybe—if the beating was severe—he'd pass out. It was all he could hope for. And Doug was wrong if he thought he could just keep beating him and not end up by killing him.

He twitched as Doug jerked down his pants until they were bunched around his ankles.

"I forgot to mention," Doug said—was he smiling cruelly as he spoke—"pain and *humiliation*."

No, Bob thought. Doug couldn't mean what he thought he did.

"Then maybe not," Doug said. Bob heard a rustling of clothes behind him. "Maybe it wouldn't be humiliation at all. Maybe you'd enjoy it. Maybe it's exactly what you've been dying for ever since we started out."

The rustling of clothes ended. Bob heard Doug making tiny sensual noises behind him. "Gotta get it ready for you, baby. Hot and ready."

"Doug, for Christ's sake . . ."

"No, no, not him," Doug said with amusement. "He was straight." He chuckled. "I *think*." He laughed. "Wouldn't that be a kick in the ass to the Church if they found out that their Son of God liked to take it up the ass."

"Doug, you are destroying your life!" Bob cried.

"Oh, no, babe, I'm destroying yours," Doug answered.

Bob turned his head as Doug moved into view. He made a feeble noise of disbelief, grimacing at the sight of Doug. Except for his boots, he was completely naked, gripping his erected penis with his left hand. Bob felt a chill at the size of it, knowing now what Doug intended to do.

"I saw the way you looked at me the other night when I was naked," Doug told him. "I used to see the way you looked at my bathing suit when Nicole and I were swimming at your house. As though you were dying to jerk it down and put my cock in your mouth."

"Oh, God, Doug, God." Bob shook his head.

"He isn't here, I keep telling you, babe," Doug said.

He moved out of sight now, Bob saw as he opened his eyes.

"Doug, for Christ's sake, don't *do* this," he said.

"Looking forward to it, are you, Bobby boy?" Doug said. "I know I am. I'm going to shove my cock all the way up your hot, virginal asshole and I'm gonna love it. Once I'm in there, let's see what your damn spiritual insight can do to comfort you. Nothing, I suspect. It's just gonna hurt like hell. And the hornier I get, the more it's gonna hurt. Mmm, I can hardly wait."

"Doug, for Christ's sake, don't do this!" Bob cried.

"Oh, now it's for *his* sake," Doug said; he sounded amused. "You're regressing, Bobby. Did you just become a born-again Christian? Give yourself to Jesus and all will be hunky-dory? I don't *think* so," he finished in a singsong voice.

"By the way," he added. "If there's no such thing as an accident, that must mean I intended to fuck your asshole right from the start."

"Doug, don't. *Please*." His voice sounded weak and pitiable, now.

He heard Doug doing something behind him. Then Doug came back. "Gonna make it easy for you, babe," he said.

Bob jerked, gasping, as he felt Doug's fingers start to probe into his rectum; there was something wet on his fingers. "Just a spoonful of olive oil makes the dicky-wick go in, the dicky-wick go in, the dicky-wick go in," Bob sang, paraphrasing Mary Poppins's song. He's gone insane, he really has, Bob thought in horror, gritting his teeth as Doug continued probing with his fingers, moving them deeper into Bob. "Just a little preview, Bobby. A coming attraction."

His fingers pulled out and Bob made a sound of fright as Doug was suddenly behind him, clutching at his sides with digging fingers. "And now," he said, sounding aroused. "Now, Bobby boy. The pièce de résistance." His laugh was like a bark. "Although you can't resist my piece, can you?" Bob twitched as Doug kissed his shoulder. "Not that you'd resist at all. I don't have to tie you to this tree. If I untied you, you'd be on your knees in a second, begging for my cock inside you."

As he spoke, he pressed the head of his penis between Bob's buttocks and began to push. The pain began immediately. "Doug, don't," Bob pleaded desperately. "For God's sake, *stop* this."

"Too late, Bobby boy," Doug said.

Bob caught his breath with a dry gasp. "Oh, goody." Doug sounded delighted. "The head just popped in. *Mm.*" He writhed against Bob. "And now—" he said.

With a snarling sound, he jammed himself against Bob's body, entering him all the way. Bob cried out in anguish, his head thrown back, his closed eyes flowing tears as he felt the tearing of tissues inside himself.

"Now I just move back and forth, back and forth," Doug said. He started kissing Bob's neck and shoulders, grunting with excitement. "Oh, God, take it, baby, take it."

Bob couldn't speak. He could only utter feeble sounds of pain as Doug slowly sodomized him, groaning, grunting, licking the back of Bob's neck, saliva running off his tongue. "Oh, God," he muttered. "God."

"Did you know Nicole talked about you all the time?" Doug said, breathing hard. "I think she wanted to suck you off. You think Marian wanted to suck me off? Ooh, I bet she did, I bet she did."

Bob's face became a rigid mask of resistance to the pain. It has to end, it has to end, he kept telling himself.

Doug's breathing became more rapid now. "Oh, Bobby boy, this feels so *good*. It's like the hottest, tightest pussy in the *world*, the *world*, the *world*." Each repetition of the word was accompanied by a spasmed shove inside Bob, making him moan in pain.

"Wouldn't you have loved a nice, hot, drunken, bisexual orgy with the four of us?" Doug said, gasping for breath now. "Wouldn't you have loved to watch Nicole and Marian eating each other while you and I were sixty-nining next to them? Oh, yeah, you would, you'd have loved it—loved it."

"Oh, my God," Bob murmured. Doug's penis was beginning to swell, increasing the pain more with each second. "I'm gonna cum inside your asshole, Bobby boy," Doug said, panting for breath. "I'm gonna fill your asshole with hot, white cum. You'll love it, Bobby boy. You'll *love* it."

A few seconds later, Doug cried out dementedly, his fingers gouging into Bob's hip flesh, his body jammed up tight against Bob as he had his orgasm. Bob felt the hot liquid spurting into his rectum. I'm going to kill him, he suddenly thought. I don't care what I believe, I'm going to kill the son of a bitch!

When Doug had finished coming, he drew back. Bob winced and gagged at the feeling. Then the pain was gone, replaced by a burning ache inside him. He felt Doug's semen running down the back of his legs. Fuck philosophy, he thought with mindless hate. Fuck the meaning of life. Fuck afterlife and reincarnation and all of it.

As soon as he could he was going to murder Doug.

11:21 AM

Doug kept him tied to the tree while he dressed leisurely, humming to himself, "I could have danced all night." He seemed at peace now, totally relaxed. Sated, Bob thought with trembling rage. Like a well-rutted animal.

"You know, I don't think I planned on this right from the start," Doug said, stopping the song, "I think it just came up." A laugh burst from him. "There I go again," he said, imitating Ronald Reagan. "Can't control those double entendres. Naughty, naughty. That nasty old subconscious."

After he'd dressed, he untied the rope and released Bob. Bob's legs felt limp at first, almost giving out beneath him. Then he straightened up and, bending over, pulled up his pants.

"Don't you want to douche first?" Doug asked lightly. "Might get pregnant otherwise. That would be embarrassing."

Bob didn't speak. He stared at Doug who was sitting with the golak lying across his lap.

"What's the matter, afraid I'll attack you?" Bob asked coldly.

"I presume you don't mean sexually," Doug said.

Bob only stared at him.

"Well . . ." Doug gestured with his hands. "Never can tell. You might go nuts. After all I've violated the sanctity of your virginal asshole."

Bob felt his stomach muscles tensing in. Should he make a run at Doug? He hated him enough to do it. But he knew, his brain still intact and functioning, that Doug could kill him with a single slash of the golak. He remembered the deep, flesh-exposing cut he'd made on the doe. He'd have to bide his time.

Carefully, he sat down on the ground, making an involuntary sound of pain.

"Hurts a little, doesn't it?" Doug said as though sympathizing. "It's like that the first time. You'll get used to it."

Bob's muscles seemed to tighten of their own accord. The first time? Was Doug planning on doing it again? He'll have to kill me first, he resolved.

Doug chuckled. "I can see what you're thinking, Bobby. You can relax though. You aren't that good a fuck. There were guys in the reformatory who could screw you under the table."

"I thought you beat up the 'big guy' in the reformatory so they'd leave you alone," Bob said.

"I did," Doug said. "And they did." He grinned. "I didn't say I left them alone, though." He squeezed his groin with a sensual sound. "Got so I really liked it. In the mouth, in the ass, you name it. I tried to talk Nicole into letting me fuck her ass but she wouldn't do it. Too bad. She might've liked it."

He picked up the golak and pointed it at Bob. "Sure you wouldn't like to stay and have more fun with me?"

"Fun?" He glared at Doug. If I had a gun, he thought, I'd risk my soul to blow him away. Right now.

"No, I guess not," Doug said pityingly. "You're as straight as a fucking arrow. It's Marian or no one, right?"

Bob didn't answer, trying hard to think how he could do something to get the advantage over Doug.

"Besides," Doug said with a mocking grin, "it's karma, isn't it? There are no accidents, you said so. Which means you probably raped some poor slob in the nineteenth century, or earlier. Maybe you were the guy who buggered Jesus. And now you've paid the price, right? An ass for an ass." He threw his head back with a coarse laugh. "Pretty good. That just came out o' me by accident. An ass for an ass. That's marvelous. I'll have to remember that."

He laughed again. "Which means it was my fucking karma too." Another laugh with his head thrown back. "Jesus Christ, I did it again. Fucking karma. That's what it was. *Fucking* karma. I had no control. What did Malkovich say in that movie? 'It's out of my control'?" He laughed again. "Oh, God, I'm really rolling now.

"You know," he went on as though contributing to his half of an amiable chat, "this really shouldn't surprise you, considering that you're such a cynic about this life and see injustice everywhere."

"I never saw it in you," Bob told him somberly. "I trusted you. I thought you were my friend."

"And now you've found out that I'm actually your karma. How about that? Is that injustice or what?"

Bob didn't answer.

Doug sighed. "I could use another cup of coffee. I'll make some after you've gone. With brandy, of course."

Bob felt himself going rigid. After you've gone?

"It's just as well you don't want to hang around and have a party. It would just spoil the game."

The game? Bob wanted to ask it aloud but couldn't speak.

Doug rubbed his shoulder, wincing. "Hurts like hell," he said. "Gives you a slight advantage anyway. Not much of one but—any port in a storm, hanh?" He took out his handkerchief and dabbed at his nostrils. "Nose still hurts too. But that won't be an advantage. That'll just make me more intent on catching you."

"You just don't see what you're doing to your soul, do you?" Bob said.

"No, Daddy, tell me. What am I doing to my soul?"

"Blackening it," Bob told him.

"Ooh." Doug made a mock face of fear. "And that means?"

"That means payment will come due," Bob said.

"Payment." Doug nodded, looking bored. "Oh, you mean, in my next life." He grimaced melodramatically. "Or my next. Or my next. Or who the hell knows?"

"Or this life," Bob told him.

"Really." Doug pretended to look fascinated. "And who'll do that? Who'll make me pay?" He leaned forward, an expression of dark glee on his face. "You, Bobby? You're the one who'll make my payment come due? I don't *think* so!" he finished jeeringly, using the singsong voice again.

Bob knew there was no point in discussing this with Doug. The subject was completely out of Doug's realm of thinking. He thought it was all bullshit. He'd said so. No matter. He'd said what he had to say. Let the rest go.

"Okay, now," Doug said cheerfully, acting as though their relationship was perfectly equitable. "As to details. It's a contest. I give you a two-hour head start, three if you insist, it won't matter any. You take with you anything you want"—he grinned—"other than the golak and the bow and arrows, of course. Anything else though. Food. Water. Toilet articles if you want them. Your ground pad and your sleeping bag, of course.

Although you may not last long enough to *need* your sleeping bag."

Bob shuddered, staring wordlessly at Doug.

"But let's assume the best scenario," Doug said. He seemed to be reciting the rules of some intriguing game. "You stay ahead of me. The cabin's about two days from here, moving fast that is—I suggest you move fast, of course. There's the Wiley place a few miles down the hill from my cabin. Good landmark. I'll let you have the compass, by the way. You just keep moving southeast and you'll be all right. You with me so far?"

Bob didn't speak. I haven't been with you since the day we met, he thought.

"Okay," Doug said. He clapped his hands together once. "You reach the cabin first, you win. I catch you first, you lose." He smiled benignly. "And, of course, you know what that means."

Bob had to ask. "And if I win, what then? You apologize for raping me? You tell Marian you're sorry that you raped me? You perform social work to make up for raping me? You get therapy because you raped me?"

"Whoa, whoa," Doug said, chuckling. "You're not going to win. You really think you can outrun me? The klutz backpacker of the century? Please. Give me a break. Or, as they used to say when I was a kid, 'No way, José.' "

They sat in silence for almost a minute, looking intently at each other. I mustn't blink. For some inane reason, it was all Bob could think.

"So when do you want to leave?" Doug asked. "You want a little more to eat first? A cup or two of coffee to brace you? Name it, Bobby boy, you've got it."

Bob didn't speak. Doug's features tightened. "Well?" he said.

Another few moments of silence.

"When do you want to leave?" Doug demanded.

"Never."

Doug looked honestly taken back. "What?" he asked.

"You seem to forget," Bob told him. "You've picked the wrong guy . . . *Douglas.* Your threat to kill me doesn't mean a thing to me. Remember me? I'm the guy who's not afraid of death."

He managed a chuckle. "You look confounded," he said, almost amused.

Doug was expressionless for several seconds. Then he said, "Let me get this straight—as they say in the beginning of every stupid letter to the editor . . . if I were to pick up my golak now and make a move toward you, you wouldn't do a thing about it?"

"I didn't say that," Bob responded. "If you make a move toward me, I'd defend myself—and hurt you any way I could. Kill you if I could."

Doug seemed to brush that possibility aside as not worth consideration. "You mean, if I picked up my bow and put an arrow in it and said I was going to shoot it straight into your heart, you'd let me? You wouldn't say, okay, I'll take the head start, just don't kill me?"

Bob only gazed at him. Odd, he thought, that at this moment of complete vulnerability to Doug, he felt, somehow, superior to him.

"You've already done your worst," he said. "Kill me if it pleases you. My soul will just move on. Yours will enter an eternal night." He finished almost fiercely.

"Oh, dear," Doug said. "You know, I think you really mean what you say. You're *not* afraid of dying. I could make you hurt, give you lots of pain—but eventually you'd die and I'd lose my game."

"I'm sorry if I'm ruining your day," Bob told him with an icy tone.

"Oh, you're not, you're not," Doug said. "Because you've overlooked a key part of our little game."

He smiled at Bob, obviously waiting for him to ask, What part? Bob wouldn't give him the satisfaction.

"Okay, I guess I'll have to satisfy your unspoken curiosity," Doug said. Bob felt a coldness on his back that made him shiver.

"The key part of our little game, audience?" Doug said as though he were a game-show host. A pause. His smile was almost merry. "Right!" he said. "The key part of our little game is—Marian!"

Bob seemed to feel every muscle in his body becoming taut. He looked at Doug with hatred. "What are you planning to do?" he asked in a low, trembling voice. "Rape her? Hurt her?"

"Oh, no." Doug sounded as though the question had hurt his feelings. "No, not at all. I wouldn't hurt Marian. I like Marian." His smile grew venomous. "You might say that I *love* her."

Despite the golak, Bob could barely restrain himself from lunging forward and grabbing Doug by the throat. Only at the last second, did his mind warn him: You can't help her if you're dead.

"You see, I have a much more interesting scenario in mind," Doug went on. "You might say"—he grinned—"the performance of my life."

"What do you mean?" He had to know, immediately. Even if he had to ask.

"Well, here's the plot," Doug said as though he were making a story pitch to a producer. "I catch you—as I will, of course. I kill you—as I will, of course. I cut you into pieces and bury them far apart from each other. Some parts may be dug up by a bear and eaten. That would only enhance the plot, you see, because, later on, they might find a leg bone or an arm bone or something. I hightail it to the cabin; I can make it in a day if I really rush, get there by late tonight." He smiled again as though looking for Bob's approval of the clever plot he'd created.

"Now," he said, holding up the index finger of his right hand, "comes the good part. The Academy Award part. I show up at the cabin in a state of near hysteria. I cry, I groan, I blame myself for everything. You went out in the dark to go to the bathroom and I never saw you again. I should have gone *with* you. I searched everywhere but couldn't find a sign of you. A bear or a mountain lion must have gotten you. We'll call the forest rangers and initiate a search—I won't tell them where we were, of course, I'll take them someplace else. I'll keep on crying, sobbing, not too much of course, just enough to be convincing. Oscar-caliber, believe me." He leaned forward, looking fascinated. "They never find your remains, of course. Finally, I drive Marian home. I stay with her to comfort her. I'm always with her. She can lean on me, trust me. I'm a damn good actor, maybe you don't know that. She'll buy it; she'll be totally convinced that I've been traumatized. I was supposed to take care of you and I didn't do my job. I'll cry some more. I'll drink, she'll drink. I'll be the—what's the fucking word?—oh, yes, I'll be the epitome of caring, the fucking quintessence—ooh, I got that right away—the quintessence—love that word—the *quintessence* of compassion. In time, Marian will come to depend on me, to need me, to—dare I speak the word?—to love me. We'll get married—" His eyelids lowered halfway, his smile gone sardonic. "And I'll fuck her asshole legally. Won't that be a gas?"

Bob was unable to speak. He could only stare at Doug, believing himself to be in the presence of a madman. A madman he had to kill, somehow, someway.

Finally, Doug spoke.

"That puts a slightly different complexion on the game, doesn't it, Bobby boy?" he said. "Still want me to kill you now?"

The murderous fury he'd felt while Doug was sodomizing him erupted so suddenly that the words spewed forth without thought. *"You miserable son of a bitch!"*

Before the sentence was finished he'd lunged to his feet and flung himself at Doug, hitting him so fast and hard that Doug, completely caught off guard, was unable to grab the golak from his lap.

Knocking Doug back with the impetus of his charge, Bob started pounding at his face as hard as he could. Doug raised his arms to block the punches but couldn't prevent some of them from driving into his cheeks, his eyes, his mouth. *"Damn!"* he snarled.

Bob couldn't speak. Fueled by his rage, he only wanted to keep hitting Doug, pounding him unconscious, killing him if necessary. Thought was gone. He could only concentrate on one thing: stopping Doug, *now*. It gave him a wild, perverse pleasure to see the look of startled amazement on Doug's face, hear the muffled flooding of curses from him. *Hit* him, *hit* him! The words were shouted in his brain by a voice he'd never heard before.

Then Doug's knee was driven up into his groin and, with an instant flare of pain, the fight was ended. Rolling on his side with a groaning cry Bob drew up his legs with convulsive suddenness and, abruptly, lay in a taut fetal position, unable to catch his breath, eyes slitted, teeth bared in a grimace of agony. Vision blurred, he watched Doug stagger to his feet. "Motherfucker," he was mumbling. "Mother*fucker*."

Now Doug loomed over him, nose bleeding, cheeks bruised, an expression of demented malice on his face. "You bastard," he muttered, "you dumb fucking bastard." Bob watched his right arm raise up, the golak clutched in his hand. *"Now you die."*

Bob closed his eyes, tensed for the violent stroke of the golak that would end his life. *Protect Marian*, he thought, having no idea to whom the plea was being sent. *Please protect her!*

When the blow from the golak didn't come, he opened his eyes and looked up in pained curiosity.

"Oh, no," Doug was saying. "No. Too easy, motherfucker. You are going to die but not this easy, not this easy. Oh, no, not this easy, motherfucker, not this easy."

Reaching down, he grabbed Bob by the hair with his left hand and yanked him to his feet. Before he was up, Doug had reared back his right fist and driven it as hard as he could into Bob's jaw.

Bob reeled back and fell, collapsing to the ground, darkness flooding across his brain. He felt Doug drag him up by the left arm and drive another violent blow to his abdomen. As he doubled over, gagging, Doug jarred him erect with an uppercut to his jaw. Now the darkness was almost complete. He felt himself sinking into it, his face and body almost numbed by pain. As though through a film he saw Doug's face, his twisted look of fury. Then, unexpectedly, somehow more horrible than the expression of malevolence, a smile of fierce pleasure.

"Now the game begins," he said.

He let go of Bob who crumpled to the ground, legs drawn up again, soft groans of pain filling his throat.

"You hear me, Bobby boy?" Doug asked. He sounded almost happy. *"Now the game begins."*

1:48 PM

He had to stop and rest for a while. He'd been trying to walk rapidly, sometimes trot, but he simply couldn't manage it. The backpack was considerably lighter—just the bare minimum of equipment and supplies to keep him going—but it still dragged at his back; and his body and head still ached where Doug had punched him so sadistically.

Taking off his pack, he lay down on his back and started doing stretching exercises he hadn't done in years—pelvic thrusts, raising his legs one at a time, then both together, drawing up his knees. He groaned in misery as he exercised. How the hell am I going to make this? he wondered. Doug was fit and strong; he was unfit and covered with pains and aches. For a while, a rush of despair engulfed him. It was hopeless. He was kidding himself. Outrun Doug? Nothing in the world seemed less possible to him at the moment.

His legs fell heavily to the ground and he groaned, partially in pain, mostly in despondent recognition. There was just no way—

"Shut up!" he ordered himself. He had to survive—for Marian's sake if not his own. Doug's diabolical scenario must never take place. Never.

He looked at his wristwatch. He'd been gone a little more than an hour now. Would Doug really wait three hours before following him? Or had that been a cruel joke?

He jerked his head around, hearing a noise to his left, a crackling sound. Was Doug already here? He sat up fast, wincing at the pain it caused. Listening intently, he sat without moving.

Then he thought, no, Doug wouldn't make any noise. He'd come stealing up like an Indian tracking prey. He'd never hear a sound. The first thing he'd know Doug's presence would be the whistling streak of an arrow and the final pain of it burying itself in his back—or his chest, depending on which way he was facing.

For several minutes, he tried to convince himself that Doug wouldn't actually stoop to murder. The rape he understood—to agonize and humiliate him. But actually kill him? Surely, Doug had no such intention.

He scowled at his Pollyanna figment. Doug would kill him all right. He said he would, and if he caught up, that was exactly what he'd do.

He groaned again as he stood. I am in such miserable shape, he thought disgustedly; a regular goddamn athlete.

"Well, what do you expect?" he assailed himself. "You hadn't planned on being chased by a homicidal maniac." The remark made him grunt with a humorless smile. If I wrote this in a spec script, they'd throw me out of the office.

But it was really happening, that was the rub. Truth really *is* stranger than fiction, he thought. As far-fetched as it was in a creative way, it was darkly, horribly true. It was happening. The man who was going to take him on a pleasant research backpacking hike was now intending to murder him. Cut me up in pieces for Christ's sake! he thought. He *is* a fucking maniac. He *is*.

He pressed down gingerly on his right foot. The blister was still there, probably broken open by now. He'd have to put a clean bandage on it later. Sure, he thought in bitter amusement. Got to protect yourself from that lethal blister.

He put on his pack again, took a drink from his water bottle, and started off. Was he going to have enough water to last him? He couldn't ration it too much; Doug had made that point clear enough. But was he going to run across drinkable water? That Doug hadn't told him as he'd left.

"Much he cares," Bob muttered as he tried to walk in long, even strides.

He stopped walking suddenly. He'd never manage to out-run Doug and there was only one alternative.

He had to lay in wait for Doug, attack him somehow, kill him. It was the only possibility. He felt too weak and sick to outdistance Doug's pursuit.

But how? he asked himself. *How?*

Again, there was only one possibility.

Taking off his backpack, he pulled out his hunting knife and looked around for a branch thin enough for him to cut into a cudgel he could hit Doug in the face with, lunging out from behind a tree.

As he searched, he considered the possibility of improvising a spear with the knife and a branch, fastening the knife to the branch with shoelaces. Immediately, he discarded the notion. What if the knife wasn't fastened to the branch tightly enough, slipping off or, at best, shifting to one side as he tried to drive it into Doug's chest. No, a cudgel was the only way. Smashing Doug across the face. A lunge from behind a tree and smashing him across the bridge of the nose, trying for an instant kill.

Instant kill. The words were sickening to him. Still, there was no other choice. He was too weak to move out quickly. It was self-defense: kill or be killed. Not just for himself. It was to protect Marian from Doug's deranged plan. That was what he had to do; no choice. No choice whatever.

Blanking his mind, he kept looking until he'd found a fallen tree, a small branch jutting up from its surface. Slowly, grimacing at the weakness in his arm, he began to hack and saw away at the base of the branch. Doug had been right. His knife seemed almost worthless. He wished to God he had a golak too. With a few hard strokes, the branch would be off. Hell, the thought occurred. If he had a golak, he wouldn't need the cudgel. He could drive the golak blade across Doug's face, plunge it into his chest. Involuntarily, he found the vision deeply shocking. No *choice*, Bob, he commanded himself. *No choice at all.*

It took him more than fifteen minutes to cut the branch loose and shorten it into a cudgel about two and a half feet long.

That done, he sat on the fallen trunk of the tree and, for a short while, examined his improvised club.

It was about three inches thick. The bottom half, the part

he'd hold, was straight for almost a foot and a half. The upper half twisted sideways, small stumps jutting out from it. He touched the ends of the stumps with his right index finger. They all felt sharp to the touch. Again involuntarily, he visualized the stumped end of the cudgel hitting Doug's face, digging into his cheek, perhaps gouging out one or both of his eyes.

He clenched his teeth and willed away the image. No choice, he told himself again and again. *No choice.*

He examined the cudgel for almost ten minutes before realizing that his plan had gone no further than the preparation of the club and the vague idea of him stepping out from behind a tree and smashing Doug across the face with it.

Idly, he plucked loose three small dead leaves from the upper half of the club. How much time had he used now to prepare it? He looked at his wristwatch. He'd wasted—*utilized!* he berated himself—almost twenty minutes now. If Doug had told him the truth, he'd have to wait in hiding for more than two hours.

Doubts began to pile up in his brain. What made him assume that Doug would come this way? What if he hid behind a tree in waiting only to have Doug bypass him by a hundred yards, *two* hundred? Then his plan was worthless.

Worse, what if Doug *did* come by this way but from a different angle? He might very easily spot him hiding behind a tree, casually notch an arrow into his bow, and let it fly. He wouldn't have to be anywhere near Bob to kill him.

Worse still, what if Doug's plan was to bypass him anyway, hurry on to the cabin, play out his lachrymose scene for Marian, and talk her into driving away with him to find the nearest ranger or sheriff's station? By the time he reached the cabin—

presuming he'd reach it at all, Marian could be gone. How could he conceivably make his way out of the forest to find help? He'd end up hopelessly lost, finished. In his condition, he couldn't possibly endure another extended hike through the forest. Lost—or killed by some wild animal—he'd die knowing that Marian was now the unwitting victim to Doug's ungodly plot.

The more he examined the possibilities, the less sense his plan made to him. Doug was too skilled to be caught by surprise, and he might never even *see* Doug. No, it made no sense, no sense at all. To wait here, lurking behind a tree, his only chance the improbable appearance of Doug in such a convenient way that he could jump out at him and smash the club across his face. Jesus Christ, Hansen, he scorned himself. Great plan. He was sure to fail the attempt, lose everything, his wife, his children, his life. You're out of your mind, he told himself. Absolutely out of your mind. There was only one hope he had. To reach Marian before Doug could overtake him. That was *it*. As weak and physically depleted as he was, it was his only hope.

He scowled at his own unthinking gullibility and looked at the compass Doug had given him. Doug had told him that the cabin was on a magnetic bearing of forty degrees from where they were standing. He had turned the compass housing to the forty-degree bearing, then turned the entire compass until the red end of the needle was lined up with the N arrow on the bottom of the circular housing.

"Now you're oriented," Doug had told him as though lecturing a student on some casual direction-finding problem. "Just turn the compass until the red end of the needle is pointing north, then turn the base plate until the direction-of-travel needle points toward a forty-degree bearing—got it?"

Bob turned the compass until the needle was pointing at N on the compass. He was off the mark by twenty degrees. Turning, he pointed himself in the corrected direction. What was it Doug had said, trying to be "so helpful"—something about picking out a distant landmark. Looking up, he saw a mountain peak on approximately the forty-degree bearing; maybe it was forty-five. He could adjust to that.

Nodding to himself in satisfaction (oh, now you're an official backpacker, his brain mocked him), he started walking again.

Was it possible that Doug had lied to him completely about the bearing to follow to reach the cabin? That he was actually sending him into untraveled forest, planning on him getting lost, dying of thirst or hunger, maybe even being killed by a wild animal? The idea made him ill.

No, he told himself then. No, he wouldn't do that. What if he goes right to the cabin and tells his story and I survive and show up? That would be too much of a risk. He has to kill me, he realized. There was no other way.

At first, he thought it was the idea of Doug sending him into impenetrable wilderness that was making his stomach churn. Then he realized—"wonder of wonders," he muttered—that he had to move his bowels.

He did what Doug had suggested (well, he's done that much for me anyway, the bizarre thought occurred) finding a fallen log and sitting on it, hovering his rear end over the ground.

It was hardly the best bowel movement he'd ever had but he groaned and sighed in relief as he emptied his bowels. In a few minutes, he sat motionless, smiling despite the dire circumstance he was in. He listened to the faint soughing of the wind in the high trees, admired the colors of the leaves, the massive silence of the forest.

The momentary pleasure ended as he wiped himself, seeing the bright blood on the tissue. "Bastard," he muttered. "Son of a bitch." He sighed wearily. A far remove from metaphysical reflection, he thought. Hanging off a log, wiping blood from my ass.

He looked at his watch as he kept moving, managing to achieve a certain rhythm and timing to his strides. He'd been gone more than two hours now. If Doug had been honest about the "rules" of his lunatic game, he'd be starting after Bob in less than fifty minutes. He visualized Doug, smiling excitedly to himself, lunging into the forest, intent on his prey. How would he know which direction to take? Had he backpacked here often enough that he had a built-in compass in his brain? Bob didn't know. All he did know was that Doug would be on the move with a zeal that was near crazed.

He was sure of that.

Still, he thought, Doug couldn't have been planning on this right from the start. Why impart any woodlore at all if he intended killing Bob from the very beginning? No, the anger and resentment had built up in the last two days. Now it had crested and erupted like a mental volcano.

When? he thought as he walked steadily. When had it all begun? What had he said to generate this madness in Doug's mind? Was it any one thing he'd said? Or was Doug primed for this from the beginning, needing only constant exposure to

Bob's thoughts and words to be aroused to murderous rage? And it *was* rage. Doug could act as "cool" as he wished—but flowing under his mock-amused behavior had to be raw, untrammeled rage, which now was out and flourishing.

He suddenly recalled what Doug had said about the vivid panoply of hues in some of the trees. It signified the destruction of the leaves; they were dying in a blaze of color. How appropriate a memory, he thought.

It occurred to him—causing a chill to wrack his body— that Doug didn't have to kill him with an arrow, dismember him and bury the parts. He could just as easily, catching up to him, throw him off a cliff or drown him. That way, he could still enact his "Oscar-caliber" performance for Marian and the authorities. An accident. He tried to protect Bob while they were climbing, while they were crossing that river. It just happened so fast. Tears and sobs. Guilt presented with performing skill.

"No," he said. "No good." Doug wanted to kill him with an arrow, two arrows, then use his golak to hack him up. Why was he so sure of that? He just was. It was as though he'd seen, full measure, into the blackness that pervaded Doug's mind and there was no room for any further doubt.

Doug would do what he said he would.

"If I let him," Bob muttered angrily. "But I won't. *I won't.*" Never mind what he believed. It wasn't of any significance at the moment. At the moment, he almost agreed with what Doug had said to him just before he left.

"Your philosophy is shit, Bobby. A lot of stupid words. You have to fight for what you get in this lifetime, not fucking meditate on the glories of the fucking universe. You grab and you take—that's the only way to live. Survival of the fittest, Bobby. Ever hear of that? Well, you better take it to heart or you'll be skewered before sunset."

Still, as he walked, he began to wonder that if the moment had actually occurred, that his ploy of waiting behind the tree had worked, that he'd actually been able to lunge out from his hiding place and use the club on Doug, would he really have been capable of killing Doug? Easy enough to rationalize that it would be self-defense, kill or be killed. But what he'd be doing was committing a violent homicide. Despite all considered facts of the situation, would he have been able to live with the realization that he was now a murderer?

He didn't know. He simply did not know.

His jaw dropped as he crossed the brow of the hill and saw a lake below.

It was a big one, deep blue, with a tidal current of its own. Should he go down there and refill his water bottle?

Leaning against a lodgepole pine, he took out the compass to check his bearing. Jesus Christ, he reacted. The forty-degree bearing was straight across the lake. Did Doug know that? Son of a bitch, he thought. He looked up at the distant mountain peak; grimaced. The view of it was also straight across the lake.

He put the compass back in his pocket and checked his watch. There was a cold, dropping sensation in his stomach as he realized that Doug was on his way now, probably running through the forest with a crazy glint in his eyes, the hunter tracking the hunted, never doubting for a moment that he'd overtake his prey and kill it. *It,* he thought. That's probably exactly what he was to Doug now. An animal without an identity. A quarry not to be concerned about but run to earth and dispatched with quick efficiency.

He shook himself. Stop brooding about your crazy stalker and start planning your escape. Escape? challenged his mind. You think you're going to escape?

"Yes!" he cried.

All right. First step: He should refill his water bottle, drop in several iodine tablets to purify it. How did he know if there would be any other water once he left the lake behind? Of course, he'd have to move around the border of the lake; the left side looked more possible than the right, which was so far away he couldn't even see it. Then, when he'd circled the lake, he'd relocate his bearing again, move on toward the mountain peak.

The descent to the lake was steeper than he'd thought it was. Almost immediately, he slipped and started to slide down on his back. Oh, Christ, don't break a bone! he thought in panic as he half thrashed, half slithered down the overgrown hill, wincing as he brushed against bushes, bounced over stones. Stop! he told himself. For Christ's sake, stop!

He managed to grab on to the trunk of a small tree as he passed it. The wrenching on his arm and shoulder made him cry out but his rapid, uncontrolled descent was stopped. He dug his boot heels into the ground and drew his hand away from the tree trunk. "Oh, *God*," he muttered, wincing in pain. Now I've sprained my arm and shoulder. What more can I do to make my flight impossible? He closed his eyes with a groan. "Jesus, Jesus, Jesus," he murmured.

The name made him think—more wish, he sensed—that taking all his grand beliefs into consideration, he could convince himself that "outside" help was available. *Pray?* he thought. Oh, yeah, that would do a lot of good. The Lord helps those who help themselves, Bobby boy, his mind chattered irritatingly. Thanks a lot, he answered it. Very reassuring.

He sighed heavily. Well, he already knew that was the case. No white-robed angel with fluffy wings was going to swoop down, pick him up, and carry him to sanctuary. He could pray until the snow fell but he'd still have to make his way to safety on his own two weary, aching legs.

For a moment, what he suddenly saw was so astounding to him that he was unable to react.

Then he gasped. "My God," he said, his voice barely audible.

A boat had appeared from behind the headland of a cove, moving across the lake. It was a motor launch with an awning roof, three people sitting inside.

"Oh, Jesus Christ," he said. He shouted. "Hey! I'm up here! Wait for me!"

He knew he wasn't loud enough and, hastily, took a sip of water, threw back his head and gargled with it, spit it out. *"Hey!"* he cried as loudly as he could. "Come *back*! I need a ride!"

He stared at the boat. Surely, they'd heard. It seemed to him that his voice had rung out across the lake, so loudly that he felt an uneasy tremor, wondering if Doug had heard and now knew exactly where he was.

No help for it. He had to get on that boat.

"Hey! I need your help! Please! I'm in danger! Come back! I need to cross the lake!"

The boat kept moving steadily through the water. Did he actually see it—his distance vision was far from perfect—or had a man in the back of the launch gestured across his shoulder with his right thumb. He couldn't be sure.

"Please!" he screamed with all the power he could summon. "I need your help! Please come back! *Please!*"

The boat did not turn but kept gliding across the lake, leaving behind a narrow wake, its prow cutting knifelike through the dark blue water.

"Oh, God." Bob's voice broke in a sob; he felt tears flowing from his eyes, running quickly down his cheeks. If this is my karma, I hate it, I *hate* it! he thought.

"I'm finished," he muttered. "There's just no way."

It took ten minutes of surrendering agony to regain himself. He hadn't cried like this since he was a young boy. Or since you watched the last scene of *The Miracle Worker*, his mind, irritating once more, reminded him. Oh, shut up, he thought. But there was no strength to his retaliation. It was weak and unconvincing.

All right, he thought, I can't just sit here, waiting for my murderer to reach me. There was still Marian. He had to reach her and protect her.

"Okay," he told himself determinedly. "Go down and get your water and move on—fast. That son of a bitch is probably bounding through the woods like Bambi."

The image made him smile despite the sense of near futility he felt.

Carefully, he worked his way down the remainder of the slope, using his boot heels to dig into the ground and prevent another slide. He tried to feel what new bruises and scrapes he'd added to the list he'd already had. Fuck it, he thought.

What's the difference? If I can move, I'll keep on going—and I can move.

The slope became a more gradual decline now, and in less than fifteen minutes, he had reached the edge of the lake. Had Doug actually *heard* him before? That wouldn't help the cause. Not at all.

Kneeling on the bank of the lake, he took a long swig from his bottle—the new batch wouldn't taste so good with iodine tablets in it—then pushed it below the surface of the water until it bubbled, full.

He added two iodine tablets to the bottle, recapped it, and returned it to his pack. A lot heavier now, he thought. Well, there was no help for that either. He had to have water. He'd keep the small water packets for an emergency.

He chewed on dried fruit—apricots, peaches, and pears—and an energy bar as he started around the lake. I should have brought dried prunes, he thought. Or even prune juice. Again, too late for regrets.

As he turned around the headland of the cove, he saw the dock.

"Oh, wow," he said. Was it possible that the launch made regular crossings and he could get a later one before Doug got here? Grinning hopefully, he saw himself sitting on the launch as it crossed the lake, telling the driver (the captain?) what had happened to him. On the other side, there had to be a telephone. Hell, the driver of the boat might even have a cellular phone; practically everyone did these days. He could call the state police, have them waiting at the cabin when Doug got there, and incarceration. Perfect!

He moved as quickly as he could toward the small dock. There was what looked like a bulletin board attached to the dock. The schedule, he thought. It had to be once an hour, something like that. He could be out of here long before that bastard reached this point.

He got to the dock and moved to the bulletin board, his heart beating heavily. Every hour, he primed himself. It has to be every hour. That made sense.

He stood in front of the bulletin board, staring at it blankly.

There *was* another pickup time.

At six o'clock.

That glacial sinking in his stomach again. He looked at his watch, already knowing the answer.

Three-sixteen.

Doug would get here before the launch.

He couldn't wait for it.

He closed his eyes. Goddamn it, don't cry again! he ordered himself. He felt like crying though. Hopelessness was like an icy shroud weighing him down. I'm not going to make it, he thought, frightened and incredulous.

I am simply not going to make it.

4:09 PM

He kept on going as long as he could. Finally, he had to rest. Locating a small glade surrounded by high bushes, he put down his ground pad—the earth was still damp from the rainstorm—and lay down on his back, resting the pack against a fallen tree. Sighing, he closed his eyes.

Almost immediately, he felt darkness begin to cloud his brain. He opened his eyes abruptly. No sleep, no sleep, he told himself urgently. You can't afford the time. Not with that crazy man in pursuit of him. He scowled. Why do I try to lighten things by calling him "that crazy man"? It wasn't serious enough by half. Doug had to be considered insane by any standard. No matter how many times he tried to convince himself that maybe it was all a joke, a prank, a game, he couldn't do it. Of one thing he was—and *had* to be—convinced.

If Doug overtook him, he'd use his bow and arrow. Or, worse, his golak. His last moments would be horrible. That was a given. It had to be if he was to survive.

He wished that he could settle on one state of mind. It was disconcerting if not completely distressing to keep fluctuating between total resolution and total surrender. He *had* to survive; for Marian if not himself. For his kids.

He did believe that he'd survive death however horrific that death might be. But he couldn't leave Marian behind, subject to the demented blandishments of Doug. He had no doubt that Doug would do exactly what he said in regard to Marian. The image of it chilled him and enraged him at once.

God, if I had a gun, he thought. Me, the sturdy advocate of gun control. I wish I had one now. For one use. To blow a goddamn hole through Doug. If there was punishment later for his murdering Doug, he'd accept it willingly. Self-defense, he thought. That would get him off the hook on this plane. Beyond . . . well, he'd accept whatever came his way.

He slipped out of his pack and took out his supply of food. Much good most of it would do him now. He knew now why Doug snickered as he watched Bob pack his food for the flight. He glared at the packets for almost a minute before crawling over to them quickly and picking them up. You *are* stupid, he told himself. Environmental concerns when your life is in jeopardy?

He put the envelopes back in his pack and made himself a cheese sandwich, starting to eat it with some nuts. It tasted good; he was hungrier than he realized. He took sips of water between his bites and swallows.

For dessert, he had an orange and an energy bar. Gourmet dining, he thought. Well, at least it was nourishing and filling him. He washed it all down with a big swallow of water, put the food supply in his backpack, and leaned back against it.

He threw the orange peels away. I'm *not* going to take them with me. Sue me, forest rangers. Anyway, they'd rot in time. So would you, his brain insisted on tormenting him. For several seconds, he could not prevent himself from visualizing his corpse lying on the forest floor, most of its flesh gone, eaten by bears or mountain lions.

"Oh, for Christ's sake, lay off, will you?" he pleaded with his noncooperating brain.

It had always been like that. The writer's mind, he thought. Victim of its own imagination. Not only story notions but personal ones as well, occasionally gratifying, mostly dark and negative. Shut up, he told it, knowing that it wouldn't, that it would patiently lie in wait, always prepared to pounce on him with some disturbing vision.

He tried to blank out his mind by staring up at the sky. After a while, he saw a lone hawk wheeling and banking gracefully, floating on the currents of air, looking down for prey—a mouse, a rabbit, whatever.

Like Doug, he thought . . . Patiently moving, waiting to dive down on his prey. No mouse or rabbit. Robert Hansen, freelance quarry.

Oh, for God's sake, shut up, please, he told his brain with angry depression.

As he thought it, he saw the hawk suddenly dive to its right. Then he saw the small bird trying to escape; in vain. The hawk's talons clamped onto it and the hawk swept out of sight. To dine in a treetop no doubt, he thought.

A most encouraging sight for a man on the run.

"Oh, God," he murmured.

Again, he tried to blank his mind but, in moments, found himself thinking about Doug again.

Doug had always maintained such a careful image. Dressed well, earned money, seemed to live a life beyond reproach. Well, not excessive reproach at any rate.

But it was pretense. Who was it that coined the phrase "people of the lie." Dr. Peck. Well, that was Doug. Was he aware at all of the darkness in his mind? He doubted it. Doug had, he believed, always built a shell of nonawareness around himself. He'd simply shunted aside any evidence of imperfection. Dr. Peck had called it "malignant narcissism." Perfect description of Doug's state of consciousness. He could, if he chose, avoid all this by backing off. But of course, he wouldn't. Not now.

If Doug had any perception of the hidden malignities within himself, how could he have done what he did this morning? How could he be doing what he was doing now? He had to be blinding himself to his own profound and murderous sickness. He had to force himself to be motivated by self-justification.

Killing Bob simply had to be done.

Hunted past reason, he thought. He winced at the phrase, wondering where it had come from.

He remembered then. Somewhere in *King Lear*. A perfect description of what he was going through.

He stretched his legs and arms, groaning at the multiple pains and aches he felt. How can I possibly outrun him? he thought.

Just don't think, he ordered himself. Just . . . stare up at the blue sky and the white clouds. Just rest awhile and then move on. You have a three-hour head start. If Doug had told the truth, of course. He had to have told the truth. This was a game to him. He'd played games by the rules.

The sky, the clouds, he thought. The sky, the clouds.

4:47 PM

He jolted spasmodically and opened his eyes. "Oh, *God*, no," he muttered, not even aware of speaking. He jerked up his left arm, wincing at the pain it caused. Oh, Christ, he'd slept more than twenty-five minutes!

"No good, no good," he said. I can't afford to *do* this. God knew how he was going to sleep at night, considering that Doug might well keep going in the darkness, using his flashlight. But he definitely could not afford to nap in the daytime. "Jesus, get up and move," he told himself.

It was a strain to get to his feet. What if he'd slept for an hour, more than an hour? He'd be dead already. Doug was undoubtedly coursing through the forest like a long-skilled Indian. He'd been here before as well. "Oh, Christ, move on," he told himself. "And fast."

Hastily, he put away his ground pad. It was wet on the side that had been on the ground but there was no time to worry about that. Slipping on the pack—at least he could do that efficiently now—he started walking quickly through the forest, mostly pine now, towering above him.

He stopped for a few moments to check the compass, reset himself again, and move on. The forest was too thick for him to see the mountain he'd been using as a landmark. Maybe later. He willed himself into a steady pace, striding as rapidly as he could, teeth gritted as he tried to ignore the constant flares and stabs of pain in his body and legs. I am in pitiful condition, he thought.

So what?! he countered angrily. You still have to move and move fast. Just grin and bear it, Chauncey.

His smile was scarcely one of amusement. I'll bear it but I damn sure won't grin, he informed his annoying mind.

He was crossing a sedge-covered meadow, the high growth slapping against his legs. What if I step on a rattlesnake? he thought. He kept staring at the ground, listening hard for the warning buzz of a rattlesnake tail. At least they did that. The "gentleman snake," he thought. Where had he read that? Or was it something Marian had said? On those rare occasions when they'd seen a rattler on their property, she would never allow him to kill it or phone the fire department for them to come and kill it. "It'll go away," she always said, "it's more afraid of us than we are of it." Unfailingly, he'd smile and shake his head at her kind regard for all living things, including rattlesnakes and tarantulas. She was frightened terribly by tarantulas but wouldn't kill them either or allow him to kill them.

Looking up, he saw that he was headed into a canyon bordered by dark pines. He wondered where it led. He hoped that—

"Whoa," he muttered.

A porcupine was waddling across the ground in front of him. He stared at it, wincing as he thought of what might have happened if he hadn't caught sight of it in time. Those quills looked awfully sharp. That would be all he needed to enrich the day, a bunch of porcupine quills imbedded in his legs.

He was going to say something to the porcupine like— "the right of way is yours, pal"—then changed his mind. The sound of his voice might alarm it.

After the porcupine had disappeared, he continued on, leaving the meadow and moving into the canyon.

He noticed that the ground on each side of his movement was rising, more and more precipitously as he walked. He thought of turning back and looking for another, more open route, but didn't dare. He couldn't afford to backtrack. He had to keep going forward.

Which made the moment all the more dismaying and disheartening to him as he moved into an open area of ground and discovered that he'd been advancing unwittingly along a dead-end pass.

Ahead of him lay a rocky wall, mostly bare with an occasional clump of manzanita or grass clumps growing out of its crevices.

He couldn't go back. It would be far too time-consuming. He might well run directly into Doug if he was getting close.

He was trapped.

A cold wave of panic swept through him. My God, I'm going to *die*, he thought.

"Jesus Christ." His voice was faint and trembling. Doug had won this awful game already.

He stood rooted to the spot, racked by convulsive shudders. He had never felt so helpless in his life. What now? his mind kept asking like a terror-stricken boy. What now? What now?

Then reason set in. Or what passed for reason, it occurred to him.

Was he just going to stand here and let death come visiting? Without resistance of any kind? What about Marian?

He drew in a deep, laboring breath.

"All right," he said. "All right, goddamn it."

He'd climb the fucking wall.

What?! his mind screamed. Climb it? Are you out of your goddamn mind?!

"Well, what would you like me to do, you idiot?" he growled at it. "Just stand here until transfixed by goddamn arrows, chopped to pieces by that goddamn golak?"

Okay, okay, his mind submitted. I guess it's better to die trying than doing nothing.

For a few moments, he thought excitedly that if he could make it to the top and Doug showed up down here, he could roll a boulder from the top, hit Doug, maybe even start a landslide—a goddamn avalanche.

"Well, don't go overboard," he told himself. "Just get up the damn wall first." He felt amused, almost exultant that he'd resolved to try to climb the wall. Doug wasn't going to paralyze him with fear, goddamn it! He was going to make it up this goddamn wall. "Damn right," he said. "*Damn* right."

Until he took a closer—more practical—look at the stone wall.

It was exactly that, a wall. Granted there were clefts in it, fissures, indentations, places he could place his feet, grab with his hands. But he had no experience at this kind of thing.

He had to be successful on his very first climb. There was no such thing as a second chance here.

"Shit," he muttered. If he only had that long rope Doug had—the memory made him wince—tied him up with. That way, he could fasten one end to his pack, climb with only the other end of the rope to worry about, haul up the pack after he'd reached the top.

That was impossible though. Nor could he just leave the pack behind. He couldn't survive without his food and water, sleeping bag and pad, medical supplies. They had to go with him.

First of all though, he had to examine the wall ahead of him to try to calculate a route to the top. He couldn't just start up blindly, find himself stranded halfway up.

It wasn't a smooth face, thank God. There were ridges and indentations, and he could see, on close examination, that it wasn't totally vertical after all but rose more at an angle. A steep angle, yes, but not a vertical one. And halfway up was a ledge he could rest on. If you reach it, that is, the mocking voice addressed his mind. Oh, just shut up, he answered it.

There were also bushes growing out of the wall that looked secure enough to support his weight if he took hold of them. Nodding to himself, he ran his gaze over the irregularities in the wall, some of them long cracks he could slip his feet into. He visualized a basic route for himself. With luck, he could make it. Never mind luck, he told himself. He *had* to make it.

Doug was never going to get his hands on Marian.

He realized now, however, that he had to lighten the load on his back. He'd never make it with this heavy pack dragging him down. He'd have to leave behind anything of severe weight.

First of all, the water bottle. Unscrewing its cap, he took a long drink, then emptied out almost all the remaining contents of the bottle. Was this a bad mistake? he worried. What if he didn't run across more water? Dying of thirst was not a risk he wanted to take.

He scowled at himself. First things first, he told himself. You have to make it up this wall or be caught by Doug. Nothing else mattered. Worry about water later. If you make it; the mocking voice again. Shut *up*! he told it angrily.

All right, what next? he thought. What did he absolutely have to take with him? The sleeping bag, of course. He couldn't possibly reach the cabin today; hopefully tomorrow. So he'd be sleeping out tonight; he needed the sleeping bag's warmth. He could probably do without the pad but he had to have the sleeping bag.

What else? he thought. Light stuff. Water packets. Dried fruit. Candy. Nuts, raisins. Energy bars. Jerky. Some bread. One mini-bottle of vodka. And, of course, your turkey tetrazzini, he mocked himself consciously. Yeah, he responded. Get back to reality now. Granola. Powdered milk. He'd pour out half of them. And coffee? Definitely; even if he had to drink it cold in the metal cup. He'd put the packages in his shirt pockets, under his shirt if there wasn't enough room in his pockets. It might all weigh down the front part of his body, but that would be the part against the wall. As little as possible on his back so he wouldn't be overweighted there. The sleeping bag, nothing more. He'd put the water bottle in his jacket pocket.

What else? He thought hard. The compass naturally. Sunglasses. Matches. The first-aid kit. Binoculars. Eyeglasses. The flashlight; he'd put that in his jacket pocket too. And his knife, of course.

That would have to do him.

He had his pack off now. Removing the sleeping bag, he started to roll it tight. Don't roll it, Doug's reminder struck him; ruins the fibers. Yeah, sure, he thought. I wouldn't want to ruin the fibers.

With his knife, he cut off the waist, shoulder, and sternum straps from the pack, tied them around the sleeping bag and fastened it to his upper back, a strap under each arm. Then put all the food bags and packets in his shirt and under it.

The discards he stuffed into his backpack, which he pushed behind some bushes. Why bother? he asked himself. Doug would undoubtedly find it. He shivered. Was he starting to imbue Doug with superhuman skill at tracking? He wasn't *that* good, was he? He had to have a *few* defects. Count on it anyway, he told himself. Maybe Doug wouldn't find the hidden pack or maybe he'd be astonished at the idea of his pathetic prey ascending this wall. Maybe.

He'd try to believe it anyway.

In the shirt pocket where he'd put it, he found the little booklet Marian had given him: *Survival in the Wilderness.* Of any value to him? he wondered. "Oh, what the hell," he muttered, sliding it back into his pocket. He drew in a deep breath. He was ready to go.

As ready as I'll ever be, the thought chilled him.

5:14 PM

The wall really wasn't as vertical as it first appeared but it was steep enough, Bob saw as he started climbing, carefully searching for, then using foot- and handholds in the rock. He tried to find handholds no higher than his head; somehow, it seemed to him that handholds higher than that would be more difficult to navigate. He climbed slowly and, as best he could manage, methodically. The weight of the tightly rolled sleeping bag on his back felt minimal. He'd made a good choice lightening his load that way.

It soon became clear to him that he only felt safe moving one hand or one foot at a time. He made certain that he kept his body in balance before releasing a hand or foot. The careful, snaillike progression of his upward movements pleased him somehow. Now he was intelligently fighting for his life. That was good.

He tried not to let himself become disturbed by the fact that he was getting thirsty. He could scarcely stop for a drink. Hold on 'til you reach the top, he told himself, forcing himself to believe that he was confident he'd reach the crest of the wall. Every time a twinge of doubt threatened to undo this certainty, he willfully blanked it out.

After a while, he stopped to rest although it hardly seemed like rest, clinging to a rock face like some ungainly insect. Still . . .

Against his preplan, he looked down, shutting his eyes immediately and hissing, teeth clenched. Jesus Christ, he thought. He had to be at least thirty feet above the floor of the canyon. He felt his heartbeat quicken, his breath labor, his stomach writhe. Easy, he ordered himself. Don't—look—down. You're going to make it. And if Doug comes this way—which he undoubtedly will, he'll have to climb this wall as well. With his full pack, tent, sleeping bag, grate, bow and arrow, et al.

The vision managed to amuse him. Then again, would Doug do the same thing he did, scrap everything but absolute necessities? No. He couldn't see Doug getting rid of all that expensive equipment, which would make this climb ten times as difficult. Maybe he wouldn't even attempt it, go back down the canyon, looking for an alternate route, lose time.

Better still, maybe he would attempt the climb, slip, fall, and crack his damn head open on the rocks below. That image pleased him even more. Let it be that way, he thought.

The handhold above him looked unsound. How was he going to test it?

After a minute or two of thought, he decided to hit the handhold with the heel of his right hand. Reaching up, he carefully did so, gasping as, momentarily, he felt as though he was going to fall backward. He pressed against the stone wall as hard as he could. Easy, easy, he told himself, swallowing dryly. Thirsty, he thought. He scowled. Just climb, he ordered. Forget about water.

After several moments, he reached up again and hit the handhold more cautiously with the heel of his right hand. The rock sounded hollow to him. No good, he thought, seeing himself for several seconds, as some canny mountaineer. Yes, yes, he heard himself lecturing his novice class. If the handhold sounds hollow when you hit it with the heel of your hand, it is inferior, you must find another handhold to replace it. Selah.

He grimaced, realizing suddenly how sore the palm of his right hand felt. He looked at it, wincing at the sight of the bruised skin, some of it oozing blood. He should have worn something over his hands. What, gloves, you idiot? he castigated the notion. Well, something, his mind defended. He'd think about it. If he ever got the chance to do anything, of course. Maybe clean off his palms—both of them were dirty and abraded he now saw—with some Bactine, put a little salve on them.

Which would make them slippery, you moron, scorned his mind. He sighed heavily; for a few long moments suffered a surge of negative despair washing over him.

The sun came out from behind white clouds as he continued climbing. He hadn't been aware of it but the climb, until now, had been a relatively cool if difficult one. Now he felt the heat gathering under his jacket and was glad he still had the hat on. He probably should have brought the sunscreen along as well. But, you didn't, so just forget it! he thought angrily. He felt sweat beginning to trickle across his temples and down the back of his neck. Just climb, he told himself. Ignore everything but the climb. Concentrate, Hansen.

A bush above him. He reached up and took hold of it, pulling downward.

No good! The bush pulled loose, raining dirt on his hat. It bounced off his head, making him gasp with pain. He pulled it off himself and tossed it away. So much for the aid of bushes, he thought in angry submission. He reached up carefully with his left hand and took off his hat, shaking off the dirt collected on its crown. At least, he hadn't lost his balance.

Looking up, he saw a small growth of rock jutting out

just above eye level. He took hold of it with a tight, clinging grip, then lifted his right leg to the next foothold and forced himself upward, groaning at the ache in his leg. *Am I really going to make this?* he wondered.

He elected not to think about an answer to the question.

Just above him, he saw the ledge he'd picked out when he'd mapped his climbing route before starting out. *Thank God,* he thought. *A chance to rest.* He reached up eagerly to pull himself onto the ledge.

Moving too fast, he started losing his balance. *"No!"* he cried out, panicked, pressing himself against the rock face as tightly as he could, wavering between balance and loss of it. Gasping for breath, he clutched as hard as he could at a rocky outcrop on the ledge. *Don't fall, don't fall,* he told himself, jamming both feet in their holds as rigidly as he could. *Don't fall!*

Balance returned at long last and slowly, carefully, using his legs more than his arms, he worked his way onto the ledge and eased himself over onto his back. He shifted the sleeping bag upward to form a pillow and groaned in relief, eyes shut, mouth open as he sucked in air. It seemed harder to breathe now. Was it because he was up higher or was it just his exhaustion? No answer to that, he realized.

After several minutes, he unzipped his jacket and felt around in his shirt pockets until he located the small bottle of Bactine. *My God, they're shaking,* he thought in dismay, looking at his hands. He'd never make it to the top if he couldn't control that.

He put down the bottle on the ledge and stretched out his

arms, shaking them to restore circulation. Then he opened the bottle of Bactine and rubbed some on both palms, wincing at the sting. Putting away the bottle, he wondered what else he *could* do for his palms since rubbing salve on them would be stupidly impractical.

Tape, he thought, wondering where the notion came from. He reached around inside his jacket again until he'd located the roll of bandage tape. Removing it, he tried to find the end of it; it seemed impossible with his shaking hands. "Come on, come on," he muttered. "Where the hell are you?"

It took him more than a minute to find the end of the tape. Pulling it loose, he began to turn the roll tightly around his right hand, grimacing as the tape was pressed across the palm. Okay, that's enough, he thought, do the left hand now.

The tape ran out when he had only wrapped a few turns around his left hand. "Damn," he said. Why didn't he bring a new tape instead of taking the used one from the bathroom cabinet? "Shouldn't you be buying yourself a new first-aid kit?" he remembered Marian saying. "Honey, I'm only going to be hiking for a few days, I'm not going to need major medical attention," he'd replied.

"Yeah, sure," he said. "Idiot." He tossed the used tape roll off the ledge, heard it bounce once off a rock below then heard no more. Messing the environment, Dougie boy, he thought. So sorry.

He drew in a long, shuddering breath of air and stared up at the sky. It was brilliantly blue with puffy white clouds drifting slowly. Beautiful, the thought came, unbidden. Immediately, he reacted against it. What the hell does natural beauty matter when a crazy man is tracking me to kill me?

He sighed wearily. Should he try a ten-minute nap? the

thought occurred. Sure, that's a good idea, he told himself. Turn on your left side to get comfortable and plummet to your death.

Bracing himself, he forced his gaze downward. "Jesus," he muttered. He must be more than a hundred feet up by now. Quickly, he averted his eyes, feeling his heartbeat jolt, his stomach roil again. *Don't-look-down-for-chrissake*, he ordered himself. Yessir, he answered.

He considered, for a few moments, getting one of his water packets out, vetoing the idea almost immediately. He might need that water desperately later on. And he couldn't assume that he was going to run across some water later— a lake, a river, a stream, a creek, a pond even. No, he'd wait, be sensible.

He caught his breath as he looked up at the sky again. A butterfly was fluttering a few yards above the ledge. It was multicolored, its wings looking as though they had been painted by some artist with a stunning taste in color and design. He saw green and brown and yellow, even tiny spots of red.

Well, hell, he thought. It's beautiful, no other word for it. It was ironic that at this perilous moment in his life, this exquisite life form should be fluttering above him like this. It's a sign, he imagined. Something is telling me that there's still beauty in the world so I won't give up, so I'll keep trying.

His smile was sad but accepting. No sign, he thought. No message from the cosmos. Nonetheless, it did provide a brief, pleasurable moment for him. It was true.

In spite of everything, there was still beauty in the world.

Standing carefully, he ran his gaze across the rock face just above him, then placed his right foot in an opening in the rock just above his knee. The opening was deep and gratefully he pushed his entire foot inside it, wedging it there.

The handhold above was a wide vertical crack in the granite. Tentatively, he put his hand inside it, trying to locate a grip. But the opening was too wide. After several moments, he fisted his hand, his palm facing the left side of the crack. He did the same with his left hand, then started to lift his right foot.

It wouldn't move, it was stuck.

"Oh, God," he murmured. What now? He realized that he shouldn't have put his entire foot into the opening. He wiggled his boot, trying to free it, realizing that his left leg was now forced outward, that he was losing balance. No, he thought. After all this? To fall now? It was too much.

"No, goddamn it, no," he said, enraged and terrified at once. "I am not going to fall. I'm not!"

He moved his right boot more strenuously, trying to release it from its trap. His fisted hands began to ache. He ignored them. Get the goddamn foot out first, he told himself.

The right boot jerked out from its hold and suddenly he was hanging in space, held up only by the two fisted hands inside the vertical crack. The pain in them was agonizing, the pull on his arms excruciating. All right, this is it, he thought abruptly. Give it up. Forget it. Just let go. Fall. Die. There'll be pain but then it will all be over. You'll survive, move on. Time to test your beliefs, boy. Let go, maybe this won't qualify as suicide.

But the entire time he thought it, to his astonishment, his legs were straining upward, right foot feeling for the hold it had been in before.

He found it and instantly the pain in his fisted hands and

hanging arms was eased and he was standing against the wall again, still alive. Son of a bitch, he thought. Son of a *bitch*. I really don't want to die. To die would be too easy actually. He had responsibilities.

He found himself chuckling at the notion, amused at himself, amused at life. One clung to it as hard as possible. Funny. Crazy. But funny.

He gritted his teeth. All right, he thought. Pain and all, he was going to keep on climbing. He was going to reach the top. He was going to protect his wife. He was going to kill Doug Crowley. Many responsibilities, he thought. Too many to let yourself die. Forge on. You're a total mess but forge on.

Slowly, teeth remaining gritted every moment, he climbed the vertical crack, using his fisted hands—the tape *did* help somewhat he was glad to note—and, very guardedly, putting his right foot, then his left into the crack, twisting them slightly to strengthen their hold but careful not to wedge them in too tightly and make them difficult to pull free.

He fell into a slow, unthinking rhythm of movements as he ascended the crack. Right foot, right hand, left foot, left hand. Maybe I'll go into rock climbing, he thought once. Then, after scorning the idea, shutting down his brain again and keeping himself a slow, laborious climbing machine, inching his way up the rock face.

At one point, he began to suffer spastic contractions in the muscles of his legs. As though he had expected this, with no reaction of surprise or fear, he hung down one leg at a time until the contractions eased. Then he started climbing again.

He lost all sense of time. Life had diminished to the climb. There was nothing else but the climb. He forgot about Doug, about Marian, about his very existence. There was only one thing. Climbing to the top of this wall. Slowly. Carefully. Patiently. Methodically. Reaching the top.

Nothing else mattered.

When he reached the crest of the rock face and raised his head above the edge, he found himself looking directly into the dead eyes of an enormous rattlesnake.

Expressionless, he stared at the snake as its tail buzzed loudly, vibrating back and forth so rapidly he couldn't follow the movement.

This is too much, the thought came quietly. It can't be true. I made the climb just to end like this?

He didn't move. The rattling of the snake's tail slowed.

Remembering the bear, then, he began to speak.

"Listen," he said, "I'm not going to hurt you." As if I could, added his mind. "And you're not going to hurt me. Just . . . turn around and move away so I can get up here. *Come* on. You're just scared to see me. You don't want to hurt me. Just turn around and go away. That's a boy."

The snake remained motionless. Its tail was still now. It didn't move though. Its lifeless eyes kept staring into Bob's.

"Come on now," he told the snake in as gentle a voice as he could summon being breathless, his throat dry.

The standoff seemed to continue for minutes but Bob was sure it hadn't been that long before the snake abruptly uncoiled itself and glided away, disappearing into some brush.

Bob crawled weakly onto the crest of the rock wall and fell on his back, breathing with difficulty. Jesus, he kept thinking. *Jesus*. I did it again. First the black bear. Now the rattlesnake. What am I, some animal guru?

For some reason, he began to think about karma. He believed in it, didn't he? That being the case, what in the hell had he done in his last lifetime or lifetimes to justify all these things happening to him? Who was he, Judas Iscariot for God's sake?

He realized then that, as far as he knew, snakes probably couldn't hear. They kept sticking their tongues out—why, to smell or what? They could probably feel vibrations. But *hear*? Not likely, and there he'd been emoting philosophy to the snake. "Jesus Christ," he muttered. Don't make a spiritual experience of this, Hansen. He hissed, shaking his head. What a dimwit.

He made himself look over the side of the rock wall. It was a cliff, by God, that's what it was. He gaped down at the floor of the canyon far below. My God, he thought. *I* climbed up here? *Me*, the worst-conditioned man in California?

It seemed an inappropriate time for laughter but he couldn't help it. And Doug would have to climb it carrying all that crap on his back! It was hysterical. He couldn't stop laughing at the thought, his body shaking, tears running down his cheeks. Unbelievable, he thought again and again. *Unbelievable*.

After several minutes, he checked his watch.

It had taken him more than an hour to make the climb. No time to rest.

He had to move on.

6:37 PM

The sun was going down now. How soon before darkness? he wondered. That would be a fearful time. Should he keep going in the dark? It might gain him time over Doug. But was it safe? Animals came out at night. He might inadvertently step on a rattlesnake. He might slip and fall, break a bone. Anything might happen.

He'd think about it later. While it was still light, he had to put some distance between himself and Doug. Despite a body that felt more exhausted and aching with every passing hour, he had to keep going. For a short while after successfully climbing the rock face, he'd felt exhilarated, as though he was getting his second wind.

Not now. He knew exactly how tired he felt, how many aches and pains he felt. When he'd pulled the tape off his hands—he should have left it on—he'd pulled away loose skin. Now his palms were partially raw, still oozing blood. He'd put a bit of Bactine on them, stinging them, but did it help any? Maybe he'd try to bandage them later if there was time.

He walked infirmly through shadowy ravines and canyons. He suspected that some of the plants he was thrashing through were poison ivy or poison oak because of their three-leaf pattern. All I need, he thought, smiling despite the uneasiness of the thought.

Trudging through a spruce and hemlock grove, he heard the sound of moving water ahead. Thank God, he thought. He'd finished what little water he'd left in his bottle. He'd been desperately afraid of finding no more water. That would be a real catastrophe. The packets of water wouldn't last long at all.

Emerging from the grove of trees, he saw a quickly moving stream ahead, its current splashing over gray rocks, spraying in the air.

Moving down to the stream, he lay in front of it gingerly and used his hands to ladle water into his mouth. It was icy cold and the taste of it made him groan with pleasure. It felt good on his hands as well.

He filled his water bottle, added two iodine tablets—he hoped he hadn't made a mistake drinking directly from the stream—then slumped down to sit beside the stream, hissing at the biting pain in his rectum. *Bastard*, he thought.

Where was Doug now? he wondered. It was the first time in hours he'd allowed himself to estimate how close Doug might be behind him. He *was* behind, wasn't he? He had to be. If he had really abided by the rules of his demented game, he'd given Bob a three-hour head start. The main question now was: Did he also climb that rock face? Or did he backtrack, knowing a faster way to overtake Bob? If that was the case . . .

He shivered convulsively. There was the problem. He couldn't outthink Doug. He simply didn't understand him. He was sure of only one thing: that Doug would persist in this madness until the very end. He probably wasn't even allowing himself to consider that what he was doing was insane. He's crossed the line and feels justified, Bob thought.

And, of course, he couldn't let Bob live now, not after everything that had happened.

Bob had to die.

He swallowed dryly, took another swallow of the cold water from his bottle.

Or Doug had to die, the reverse thought came.

One of them wasn't going to survive this insanity, that was certain.

I really should move on, he thought. But he was so *tired*. He had to rest awhile longer, he just had to. I'm so tired, so damn *tired*, he thought. And I hurt so much. He'd like to just give up. If I was single, I *would*, he realized. But he had to get to Marian before Doug could reach her.

Get some goddamn energy inside yourself for chrissake, he told himself suddenly.

"Yes," he said. Unzipping his jacket he took out an energy bar and some dried fruit, began to eat. What else was there? He felt around in his shirt and, feeling the booklet, drew it out. He took the folding glasses from his jacket pocket and put them on.

" 'Survival in the wilderness,' " he read aloud, adding, "Subtitle: *With Some Crazy Bastard Chasing You. Life Support Technology, Inc.*"

He opened the booklet and read the copyright date: 1969. Right up to date, perfect, he reacted. He looked at the opposite page. *Although we may be unable to control our circumstances,* it read, *we can control how we operate and live within them.* True, he thought. But will I be capable of doing that?

He turned to the next page and read: "The purpose of this booklet is to aid and insure your survival and rescue under wilderness conditions in North America."

Reassuring, he thought. Except that the booklet lacks a chapter entitled *What to Do If a Maniac Is Chasing You to Kill You.*

The introduction mentioned five basic needs. *Water. Food. Heat. Shelter.* The last one surprised him. *Spiritual Needs.* Sounds good, he thought, although I'd be glad to exchange all those needs for a loaded rifle. Whoever wrote the booklet simply hadn't prepared it for a prey in flight. He drew in deep, trembling breaths. Maybe Spiritual Needs *was* a necessity. He'd hold that in abeyance.

Remember, the booklet read, *we tend to magnify the hazards of strange and unfamiliar surroundings.* True enough, he thought. But how was it possible to overmagnify Doug chasing him with a bow and arrow through these unfamiliar surroundings.

"Oh, well," he said. Another trembling breath. The booklet wasn't designed for that sort of thing. What it *was* designed for could well be of value to him. Bless Marian for secreting it in the pocket of his shirt. It might make all the difference.

He ran his gaze down the list of basic suggestions. Treat injuries. Shelter and fire of prime concern. Select a site close to water. Signal fires? Hardly. *Assume that you are going to have a few days' wait for rescue.* Double hardly. He had to keep on moving.

"Stay clean," he read. A daily shower with hot water and soap. Keep underwear and socks as clean as possible. Keep your hands clean. Avoid handling food with the hands. Sterilize heating utensils. Hardly again. He just wanted to make it alive and first to Doug's cabin, then drive away with Marian like a bat out of hell. A shower a day with hot water and soap? Sure.

" 'Fear of the unknown weakens one's ability to think and plan,' " he read aloud. That I buy, he thought. I'm not going to let that happen though.

He turned the pages rapidly. No point in studying anything until (or unless) the need came up. *Snow Blindness and Frostbite.* Not likely he'd need to consult that section. *Snake Bite.* He hoped he wouldn't need that entry. *Fire Starting.* Absolutely. Bless you again, Marian. *Water.* Undoubtedly.

Temperature and Wind Chill Chart. Doubtful. *Shelters.* More than likely. *Food.* Definitely; he hoped the booklet described wild food he might run across—berries, seeds, roots, plants. On that the booklet could prove invaluable. *Signaling.* Not very likely. *Snares.* Wouldn't it be wonderful if he could catch Doug in one of the illustrated ones—the hanging snare, the dead fall, the "twitch up" trigger snare. But they were all for smaller game. And how could he possibly guess exactly which way Doug was going to come? Moreover, even if he set up a snare, Doug would certainly recognize it in an instant and all that careful preparation would turn out to be a waste of time.

Fishing Hints. Definitely a possibility. He was going to need some solid food if he was going to maintain the strength to reach the cabin. *Knots.* Probably useless—unless he could get one of them around Doug's neck. Didn't he wish.

"Travel" was the last section. He saw the opening sentence. THE BEST ADVICE IS: STAY PUT.

"Sorry," he said. "Bad advice."

He turned to the last page and, despite all weariness and anxiety, had to chuckle at the titles of reference books by Euell Gibbons. *Stalking the Wild Asparagus; Stalking the Blue-Eyed Scallop; Stalking the Healthful Herbs.*

"Those are the titles I really need," he said.

He stiffened abruptly at a noise across the stream.

Frozen, heart beginning to throb jerkily, he saw, in a clearing some fifteen yards distant, a bear with two cubs.

He assumed that she was a black bear—didn't Doug say they were the only bears in this region? This bear was cinnamon-brown though and while one of the cubs was the same color, the second one was dark brown with orange tips on its ears.

What do I do now? he thought. He saw no answer but one—to remain immobile. If he jumped up and ran, the mother bear, thinking to protect her cubs, would likely pursue him. He doubted if shouting at it and waving his arms would dissuade a mother bear. And certainly he could not expect to speak it out of attacking. All this thought in a few seconds as he sat unmoving, afraid he might cough or sneeze or make the slightest noise.

A swooping movement in the air caused his gaze to jerk upward. A huge bald eagle was descending quickly in a shallow glide, then hovering above the bears. The cubs scattered in terror, followed protectively by their mother.

But the eagle wasn't interested in them. Could it have possibly lifted one of them if it *had* been interested? Bob wondered.

It paid no attention to the cubs though, instead suddenly sweeping over the stream, braking wildly, then dropping like a stone into the water to grab a large fish in its talons.

Bob twitched as the mother bear came charging across the clearing, heading for the stream. As it thrashed into the water in an ungainly lunge, the eagle tried desperately to rise and carry away the flopping, struggling fish. It wasn't strong enough however and as the mother bear came too close, it let go of the fish and soared up rapidly into the air. The bear braked clumsily in a splash of water and seized the fish in her mouth, then carried it back to her cubs.

As the three of them disappeared into the woods to supper on the fish, Bob stood on unexpectedly shaky legs, braced himself, then started along the bank of the stream as quickly as he could.

He'd cross it later. When he was—hopefully—well out of range of mother bear and her cubs.

7:22 PM

How soon would it be dark now? he wondered. Did he have another hour of light—or, at least, enough light to see his way? He'd have to hope and pray for that. *Pray?* he reacted. Somehow, the notion struck him as hypocritically absurd. He had to make this on his own. Whatever his beliefs, he had to go it alone. There was no other way. Prayer would only distract him now—or worse, give him false hope.

Up ahead, he heard the sound of water. This was much louder than the sound of the stream; rough and rushing water, how wide he couldn't imagine. Would it even be possible to cross?

Four minutes later, he knew. This was a river, more than twenty feet wide, its current so rapid that he knew immediately he couldn't ford it as he and Doug had done yesterday. There was no possible way he could wade across it; he'd be instantly swept away in the racing current.

Did he *have* to cross it? he wondered suddenly. Reaching into his jacket pocket, he took out the compass and checked it.

His cheeks puffed out as he released a dismal exhalation. *"Naturally,"* he muttered. The river had to be crossed. Unless Doug had given him inaccurate instructions about using the compass. Was that possible? He found himself unable to believe it. Above all, Doug would want this chase to be authentic.

It would be of no satisfaction at all to him to win this game by cheating. He didn't have to cheat anyway. Bob was sure that Doug had total confidence in his ability to win this awful game.

But how was he to cross the river? There seemed only one way and that a perilous one—to step—or jump—from one boulder to another. But where? He moved along the bank of the river—its current sounded thunderous to him—looking for a grouping of boulders that might serve his need.

About fifty yards down he came across a spot where the river seemed somewhat narrower and a possible crossing existed in a pattern of boulders. He stared at them uneasily. They were certainly big enough to step on but all of them looked wet from the rush of water splashing over them. Keep looking, he thought. He couldn't though. There wasn't time for a leisurely search of the river, looking for possible crossing spots. How far could he assume that Doug was behind him? *Had* he climbed the same rock face? Or had he taken another route? An easier route.

A faster route.

Shuddering, Bob realized that he had to make up his mind immediately. He'd try stepping—once jumping—from boulder to boulder. What else could he do?

He stood motionless by the bank of the torrentlike river and tried to brace himself for the attempt at crossing. He couldn't fall in; that was out of the question. Out of the question? he thought with a bitter smile. It wasn't out of the question at all. It was a matter of life or death. If he fell into the river, he'd be drowned or smashed to pieces against a boulder.

He sighed exhaustedly, almost allowing himself the option

of simply sitting down and waiting for Doug to overtake him, kill him. God knew it would be easier than what he was planning to do on the slippery boulders. An arrow in his chest— more likely in his back—and it would all be over. This part of the torment anyway. He knew that he'd survive his death. What came afterward, he'd have to face, have to accept.

But then, again—always again—there was Marian. He simply couldn't leave her to be victimized by Doug. He had no doubt whatever that Doug would do exactly as he said— cajole and sympathize, pull out every performing stop until he'd finally managed to convince Marian that he had died accidentally, that Doug felt desolate about it, that he'd start to move in on her, psychologically at first, then physically.

Bob felt his body tensing at the image—No, goddamn it, he thought. "No, goddamn it!" he said furiously. It wasn't going to happen that way. He was going to live. Dying was too easy. He wasn't going to take that route. That route was surrender.

He untied the sleeping bag and removed it. It would throw him off balance on his back. He hung it loosely around his neck—when he got far enough across the river he'd toss the bag to the opposite bank. He had to keep his boots on; he knew that. Barefooted, he'd slip on the boulder tops almost immediately.

He emptied his water bottle. That took some weight off him. Maybe he could throw the bottle to the opposite bank as well when he'd gotten close enough to it.

What else? Any other weight he could eliminate? No, there was nothing. It was time to go.

The first boulder was about five feet from the bank. Too far to jump. He'd have to get his boots and socks wet, no help for that. The current along the bank was slower than it was in the center of the river—a massive boulder farther back divided the current and decreased its rushing impetus.

Taking a deep breath (Okay, if I really *do* have a guardian angel, this is the time for you to help me out, the thought flitted across his mind), he stepped into the water and moved quickly to the first boulder, clambered onto it with both knees. The water was, as expected, icy cold and the boulder slippery wet. He wavered to the right and left, until he'd managed to get balanced.

Okay, first step, he thought. It was amazing to him what a sense of satisfaction he felt. Like the feeling he'd gotten after successfully climbing that rock face. I'll beat you yet, you son of a bitch, his mind addressed Doug.

Now the current of the river was at full speed. With infinite slowness, he braced himself on one foot, then the other and stood, holding both arms extended to help him maintain his balance. Next step, he told himself.

He drew in several deep breaths and stepped across the small gap onto the next boulder. Here we go, he thought.

He gasped in sudden shock as his right boot sole slipped on the wet boulder top. "No!" he cried, falling to his knees on the boulder and rocking back and forth, arms extended again, rising and lowering quickly like the wings of a bird in a frantic attempt to gain his balance.

When he felt secure, he drew in deep, shivering breaths and stared at the plunging movement of the river in front of him. I'm not going to make it, he thought. The next boulder was more than two feet away, the one beyond that even farther away.

A wave of despair made him groan. For moments, he had

an urge to throw himself in the water and let the river take him where it chose, whether to safety or, more probably, to battered death. He had to struggle against the urge. Live! he ordered himself. You have to live! This time the order almost didn't take, he felt so helpless, so completely desolate.

Only after several minutes of crouching on the boulder had passed did he reacquire enough resolution to go on. Inching himself around, he took several chest-filling breaths, then raised himself slowly and after several moments' hesitation, stepped back to the boulder he'd left. This time, he didn't slip. He considered jumping to the bank, then dropped the idea. Why bother? he thought. My shoes and socks are already wet anyway.

Stepping down into the cold water, he regained the bank, thinking one word, over and over.

Retreat.

He had to walk along the riverbank for almost twenty minutes before he came across the fallen tree. It lay like a bridge across the now slightly narrower river, its pulled-up roots on one side, its foliage on the other. The foliage was still fully grown; the tree must have fallen recently. Good luck for me, he thought. Maybe I have a guardian angel after all.

The problem was that light was fading quickly now. Up above the forest growth, it was probably still daylight. But under the heavy growth of fir and spruce, shadows were darkening. He had to cross the river fast. His compass heading was still the same.

Fortunately, the huge roots on the bank and the limbed and branched foliage on the opposite bank held the trunk of the tree well above the surging current. It looked as though he could ease along the trunk, a leg on each side, his boots a few inches above the swift movement of the water.

He checked his watch. It was getting close to eight o'clock. Thank God for daylight saving, he thought again. But it was going to be dark soon. He'd have to stop, try to light a fire Doug couldn't spot, try to get some sleep and be off again at the first moment of dawn.

Climbing over the damp, gnarled roots of the tree, he crawled out onto the trunk, then straddled it. He'd guessed— barely accurate—that the darting surface of the river was several inches below the bottoms of his boots.

Methodically, he began to inch his way along the rough texture of the trunk, wincing at the pain each movement caused, particularly on the rawness of his palms. Why did he pull off the tape before? He could have left it on until he reached the cabin.

Reached the cabin . . . he thought. Was it really going to happen?

"Well, if it isn't, what the *hell* are you going to all this trouble for?" he snarled at himself. Get *with* it, Hansen. You're crossing the river successfully. You're still ahead of Doug. You may ache and throb and smart and God knows what but you're still alive. That's what counts, isn't it?

He saw now that he was close enough to the opposite bank of the river to throw his sleeping bag there, his water bottle. Stopping, he carefully removed the sleeping bag from around his neck and began to fasten the straps around it as tightly as he could so that it wouldn't open up when he threw it.

First, he threw his water bottle across the remaining space, gasping in dread as it bounced off the tree foliage; for a few seconds, it looked as though it was going to be deflected into the river. Then it fell to the ground of the bank and he groaned with relief. He had to be more careful with the strapped-up sleeping bag.

It was easier than he thought it would be—although the tree trunk shifted slightly under him as he raised his right arm to fling the sleeping bag, the tightly strapped bag flew past the edge of the tree foliage and landed smartly on the riverbank. Good! he thought. Maybe things are going my way at last.

Then it happened.

Stunned, his hands jerked off the tree trunk and he toppled to his right as, in the distance, high and echoing, he heard Doug shouting *"Bobby!"*

The second echo was engulfed by roaring water as he plunged beneath its leaping, frigid surface. Instantly he was swept along by the swirling, plummeting current, feeling the icy cold of it knifing through his clothes. He fought to reach the surface and, for a flash of seconds, was able to gulp in air. Then he was beneath the water again, kicking and flailing helplessly against its surging pull.

He surfaced again and watched in shock as he was hurtled by a huge jagged rock. If I'd hit it! The horrifying thought coursed his mind. Then his brain was blanked as he continued tumbling over and under the rushing water, trying in vain to struggle toward the riverbank. He had to reach the bank. If he kept on tumbling this way, he'd be pounded to death on the jagged boulders all along the river.

He had no control though. Like a weighted cork, he was flung above and beneath the turbulent velocity of the water. He had to get to the other bank. If he stayed in the river, sooner or later he was bound to be smashed against a boulder or a sunken tree.

Suddenly the river swept him into a boulder-rimmed pool where he was dragged into an overhang and felt himself being tugged down by the cold, dark water. He tried to lift his legs but it seemed as though a huge magnet were holding them down. Unable to fight his way up, he felt the maelstrom sucking him down. Abruptly he was dragged down more then ten feet and his ears began to pop. I'm dead! he thought. It's over!

With unexpected suddenness, he heard a voice shout in his ears, "Swim out of it!"

Unquestioning, he forced himself onto his stomach and began to kick as powerfully as he could, breast-stroking with all the strength he could summon. His lungs and chest ached from held breath, his eyes were wide and staring, terrified.

Abruptly he was flung from the whirlpool as though some unseen force had grabbed his body and hurled him through the water.

He gasped in air as he burst through the surface. Just in front of him, he saw another fallen tree, a number of logs trapped against it. Frantically, he clutched at a branch of the tree, breath laboring, his expression blank as he looked around expecting to see Doug on the riverbank; someone; anyone. There was no one though. He stared into the confusion of his mind and thought: *Who shouted at me?*

9:09 PM

When he had dragged himself infirmly from the river, he found himself unable to stand. He tried repeatedly; in vain. His legs felt devoid of strength and he kept flopping over like some hapless rag doll.

Finally, shaking with cold, his entire body aching from his

harrowing experience in the river, he half crawled, half pulled himself away from the riverbank until he reached a fallen tree. Working his way beneath its trunk, with weak, fitful movements, he pulled as many dead leaves around himself as he could reach. It helped a little to abate his chilled body. Shivering, with occasional violent spasms, he lay beneath the tree, his body feeling so heavy he was sure he would never be able to move on again.

Only his brain kept moving.

Had it been an actual voice? Had something beyond himself come to his rescue?

He didn't realize that he was smiling cynically at the concept. What he had heard, undoubtedly, was an audible expression of his own subconscious. Somewhere along the line, he had read that the only way to escape a whirlpool was to swim out of it. Now that he recalled, it was Randy who had told him that. He'd gone on a river rafting trip, been tossed from the raft, and sucked down into a whirlpool. He must have read about swimming out of it and had done so, thank God.

Anyway, he'd told his father about it and, obviously, Bob had remembered it and, in the extreme peril of the moment, had produced what seemed to be an audible voice telling him to swim out of the whirlpool. It would be comforting to believe that a guardian angel had saved him. But he couldn't. He couldn't allow himself to slip into such a deluding state of conviction. He'd become dependent on it. God forbid, complaisant in it. And that was out of the question, unacceptable. He still had to depend on himself to reach Marian. And there was a far more serious threat extant than whirlpools.

There was Doug.

A shudder racked his body. God, he was cold! He was

going to have to move and soon. He had to retrieve his sleeping bag and water bottle, try to light a fire, attempt to dry his clothes—or, at least, dry them as much as he could. He hated having to go back up the river. He must have been swept along for quite a distance, perhaps gaining an unlooked for gain on Doug. But there was no help for it. He had to have the sleeping bag or he'd never make it through the night.

He tried to avoid thinking about where Doug was but it was impossible for him to do it.

He couldn't believe—he mustn't *let* himself believe—that Doug had actually seen him crossing the river on the fallen tree. The forest growth was just too thick— and Doug's echoing shout had come from high above.

Most likely—he hoped—Doug had been high on a ridge and had—with terrifying coincidence—shouted Bob's name simply to remind him that the pursuit was still on. Not that he needed reminding. He knew Doug had no intention of abandoning the chase.

The thing was —the question made Bob shudder uncontrollably—how far behind *was* Doug?

Leaving the question that preyed on his mind almost every moment, consciously or otherwise.

Was he going to make it?

By the time he'd found the sleeping bag and water bottle, darkness had fallen.

Fortunately, his flashlight still worked. If it hadn't he would never have been able to locate the sleeping bag.

He unstrapped it, opened it up, and put it across his shoulders to try to warm himself a little. As the darkness deepened, the air grew more and more chilly, making him shiver almost constantly. I'm going to get sick if I don't start getting some warmth in my system. God, but he could use Doug's brandy flask right now. He'd save his one bottle of vodka.

Filling his water bottle from the river and adding two iodine tablets to it, he moved away from the river, into the forest, shining the flashlight beam on the ground so he wouldn't accidentally run across a rattlesnake or step on a rock or into a hole and damage himself worse than he already was.

His mind wandered uncontrollably as he moved through the forest. Could Doug see his flashlight beam? Was Doug evil? Anagram: vile. And evil spelled backward is *live*. Any meaning there? Probably not. Is it evil to live? Evil *not* to live?

A wet sneeze broke his idle train of thought. Great! he thought. Next stop, pneumonia.

He heard Marian's voice in his mind, telling him, "Now you know you're going to enjoy it, Bob."

Right, Marian, he answered her mentally. Loving every moment of it. Wish you were here.

He sneezed again, more loudly. Damn it! his mind raged.

Well, forget the anger, he ordered himself. Find a place where you can stop for the night, get a small fire going, eat some food, start to dry your clothes as best you can.

He realized, for the first time, that his hat was gone. Oh, big surprise, he mocked himself. It probably went the first second you fell into the river.

He ran across a patch of berries and checked the survival booklet. They were blackberries, edible. He stopped long enough to eat some and put a few handfuls of them in his jacket pocket. Stalking the Wild Blackberry, his mind felt compelled to observe. Oh, shut up, he responded irritably.

He came across a ring of boulders near a steep rise. Perfect, he thought. He climbed inside. Was it just his imagination or was it warmer there? Possible, he thought. The boulders might have been in sunlight all or most of the day and, now, were radiating some of the absorbed heat. Whatever the case—he'd even accept imagination if it came to that—it did feel slightly warmer inside the boulder ring. Maybe it was because there was no movement of air. Whatever, he thought. It felt good.

As quickly as he could, he clambered out of the ring, leaving his water bottle and sleeping bag there and, hastily, gathered some dry grass and twigs for kindling, a few small branches. Did he dare look for a log? He shook his head. He could only afford to burn a fire—and a small one at that—for a short while; long enough to help him dry his clothes a little bit. He had no hope of drying everything completely; they were too wet—especially his boots.

Returning to the ring of boulders with his fire makings, he scraped and dug a hole with his knife and lay the dry grass in its bottom. Happily, the match container had remained dry and he ignited the dry grass, laying the twigs across it one by one until all of them were burning. The smoke stung his eyes a little but he ignored it, the warmth of the flames felt so good to him.

As fast as he could move, he removed his jacket shirt and undershirt and wrung them out over a boulder, squeezing as much water out of them as he possibly could. The open sleeping bag wrapped around him, he began to dry first the undershirt, then the shirt. He had removed all the food packets from his shirt and jacket pockets. Most of it was intact except for the bread, which had been turned into a soggy mess by the river. He tossed it over his shoulder, thinking how nice it would be if some stern-visaged environmentalist would suddenly materialize to scold him for tossing away the bread so carelessly.

"I'm sorry about that," he heard himself addressing the nonexistent environmentalist. "By the way, could you help me to escape a maniac who's chasing me?"

While he did what he could to dry his wrung-out undershirt and shirt, he ate an energy bar, some turkey jerky, the rest of the cheese, and some blackberries, washing it all down with cold water. He hoped he wasn't eating too much. How much more was he going to need? Was he going to reach the cabin tomorrow?

He fantasized briefly about roast chicken. The way Marian made it, with apricot sauce. How he'd love to have some of it right now. Was it possible that he could catch a trout tomorrow? That would taste wonderful. He remembered how delicious it had been when Doug fried one up.

Somehow, that seemed ages ago, the thought occurred. It was almost impossible for him to recollect. The two of them sitting together, well fed, brandy-laced coffee to drink, conversing amiably—well, almost amiably.

And now Doug was chasing him like some hunter tracking an animal.

He couldn't help shaking his head. How could he have known Doug all these years, yet never had a hint, an inkling, of what lurked beneath that bluff, seemingly affable demeanor?

The answer, of course, was obvious now. He'd never really known Doug at all. Doug *was* an actor after all, and in life, he played as convincing a role as he had, many times, in television, films, or on little theater stages.

Add to that the fact that their relationship had been completely superficial, based almost entirely on casual socializing with Doug and Nicole.

Now he could consider it all with more depth.

Doug was overly proud. He denied—to himself and certainly to others—whatever moral imperfections he had. He had developed an arrogance—disguised as pretension-laced humor—that made him reject—even personally attack—any evidence of those imperfections. What did Peck call it?

In a few moments, he remembered, nodding. "Malignant narcissism." Everybody out of step but you.

Every submission to the dark temptations engendered by his moral imperfections undoubtedly made Doug weaker by the year, constantly opening the path to further—darker—temptations. Now he had submitted to these temptations without recognizing them as submissions. He had lost his freedom of choice. Good was lost as an option. Only evil remained.

Was it the cold or the thought that made Bob shudder so convulsively? He didn't know. But *was* that the actual answer? That Doug was uncontrollably evil now?

Did evil run in families? Was it passed along from generation to generation by some terrible genetic regression? Had it been Doug's father? His mother? Was he actually not to blame for all this, in essence a victim of a dark transmission of genes he knew nothing about?

Was Doug suffering for any of this? He didn't seem to be. Or maybe it was all willpower, a determination not to allow himself to suffer. To maintain an unyielding conviction that he was in total control, "on top of things."

Yet, somewhere, deep inside—how deep only God knew—there might well be some kind of fear, a dread that his constant pretense would break down and be lost. That he would then be forced to come face-to-face with the actuality of his nature.

No. Bob shook his head. He couldn't believe it. Doug had surrendered any possibility of self-awareness. His conscience had been, to all intents and purposes, obliterated. Only his will was left.

The fire didn't burn very long. And Bob felt too exhausted to climb out of the ring and find more branches. He had managed to almost dry his undershirt, underpants, and socks, half dry his shirt and trousers. His jacket would have to stay wet. In the warmth of the day tomorrow—God help me if it rains, he thought—the jacket might not be too uncomfortable. If it was warm enough he could even drape it over his shoulders and hope the sun would dry it.

As for his boots—hopeless.

He was getting sleepy now; it was almost ten o'clock. But he thought it advisable—maybe it was little more than a ghoulish impulse—to take an inventory of his physical afflictions.

1. His right wrist still aching from when Doug had dragged him out of the water.
2. His right palm bruised and infected, his left palm abraded, both of them scabbing.
3. His back and stomach still hurting from where Doug had punched him.
4. His right side still aching from his fall on Sunday.
5. His right arm and shoulder still hurting from grabbing onto that branch when he slid down that slope.
6. His back hurting where Doug had jabbed him with his golak.
7. His forehead aching where Doug had knocked it against that tree trunk.
8. His rectum aching badly from the rape.
9. A blister on his right toe and two more on the heels of his feet, the raw centers of them ringed with blue.
10. His right cheek stinging, undoubtedly infected. The rest of his face feeling sunburned.
11. Overall, every muscle in his body aching and totally exhausted.

God but he felt like an idiot for having developed his metaphysical muscles so well and let his physical muscles go to hell.

He was thinking that when, the fire out, his body huddled in his zipped-up sleeping bag, he felt the bottom drop out of his consciousness and fell into a dark, troubled sleep.

———

Despite his exhaustion, he couldn't stay asleep; he woke up, his brain churning out dreads, apprehensions, dark imaginings. His mind seemed alive with thoughts, like maddened ants racing across it; it seemed as though he could almost feel them moving there.

Where was Doug now? Was he stalking through the darkness, using his flashlight? Had he climbed the same cliff? Was he sleeping at all? Or subsisting on those ten- and twenty-minute naps he'd mentioned? He had to rest sometime; he really wasn't Superman. What was Marian doing? What were Randy and Lise doing? How would they react if they found out about what was happening to their father?

He began to think about Randy and Lise, what it was like when they were born, what it was like raising them. What lovely children they were, how well they did in school despite occasional, expected slips. How he and Marian had enjoyed them both, how satisfying—yet, somehow saddening—to see them growing into teenagers, then college students, both of them at U.C.L.A., Lise planning to act (for her sake, he disliked the idea, knowing from personal experience what a draining lifestyle it could be), Randy drawn to writing. (Another possibly draining lifestyle but he couldn't very well try to talk him out of it, any more than he could try to discourage Lise. Especially when Marian was so supportive of them.)

He grimaced, trying not to think about Marian and the kids. In some unnerving way, it was as though he was mentally saying good-bye to them.

He tried to shake himself out of thinking at all. He had to sleep. God only knew what kind of day tomorrow was going to be. He thought again of giving up—or, with probably hope-less reasoning—waiting for Doug and trying to talk him out of this madness.

His thoughts were broken off by the sound of something moving in the darkness.

Had Doug caught up to him already?

Then he heard the huffing cough of a bear and stiffened, face a mask of dread. Should he have tried to hang up his food? he wondered, then realized that he had no way of hang-ing it up. Anyway, all he had in his pockets was dry food. Surely, the bear couldn't smell *that*.

He lay motionless except for his uncontrollable spasms of shivering, waiting for the bear to go away. Fighting off the perverse image of the bear climbing into the ring of boulders and tearing him to pieces.

He didn't know how long it took for the bear to go away. At last, it did though and with startling suddenness Bob felt a cloud of sleep enveloping him.

Wednesday

7:01 AM

It was a difficult set of steps to ascend; they seemed to go on endlessly. He felt his breathing get more and more strained. "I have to warn him," he kept muttering to himself. The man had to leave right now or he was doomed.

Finally, he reached the door—it was made of thick, heavy wood. He pounded on it with the side of his right fist, wincing at the tenderness in his palm.

There was no response and he pounded on the door again. "Come *on*," he shouted. "For God's sake, answer the door!"

No response. He looked around. Was there a window he could break, maybe kick in? No; the outside wall of the cabin was solid. "Goddamn it, what's the matter with you?!" he cried.

He had just raised his fist to hit the door again when the door was yanked open by an irritated-looking man. "What the hell is it?" he demanded.

"What the hell is it?" Bob raged. "Don't you know what's going on, for Christ's sake?"

"No, tell me," the man said mockingly.

"Goddamn it, man, the mountain is getting ready to blow!" He looked across his shoulder at the mountain and saw the dome on its side swelling quickly.

"You have to get *out* of here," he told the man. "Can't you see that?"

"Listen," said the man. "I have a job to do. You want to take a powder, do it. I'm busy."

"For God's sake, man, the mountain is going to explode any second now! Either you—!"

At that moment, he saw the man look across his shoulder, an expression of shock on his face. Jerking around, he saw that the dome had exploded, sending a dark cloud of smoke high into the sky. "Oh, Jesus," he muttered. He couldn't understand why there was no sound to the explosion.

He looked back at the man but he was no longer in the doorway, running to a radio transmitter. Picking up a microphone, he shouted into it, "Vancouver, Vancouver, this is it!"

Bob whirled to see a cloud of gas rushing at him, a torrent of mud and rocks hurtling toward the cabin. Too late! he thought. Dear God, he'd never escape now. He was finished.

He felt his body twitch so sharply that it woke him up. He sucked in at the chilly morning air. Dear God, he thought. It had been so real. But why such a dream now? Because it was a way for his subconscious to express itself because he was afraid he'd never escape from Doug?

He shuddered and swallowed. His throat was dry. Feeling around for his water bottle, he found it, picked it up, unscrewed its cap, and took a swallow of the cold water, then managed to swallow two multivitamins.

Putting the cap back on the water bottle, he slumped inside the sleeping bag. He still felt tired, bone tired. And yet he had to get going; he had no choice.

He recalled the time he and Marian had driven up to the Mount St. Helens display building and seen the film there, the one that began with the last words of the observer in the area—"Vancouver, Vancouver, this is it!"

The film had been horrifying. No sound of explosion because it traveled straight up—but a river of mud and rocks and magma hurtling down the valley at a hundred eighty miles an hour, the observer dying almost instantly, a man living miles away telephoning Vancouver to report that he had just seen the observer's car and cabin engulfed by the rushing wall and that it was headed for him. "And now it's going to get me," the man said in a dreadfully calm voice. Then he was gone as well.

Bob shuddered convulsively, then checked his watch. Not quite quarter after seven. He had to move on right away. His clothes still felt damp but there would be no opportunity to dry them any further. He decided that he'd leave the sleeping bag behind, trusting the assumption that he'd reach the cabin today; anything to help him move faster.

He winced as he realized that his face felt hot. He pressed a palm against his forehead. It felt warm but not as hot as it would if he had a fever. He realized then how badly he'd become sunburned. He gritted his teeth in a scowl. Sure, why not? he thought. Add it to the list.

When he sat up, he saw the headless rabbit. It was impaled on an upright piece of branch the other end of which was pushed into the ground between two of the boulders.

At first, his mind could not react. He stared at the rabbit blankly, then a rush of ice water flooded his chest and stomach.

Doug.

He gaped at the rabbit in sick, mindless terror. It had been skinned, its hide split open from tail to throat and peeled off carefully, its genitals and musk glands removed, internal organs lifted out, its bladder carefully cut away. Blood and transparent liquid dripped from its flesh.

Thought suddenly returned to him, searing his mind. Why was he still alive? If Doug had caught up to him, why hadn't he hacked him to death with the golak? It didn't make sense and, in a way, was more frightening than the idea of him being killed as soon as Doug overtook him.

Then he saw the note. It was impaled on a standing twig, written on a piece of cardboard torn from a box. One that he had or one that he found? he wondered pointlessly.

For almost a minute, he could only stare at the piece of cardboard, unable to move, feeling that he was destined to be killed by Doug. But why the note? Why the rabbit?

Reaching out a shaking hand, he pulled the piece of cardboard from the twig. The note was printed in small, uneven letters of ink.

Bobby boy: Your giving me ambivalence, babe. It's too damn soon for the game to end. Can't you do a little better? I give you points for climbing that wall, that impressed me. I didn't bother trying it, dubled back and took another—shorter!—rout. That's how I caught up to you so soon. Looking down at you now, your sleeping like a baby—a tired one, I'll bet!

Tell you what I'm going to do. When your ready to take off, blow your whistle twice. I'll give you a two-hour head start. How's that for fair? Good luck. You aren't going to make it but it's only decent of me to wish you well. I'm looking forward to catching you today. Getting the hots for you again. Maybe I'll fuck your asshole before you die. Or after *you die! There's an idea! Always thought the idea of neckrofilia was kind of exciting.* Yum. *Going now to get some winkem, blinkem and nod. See you soon. Your friend and lover. Doug.*

Conflicting thoughts raced through Bob's brain, dread competing with fury. *Goddamn the man.* It's still a game to him, a sick, exciting game. He'd been here. *Here.* He could have murdered me in my sleep. But he wants the chase to go on. Never had he felt more distant from Doug's mind. He was sociopathic, that was certain now. How had he functioned as an actor all those years, as a husband, as a father, as a human being? Well, he hadn't, that was undoubtedly the answer. He'd hidden his diseased interior self with the skill of a trained performer. Now it was out in all its aberrant glory. The man who wanted to kill him was deranged.

"Well, goddamn it," he said in sudden rage. "I'm not going to play the role of helpless victim for you."

Moving fast, he unzipped the sleeping bag, pulled it off and slung it aside. Environmentalists, go screw yourself, he thought. He shivered, his clothes still damp, especially his jacket. For several moments, when he stood, all his angry resolve evaporated as he almost lost his footing, his legs feeling weak and rubbery. No! he commanded himself. Pulling on his boots quickly and fastening their laces, he stamped his feet on the ground to get their circulation going. That was better. He was going to move and move with speed. Doug had underestimated him. He shunted aside the realization that Doug had already caught up to him once. Well, it wouldn't happen again. It just wouldn't.

He had the whistle to his lips when the idea came. Well, thank you, Doug, you idiot. I need protein and you've provided me with some, you dumb son of a bitch. You even prepared the rabbit for me. Thanks again.

As quickly as he could, he opened his knife and hacked away a chunk of the rabbit's flesh, stuffing it into the right side pocket of his jacket. I'll cook it later. Now—

He raised the whistle to his lips and blew it twice, as strongly as he could. He had no doubt whatever that he had two hours to get the jump on Doug who, in his own psychotic way, would abide scrupulously by the rules of the game.

The rules of the game, he thought in sickened disgust. A game that belonged in another time, another place, not in California, U.S.A., in the twenty-first century. Well, so be it. Let the grinning sociopath play his crazy game. He'd play another one titled Escape and Revenge.

Chewing on turkey jerky, he began to move as rapidly as he could through the forest. He had to force himself to move at a quick pace, force himself to ignore the aching pains in his body. He wasn't going to lose Doug's stupid, bloodthirsty game, he vowed. Allow him to take over Marian's life? Never!

"You can't even spell, you stupid bastard!" For some bizarre reason, the thought pleased him.

9:12 AM

He kept thinking it over and over as he struggled through the forest, eyes staring, almost unfocused.

Easy enough to say.

Easy enough to say he was determined to live, determined to reach the cabin and get Marian out of there.

How did he convince his body of it?

He felt exhausted again, every muscle seeming to ache. He'd stopped once and attempted to move his bowels; completely in vain. Every effort to empty them drove streaks of pain through his rectum. Finally, he gave up, pulled his pants up, and continued on.

His legs seemed strengthless now. He kept stumbling, tripping, stubbing his boots on the ground. How can I go *on* like this? he thought. He had the feeling that if he threw himself down and allowed himself to rest, even to sleep, he'd never be able to get up again, he'd be lying there, inert and helpless when Doug caught up to him, pulled out his golak, and hacked him to death. I can't let that happen, he told himself but with less and less assurance. He had the frightening impression that he *wanted* to fall, to rest, to sleep.

To surrender.

Still, he kept on going, his movements more labored and erratic as the minutes passed. He fell more than once, pushing to his feet each time, starting forward once more, as though he was impelled by some kind of mechanical force, walking like a robot, stiffly, devoid of will, unable to stop, his expression blank, his gaze directed ahead of himself yet seeing nothing but forest, forest, forest.

Once, as he crossed a sunlit clearing he thought: I've paid no attention to the house I live in. I've spent too much time thinking about where I was going when I left the house, in the meantime letting the house get run-down and in desperate need of repair.

Now that house was on the verge of collapse, ready to fall because of his neglect.

Then he was in the forest again, his mind unable to concentrate. There was only one thought he could manage. How far behind was Doug? Had he already recommenced his stalk? Goddamn the man, didn't *he* ever get tired? Who was he, goddamn Superman?

He stumbled over a fallen branch and, without volition, reached down and used his boot to break off a piece of it, strip away its twigs and leaves. A cudgel, he thought. Good. If he had the chance, he'd use it on Doug, kill him if he had to. He knew it was an unlikely weapon since Doug had the bow and arrow and could kill him from a distance. But if he could hide somewhere, so that Doug came close without knowing he was there. A sudden blow then, directly on Doug's skull.

He frowned in confusion as he stumbled on. Hadn't he already thought about waiting to ambush Doug? And didn't he discard the idea as unfeasible?

He grunted, gesturing weakly. Just keep walking, he told himself. Keep walking as fast as you can. He checked the compass again. He was still moving in the right direction. He'd use that distant pine tree standing by itself as his immediate target. Walk, he told himself. Keep walking. Fast. Forget about your body. Your body is irrelevant. Will yourself on. No other way. Try to ignore—no *ignore!*—the aches and pains, the devouring fatigue that threatened him, at every moment, with collapse, surrender. Keep moving. Move. Move.

He tried to deflect his sense of exhaustion by looking at the area he was passing through. On each side of him were darkly forested hillsides that disappeared in heavy mist. The entire valley he was walking through had a low ceiling of mist, lying like pale wool above the trees. He could barely see the target pine tree through the mist. The valley was dead still. The only sound he could hear was the crackling stumble of his boots. He hoped he would be out of the misty section of forest soon. His jacket, still damp, felt cold on him.

Still, the silent valley was extremely beautiful, he thought, then recalled that, somewhere he had read that, just before death, everything looked beautiful. He forced away the notion but realized that his resistance was becoming weaker and weaker. He had to face the facts. At any moment, he might break down, crumple to the forest floor, and lie there helplessly, unable—even unwilling—to go on.

Don't, he pleaded with himself. Just keep moving, moving. Doug couldn't run after him; he had to be tired too. His grip tightened on the cudgel. Just keep on, he thought. Keep on. Keep on.

Keep on!

10:48 AM

His gaze nearly out of focus, he almost walked directly into the mountain lion.

With a dry gasp, he recoiled, hearing the hiss and snarl of the lion; it was big, its tawny body eight feet long. He froze, preparing himself to die. There was no possible way he could escape.

But the lion didn't attack. As he stared at it in terror, he saw it slump back on the ground, its greenish-gray eyes fixed on him, its mouth open, teeth bared in a threatening growl. Why doesn't it attack? he wondered. Surely, this was not another apparent miracle of protection.

Then he saw the reason. The mountain lion's right rear leg was pinned beneath a fallen tree, it was unable to do more than try to stand on its front legs.

"Oh, you poor thing." Bob couldn't help but feel sorry for the trapped cat. "How long have you been that way?"

The mountain lion growled again, a rumbling in its throat and chest.

"It's all right," Bob told it. He quickly put down his branch cudgel. "You don't have to growl." He made shushing noises until the mountain lion grew still. Bob saw now that its tongue was hanging out and it was panting. "You're thirsty," he said. "Well . . ." He couldn't very well put water in his palm for the cat. He'd lose his hand if he tried.

He stood immobile for a while, wondering what to do. Practicality advised that he move on, Doug was still after him.

He couldn't though. He knew that if Doug ran across the mountain lion—and he probably would—he'd immediately fire an arrow into the trapped cat. Or cut off its head with his golak.

He couldn't allow that. I'm not *like* him, he thought. I can't just leave it here. I *won't*, goddamn it. *I just won't.*

He looked around and saw that the trunk of the fallen tree had some bark torn away. Maybe he could . . .

Taking out his knife—the movement made the lion growl—he began to peel away a section of bark several feet in length.

"You don't have to growl now," he told the cat in a gentle voice, "I'm going to see if I can give you a drink. Just lie still now. Shh. Shh."

The cat became quiet and watched, seemingly curious as to what he was doing. "That's right," he said, "I'm going to try and give you a drink, okay?"

Now the mountain lion's mouth was shut except for the tip of its red tongue protruding slightly. It watched as Bob peeled away the section of bark. "Now," he said, "let's see if this will work."

The strip was already curled up on both sides. At first he considered trying to use it as a trough through which he could pour the water into the cat's mouth. He gave up that idea immediately. Cats didn't drink that way.

Carefully, he began to bend up one end of the curled bark strip. It wouldn't hold, making him frown. If he only had one of those backpack straps now, he thought. He looked around. Something to tie up the end with, he thought. Something to—

"Ah," he said. He reached into his trouser pocket and took out his handkerchief. It was still damp but that didn't matter. He twisted it again and again until it formed a kind of thick, white twine that he used to tie up one end of the bark length. Then, pouring water from the bottle into the curved bark, he began to slide it slowly toward the lion. A rumble sounded in its chest. "No, don't growl," he told it quietly. "I'm trying to give you a drink. Don't growl now. Shh. It's okay. I'm just trying to give you a drink."

The bark-held water was close enough now for the cat to drink from it but it only eyed the bark suspiciously, not moving. "Go on," Bob told it softly. "Water. It's water."

The mountain lion extended its broad white paw and hit the bark, knocking it aside as the water spilled on the ground. "Aw, *no*," Bob said. "Don't do that. I'm trying to give you a drink. Come *on* now."

As he pulled back the length of curved bark, Bob wondered if he was committing suicide by staying so long with the trapped lion. He made a hapless sound. "What am I supposed to do, just let it die?" he asked, of whom he had no idea.

"All right," he said, "I'm going to try again. Now just don't knock it over. I know you're thirsty."

Pouring more water into the curved bark, he pushed it back toward the cat. "All right, I'm doing it again," he said. "Now *drink*, will you? Just drink?"

The cat slapped at the bark, spilling the water again.

"Oh, for Christ's sake, pussy," Bob said unhappily. "I can't stay here all day, trying to give you a drink of water. A crazy guy is after me and wants to kill me."

Again, he put water in the bark, holding the bottle higher so the cat could see the water being poured. "See?" he said. "Water. I *know* you're thirsty. Now you're going to drink this time, all right? Water. Water."

The cat watched him push the length of bark to it. This time it didn't move. "Come on," Bob said. "Drink. Drink."

He felt an unexpected rush of joy as the lion lowered its head and began to lap at the water with its tongue. "That a boy—or girl—I don't know which but I'm not going to check," Bob said, feeling a strange flow of happiness inside himself. "Drink. Good water. Good."

When the lion had drunk all the water, Bob leaned forward without thinking to pour more into the bark. The cat jerked up his head to stare at him but for some reason, Bob didn't feel alarmed. He poured more water into the bark. "There you go," he said. "Have some more."

Without a sound, the mountain lion lowered its head and lapped up the new supply of water. "That's the way," Bob told it, smiling. "You're really beautiful, you know that?"

The cat *was* beautiful, its head covered with multishades of brown, gray, and beige all blended perfectly, its nose dark red, the fur beneath its nose and on its chin a snowy white, its whiskers and hairs sticking out above its eyes also white. Its long body was a soft, tawny brown, its chest white.

"You *are* beautiful," Bob told it. "And I'm going to get you out of here right now."

He blinked at his audacity. Get it *out* of here? *How*, for God's sake? He couldn't get close enough to the lion to try to raise the fallen tree. The cat would kill him. Maybe glad to get that water but not suddenly domesticated.

Bob looked around uneasily. I have to get out of here myself, he thought. I can't waste any more time. But, again, the conviction gripped him. He simply could not leave the mountain lion for Doug to slaughter. No matter how long it took to—

"*Ah!*" he said. Another inspiration. Well, a workable idea at any rate, he decided.

He moved to the fallen tree. A branch wouldn't be strong enough; he had to have a limb. Fortunately, in its fall, one of the limbs had almost cracked away from the trunk. Bob took out his knife and hacked at the splintered wood holding the limb in place. Could really use that golak now, he thought, wincing at the image of how deadly a weapon it was. Not that it was designed to be exclusively a weapon. That was, of course, how Doug regarded it though. He tried to rid his mind of the image as he cut the limb free.

It took only a few minutes for him to cut away the branches. This should do the trick, he thought. "I'm going to get you out of here, pussy," he said. He grimaced at himself. *Pussy?* This was no house cat. He recalled, fleetingly, Doug calling him that. Bastard, he thought.

The limb was ready now. He moved to the opposite side of the tree and spoke across the foliage to the mountain lion.

"I'm going to raise the tree now," he told it. "When I do, pull out your leg and move off. I hope your leg isn't broken. However . . . just don't kill me after you're free, okay? I really don't deserve it. Right. Let's see what happens."

He pushed the end of the limb as far beneath the trunk as possible, keeping it away from the lion's trapped leg. "All right," he said. "Archimedes's principle, pussy. The lever. Get yourself ready."

He pressed down on the end of the limb. Nothing budged. "Oh, Christ, I hope it's not too heavy," he muttered. He pressed down harder, using more strength. The effort sent barbs of pain through his lower back. "I'm not sure I'm going to be able to do this," he told the cat and himself. "Jesus, don't let the tree be *too* heavy."

He pressed down harder, teeth clenched against the pains it caused in his back. "What am I doing this for?" he muttered. "Trying to save you, I'll ruin myself. Is that fair? *Ah!*" A quick smile pulled back his lips. The tree was lifting off the ground. "Get ready, pussy, get ready," he said, breathless now. "Pull out your leg."

The cat remained motionless, its throat filled with vibrating growls.

"For Christ's sake, pussy, pull your leg out," he begged. "I can't keep holding up the tree." Wasn't there enough of it lifted for the cat to free its leg? he wondered. He groaned in agony as he pushed down harder on the limb. "Come on," he said through gritted teeth. "Pull out your leg. I can't keep—"

He broke off in shock as the limb snapped and the tree trunk fell back on the mountain lion's leg. Its high-pitched scream of pain horrified Bob. "Oh, God, I'm sorry," he said, barely able to speak. "I didn't mean for that to happen. It wasn't me, it was the limb. It broke, it broke."

The mountain lion uttered an unearthly sound of pain and fury.

Suddenly, uncontrollably, Bob began to cry. "I'm sorry, I'm sorry," he said brokenly, tears pouring from his eyes. "I didn't mean to hurt you. I'm trying to help you get away." He could hardly speak he was sobbing so hard. "You can't stay here, you'll die. Don't you understand? You have to move or you'll die."

Fury filled him with startling abruptness. "Goddamn it, pussy!" He began to rage. "Are you just going to give up and die?! Don't you want to live?! Don't you?!"

With a sudden move, he grabbed hold of a still intact limb and struggled to lift the tree. "Damnit, you are going to live, you hear me?" he told the cat in a fury. "I'm going to lift this goddamn tree, and when I do, you're going to pull your goddamn leg out, do you hear me? Do you *hear* me, cat?!"

Later, he wondered where on earth the strength had come to him to raise the tree trunk. Was it the kind of desperate strength that helped tiny women to lift the weight of a car off their child's leg? He never knew. All he knew, at this moment, was that his body felt suffused with a kind of maddened power that enabled him to lift the tree trunk from the mountain lion's pinned leg.

"Now move, goddamn it! Move! Pull out your leg! You hear me, goddamn it! Pull out your fucking leg!"

The mountain lion suddenly lurched free and leaped to its feet, growling fiercely.

All rage vanished in an instant, all unnatural strength. He

stood frozen, watching the mountain lion starting to limp around the tree to get at him.

"Now come on," he pleaded. "I just saved your life. I gave you water. I lifted the tree and freed your leg. You don't want to kill me. You know you don't."

The mountain lion stopped its limping move around the tree. Was it the sound of his voice, no longer furious but, once more, gentle? He had no idea but kept on talking.

"Just move on now, pussy, just move on," he said. "If your leg is broken, there's nothing I can do about that. But at least you aren't trapped. My crazy friend can't kill you now." He broke into a bitter laugh, causing the cat to cock its head and gaze at him curiously. "He's not my friend. He's nuts. He wants to kill me. I'd love it if you got *him* instead of me. But just move on. I'm going to turn and get on my way. Don't jump on my back now, please. Just stay here 'til I'm gone, then move on. Okay? I'm going to turn and walk away now. Just stand still. I wish you well. Good-bye now."

As slowly as he could, he picked up the cudgel, turned and started off into the forest, chills lacing up and down his spine as he walked, anticipating a dreadful roar behind him, the sound of the huge cat's thrashing body, the crushing weight of its body leaping on his back, the claws digging into him, the sharp teeth rending at his flesh. Much good the cudgel would do him.

Nothing happened though. After a minute had passed, he stopped and turned around. The mountain lion was standing motionless, watching him go. Without thought, he raised his right arm. "Bye," he said. "Take care of yourself."

He turned around and walked on into the forest. A miracle? he wondered. Or simply that the mountain lion knew he'd saved its life?

He sighed. At least that bastard Doug would never get to kill it now.

12:09 PM

He'd followed the instructions in the booklet Marian had given him, found a flat, concave stone and heated it over a fire. Then, when the rock was hot (he'd put drops of water on it until the last one sizzled) he'd placed the rabbit, open side down on the rock and fried it as long as he dared.

It was barely done, but it tasted magnificent. He was conscious of tearing at it like a wild animal, ripping off large chunks of it with his teeth, chewing it noisily and probably swallowing it too soon. But it tasted delicious and he ate every scrap of it.

Now the coffee was steaming. Using his shirttail to hold the hot metal handle of the cup, he sipped at the coffee with powdered milk and sugar in it. It tasted wonderful too. He ate an energy bar and took continued sips from the metal cup. As he did, he kicked dirt onto the hole in which he'd placed the rabbit directly on the stone, turning it over and over, blackening it on the outside, hoping that the inside would get cooked enough to make it edible.

He looked at his watch. He'd been here almost twenty-five minutes. Had it been too long? There was just no way of knowing where Doug was, how fast he was moving in his demented pursuit.

No matter. He had to eat and he did. The rabbit, probably

more raw than cooked, sat in his stomach in lumps. To hell with it, he told himself. He needed protein, he had it now.

He finished putting out the fire and kept sipping at the hot coffee, nibbling at the rest of the blackberries in his pocket. He'd finish the coffee, then move on. Even sitting, he was aware of every ache in his body. Never mind, he thought. You saved that mountain lion, didn't you? He had the time. Even as he thought it, he realized that the logic made no sense at all. Yet, somehow, it was satisfying to him. He was amazed that he was even able to stand after the strain he'd put on his back, lifting that tree. Adrenaline, he thought. There really was something to it. To his knowledge, he'd never consciously experienced its effect before. He sure did this time though.

It came to him, as he thought, that his belief system had value to him only as a philosophy that had no tangible effect on the realities of his life. Perhaps if he was so spiritually advanced he would actually control those physical realities. He wasn't though. He had the belief system, period.

So he believed in life after death. So what? It didn't make his plight any easier to endure. Surviving death, however certain it might be, didn't alter by a single detail the knowledge that a madman was chasing him, planning, after the killing, to move in on Marian. Under these circumstances, his belief system was of limited or no use at all to him. He didn't have the time to sit on a log and ponder on the infinite.

Karma? Sure, maybe this entire terrifying experience *was* part of his karma. Again, so what? Believing that Doug would eventually pay the price for what he was doing didn't help a bit. Big deal, he thought in disgust. The only thing that mattered was staying alive; and the details of living were up to him.

Maybe he'd spent so much time thinking about the meaning of life that he'd almost overlooked the fact that he was alive.

It was a bizarre notion but, in a real sense, maybe Doug was doing him a favor. He knew very well that this was the last thing in the world Doug intended. It was true though.

By threatening him with death, it was just possible that Doug had reacquainted him with life.

2:16 PM

He emerged from the forest and saw an open, boulder-strewn slope in front of him at the bottom of which—about fifty yards distant—was a cliff overlooking distant forest and mountains.

He felt a stab of dread. Had he miscalculated the compass reading? Hastily, fingers trembling, he removed the compass from his jacket pocket and took a reading. An even more severe stab of dread now. The route Doug had instructed him to follow pointed directly toward the cliff. He couldn't possibly climb down that. Had it been a ruse on Doug's part after all? A ghoulish trick to lead him to this hopeless end?

"No, wait," he muttered. "Wait." Doug had told Marian that she'd enjoy the cabin's deck, which overlooked forest and mountains. This had to be the view he was describing to her. He must have drifted to the left or right, probably the left, he decided. Looking into the distance, he saw what appeared to be a turn to the cliff top. At this right turn, the forest continued. He'd keep moving into it. Eventually, the cliff would turn toward the north and the compass reading would lead him on correctly. He had to believe that anyway.

He went back into the forest and kept on walking as rapidly as he could. If the cliff was here, maybe the lodge Doug had mentioned was just ahead.

He was sitting in a blackberry patch, eating some of them, when a black bear pushed its way into the patch.

"Oh, my God," he muttered.

Without thinking, he immediately rolled himself into as tight a fetal position as he could, thinking about having his flesh clawed open.

Ignoring him completely, the bear turned and ambled out of the blackberry patch.

Bob unrolled himself and sat up. "It wasn't a grizzly bear, it was—"

His words broke as he began to laugh softly and uncontrollably. It didn't even pay attention to him for chrissake! It must have thought: Who in the hell is that idiot rolling himself into a ball? Bob laughed until tears were running down his cheeks.

Then he went on eating blackberries and washing them down with water.

A few minutes later, his bowels moved so quickly, he barely had time to pull down his pants and assume a squatting position.

He'd been moving steadily for the last hour, walking as fast as he could, deliberately ignoring the aches and pains he felt. Taking three aspirins had helped. He didn't dare take any more and risk possibly falling asleep.

At least, he seemed to be still ahead of Doug. To say the least, it was encouraging. Maybe he'd reach the cabin today after all. If his luck held out.

He was traversing a slope with a ten- to fifteen-degree decline toward the cliff edge. He leaned away from the edge as he walked, feeling edgy at being so close to that tremendous drop.

Suddenly, catching him completely by surprise, a burst of wind hit him, throwing him down to the rocky ground, tearing the cudgel from his grip. My God, where did that come from? he thought.

He started to stand, then found himself slipping on the layer of pine needles on the slope. He struggled up to his knees and tried to stand again. The pine needles slipped out beneath him again and he fell on his chest and stomach.

To his horror, every move to stand he made caused him to fall again and begin sliding backward toward the cliff edge. "Oh, no," he muttered. Was this the way it was going to end, falling thousands of feet to a horrible, crushing death?

He tried to crawl away from the cliff edge and found himself slipping backward again, the pine needles shifting constantly beneath him.

"No," he said, terrified. He tried again, more desperately this time, to crawl up the slope. The movement only caused him to slip even more.

Spread eagle, the thought came abruptly. He stretched his legs and arms to the side, lying motionless, feeling his heartbeat pounding at the slope.

Now what? he wondered. He thought hard, then, very slowly, using his right hand, he brushed away the pine needles in front of him.

His gaze scanned the rocky face. With the pine needles gone, he could see that the surface of the slope was uneven, cracks here and there.

Very carefully, again as slowly as possible, he reached up and curled the fingers of his right hand into the tiny crevice. His fingers dug in tightly, and grunting from the effort, he pulled himself up to the crack, using only the strength of his right arm to get him there, the pain in his right wrist, arm, and shoulder making him groan.

Reaching forward, he brushed away more pine needles. This time there was a crevice nearer his left arm and reaching forward he dug the fingers of his left hand into the crack and pulled himself forward, this time forgetting and trying to use his feet, causing himself to begin sliding back again. He grasped at the crack as hard as he could and, with straining effort, pulled himself forward again.

In this way, with agonizing slowness, he managed to reach the top of the slope and regained his footing.

The explosive shot rang out ahead of him and suddenly the tree beside him was gouged by a bullet, detonating splintered fragments of bark by his face, some of them shooting into his cheeks, making him cry out in pain. He fell to the ground in shock, his thoughts a tangle of confused feelings, the main one being—totally stunned—*Where did Doug get a rifle?*

When there were no further shots, he pushed up on his elbows and half crawled, half pulled himself across the rough ground until he reached a clump of bushes. Pushing his way through them, he got a glimpse of the slope.

A man was standing by a boulder, wearing a plaid jacket and hat, a rifle poised in his hand as though in readiness to finish off his prey.

"Goddamn it, what's the matter with you?!" Bob yelled. Even as he did, he wondered why he was yelling at a man who could save his life.

The man's eyes squinted as he looked toward the bushes. "Where are you?" he asked; his tone more irritated than repentant.

"Here," Bob said, "don't shoot at me again for Christ's sake."

"Well, I thought you were an animal," the man said grumpily.

Bob struggled to his feet and limped toward the man. "Do I look like a fucking animal?" he demanded, still unable to understand how he could speak so furiously to a man who might well be his salvation. "This is not a hunting area, you know! It's a national forest!"

"Well, no one told me that," the man answered resentfully.

As Bob neared him, the man grimaced in revulsion. "Jesus Christ, what happened to you?" he asked. Bob winced, realizing how terrible he must look.

"Listen," he said. "I need your help."

"You sure as hell look as though you could use somebody's help," the man responded, still making a face at Bob's appearance.

"There's a man chasing me," Bob told him. "He intends to kill me with a bow and arrow—or a golak."

The man's expression made it clear that what he had just been told didn't really register on his mind. "What?" he asked.

"A man is chasing me," Bob said. "He means to kill me."

"Why?" the man asked, still looking confused.

"That's besides the point," Bob told him urgently. "I need your protection."

"My protection." Now the man looked suddenly alarmed and cautious.

"I need your rifle to protect me. Don't you understand?"

"My rifle?" The man's seeming inability to understand what he was being told incensed Bob.

"Yes!" he cried. "I either need you to protect me or I need your rifle!"

"I'm not giving you my rifle," the man said, sounding offended.

"Then protect me!" Bob said furiously. Was the man an idiot?

"From what?" the man demanded.

"I've already told you! There's a man chasing me who means to—!"

"I know what you told me!" the man interrupted, suddenly angry himself. "How do I know what you're telling me is true?"

"It is true, damnit!" Bob raged at him. "Do I look like I'm crazy?"

"You look worse than crazy, pal!" the man said; he seemed to be regaining confidence now.

"Goddamn it!" Bob abruptly struggled for composure. It was obvious that the more he ranted, the less the man would believe him. He noticed the man's guarded look at his cudgel and threw it down.

"Listen to me," he said. "My name is Robert Hansen. I'm here from Los Angeles. I came out here to backpack with a friend of mine—"

"A friend?" the man said suspiciously.

"I *thought* he was my friend." Bob felt himself losing control of his temper again and fought to hold it in check. "He's not my friend. He's crazy. He's chasing me—"

"I know; you told me," the man said. Bob felt incredulous. The sound in the man's voice was cynically dismissive now. He couldn't believe what was happening. The man had a rifle, he could bring down Doug and end all this.

"Listen," he said, as calmly as he could. "You have got to shoot this man before he can kill me."

"What?" The man's voice was querulous now, his expression unbelieving. "Shoot a perfect stranger? Are you nuts or something?"

"No, *he's* nuts," Bob snapped back. He was not going to be able to control his anger much longer, he knew. "Listen," he said. "*Sell* me your rifle then."

"*What?*" The tone even more querulous, the expression incredulous.

"I'll pay you any price you ask," Bob told him. "I'm a writer, I have lots of money."

"Writers don't make money," the man said contemptuously.

This is a fucking nightmare, Bob thought. The man didn't understand any of this, was totally unwilling to help him.

Abruptly he grabbed the rifle by its barrel. "I'm sorry, I have to have this," he said, his voice trembling.

"What the hell do you think you're doing?" the man said, his tone aghast. "Are you *nuts?*"

"I need to kill this man," Bob said, teeth clenched. "It isn't only me he's after, it's my wife as well."

"Oh, well, you're insane, man." The hunter pulled back at the rifle. "You belong in a nuthouse."

"Goddamn it, I need your rifle!" Bob screamed in his face.

They were wrestling for possession of the rifle, boots scraping and stumbling on the ground, when the buzzing sound streaked past Bob's ear. The man's cry was startled, like a child's.

Imbedded in his neck, its bloody point protruding from behind, was an arrow.

Bob recoiled in shock, staring blankly at the man, whose expression was dazed, confused. "What the—?" he began to say.

The next instant, he had toppled backward, the rifle still grasped in his hands. He was dead before he hit the ground.

Bob whirled and stared into the forest. There was no sign of Doug. And yet he had to be there. Was that a movement in the distant brush?

Abruptly he twisted around and, dropping to his knees, tried to pull the rifle from the dead man's hands. His grip had frozen on the rifle though. Bob pulled at it desperately.

Another buzzing sound, an arrow hitting the ground several inches away, head buried in the soil. Dear God! Bob thought. He pulled at the rifle in panicked anguish. He had to have it or he was finished!

Another buzzing sound, the arrow shooting past him to imbed itself beside the last one. Then Doug's voice, shouting from the forest. "*Better run, Bob!* You aren't going to get that rifle!"

A burst of mindless terror drove Bob to his feet. He stumbled, almost pitched forward, then was able to regain his balance and break into a run for the nearest trees.

"That's right, Bobby! Run like crazy! I'll be with you in a little while!"

Bob lost all sense of time and direction as he fled through the woods, stumbling more than once, once falling across a tree root, gasping with pain. Ignoring the pain, he struggled to his feet and ran again, unthinking, stupefied, a brainless, fleeing animal.

Finally, he had to stop, he couldn't find the breath to continue.

Panting, sweat running down his face, mouth hanging open, eyes staring sightlessly, he turned. He had to know if Doug was running after him.

There was no sign of Doug. Where was he? Beside him in the forest? Ahead of him?

He had to know. He simply had to know.

With what remaining strength he had, he managed to pull himself up into a tree that had branches he could step on starting close to the ground. He kept climbing, visualizing, as he did, Doug appearing just below, looking up with a grin as he notched his arrow into the bowstring, aimed, drew back the string, and shot an arrow into his heart.

Using his tiny binoculars, he looked down, surprised that he could see the dead hunter.

What else he saw made his skin crawl and his stomach almost lose its contents. He made a gagging sound, spit out wet pieces of rabbit, and stared at what Doug was doing: removing the arrow from the dead hunter's throat, pulling it out from the front so the barbs of the arrowhead wouldn't get caught in the man's flesh.

As he watched, he saw Doug—teeth gritted with the effort—yanking at the arrow until it suddenly came free, its feathered end soaked with the hunter's blood.

Doug poured some water on the feathers and the arrowhead, cleaned them off with his fingers, and slipped the arrow back into its quiver; the two other arrows were already there. The rifle was nowhere to be seen. Doug must have flung it off the cliff.

"No," Bob murmured, his expression suddenly twisted, sickened.

Doug had taken the hunter's boots in his hands and was dragging him to the slope that ended at the edge of the cliff.

"You son of a bitch," he murmured weakly. "You goddamn son of a bitch." Slip on the pine needles the way *I* did, he thought. Fall to your death.

But Doug seemed to know about the pine needles. He stopped dragging the dead hunter to the place where the pine needles became a problem and laid the body parallel to the edge and sat down close to it, pressing his boots against the hunter's side.

With a sudden lunge of his boots, he shoved at the body violently. It rolled over and over, sliding on the pine needles until it reached the cliff edge.

Then it was gone.

Bob's stomach convulsed and, opening his mouth wide, he vomited, gasping, groaning.

If there had ever been the remotest chance that Doug would change his mind, relent, that chance was gone now.

If he failed—and how in God's name could he succeed?— to kill Doug, Doug was certainly going to kill him.

It seemed as though, for the first time since all this had begun, he felt the actual, icy presence of death gathered around him.

With a sob, he threw his head back, staring at the sky through tear-blurred eyes.

"You aren't going to help me, are you?" he said in a choking voice. "You're there but you aren't going to help me. I have to do it all myself, don't I? All the lip service I give you isn't worth a damn, is it? I save myself or I die." He was crying now, disabled by fear. "Well, thanks a lot," he sobbed. "You've been a great help." His teeth clenched in an expression of rabid fury. "Guardian angel, my ass!" he snarled. "Ever-present consciousness, my ass! Wherever you are, you're not worth a pile of shit to me!"

He leaned his forehead against the tree, weeping bitterly, no longer certain if he could conceivably survive this. Suffering with a sense of horror at the idea of leaving Marian to Doug's insanity, but totally unable to believe that he could do a thing to stop it.

4:22 PM

Nevertheless, I go on, he thought as he walked unevenly, almost staggeringly through the forest. He simply could not stay in that tree and wait for death. Once his initial sense of despairing submission had eased, he'd climbed back down. Doug was obviously confident in his ability to overtake him. Bob's last view of him was Doug sitting on the boulder the hunter had been standing by, casually eating.

He *is* insane, Bob thought as he continued through the forest. He just murdered a man, yet there he sits calmly, eating. There were probably blood splashes all around him. Did they bother Doug? He had to assume that they didn't. He'd just pushed the hunter's corpse off the cliff. Why should a few bloodstains bother him?

It was clear now that Doug did not intend to pay the price for either the hunter's death or his. He'd find a way to dispose of his body as well. Then on to the cabin and the performance of his life—anguish, guilt, tears, sobs of utter desolation.

He could almost see Doug telling Marian the heartbreaking story— Bob getting lost, Doug searching in vain for him, then finally rushing to the cabin so they could drive for help; more of his stellar portrayal of the broken man to the authorities. That was the horror of it. Anyone else would arouse suspicion. Doug was not just anyone though, lying unconvincingly. He was an actor playing a chosen role. Not to the hilt either. No, he'd gauge it perfectly, keep it under skillful control.

And where will I be? Bob wondered. No doubt off the same cliff as the murdered hunter. Two corpses shattered on the rocks below, probably never to be found. And even if they were eventually found, would there be any way to implicate Doug? For all he knew—now that it occurred to him, it seemed obvious—Doug had thrown his bow and arrow off the cliff as well; less evidence against him.

Bob scowled. Then why remove the arrow from the hunter's neck? Unless—more than possible—he'd thrown, or would throw, the bow and arrow off the cliff far from where the hunter's remains lay splattered on the rocks.

He might even bury the bow and arrows, kill Bob with the golak; it seemed obvious, for some time, that he'd prefer to murder Bob that way. When he tossed Bob's body off the cliff, the broken and bloody appearance of his body would most likely obscure the golak slashes.

Then on to the cabin, he thought again. Marian. The performance. Anger made him tremble at the image in his mind. But what could he do to defend himself? He was beyond exhaustion now, on the verge of collapse. It seemed as though only mindless habit kept him going.

He had been so engrossed in dark thoughts that he didn't see the lodge until he was almost up to it.

A sudden burst of hope mantled his mind and body. My God, it's there, he thought. I've made it. If Doug had told the truth, the cabin was on the steep hill beyond the lodge. He might make it after all. He couldn't understand how he was still ahead of Doug but never mind, he thought. He still had a chance to reach Marian and get her out of the cabin, away from Doug.

His burst of eager optimism was dispelled in an instant.

"Well, I see you made it, Bobby boy!" Doug's voice rang out behind him.

He jerked around, breath catching in his throat.

Doug stood about fifty yards away, grinning like a happy kid. Bob saw that he was right. The bow and arrow were no longer evident; he *had* gotten rid of them.

His heartbeat lurched inside him as he saw Doug shuck his backpack and toss it aside, then slowly draw the golak from its sheath.

"Time to say bye-bye, Bobby," he said, still grinning. "I'm about to cut you up in little pieces now."

He started forward.

Bob whirled and ran toward the lodge, terror fueling his body with adrenalined strength.

"Oh, you can't get away from me now!" Doug called. "You've had it! I'm surprised you made it this far but it's the end of the line now, Bobby! You are finished!"

Bob dashed inside the lodge, tripping over a raised board and sprawling onto the floor. Shoving up with a gasp, he looked around the shadowy, rancid-smelling entry hall and saw a flight of stairs across the way. Why don't I have that club now?! his mind cried.

"Here I come, ready or not!" Doug called outside. Bob heard the crackle of his boots as Doug came walking through the dry grass toward the lodge.

He started up the stairs, trying to manage two steps at a time. Halfway up, his right boot crashed through a rotted step, his leg plunging down to its knee; he felt long splinters driven into his leg through his pants.

"Time to find out if there really *is* an afterlife, Bobby!" Doug called. "Aren't you excited?!"

Bob fought to lift his leg from the jagged hole in the step. At first, he couldn't pull it up because his pants leg was pierced by the splinters. Oh, God, not like this! the terrified thought exploded in his mind. He jerked up at his leg convulsively.

"Here I come, Bobby boy!" Doug called.

With a hiss of frenzy, Bob yanked up his leg again, tearing his pants free and pulling himself loose. He started running up the steps again, now sticking to their sides, using his grip on the banister to pull himself faster, hissing as his palm and fingers were imbedded with more splinters—

"Bobby!"

Bob jerked his head around to see that Doug had just run in below. At first, Doug didn't see him, looking around with quick movements of his head.

Then he saw Bob near the head of the stairs and said, with joyous expectation, "*Ah!* That's good there, Bobby boy! Don't make it *too* easy for me, that wouldn't be any fun. Act three, baby. Needs to wind up with a bang." His laugh was more a breathless croak. "And when I say a bang, you know exactly what I mean. I'm getting hard already."

Bob twisted around and dashed along the second-floor hall.

"Look out, look out, wherever you are!" Doug called. Bob heard his footsteps thumping slowly, loudly on the stairs. "Here comes a candle to light you to bed!" Doug said with obvious relish. "Here comes a golak to chop off your head!" His laugh chilled Bob as he reached the door to a room and ran inside.

It had obviously been the master bedroom of the lodge, he saw, about twenty feet long and fifteen wide. There was still some furniture inside it, a rickety chair and, against the far wall, a heavy bureau.

Hastily, he reached down for the chair. One of its legs was almost broken off. He grabbed it and pulled hard, teeth bared. The leg broke off. Okay, he thought, you'll have to fight me now, I won't just stand here, waiting.

He started across the floor, only, at the last moment, seeing that the large, moth-eaten rug was sagging in the middle. There had to be a hole in the floor.

"Here I come, lover!" Doug was in the hallway now.

As quickly as he could, Bob pulled the edge of the rug until it lay flat, hiding the hole that had to be beneath its center.

He moved around the rug as quickly as he could and moved to the end of the room. The bureau stood several feet from the wall; it looked enormously heavy. He moved behind it, staring toward the hallway door. His heartbeat pounded, drumlike, in his chest. If Doug would cross the rug, he thought.

Doug entered the room. "You in here, Bobby boy?" he asked. He peered across the shadowy room. "Oh, there you are, you little devil, hiding behind—what is that, a bureau?" His chuckle made Bob shudder. "Isn't going to save you, baby. Nothing's going to save you now." His voice grew suddenly vicious. "You're a dead man, Bobby. I am going to fuck your dead ass, then go up the hill and fuck—oh, no." His tone abruptly lightened again. "I'll fuck her, yeah, but not until we're married. Won't that be a kick in the head, Bobby boy?"

He started forward slowly, the golak in his hand.

"You notice that I haven't got the bow and arrow. Might make bad evidence against me if they find that stupid hunter."

He brandished the golak in front of him. "But this will do the trick."

Step on the rug, Bob thought. Just step on the rug.

"Oh, this is going to be a ball," Doug said. "First I kill you, then I fuck you. Doesn't that sound yummy? Jesus, I am getting hard. I can hardly wait to jam it up your ass again."

The rug, Bob thought. Cross the rug.

"This shouldn't bother you too much," Doug said. "A little pain and then you'll be in paradise, schlepping around in a purple robe. Won't that be a gas? While I'm down here, sliding my cock in and out of your hot ass." He laughed. "Before it gets cold, of course."

That's it, Bob thought. The rug. Come right across the rug.

"If you feel the need to offer up a prayer, now's the time to do it, Bobby boy. Because I'm gonna—oh, now, wait a second."

Bob looked at him in sick dread as Doug stopped and looked down at the rug.

"You trying to fool me, Bobby boy? You clever bastard you. Oh, my."

Bending over, Doug put down the golak and grabbed the edge of the rug. He yanked it hard across the floor, revealing the gaping hole. "Oh, nasty, nasty," he scolded. "You meant for Dougie boy to go right through this hole, didn't you?" His voice hardened as he picked up his golak. "Didn't you, you stupid fuck?"

He started across the floor again, moving around the hole. "You really thought you could fool me, didn't you? Well, that'll make it all the more delicious hacking you to pieces . . . you stupid, fucking son of a bitch."

Bob slung the chair leg at him, hitting him on the chest and knocking him back. Doug cried out in shock, then pain. He lost his footing for a few moments, staggering toward the hole. Fall! Bob's mind screamed. Fall, you bastard!

Doug regained his balance now and rubbed his chest, grimacing. "You son of a bitch," he muttered. "You really think you're going to live? Oh, no. Oh, no. You're going to die. In agony. I'll make it last a long time, babe. A long time," he repeated, his voice shaking. Slowly, he advanced on Bob, the golak raised to strike.

Where the strength came from, Bob never knew. Terror? Fear of dying? Determination to save Marian? No way of knowing.

All he knew was that—with a sudden, maniacal snarl— he shoved the bureau directly at Doug; he hadn't realized that it was set on wheels. Shoved with such violence, it rolled quickly across the floor and struck Doug head on, knocking him back.

With a hollow cry of astonished dismay, Doug fell into the

hole and disappeared. Bob heard the crash of his body in the room below. The bureau, too big to fall through the hole, sagged over on its edge, wheels still spinning.

At first, he couldn't move. After all he'd been through, he could not believe that it was over, even more impossible to believe that he had won, that he had beaten Doug.

After several minutes of paralyzed debility, he found the strength to walk infirmly to the hole and looked down.

It was too dark below for him to see anything, and for several moments, he had the horrified apprehension that Doug wasn't there, that he'd fallen on something soft and was already coming up again.

Then—miraculously it seemed—he remembered his flashlight and switched it on, pointing it downward through the hole.

Doug was lying on his back, eyes closed, a twisted expression of pain on his face. Bob tried to see if there was movement on his chest. He saw none. The fall had to have killed him.

At first, he cried out with a sense of rabid exultation. His tormentor was dead! Good! Good!

Then revulsion came, sadness, even guilt. All right, it had been self-defense; no doubt of that.

But he had never killed in his life, not even an animal. Now this.

"Oh, Jesus Christ," he muttered, feeling nauseous. "Why did we ever come up here. Why?"

He took out the small bottle of vodka and drained it in a swallow. It didn't help. It only made him cough.

4:59 PM

What do I tell her? he wondered as he struggled up the hill. That I killed Doug? The details of the last three days swamped his mind. Where do I begin?

He gulped in air and belched dryly as he was forced to bend forward to make it up a rock-strewn slope. No matter, he thought. We have all the way back to Los Angeles for me to tell her all the details of Doug's increasingly insane behavior since Sunday.

Then again, of course they'd have to stop at the first police or sheriff's station they came to, let them know what happened. They probably wouldn't be going back to Los Angeles after all. Not for a while at least. They'd probably have to come back here; there would likely be a forest ranger with the police or sheriff's men. They'd have to find Doug's body, later on search for the hunter's corpse.

Reaching into his jacket pocket, he drew out the note Doug had left him. Thank God he hadn't left it behind. He couldn't imagine why he'd taken it along. God knew, he'd never thought, for an instant, that he'd be using that note as evidence against Doug. What point was there in evidence now anyway? There couldn't be a trial with Doug killed. But at least, the note would allay any suspicion against him for causing Doug's death.

"Oh, God," he said in an exhausted voice. All he wanted to do was go home with Marian and try to forget everything that had happened. Impossible, of course. There was no way of estimating how complicated and time-consuming the investigation would prove to be after he reported what had taken place. They probably wouldn't be allowed to return to Los Angeles for some time; they might have to stay in a local motel until things were settled.

"Okay," he muttered. Even that would be acceptable. A hot shower, cuts and bruises treated, splinters removed, a decent meal— and then a long sleep lying next to Marian. It sounded like heaven.

The hill seemed to get steeper now. Instead of straining up it, leaning forward, he was forced to climb, reaching ahead to pull himself upward, using bushes, boulders, scrub-growth trees. His breath grew more and more labored, his chest heaving with gasped-in breaths. No matter, he told himself. The cabin would be at the top of the hill. Marian. Safety.

Escape from the nightmare.

Reaching the top of the hill, he straightened up, panting, looking around for the cabin.

There was no sign of it.

"Oh, no," he said. "Oh, no." He felt tears rising in his eyes. It couldn't be. It mustn't be. The cabin wasn't here? Doug had lied to him right from the start?

"No. No," he muttered, refusing to believe. It couldn't be true. He'd followed the compass setting. Hadn't he found the lodge? Why should Doug have told him about the lodge, then lied about the cabin being up the hill behind it?

"Doesn't make sense," he mumbled. "No. It simply doesn't make sense."

He twisted his head around, a look of crazed, incredulous panic on his face. "It doesn't make sense!" he cried, his voice hoarse and trembling.

Fingers almost vibrating they shook so badly, he took out the compass and checked it. He was a few degrees off but not enough so he would fail to see the cabin if it was anywhere in the vicinity.

It wasn't.

Doug had lied to him. He had no idea whatever where the cabin was.

He was lost again.

His legs gave out beneath him and he sank down on the hard rock surface of the hilltop, slumping there, a sense of total hopelessness assailing him again. He'd thought the nightmare was over, that the cabin would be up here, Marian waiting for him.

"Oh, God," he muttered, half sobbing the words. After everything he'd gone through, he was little better off than he'd been from the start. All right, Doug was dead, he didn't have to dread being murdered.

But now he was lost, without an inkling of which way to go. He could still die. His food was virtually gone, all he had was water. That would sustain him for a while.

But which way was he to go?

He could go hopelessly wrong in whatever direction he took. Become so lost that no one would ever find him.

For several moments, he had a vision of his body lying dead in the woods, eyes staring, face mummylike, mouth ajar, an expression of terrified surrender printed on his features. He'd described such things in novels and in scripts. It had never crossed his mind that he was describing his own demise, preparing his own epitaph. HERE LIES ROBERT HANSEN / PERISHED IN THE WILDERNESS. A grotesque, staring corpse in the forest. Probably—the thought made him shudder and groan—eaten

by bears or mountain lions. His writer's mind, even in this
moment of utter despair, could imagine the mountain lion he'd
saved dining on his flesh and gnawing on his bones.

"Oh, shut up!" he raged. He pushed up dizzily, almost fell
again, then staggered and regained his balance. You're not dead
yet, he berated himself. Keep moving. You'll see something,
find some way to escape all this. He'd thought himself helpless
to defend himself against Doug, hadn't he? Well, he'd won
that battle, Doug was dead. He'd win this battle too. Goddamn
it if he wouldn't.

He started along the crest of the hill, knowing very well
that he was whistling in the dark. Trying to ignore that feeling
though, repress his sense of helplessness, keep going on. I will,
he told himself. I will. I will. I will.

As he moved around a clump of boulders, he saw the three
coyotes standing twenty feet ahead of him. They were staring
at him, bodies tensed, lips drawn back from pointed teeth, deep
growls rumbling in their throats and chests.

He stood frozen in his tracks, staring back at them.
They're going to attack, an insanely calm voice addressed his
mind.

He didn't know until it was over exactly what had happened. All he knew was that, abruptly, there was one thought
in his head.

After everything I've been through, *this?*

Something snapped inside him and suddenly he went ber-
serk, rushing at the coyotes, a demented, animallike scream of
fury pouring from his open mouth, his arms thrown up, his
fingers curved like talons.

The three coyotes twitched back, growling. Then abruptly
they jumped around and ran away from him.

Bob stopped, scarcely able to catch his breath. That's right, you crazy bastards, run away from me before I kill you, he thought.

Then sanity returned and he was shivering from head to toe. My God, I went insane there, totally insane. But I wasn't going to let it all end by being killed by a trio of damn coyotes. I just wasn't.

His shoulders slumped, he exhaled hard.

Then, suddenly, he whirled, a look of startled amazement on his face. A distant voice, very faint.

Marian's.

"Bob?!" she was shouting. "Bob?!"

He broke into a shambling run toward the sound of her voice. "Yes!" he called. But his tongue was too raspy, he had used up his voice screaming at the three coyotes. Nonetheless, he cried out again in answer to her. "Yes! I'm here!" He couldn't believe she'd hear the hoarse croaking of his voice but kept on shouting anyway. "I'm here! I'm here!"

"Bob?!" Her voice was closer now, clearer. "Bob?!"

"I'm coming!" he cried.

She kept calling his name, the sound of her voice becoming more distinct each time she called his name. "Oh, God, I'm here," he said, legs moving under him like pistons, totally without strength, driven on by joy and exultation. He had found her!

Now, through the trees, he caught sight of the Bronco, then, beside it, the cabin. On its deck, Marian was standing. *"Bob!"* she cried out, catching sight of him now. "Oh, my God! *Bob!"*

She was running down the deck steps now, rushing to meet him. Oh, thank God, thank God, he thought. He stumbled, almost fell, then caught his balance once more and ran on.

They came together so hard they almost collided. Suddenly she was in his arms, her arms clutching at him; she was crying helplessly as he was. "God, oh, God, Bob, I was so *afraid*," she said, her voice shaking, almost impossible to understand.

"*Marian.*" He held her as tightly as he could. "I thought I'd never see you again."

Their lips were crushing at each other's, arms wrapped rigidly around each other.

"It's all right, you're safe now, safe," she told him, sobbing.

"If you only knew what I've been through," he said.

"I know, I know. Oh, God, I am so glad to see you, I was *so afraid.*"

"So was I," he said.

"You look *terrible*," she said.

"You look wonderful," he told her.

They kissed each other's lips and cheeks and necks, clinging to each other tightly.

"Well, you *made* it, Bobby! What a big relief!"

Bob twitched violently, looking toward the cabin deck.

Doug stood there, smiling at him.

"You really had me worried, buddy," he said cheerfully.

At first, he couldn't speak he was so stunned. All he could do was murmur a faint, incredulous "Wha'?"

"What is it, Bob?" she asked.

His voice returned then and he muttered, "Hold me, hold me." He embraced her tensely. "Put your arms around me. I don't want him coming down here."

"What is it?" she repeated, sounding even more concerned.

His mind was racing with a jumble of thoughts. He didn't know which one to start with.

He heard himself ask, "How long has he been here?"

"About . . . thirty minutes. Why?"

"What did he tell you?"

"He's really been disturbed that you were lost. He kept on searching for you—"

"Stop." He cut her off, his voice almost falsetto with throttled fury.

"Bob, what *is* it?" she asked again.

"I thought he was dead, I thought I'd killed him," he blurted, still not knowing how to tell her everything.

"What?" It was her turn now to look and sound incredulous.

"He must have—"

"Hey, lovebirds, come on up! We have a lot to talk about!" Doug called, breaking into Bob's attempt to speak.

"He must have come to, he knew how to get here faster, beat me to it." The words ran together as he spoke.

"Bob, for God's sake, *what is going on?*"

"Listen to me, I can't give you every detail but he's been chasing me since yesterday morning, intending to kill me."

"What?" Her voice sounded too loud to him and he quickly cut her off. *"Shh.* Don't talk, just listen. He is crazy, Marian. He raped me yesterday morning—"

"What?" She couldn't seem to take it all in, looking at him as though she thought him mentally disturbed.

"He gave me a head start, then chased me. He even caught up to me last night while I was sleeping, could have killed me then but left me a note, I have it in my pocket, he's *crazy,* Marian, I'm telling you."

"My God," she whispered.

"He killed a hunter earlier today, shot an arrow through his neck."

"Bob, are you—?"

"Crazy too? No. This really happened, Marian. We have to get away from him. Where are the car keys?"

"In the ignition." Her voice was trembling now. "What are we going to *do?*"

"Play along with him; we have to. I don't know what he has in mind, why he came here after everything he's done, why he didn't try to get away somewhere."

"Oh, *lovebirds!*" Doug called. "Enough smooching! Come on up!"

"Does he have his golak?" Bob asked quickly.

"His *what?*"

"Golak. That big knife, like a machete."

"Yes," she answered shakily.

"Too bad," he murmured, wincing. "We better go on up, I don't know what he'll do if he thinks we're plotting against him. He's crazy, absolutely crazy. Let me do the talking. Try not to look as panicky as both of us are feeling."

"Yes," she murmured weakly.

Bob felt numb as they walked toward the cabin. Shouldn't they run for the Bronco, hoping to reach it before Doug could catch them? He knew it wasn't possible. Doug was too fast, too clever. And he had the golak in his belt. He realized that everything he'd gone through in the past two days had given him a mindless fear of Doug, a conviction that no matter what he did, Doug would always counter it.

As they reached the deck, to his horror, Doug embraced

him tightly. "*Bobby* boy!" he said in a delighted voice. "You're safe, you're really safe!"

Bob could see that Marian was trying to control the sickened dread she obviously felt. She even managed a smile, not a convincing one but nonetheless a smile. "You both look like hell," she said. Good! Bob thought. Throw him off. Let him think he's still in charge of everything.

Doug laughed as though her words had thoroughly amused him. "That's no lie," he said. "After everything we've been through. Remind me never to take your husband backpacking again."

No fear of that, Bob thought.

"Man, I'm glad to see you safe and sound!" Doug said. He laughed again. "Well, not exactly sound. Marian is right, we do both look like hell. I know you do anyway, I can see it with my own eyes. And when I get a chance to look in a mirror, I know I'll see how shitty I look too." He babbled happily as though all problems had been solved. The actor, Bob thought. Giving his penultimate performance.

"Well, the two of you must be starving," Marian said. Bob was amazed at the controlled tone of her voice. She's marvelous, he thought.

"Yes, we are," he said. "I know I am anyway."

"Me too," Doug said as though in high spirits now. "You want to make us something, Marian?"

"How about some eggs?" she asked. Again, Bob felt a rush of admiration for her. With her help, they were going to get out of this, he vowed.

"Sounds good," Doug told her, smiling.

"Very good," Bob added.

"I'll get them right away," she said.

For an instant, Bob felt his stomach drop as she turned and went into the cabin, leaving him alone with Doug.

He started to follow her, then froze as Doug's fingers clamped on his arm.

"I hope you haven't told her anything," Doug said quietly.

"No," Bob lied. "I haven't."

"Don't know whether to believe you, Bobby boy," Doug said. "But if you're lying, she goes too."

Doug's last words made him tense convulsively. "Don't hurt her," he said.

"Warning me?" Doug said, sounding amused. *"Me?"*

"I know you want me dead. You have to kill me now because I know about the hunter; but leave her alone."

"Listen, Bobby." That same maddeningly cheerful tone. "If she doesn't know anything about what happened, I'm not going to kill her, I'm going to marry her, don't you remember?"

Bob drew in a shaking breath. "Oh, God, you're such a bastard," he said.

"That I am," Doug answered lightly. "But a clever one, you must admit. You almost got me down there at the lodge. But I landed on some sofa cushions or something. Otherwise, you would have won. But now that's out of the question, isn't it?"

"You planning to kill me in front of her?" Bob asked. "You think she'll—?"

"Oh, no, no, no," Doug interrupted. "I'll figure out some way to make it look like an accident. You wouldn't want me to kill you in front of her. Then I'd have to kill her too and you don't want that, do you, Bobby boy? So watch yourself when we're inside. Remember it's her life at risk as well as yours."

"I'll remember," Bob replied. That hopeless feeling again. Doug was invincible. There was no way to beat him. He'd even survived that fall. What chance was there that, weaponless, he and Marian could overcome him?

When they went inside, Marian was at the stove, breaking eggs into a cast-iron skillet.

"Hate to put you boys to work after what you've been through but would you mind setting the table while I fry the eggs?"

"You bet!" Doug told her, grinning.

Bob followed him to the cupboard and watched him open the doors and draw out three plates. They were cheerful-looking plates, rimmed by flowers.

He opened a drawer to find some silverware, tensing as he saw the carving knife inside.

Doug seemed to read his mind. He reached into the drawer and pulled out three forks, waggling his finger, a look of blithe warning on his face. "No, no, no," he murmured. "Leave that in there."

"What?" Marian asked at the stove.

"Bob was taking out spoons instead of forks," Doug told her, smiling.

"Oh." She held the skillet with a pot holder, tilting it to run the melted butter underneath the eggs. "Who's for over, who's for sunny side up?" she asked. Bob could scarcely believe how nonchalant she sounded.

Doug put the plates and forks on the table. "Napkins over there, Bobby," he said, pointing.

It was impossible for Bob to register that this domestic scene was taking place when, all the time, Doug was planning to kill him somehow, somewhere, "accidentally."

"We'd better wash our hands at least," Doug said. "Come on, Bobby."

His mind unable to function clearly, Bob walked after Doug into the bathroom.

In silence, Doug's eyes unmoving as he stared at Bob's reflection in the medicine cabinet mirror, they washed their hands; Bob wincing and hissing at the sting of the soap on his raw palms. "Hurt?" was all Doug said. Bob grunted, unable to answer.

They dried their hands and returned to the kitchen, sat at the table.

"I made you both some toast," Marian told them, putting the platter on the table.

For a few crazed moments, Bob imagined that she'd known about this from the start, that she wanted him to die, wanted to marry Doug and—

Oh, for God's sake, stop it! he raged at the writer in his mind. He was being as insane as Doug now. Marian was playing along with Doug as he was, waiting for the right moment.

Which came suddenly. As Doug began to butter his toast, smiling contentedly, Marian carried the skillet across the room and, twisting it abruptly so the eggs and melted butter splattered on the floor, smashed the heavy cast-iron skillet on the side of Doug's head.

With a startled cry, Doug toppled from his chair and sprawled on the floor. With a dazed look, he began to push up on one elbow. Standing so quickly that his chair fell back, Bob grabbed the skillet out of Marian's hand, dropping it with a hiss of pain as the handle burned his palm.

Doug started pushing to his knees. "Bitch," he muttered. "Bitch."

Bob braced himself and grabbed up the cast-iron skillet again, ignoring the handle's heat as he smashed it as hard as he could on Doug's head. Doug went sprawling again, unconscious now.

"The car," Bob gasped.

The two of them rushed to the kitchen door and Bob flung it open. Racing across the deck, they half ran, half jumped down the steps. Bob's legs collapsed beneath him and he pitched forward on the ground, Marian crying out in alarm as he did. He shoved up quickly. "I'm all right," he gasped as they continued running toward the Bronco.

They jerked open the doors and flung themselves inside.

"Oh, no!" she cried.

The ignition key was gone.

"What do we do?" she asked in dread.

For several moments, Bob sat motionless, his mind frozen. Then he tightened, catching his breath. *"Doug,"* he said.

He shoved open the door and slid out quickly. Glancing aside, he saw Marian getting out. *"Stay here!"* he ordered. "I'll get the keys!"

He raced unevenly across the ground. A pinecone rolled beneath his right boot and he staggered, almost falling. "Bob!" she called out anxiously.

"I'm all right!" Bob waved her off and kept on running. Rushing up the steps two at a time, adrenaline pumping strength into his legs, he reached the deck and sprinted across it, lunging into the kitchen.

Doug was starting to stand, a dazed look on his face. Seeing Bob, he bared his teeth in a grimace of hatred. "Son of a bitch," he mumbled, reaching for his golak.

Bob ran to the skillet, snatched it up, and crashed it down on Doug's head. Doug groaned in pain, stumbling back and falling to the floor again.

Bob dropped to his knees beside him and started ransacking his pockets. He felt Doug's fingers grabbing feebly at his shirt and flung them off. "Bastard," Doug mumbled.

The keys were in his trouser pocket. Yanking them out, Bob started to his feet. Once more, half conscious, Doug clutched weakly at his shirt.

With a look of rabid satisfaction, Bob clenched his right fist and struck Doug's jaw as hard as he could. "I'm not going to die, *you* are," he said fiercely.

He staggered to his feet and ran across the kitchen.

"Bastard!" Doug cried faintly behind him.

Bob rushed out of the kitchen and across the deck. He descended the stairs as rapidly as he could, his legs now feeling weak again.

Marian was standing beside the Bronco, looking anxiously toward the house. Seeing him, her expression brightened to a look of hope. "Get in!" he called.

She got into the car and slammed the door.

Reaching the Bronco, Bob pulled open the door and got in hurriedly. He slid the ignition key into its slot and twisted it. The engine started instantly. We're *safe*! he thought.

"Where was it?" Marian asked.

"In his pocket. I should have known he'd take it."

Sliding the transmission lever into reverse, Bob started backing up, looking across his shoulder.

"Is he unconscious?" Marian asked.

"Just about," he said. "I wish I'd *killed* him."

"No, you're not that way," she said.

Her words were like a balm to his mind. I'm *not* that way, he thought. My beliefs are still intact, God bless 'em.

He turned the steering wheel, backing along the curving dirt entrance. "How do you get *out* of here?" he asked.

"I had to drive in straight," she said, "I didn't see a place to turn around. You'll have to back up all the way to the road."

"Damn," he muttered.

He backed the Bronco as quickly as he could around the corner of the cabin. Up above, he saw the road. They'd be there in a few moments.

Then away as fast as he could drive.

"I can't believe it's over," he said.

"What will he do now?" she asked.

"Make a run for it, what else? Canada or Mexico. He's finished as a—"

He broke off with a hollow cry at the explosive detonation to his right.

"Oh, God," she said.

Suddenly the Bronco lurched. He tried to get control of it but it sideslipped, crashing into a dirt bank, its engine stalling.

He looked toward the house in shock.

With a look of crazed elation on his face, Doug was limping toward the car.

A shotgun in his hands.

5:12 PM

Bob's eyelids fluttered up, he gazed up blurrily. Shooting pains racked through his head where Doug had struck him with the shotgun butt.

His eyes focused on Marian. She was standing over him,

pressing a wet cloth to his forehead. For a moment, he thought it was over, that, somehow, she'd done something to stop Doug.

Then he realized that he was sitting on one of the kitchen chairs and, standing several yards behind Marian, Doug was watching them, the shotgun still in his hands.

"Does your head hurt terribly?" Marian whispered.

"I . . . don't—" he muttered, unable to answer clearly.

"Bobby boy is back with us," Doug said, chuckling.

"Oh, God, if I could kill him," Marian's whisper trembled.

"No more whispered messages," Doug said. "Don't like that."

Bob shook his head, hissing at the pain, teeth bared. "What are you going to do?" he asked, even though he felt sure he already knew.

"Oh, I have a dandy plan," Doug said; his smile was more animallike than human. "A *dandy* plan."

"Whatever you do, you aren't going to get away with it," Bob said.

"Oh, you mean my next lifetime, Bobby? No problem. I can wait for that."

"I mean *this* lifetime, you son of a bitch. You've already murdered one man—"

"Yeah, that was a shame," Doug broke in casually. "Didn't mean to kill the fucker, just meant to put an arrow in his arm or shoulder. Better take more shooting lessons." He clucked. "Well, at least he died fast. And they'll never find his body down there. It'll probably get eaten." His laugh was guttural. "Maybe by one of those mountain lions you were always worried about."

"Doug, I know you're going to kill me but leave Marian alone, *please*," Bob said.

"Oh, I'm not going to kill her," Doug said. "Not yet anyway. I have to fuck her first."

"What?" Marian's voice was faint, incredulous.

"Goddamn you," Bob said. "Let me fight you hand to hand. I know you'd rather kill me that way than—"

"Oh, I'm sick of you," Doug said disgustedly. "I'm going to blow your fucking brains out right now."

He moved toward Bob, the shotgun barrel extended.

"No!" Marian lunged for him and grabbed the shotgun barrel. *"Don't!"*

Doug backhanded her across the face, and with a cry of pain, she staggered to her left and fell on the floor. Doug came close to Bob and pressed the end of the shotgun barrel against his forehead. "Bye, bye, Bobby," he said. Bob closed his eyes, heart pounding. Marian screamed. Bob's mind pleaded, *Please watch over her!*

The loud click of the shotgun trigger made him twitch, then open his eyes to stare at Doug, a blank expression on his face.

Doug threw back his head with a piercing laugh.

"Fooled ya, didn't I?" he said. "I only had one shell left. Lucky shot I hit the Bronco tire."

Bob stared at him wondering if it was truly possible to hate anyone as much as he hated Doug.

"You monster," Marian said in a shaking voice. "You goddamned monster."

Doug grinned. "I love you too. Strip down."

She stood up slowly, looking at him as though she hadn't heard what he said.

"Strip *down,* baby," Doug ordered her. "I'm going to fuck you."

"No, you're not," she said.

"Oh, no?" Doug's smile vanished and he slung aside the shotgun. Pulling the golak from his belt, he turned toward Bob. "No!" she cried, blocking his way.

He slammed his right arm against her, gasping at the pain in his shoulder as she lurched to the side, fighting to remain on her feet.

Reaching Bob, he yanked back his head by pulling at his hair. He pressed the golak blade against Bob's throat. "Take your choice, babe," he said, his tone coldly merciless. "Either strip or watch me hack your hubby's throat to the spine."

"No, *don't!*" she begged. "All right, all right."

Doug let go of Bob's hair with a thin smile. "Isn't she accommodating, Bobby?" He looked at Bob with hooded eyes. "Didn't want to kill you anyway. Want you to *watch*. Watch me shove my cock right up into her hot cunt. *N'est-ce pas?*" he added, laughing at his humor.

Bob couldn't speak. If only he could attack Doug, golak or no golak. But he was still dazed and weak. He considered standing quickly, and trying to hit Doug with the chair but knew it wouldn't work, Doug would be too fast, able to side-step easily. Then what? Hack open Bob's throat right away? He shook his head involuntarily. He had to wait for a better chance. He couldn't leave Marian alone with Doug.

Doug had placed another of the kitchen chairs facing the one he was in, putting it next to the table. He lay the golak on the table and unbuckling his trousers, dropped them to the floor, then dropped his underpants. "Ooh, lookie, Marian. He's getting hard already, dying to get buried in your sultry snatch, Hey, that's like poetry, aren't you impressed?"

Marian had only taken off her jeans and unbuttoned her blouse.

"Goddamn it, I said *strip!*" Doug told her savagely. "I want you naked, understand. Completely *naked.*"

Marian looked over at Bob with a pleading expression.

"Marian, he's going to kill me anyway, don't let him do this to you," he said.

"Goddamn it, I am going to cut your fucking throat right now!" Doug said, infuriated.

"No!" she cried. "I'll strip."

Doug grinned at her, teeth bared. "Now that's a good girl. Do it fast. I want to see all of you."

Moving quickly, Marian removed her blouse and dropped it to the floor. Reaching back, she unhooked her brassiere and dropped it beside the blouse. Doug groaned. "*Look* at those luscious tits," he said. "Why couldn't Nicole have had a pair like that? I'm going to suck them dry."

"Doug, goddamn it, *please don't do this!*" Bob cried out in anguish.

"Don't *do* it? Are you crazy, man? I'm going to do it 'til she screams."

Marian took off her pants and dropped them. "Nice and *bushy*," Doug said. His face grew suddenly angry. "The fucking shoes and socks, I said *naked!*" he told her.

Bending over, she quickly untied the laces of her Reeboks and pushed them off, pulled at her socks. "Ooh, ooh, ooh, look at that ass," Doug said, staring at her. "That comes second."

Marian stood on the floor, immobile, shivering. Bob closed his eyes, then opened them again. He couldn't watch this. But he had to. *No*. He *couldn't*.

"Open your eyes, Bobby boy," Doug told him. "This show is for you."

"Oh, *God*, but I despise you," Bob said, through clenching teeth.

"*Oh*, dear, dear, dear. How *un*spiritual. I thought you loved all mankind."

Despite his semiconscious condition Bob tried to stand, his face a mask of hatred.

"Wouldn't *do* that, Bobby boy," Doug warned. "Unless you want to see the golak sticking out through Marian's chest."

Bob sank down on the chair, shaking his head, struggling to regain consciousness. I can't let this happen, he thought. *I have to stop it.*

Doug sat down on the other kitchen chair and shook off the logs of his trousers. Leaning back, he spread his legs apart.

"Come sit on Daddy's lap now, little girl," Doug told her. "Don't straddle me, sit with your back to me, I want hubby to see you getting fucked by a *real* man, not some pussy who keeps babbling about afterlife and reincarnation and all that stupid shit."

Marian avoided Bob's eyes, her expression one of agonized shame.

"That's it, sit on Daddy's cock. A little more. A little more. Ooh, your wife is all wet, Bobby boy," he said mockingly. "She's just dying to—"

Abruptly Marian lurched back, knocking Doug off balance so the chair began to fall. Before it hit the floor, Marian was on her feet, grabbing for the golak.

With a snarl of rage, Doug twisted around to get up. By then, Marian had the handle of the golak gripped in her right hand. She slashed down violently at Doug's back, in her desperate rage only managing to hit the edge of his left shoulder. Doug cried out in astonished pain.

Marian tried to pull the golak loose, but the blade was stuck in Doug's shoulder. She looked around with a groan of desperation, then suddenly rushed toward the front door. Bob's mouth fell open. "Marian," he called, unable to believe that she was leaving him. He struggled to his feet, an incredulous look on his face.

Doug was stumbling around the room now, making sounds of animal pain, trying to reach the golak. Every time he turned Bob saw blood running down his back. *If he gets the golak . . .* he thought, still stunned by Marian's deserting him.

On shaking legs, he hobbled toward the cupboard to get the carving knife, but Doug's stumbling lurches blocked his way and, turning, Bob weaved over to the shotgun and, falling to his knees, picked it up.

"Now," he heard Doug say in a hoarse, choking voice.

Jerking around, Bob saw Doug moving at him slowly, obviously only half conscious but fiercely determined, the golak gripped tightly in his right hand. The end of the blade was dripping his blood. Bob extended the shotgun to defend himself.

"You go first," Doug muttered groggily. "I am going to cut your fucking head off." He was breathing hard, eyes going in and out of focus. "Then your bitch wife. I am going to jam this golak up her cunt so far it'll come out her mouth. Get ready to get butchered, you son of a bitch."

He raised his arm, wincing at the pain in his shoulder, and slashed the golak down at Bob. Throwing up the shotgun barrel, Bob was able to block the downward slash, grunting at the impact.

"Wanna duel, huh?" Doug muttered, teeth clenched with pain. He swung the golak sideways and Bob just managed to twist the shotgun barrel down to deflect the golak blade.

"Might as well give up, you motherfucker," Doug gasped. With shaking hands, he gripped the golak with both of them and started to raise it for another blow.

They both jerked around as Marian came running back inside.

"All right, you die first then," Doug told her, barely able to speak now. He staggered around.

"Wrong," she said, gasping for breath.

Bob hadn't noticed what she carried. Suddenly she raised the flare and pulled its cord, igniting it. Lunging forward, she held it up to Doug's face. He screamed in pain and lurched back, throwing up his arms to protect his face, the golak flying from his hand.

A look of remorseless fury on her face, Marian kept moving at him, pointing the hot white sparking of the flare at his face. Doug screamed again, then, tripping over the fallen chair, toppled backward, landing hard.

Marian held the flare pointed at his chest as he twisted and writhed on the floor, shrieking with pain.

Bob shifted the shotgun around so that he held the barrel in his hands. He swung at Doug's head as hard as he could. The shotgun's butt end struck Doug's temple squarely and he crumpled to the floor. With a crazed sound, Bob snatched up the golak to kill him.

Marian shouted his name and he looked at her, his expression maddened.

"You're not like him!" she cried.

He stared at her in silence, breathing hard. Then, exhaustedly, he placed the golak on the table. She ran to him and he held her tightly, eyes shut. "God," he murmured. "Oh, dear God."

6:29 PM

Bob had almost finished lashing him to the bars on the Bronco roof when Doug's eyelids fluttered. As Bob tightened the final knot, Doug stared at him. "What do you think you're doing?" he muttered, his expression distorted by pain, his face and chest burned by the flare. Bob had tied him naked to the roof, his right shoulder bandaged tightly.

"I don't *think*, I *know*," Bob told him. "Hunters tie their trophies to their car roofs, don't they? You're my trophy and I'm carrying you away from here. I doubt if we'll get very far before a sheriff's car stops us. But far enough to satisfy me."

Doug twisted on the rooftop. "Cut me loose, you bastard. Or *kill* me. You're entitled. I raped you and almost raped Marian, I killed that hunter. I deserve to die. Send me to the hell you're sure I'm going to."

"No," Bob answered. "You have debts to pay on this side first. Later on, you'll pay a second time."

Doug replied through gritted teeth. "If they don't execute me, Bobby boy," he said, "I'll get out somehow and kill you. You'd better *hope* they execute me because the next time—"

He broke off with a grunt of pain as Bob clutched at his hair and banged his head down on the Bronco top. "If there's a next time," he said, "I may not be able to stop myself from killing you."

"What, and blacken your soul?" Doug said, drawing back his burned, blood-crusted lips in a deranged smile.

Bob answered, *"It might just be worth it."*

Stepping down, he got into the front seat of the Bronco next to Marian.

"Is it the only way?" she asked.

"Yes," he said, "I'm not going to kill him but this is what I want. It's the least he deserves. It's the least *I* deserve." He made a sound of strained amusement. "Don't worry, it isn't going to last too long. As soon as we're sighted . . ."

He sighed heavily.

"I should have gagged him, he may scream." He grimaced angrily. "But that's all right too, let him scream. Oh, *Jesus Christ.*"

She put her hand on his arm. "What?" she asked.

"Maybe he won after all," Bob said.

"I don't understand."

"Much good my belief system did me," he said. "I finally had to descend to his level to beat him."

"You had no other choice, Bob," she said. "Neither did I. It doesn't mean we sank to his level."

He thought about it; sighed. "I hope you're right," he said.

He glanced at her. "What made you think of that flare anyway?"

"I saw them in the Bronco when we first arrived on Sunday. It just . . . came to me."

"You saved me, Marian."

"We saved each other." She squeezed his arm. "How are

you, sweetheart? You've been through a horrible time, I know. How *are* you?"

His smile was one of weary satisfaction.

"*I'm alive,*" he said.